# Divinity

Knights of Eternity: Book Three

Rachel Ní Chuirc

Copyright © 2024 by Rachel Ni Chuirc

Published through The Legion Publishers Ltd

Editing by Anna Johnstone

Editing by Judy Roth

Cover by Rashed Alakroka

Typography by May Dawney Designs

Formatting and additional editing by Christine Cajiao

All rights reserved. This book or any portion thereof may not be reproduced in any manner whatsoever without the

express written permission of the author/publisher except for the use of brief quotations in a book review.

This is a work of fiction.

# Contents

Contents ........................................................................... 3
THANKS .......................................................................... 6
Characters ...................................................................... 7
Prologue ......................................................................... 9
Chapter One ................................................................... 15
Chapter Two ................................................................... 22
Chapter Three ................................................................ 28
Chapter Four .................................................................. 34
Chapter Five ................................................................... 41
Chapter Six ..................................................................... 48
Chapter Seven ................................................................ 55
Chapter Eight .................................................................. 62
Chapter Nine ................................................................... 67
Chapter Ten .................................................................... 73
Chapter Eleven ............................................................... 80
Chapter Twelve ............................................................... 86
Chapter Thirteen ............................................................. 95
Chapter Fourteen .......................................................... 104
Chapter Fifteen .............................................................. 111
Chapter Sixteen ............................................................. 116
Chapter Seventeen ........................................................ 122
Chapter Eighteen ........................................................... 128
Chapter Nineteen ........................................................... 137
Chapter Twenty .............................................................. 141
Chapter Twenty-One ...................................................... 148
Chapter Twenty-Two ...................................................... 156
Chapter Twenty-Three ................................................... 162

Chapter Twenty-Four ................................................................ 168
Chapter Twenty-Five ................................................................ 174
Chapter Twenty-Six ................................................................. 182
Chapter Twenty-Seven.............................................................. 189
Chapter Twenty-Eight .............................................................. 197
Chapter Twenty-Nine ............................................................... 202
Chapter Thirty ......................................................................... 208
Chapter Thirty-One .................................................................. 214
Chapter Thirty-Two .................................................................. 220
Chapter Thirty-Three ................................................................ 227
Chapter Thirty-Four ................................................................. 233
Chapter Thirty-Five.................................................................. 239
Chapter Thirty-Six ................................................................... 245
Chapter Thirty-Seven................................................................ 255
Chapter Thirty-Eight ................................................................ 261
Chapter Thirty-Nine ................................................................. 270
Chapter Forty .......................................................................... 277
Chapter Forty-One ................................................................... 282
Chapter Forty-Two................................................................... 290
Chapter Forty-Three ................................................................. 298
Chapter Forty-Four................................................................... 305
Chapter Forty-Five ................................................................... 312
Chapter Forty-Six..................................................................... 319
Chapter Forty-Seven ................................................................ 327
Chapter Forty-Eight ................................................................. 333
Chapter Forty-Nine .................................................................. 339
Chapter Fifty ........................................................................... 347
Chapter Fifty-One .................................................................... 354
Chapter Fifty-Two.................................................................... 365

| | |
|---|---|
| Chapter Fifty-Three | 373 |
| Chapter Fifty-Four | 377 |
| Chapter Fifty-Five | 385 |
| Chapter Fifty-Six | 394 |
| Chapter Fifty-Seven | 404 |
| Chapter Fifty-Eight | 412 |
| Chapter Fifty-Nine | 420 |
| Chapter Sixty | 428 |
| Chapter Sixty-One | 438 |
| Chapter Sixty-Two | 447 |
| END OF BOOK THREE | 454 |
| ARISE ALPHA | 455 |
| WANDERING WARRIOR | 456 |
| QUEST ACADEMY | 457 |
| SCARLET CITADEL | 458 |
| OVERDUE: LIBRARY SYSTEM RESET, BOOK 1 | 459 |
| FACEBOOK AND SOCIAL MEDIA | 461 |
| LITRPG! | 462 |
| LITRPG LEGION | 463 |

# **THANKS**

I'm writing this just as I penned those two fateful words—
"The End."
I can't believe we're on book three—the end of the *Knights of Eternity* trilogy. There's been lots of sitting at the keyboard with my head in my hands, an unhealthy amount of Coke Zero, and tears (mainly happy ones). Just days ago my local bookshop in Ireland hosted a book launch for me, and people showed up with zero idea what the book was about, but bought it anyway just to support me. My friends and family traveled from all over to attend, and I got to meet Chrissy, one of my wonderful publishers, in person for the first time. Usually I like to joke around a little in these intros, but I'm just sitting here feeling very grateful for the people in my life.

Thank you to Aisling O'Connell, Ilya Voulis, and Ruairí Moore for reading through this entire trilogy in its roughest forms, pointing out mistakes and ribbing me for never getting the difference between "whose" and "who's" right (I still mess it up).

To the Legion Publishers: Jez, Chrissy, and Geneva, without whom this trilogy would have languished on my computer. Thank you to my mom for buying everyone at her work a copy of my book and making me smile. And thank you to my dad—you know why.

And finally thank you to you, dear reader. This is the end of Eternity, Zara's, Lazander, and our MC's stories (she gets a name in this book, I *promise*). I really, really hope you enjoy it.

Love,

Rachel Ní Chuirc

# Characters

## Gods

Calamity (Alias: the Tyrant)

Ravenna (Aliases: Goddess of Truth, Birth Mother of Falslings)

Gallow (Alias: God of Judgment)

## Champions (servants of Gallow)

Imani

Vivek

Malik

Lazander

## Player Characters

Magnus (Earth name: unknown)

Valerius (Earth name: unknown. Aliases: Prince of Navaros, leader of the Gilded Knights.)

Zara the Fury (Earth name: SYSTEM ERROR. Aliases: parasite, girl-child, Other Zara, crazy spirit lady.)

## Vaxion

Ashira (occupation: leader of the vaxion)

Yemena (occupation: witch/*shi'ara* of the vaxion. Deceased)

Jaza

Fatyr

Esia

Himora

Tek (deceased)

## Lazander's Animal Companions

Merrin (hawk)

Galora (dragon)

Mabel (horse)

## Citizens of Earth

Noah

Adrian

Uncle Jacobi

Margaret (Maggie)

## The Gilded Knights

Marito (deceased)

Gabriel (deceased)

Lazander (former)

Valerius (former)

# Prologue

When the ambulance arrived in movies it meant everyone was going to be okay. That the good guys saved the day. At least that was what Noah always thought.

But as his aunt SYSTEM ERROR lay on the ground of the arcade, covered in blood, her lips a painful blue, he didn't think that anymore. Men and women in uniform, the same blue and red as the lights that flashed outside, surrounded SYSTEM ERROR. They were yelling things like "unresponsive." Three more were struggling to get Uncle Jacobi onto a stretcher, the crimson splotches of his gunshot wounds hidden by huge bandages.

At Noah's back stood Adrian. The paramedics had examined the mangled flesh of Adrian's ear, told him how "lucky" he was the bullet hadn't clipped his skull, and tried to put him in an ambulance. Adrian refused, begging them to focus on SYSTEM ERROR and Jacobi. He'd stayed glued to Noah's side since, one hand resting protectively on the twelve-year old's shoulder.

"Noah? Oh, thank God!" Noah heard his mom, but she sounded strange—like she was both close and far away at the same time. Suddenly arms were pulling him close, the smell of lavender and laundry detergent filling his nose. His mom was here? Why was his mom here?

"Are you all right? Are you hurt? When I got the call, my heart just about…" Her words faded to white noise as Noah spotted his grandmother running. Nana Maggie always looked *perfect*, even after a night shift at the hospital. She'd come home with a smile and a takeaway cup of coffee in hand—her hair in a neat tight bun, her nurse's uniform pristine. Now Nana Maggie's hair was down, her jacket half-open as she ran toward the paramedics, yelling that she was a nurse, that SYSTEM ERROR was seventeen years old, blood type O+, and lots of other facts about her that confused Noah.

His mom gently turned him away.

"Don't look, honey," Mom whispered, her voice breaking.

Noah thought it was a weird thing to say. He'd seen SYSTEM ERROR get shot, had pressed his school sweater to her chest and watched it turn dark with blood. What difference did it make if he looked now?

"It happened so fast," Adrian babbled somewhere behind him. "This guy showed up and demanded all our cash. Jacobi charged him, and Noah tried to grab the gun—"

"You did *what?*" Mom said, holding him at arm's length. "Noah, what the hell were you thinking?"

And just like that everything hit him at once—the sharp crack of a gunshot, SYSTEM ERROR pushing him out of the way. Her face when she collapsed in front of their favorite game, *Knights of Eternity*. The arcade door slamming shut when the gunman ran.

Noah looked at SYSTEM ERROR. She wasn't just his aunt. She was the sister who helped him with his homework. The best friend who played games with him until he smiled. Tears flooded his cheeks, unable to stop now that the dam had been broken.

"… my fault. It's—it's all my fault," Noah sobbed. "She's gonna die, and it's all my fault!"

"Shh, baby, don't say that. Nana is here, and she's gonna look after SYSTEM ERROR. It's okay, everything is gonna be okay," Mom murmured into his hair, running her hands down his back like she used to when he was small. "Why don't we step outside and get some air? Come on, we—"

"I need a crash cart, now!" one of the paramedics yelled. Two ran outside while another pressed his hands against SYSTEM ERROR's chest, pumping frantically. He wanted to tell the man to stop, that that was where she got shot, but Nana Maggie took off her jacket and knelt next to him. Mouth in a thin line, she nodded to the paramedic when he slowed then stepped in, one hand atop the other like they did in movies. She looked so calm and composed that Noah almost relaxed—until he noticed the tears streaming down Nana's face.

The arcade machines, quiet until now, lit up all at once, flashing wildly as shooters and platformers, puzzle and fighting games blasted their jaunty theme songs at full volume. Everyone but Nana jumped, her gaze focused only on SYSTEM ERROR's face as she pumped frantically.

"What in the hell?" a paramedic called, the dim arcade now a disco of lights and noise.

Amidst the chaos Noah saw one machine lay dark—*Knights of Eternity*. As if sensing Noah's gaze the blood-spattered screen came to life, but instead of the black and gold of the starting menu, a new scene appeared.

Pixelated flames licked the edges of the screen as a dark hand reached out, pressing against the glass. It gently trailed its fingers along the edges, caressing them almost, before it drew back, making a tight fist.

And *punched* the screen.

The entire machine leaped, cracks forming in the glass. Nana didn't even look up, not even when a voice echoed throughout the room, the fist drawing back once more.

**iT IS tiME**

\*\*\*

The god Calamity shook, its slug-like body swelling with stolen power. Every quest its players finished and every servant they released was a grain of sand in the hourglass that was its power. Now, after decades of planning, the hourglass was finally tipping. Flecks of mana fell from the slug's body like scales. Every drop crystalized as it fell, becoming tiny crimson grains—one of trillions in its desert prison.

The god slid across the sand, leaving flecks of slime and blood in its wake. Though it healed quickly, the wounds the rebellious player and her vaxion companion inflicted on Calamity ran deep. While it had never experienced something as mortal as "shame," the god felt something perilously close to it. Calling Magnus, Valerius, and Zara to its prison had used a piece of its godhood—the rarest substance in the universe, one it hoarded like a jealous dragon. But Calamity had deemed it necessary—its arrival was imminent, and its players were wavering. They needed to be reminded of the cost of disobedience. They needed to be put in their *place*.

Yet it all went wrong.

The player who wore the skin of Zara the Fury refused him, shifting the very fabric of the Void in the process. Over Calamity's thousand years as a prisoner, the entity had scoured every inch of the desert, searching for ways to escape. Yet the female had done what only a god could—she summoned her vaxion counterpart, a white beast with murder in her heart and death in her eyes. Together they'd rained lightning on the god's domain, nearly killing Calamity in the process. If it hadn't used another piece of its godhood to banish the vaxion, Calamity would have been reduced to particles lost to the sand.

This was unacceptable.

A whimper dragged Calamity's attention back to the present. The rebellious player knelt before him, her limbs bent and broken. Still as a statue, only the shuddering rise and fall of her shoulders revealed she was still alive. Calamity's ink-black form elongated so it could raise its head and look upon the female.

Blood poured from her ears and nose while the bulbous globs of liquid humans called "eyes" were squeezed shut. She was free of the scraps of cloth humans clad themselves in, her hairless body akin to a trembling swine.

**yOU eXIsT TO CaRRY oUt MY WiLL**

The female player hissed in pain at Calamity's words, and the god inhaled the sweet-scented terror of her mind. It chose humans from Earth as its servants for good reason. The god found their minds malleable, their souls easily molded by the gears and pulleys of pain and fear. There had been failures along the way, of course—a human's sanity was as fragile as their bones. But even those that refused him inevitably fell prey to the endless gifts the Calamity System offered—for power was as sharp a blade as fear.

It was why Calamity knew this female would kneel. It only had to find the right motivation.

**nOAH**

The female's eyes snapped open, her mind flooding with images of the arcade, her nephew, and the bullet that pierced her heart. Calamity drank in her fear, measuring it carefully.

**tAkE bACK cONTROL oF zaRA ThE FuRY**

### kILL tHE FemALE nPC ASHirA
### AnD nOAH wiLL bE SPARed wHEN thE TiME cOMEs

Calamity's mouth pressed to the human's forehead, waiting for her mind to flood with relief. The god had offered her a second chance, a superior vaxion body, and near endless power thanks to the Calamity System. Most humans would kill for such an opportunity. Magnus had. And while Valerius had resisted for a time, he too had knelt.

They were only humans, after all.

Yet at the mention of Zara's name, Calamity felt a wall form around the female's mind. Her thoughts battered at the god's presence, a kitten's mewling cry in the darkness. Tiny fists clenched, she glared with a cold fury Calamity did not understand.

"No."

The female was sure that single word meant her death, but the god felt no desire to kill her—only confusion. She must require further instruction.

A spark of magic was all it took to force her head back, her jaw opening so wide the edges of her mouth split, delicate trails of blood trickling down her cheeks. The red sand of Calamity's prison pulsed at the god's back, lifting into the air to form a column of sand no wider than a fist.

Her eyes went wide with realization, but even if she had begged and pleaded, Calamity would not have stayed its hand. She had to *learn*. The tower of sand arced above him, twisting like a tornado.

### tHE PRicE Of dISObedIENce

It drove the sand into her mouth, burrowing down her throat.

The human didn't scream. Couldn't. She made a dull choking sound, her eyes rolling back as sand filled her, her flesh undulating like rocky waters in a storm. Her body jerked and twisted, but Calamity held her there, watching.

Waiting.

"Master, can I… can I go?" came a voice.

Calamity didn't turn. The god knew Valerius lay face down, the male's skin covered in sand that burrowed into his body. He could feel the male's desperate need to wipe it away, but terror stayed his hand. He feared the god more than he feared pain.

Calamity hummed with approval. Valerius may have failed his last quest, but he had not strayed from the path—he simply needed a reminder.

**fAIL aGAiN?**

The female drowned in sand but Calamity took care to keep her heart beating, even as her lungs burned, and her mind screamed she was dying.

**AnD YoU WILL SufFeR fAr wORsE**

# **Chapter One**

In the middle of a forest lay a pitch-black marsh—the stinking bog a haven to insect and amphibian life. Rattlespiders and ripperbacks prowled the edges, searching for prey foolish enough to fall into waterlogged depths. But even predators didn't venture into the marsh's heart. It was a cold dark place, bereft of human life.

Or it was until Valerius fell from the sky, naked as the day he was born.

He crashed into a freezing pool of water with a meaty slap, mulch sticking to his skin. Shock made him gasp and stinking water rushed down his throat, choking him. In a panic, he burst through the pool's surface, grabbing at fistfuls of weeds like they were life buoys, but they crumbled in his hands.

Seconds later his foot touched the bottom of the pool, and he staggered to his feet—the water barely came up to his elbows. Too relieved to be embarrassed, Valerius hauled himself onto solid ground, sinking inches deep into the wet moss as he coughed up what felt like half the marsh. Usually he'd be furious to find himself naked and filthy in a bog. Now he kissed the ground, almost weeping with relief.

He could think again. *Feel.* The cold wet moss was a balm after the searing heat of Calamity's prison. He took a steadying breath, relishing the cold.

Three years. It had been trapped in this world for three godforsaken years. He had no idea how much time had passed back on Earth—days? Months? *Years?* All he knew was that every second he spent here, his need to return home grew more desperate. It was why he'd thrown himself into Calamity's service—the god was his only way back to Earth. Why he'd worn the guise of Valerius, Prince of Navaros, like a second skin while secretly following the fickle god's orders. The money and comfort he'd enjoyed as a prince had made his hellish life *almost* bearable.

And then the order came—*End the Gilded Knight NPCs.*

He'd murdered his fellow Gilded Knights, left the queen half dead and betrayed the kingdom the real Valerius had sworn to serve—all to bring this world closer to the endgame. Yes, some NPCs died along the way. And yes, there were some days he couldn't look himself in the mirror. But he'd had no choice, he told himself, over and over again. This was the only way.

And then *she* appeared—the mysterious player who wore the face of Zara the Fury.

His fists clenched. Everything Valerius had done as a player, she'd done the opposite. He'd shunned his game version, while she'd embraced hers. He'd kept this world at a distance, unwilling to treat the people like anything but NPCs, yet she protected them as fiercely as if they were living, breathing people. And when Calamity ordered her to kill the vaxion, she refused. He shook his head, annoyed at how close he'd come to siding with her foolishness—to giving in to the little kid in his heart who still thought he could be a hero. With a sigh he got to his feet. He didn't have time to daydream. He had to grab Magnus and…

Wait—*Magnus.*

Fueled by adrenaline, his eyes darted around the swamp—he'd completely forgotten about the mage. Magnus had been summoned with them to the Void, but Valerius hadn't seen him since. Was he still trapped there? Or had Calamity sent him elsewhere?

A flash of pale flesh caught Valerius' eye, and he spotted a body slipping into the depths of the bog. Cursing, Valerius half-swam, half-dragged himself toward it, the freezing water no longer soothing. When he spotted blond hair, long and impractical, and a slim figure that was used to being waited on hand and foot, he doubled his efforts.

Looping his forearms under Magnus' armpits, Valerius threw him onto the mossy bank with a jerk—relieved at how light the mage felt. His strength was still intact, at least.

Using the tip of his foot, he flipped Magnus onto his back. Last time he'd seen the mage he'd been on death's door, a hole the size of a fist in his gut courtesy of Zara the Fury. Now Magnus' stomach was pale and smooth, revealing no hint of the deadly wound. Even his right arm, once burned to a cinder, was now healed, the mage's long spindly fingers whole once more.

"Get up," Valerius barked in annoyance.

Calamity hadn't given them another quest, but it was only a matter of time. They didn't have the luxury of lying about like damsels-in-distress—they had to *go*.

But Magnus didn't move.

Valerius rolled his eyes and brought up the Calamity System Menu with a stray thought. He scanned the interface, breathing a sigh of relief when he jumped to the Inventory tab and saw his leather armor was still there. He summoned it, the System enveloping him in a warm glow as it automatically dressed him. He didn't enjoy being naked at the best of times—the sight of a body that wasn't his was just a reminder he didn't belong here. And being naked in a *swamp* didn't help that feeling.

He returned to the System Menu. Calamity hadn't taken his strength, or his favorite leather armor, but that didn't mean anything. Valerius had been sent to kill the vaxion—though declawed, the falslings still posed a threat to the god's arrival. But he'd failed what should have been a simple task. It didn't matter that Zara the Fury was the *reason* he'd failed—Calamity would punish him regardless. The question was, what had the god done to him? Valerius switched to his Character Sheet, scanning it.

| Current: | |
| --- | --- |
| Stamina | 1100/1100 |
| Hit Points | 1100/1100 |
| Mana | 510/510 |

Valerius frowned—that wasn't right. His health and mana should be drained after his fight with Zara. He scrolled to his base stats.

| Base Stats: | |
| --- | --- |
| Strength | 210 |
| Essence | 100 |
| Resistance | 675 |

| Recovery | 710 |
|---|---|
| Speed | 156*<br>(Note this stat is increased by 20 percent with current equipped armor.) |
| Luck | 50 |

His frown deepened. His base stats were correct. Switching back to the Inventory, he scrolled through the seemingly endless slots. While it was impossible to catalog everything, his most valuable items: Festering Wound—a sword that did necrotic damage, Twin Strike—a crossbow that fired two bolts the size of harpoons, and Titan's Judgment—a hammer that repelled magic were all there.

Feeling desperate Valerius ran his hands over his face and body, patting everything down twice. Two eyes. Two ears. A tongue. Everything was there. But he'd failed a quest! Being dragged to the Void, tortured and berated couldn't be his punishment—that was far too kind. But he couldn't figure out what else it could be...

Valerius ran through everything again, but nothing was missing. If Calamity had taken something from *inside* him, a lung or a kidney for instance, shouldn't he have noticed by now?

Nervous, he dismissed the System Menu. The marsh was silent but for the monotonous hum of insects. Black waterlogged soil surrounded him as far as the eye could see, each step promising to be his last. A gleam of eyes, yellow in the light of the sinking moon, flashed in the darkness—a ripperback, he guessed.

They couldn't stay here, not unless they wanted to end up dinner for some stinking beast. Valerius' current gear wouldn't stop the teeth of a ripperback, but it boosted his speed enough that he'd be able to outrun them, even while dragging Magnus behind him like goldfish droppings.

Speaking of...

"Magnus, enough with the dramatics," he snapped, glaring at the unmoving mage. "Calamity healed us both, so *get up*. Or I'll leave you here, endgame or not."

The man lay still as a corpse.

Valerius kicked Magnus hard enough to send him flying. He landed face-first in inches deep water, a sure-fire awakening. But Magnus just lay there, his blond hair bobbing gently around him. Valerius frowned at the water, realizing how still it was—too still for someone who should be *breathing*. Heart in his mouth, the prince grabbed Magnus by the hair and lifted him.

Dark shadows marked Magnus' eyes, and his lips were tinged blue. Valerius pressed two fingers to the man's neck, searching for a pulse.

And found none.

He stumbled backward, the mage hitting the water with a dull splash.

"Damn it. *Damn it!*" Valerius yelled, fists clenched in his hair. Why would Calamity heal a dead man? Why dangle hope in front of him, only to snatch it away?

Valerius groaned, the full weight of Magnus' death hitting him. At any other time Valerius would thank Zara for killing Magnus—he hated the man with every fiber of his being. But while Calamity had always been cagey about what would happen in the endgame, the conditions were clear—the god needed Valerius, Zara, *and* Magnus. Zara hadn't just killed Magnus—she'd doomed Valerius to a life trapped in the body of an arcade game character. A life where every moment he spent in this accursed world he forgot a little bit more about Earth. About the kid he used to be. Until one day he became convinced that *this* was the real world.

He'd seen it happen to Magnus. And the thought of ending up like him scared Valerius almost as much as Calamity did.

Fists clenched, flames of resolve burned in his chest. He'd been nothing but a puppet, and he'd accepted it—but this. This was more than he could take.

Hands glowing, Valerius summoned a dagger from the Inventory and pressed it against his throat. Blood rolled down the blade's edge, trickling over his shaking fingers.

*Do it. Come, just* do it!

He gritted his teeth, giving himself a count.

*Three.*

*Two.*

*One!*

His hands didn't move—his own fear betraying him.

With a roar, he threw his blade to the ground. It struck the moss, but stayed in place, quivering slightly. He fell to his knees, slamming his fists into the soil. The pathetic, slapping noise his hands made echoed around the swamp, mocking him.

*Stupid, pathetic* coward. *You're going to die here, and you're not even man enough to do it yourself!*

His anger died to sobs and a fear so deep he thought he would drown in it. And then Calamity spoke.

**feASt**

Valerius froze, the god growing in his mind, his power vast and endless. Calamity had always favored cryptic quests, but Valerius had served him long enough to understand him. This order, however, was nonsensical.

"Of course, Master. But what should I... feast on?" Valerius asked, taking care to sound obedient.

**foR PrIzE aNd puNIShMeNT**

**fEAsT**

Valerius frowned, looking around him. There was nothing he could eat unless Calamity wanted him to snack on moss and twigs. Nothing except…

His eyes fell on Magnus and his smooth, pearlescent skin.

"No... no, no, no," Valerius said, realizing why Calamity had healed a dead man. Why he'd taken such care to ensure that Magnus' stomach was smooth and full of flesh.

"No, please. I'll—I'll do anything else. Do you want an eye? A kidney? Take it, take anything!" he begged.

Calamity's power crackled like the first bolt of lightning in an oncoming storm.

Valerius winced, his mind splitting in pain. Images of the rebellious player flashed, her body twitching as Calamity filled her with burning sand.

**fEAsT on MaN Or DeSErT**

**ChOoSe**

Tears filled Valerius' eyes, but he crawled toward Magnus. The mage's lips were parted ever so slightly, his eyes closed as if he were sleeping. With shaking hands, Valerius grabbed his dagger, still stuck in the moss like a blade in a chopping block and held it over Magnus' stomach.

His own lurched. He fought not to vomit.

"Why?" Valerius couldn't stop himself from asking. "Why are you doing this to me? The game is ruined. You said we can't *Summon Eternity* without Magnus."

He felt Calamity pause, and he knew the god was debating answering him or punishing him for daring to ask a question. But he had to. He had to know that this wasn't all for nothing.

**fEaST**

Calamity's word echoed in Valerius head, and he flinched.

**aND HIs GIfTs aRE YoUrS**

**yOUr PoWErS DoUBLED**

**YoUr sTRenGTH uNRIvALED**

**FoR yOu WiLL SuMMOn ETerNItY iN HiS plaCE**

Valerius almost laughed. Trust Calamity to find a way to punish him and complete the game in one horrifying swoop.

He took a deep breath and closed his eyes.

*This isn't real. These people, this world—none of it's real.*

He drove the blade down and felt it strike something soft. Heard the wet slap of meat.

*Not real. Not real. Not real.*

He repeated his mantra over and over, the truth of what he was doing tearing at the edges of his sanity. Eyes still shut, he stabbed until he felt something moist and slippery. Feeling around blindly, he caught a piece of what he told himself was steak… and put in his mouth. The coppery tang of blood and bile almost made him vomit, but he forced himself to swallow it whole, gagging as he choked it down. He slapped a hand over his mouth, waiting until his insides settled.

He blindly reached out again, knowing that if he opened his eyes, his nerve would fail. He grabbed another piece of meat.

And another.

And another.

## Chapter Two

Breaker found people—usually to kill them. And she was damn good at it. The dwarf had hunted butchers and bartenders, lords and layabouts for over a decade. But in all her years, she'd never been hired to string up a *prince*. She'd laughed when first offered the contract, sure this was someone's idea of a joke, but the King of Navaros had sent Rhys, his right-hand man, and a bag full of gold as down payment.

The rumors were true then—the goodly Prince Valerius really had murdered his fellow Gilded Knights and chopped up his mommy for good measure. Breaker grinned, twirling the contract in her hands. Finding a pampered mommy's boy would be easy, she thought.

She was wrong.

Valerius' trail had gone cold. She'd tracked him to Evergarden and a disgruntled innkeeper who'd tried to pin his bill on her. Then to the Moonvale Mountains, home to the vaxion and a choice place to hide if Valerius fancied a long and painful death. A trio of gravediggers stalled her attempts to climb the mountain, the clawed bipedal birds a nightmare even to someone with her skills. She was reduced to skirting around Moonvale's perimeter like a vagrant, determined to find another way in.

Instead she found a swamp.

A child could tell it was foolish to cross, though she'd tossed in a stone for good measure. It sank instantly, the sound sending hidden rattlespiders running, their barbs poised above them. She'd been about to move on when light flickered in the sky like an uncertain star.

Breaker had seen a lot of strange things on the hunt—a pirate who'd strapped himself to the bow of a ship, pretending to be a maidenhead. A woman who'd painted herself to look like a tree, convinced it made her invisible. Even a butcher who'd tried to hide from her by sewing himself into a dead cow. Little if nothing shocked her anymore.

Nothing except the Prince of Navaros falling naked through the sky.

She slipped into the marsh, half-convinced years of sleeping rough and eating rations had driven her mad. Keeping low, she let magic instead of air fill her lungs and dull her footsteps. It was a spell unique to Breaker that she'd dubbed *Predator's Step*. It used less mana than a full cloaking spell and was often all she needed to catch her mark unawares. She took her time, picking through belching holes of muck and gently skirting a troop of rattlespiders who twitched in their sleep, unaware she was even there. Breaker forced herself not to hurry, knowing she couldn't catch the prince if she was neck-deep in a bog.

But her worries that Valerius would give her the slip were unfounded. When Breaker found him he was staring into space—suddenly clothed in leather armor that cost more than she made in a year. At his feet lay a dead man.

She squinted at the blond corpse, unable to believe her luck—*Magnus of Ashfall.* The man had a dragon's hoard of a bounty on him for kidnapping Eternity, Gallow's perfect little princess. Breaker kissed the dried bird's skull she kept hidden under her armor. She must be doing something right for the God of Judgment to drop such a gift in her lap. All she had to do was drag Valerius and Magnus back to the Ivory Keep, and she'd earn enough coin to last her *years*. The king was already building a barracks and an executioner's block for his precious son. When Valerius got the chop, she'd be sure to blow him a kiss.

It was the least she could do.

Valerius was talking to someone, his voice low and pleading. Breaker rolled her eyes—he obviously thought Magnus was still alive.

*You'd think a knight would know a stiff when he saw one. Pampered pups—the lot of them.*

Breaker drew a small blade from her wrist guard. Valerius was three times her height, a master swordsman, and had a kill count that rivaled hers. She couldn't take him in a straight-up fight, but then she never fought unless she had to.

She tapped her blade twice, activating the spell within. The edges glowed, lighting up with a paralysis spell that could down a horse. It cost her an arm and a leg but had earned that back more times than she could count.

Breaker was about to move when caution demanded she cast *Whispering Darkness*. She vanished from sight and sound, the mana-draining spell effectively rendering her non-existent. When Valerius fell to his knees and began to crawl, much to Breaker's confusion, she followed him, matching the pace and placement of his steps.

Valerius came to an abrupt stop by Magnus' corpse, and Breaker froze, only a handful of steps behind her quarry. Her blade twitched with eagerness—one nick was all it would take to down him. But she forced herself to wait. She had one chance, and she couldn't afford to be sloppy. A glow of light appeared in Valerius' hands, and Breaker frowned when it faded to reveal a dagger.

*A knight can't use magic, how did he…*

All thought left her as she watched one of the most powerful people in Navaros howl like an animal in pain and drive his blade into a dead man's stomach. He stabbed Magnus again, and again, sobbing and screaming as if he was the one being shanked.

Breaker's surprise at the prince's insanity turned to a cold pit in her chest when Valerius lifted a piece of flesh to his lips. The slurping sounds he made sent Breaker's guts roiling, and it took everything she had not to retch. She'd seen some dark things in her life—the kind of evil and cruelty that if it didn't break you, left you numb to everything, even joy. But watching a royal prince sob and scream as he ate a dead man?

In that moment, Breaker decided it was high time she retired.

She crept forward until she could reach out and touch the prince, carefully lining up her blade with the back of his neck. Her contract specified the target be brought in alive, but if she happened to "accidentally" sever Valerius' spinal cord? Well, what a shame that would be.

Valerius stilled. Breaker darted forward like a viper, driving her blade into his neck.

*Got him!* She thought, leaping back with a grin. She waited for Valerius to collapse, already planning how she'd spend her hard-earned coin. But the prince didn't move. Didn't even flinch. Panicked, she looked at her blade. The first two inches were stained blood-red—she'd cut him, she knew she had! So how was he…

Valerius shakily got to his feet, swaying like a drunk. Breaker could only watch in horror as he turned to face her, his eyes dull and unseeing, his face and chest stained with blood and gore.

*Shek!* She silently cursed, drawing her mace. He might know she was there, but *Whispering Darkness* was still active, which meant he couldn't see or hear her. All she had to do was stay quiet, drive her mace into his knees, and she could still salvage this.

And then Valerius... disappeared. There was no flicker of magic, no whisper of reeds as he ducked out of sight. He simply *vanished*.

Breaker blinked, head darting around. Ruined corpse. Bubbling pool. Bog. Bog. Endless bog. A noise made her spin, mace high, but it was just the wind rustling through the grass. The edge of Breaker's vision blurred with the telltale sign of low mana. She'd held *Whispering Darkness* too long. A more inexperienced hunter might press on, but Breaker hadn't survived this long by being stupid. She turned on her heel and ran at full speed, trusting her magic to hide her retreat.

*Fall back, let my mana replenish, then track the bastard down again. I found him once, I can find—*

Pain flared in her right ankle. She hit the ground hard, *Whispering Darkness* dissipating as her breath left her in a painful *whoosh*. Breaker looked down in horror to see a cone of ice around her ankle. It crept up her shin like ice-cold fingers, so cold it burned.

Breaker slapped a hand on the ice, flames bursting to life. The ice melted, but too slowly—she might be a mage, but her affinity lay in invisibility magic, not the elements. Sweat dripping from her brow, Breaker raised her mace, forcing herself to keep her eyes on the bog and not her slowly defrosting limb.

*Stupid, stupid, stupid. He's not alone, a mage must be helping him. Get rid of the ice and run. Now!*

Pain pressed on the edge of her skull, her body warning her of the cost of using up her mana. With a grunt, she slammed her mace into her ankle, shattering the last of the ice. Stumbling, she got to her feet. She wanted to use *True Sight* to scan the bog for hidden assailants, but she only had a shred of magic left.

Forcing her breathing to slow, Breaker gripped her mace and did what she did best—lied her pants off.

"You're either suicidal or stupid, Valerius," she called, her voice free of the panic that flooded her body. "I'm a scout for King Najar. Rhys waits at the base of the Moonvale Mountains with fifty men strong and half as many mages. Unless you want the full wrath of Navaros brought down on your head, you'll let me leave."

Silence.

Breaker backed up. The bog was eerily quiet, bereft of even the chitter of rattlespiders. A gentle breeze picked up, the smell of rotting corpses making Breaker's nose wrinkle.

She realized too late that it came from behind her.

A hand snaked out, gripping her by the neck. She swung her mace, but Valerius easily ripped it from her hand, dislocating her shoulder as he flung it into the bog. It sank instantly. Breaker's palm shot out, and she poured every drop of her mana into one last desperate spell.

The world turned white with *Sun's Glare*. The spell blinded and confused enemies—she'd once legged it from a small army using it. Kicking out, Breaker caught Valerius in the elbow, praying he'd drop her. But the man didn't even flinch, despite the searing pain he must have felt in his eyes. In a fit of panic Breaker pulled her paralysis blade from her wrist guard and drove it into his arm. She refused to give in. Refused to believe a spoiled prince in a stinking bog was how she died.

"Why. Won't. You. Go. *Down?*" she screamed, stabbing Valerius again and again. He should be a twitching puddle of drool and urine by now, but he just stared at her, his tears making tracks on his blood-spattered cheeks.

"… you will be the first," Valerius whispered.

Breaker spat a slew of curses, but Valerius' jaw snaked forward, cutting her off.

The Prince of Navaros bit down on the dwarf's throat, teeth sinking in. Her world went dark. Minutes, hours, or days later, Breaker couldn't tell, she opened her eyes to find she was lying on her side, the ground beneath her hot and rough. The dwarf shot up, falling to one knee when red sand slid under her. She was alone and naked—not the first time that had happened, but she'd never woken up in a desert with nothing but two suns in the sky for company. She didn't know where she was, or how she'd gotten here, but every instinct screamed at her to run and hide.

"Gallow protect me," she whispered, cold terror gripping her heart.

**dO nOT sPEaK ThAT NAmE**

The voice drove iron nails into her skull. Visions flooded Breaker's mind—a skeletal giant crushing a city with a single step, tornadoes of blood ripping through flesh, and a horde of dark creatures pouring into the Ivory Keep, Evergarden, and Freyley—with the dwarven woman leading the charge, a smile on her face. A hand the size of a moon reached for her through a split in the sky.

**yOU WiLL SeRVE**

**oR yOu wiLL DiE**

**ChOOSE**

## Chapter Three

"You want to kill a god?" Ashira asked, arms crossed, eyebrow raised. In the fight with Valerius, her claws and part of her fingers had been ripped clean. Yet already new pink skin stood out against nut-brown. The myriad of wounds left by the prince's blade had faded to white lines, splitting the ink black tattoos on her arms and shoulders. But no amount of vaxion healing could hide the gaping hole that was her right eye. Ashira wore no eye-patch or bandages—battle scars were proof you'd fought hard and survived. Nor did she seem remotely bothered by her injuries or the events of the past few weeks—as if servants of an evil god showing up to murder your people was an everyday occurrence. To most, Ashira was the same as she'd always been—stoic, strong, and unflappable.

But Zara the Fury knew her aunt better than that.

She saw it in the way Ashira kept Jaza close, not letting the woman out of her sight. In how Ashira insisted on wrapping the dead herself, five in total, her low voice whispering prayers to Ravenna as she dug their graves—her job now that the clan's witch, Yemena, was dead. In how Ashira tipped her head to Lukas in respect, a mongrel she would have enslaved in an instant years before. There was a gentleness to the woman Zara had never seen and wanted desperately to ignore. But this new Ashira wasn't content with clucking over her underlings like a hen mother.

No—she'd turned her eye to Zara too.

"You heard me," Zara said, her tone sharper than she'd intended. "I'm going to kill a god. Or do you think me incapable?"

They stood in what was once the main hall of the waterstone the vaxion now lived in. The huge floating rocks from which water poured, gifts from the goddess Ravenna, had begun to fall from the sky when the vaxion became sick a decade past. The clan, or what was left of it, now lived in the remnants of one.

"I think there is nothing you cannot do once you set your mind to it, little star," Ashira said softly. Zara resisted the urge to snap at her about the childish nickname—her aunt would use it anyway. "But gods are few and far between.

Ravenna, our birth mother, and Gallow, God of Judgment, are all that remain after the Tyrant's war."

Zara hesitated. She could hardly tell her aunt, *"I have no interest in Ravenna or Gallow. I seek to end the scourge of this world—the Tyrant, Calamity himself. Why? Because he forced a parasitic girl to take over my body and sentenced her to a lifetime of torture because she refused to hurt you and the other vaxion. She helped me kill Magnus, and for that I owe her a debt—and I will kill every last god in this wretched world if it means rescuing her."*

Best case scenario, Ashira would think her insane. So Zara used a strategy that hadn't failed her yet.

Silence.

Ashira sighed. "I can tell you a thousand ways to rend flesh from bone, but when it comes to besting a god, I know nothing."

Zara nodded. She should have known better than to ask. On the floor next to her, Zara's breakfast of fermented *grobz* lay untouched while Ashira's was licked clean. The vaxion she'd grown up with as a child dined alone, eating only the food they'd killed with their own claws. Now they ate together, *chatted* together. They even shared meals, as if they were mere cubs fresh from their mothers' wombs!

It was alien to her.

Zara sat apart from the other vaxion, preferring to eat in peace—or would have but for Ashira. Her aunt insisted on sitting next to her at mealtimes, even though Zara wouldn't touch her food until Ashira was gone. Zara grabbed her bowl, resolving to finish her food in her room, but Ashira stopped her with a gentle, almost shy touch on the shoulder.

Zara couldn't hide her flinch.

"When you seek to kill a stonebreaker, you speak to a witch. When you seek to kill a vaxion, you speak to me," Ashira said, smiling sadly at Zara's reaction. "And so it stands to reason that if you seek to kill a god, who better to ask than Ravenna? For a god she may be, but she is our birth mother first. Yemena… the *shi'ara* would know best, but without the witch I can only advise you to visit Ravenna's Breath. Every vaxion true has faced the trials there, and all of us have felt a kinship to her since. The maze is made of simple earthen walls, the beasts within likely long dead, but I…" She hesitated, and Zara couldn't believe her ears. Her aunt, the leader of the vaxion wasn't going to—"I can accompany you there. It is a mere three-day trek."

Silence greeted this while Ashira stared straight ahead as if she hadn't just broken the *rule,* the guiding force of the vaxion—*never* offer a hand in help.

"I am no cub who needs an escort," Zara hissed, grabbing her food and striding away. Did her aunt think her so weak? So incapable? But as she headed for her chambers, shame burned in her chest, red-hot and unwelcome.

The parasite would tell her that Ashira was simply trying to help. That Ashira also felt the weird, unbreachable gap between aunt and niece, and this was her awkward way of trying to bridge it. But Zara found herself rejecting her efforts again and again.

She told herself it wasn't her fault. After years as a slave to Magnus, she'd returned to find her people alien, their customs strange. Even Ashira, who once would have killed her for speaking with such disrespect, now not only allowed it, but seemed saddened by it.

Her temper wasn't helped by her sleep—or lack of it. The snatches she grabbed were polluted by dreams of the parasite, her mouth wide and screaming, her cries of pain a blade in Zara's heart. She awoke every morning, claws unsheathed, snarling like a trapped animal. If this kept up, she might butcher Ashira for wishing her a good morning.

She had to get it together, but she couldn't while Ashira treated her like a fragile cub. Nor could she just pack up and leave without her aunt tracking her down and asking irritating questions like, "Are you all right?"

And so the beginnings of a plan formed. Her aunt hadn't told her how to kill a god, but she'd done something almost as good—she'd given Zara an excuse. Zara's belief in Ravenna was shaky at best, but a three-day hike to Takir and the trials known as "Ravenna's Breath" was the perfect reason to get away. Not even Ashira could protest it.

The thought of a few nights beneath the stars with nothing but her claws for company made Zara smile. *There lies the problem,* she decided. *I yearn for the feel of the wind and the thrill of the hunt—not this play at domesticity. I'll grab my bag, and set out immedia—*

"Zara! I went out hunting this morning and caught not one, not two, but *three* spike-hogs!" called a voice, every word laced with a joy and energy that made Zara want to fling herself into the nearest river. "All we have to do is add a dash of mushi herbs, blast it with your flames, and we are in for a *treat* come Second Dawn!"

Lukas bounded up beside her, bits of twigs and dirt stuck in his curly blond hair. The day had only just begun, but he looked as if he'd been up half the morning already, his eyes bright, his smile wide. The man had been shunned by molger and vaxion alike, a tadpole caught between two rivers, yet he'd settled into life in the waterstone with an ease that disturbed Zara. He'd taken to shifting between his huge, six-legged molger form and his lithe vaxion beast at will, clearing the rubble from the fight and hunting in the forests as if he'd been born for this life. Even the other vaxion who would have called him "mongrel" and spurned him years before, now greeted him as a clansman.

Not mongrel, she corrected herself, the word cutting deeper than she'd like. A… hybrid. That had been the parasite's word for Lukas and now for Zara herself.

"I'm leaving," Zara said suddenly, disliking the thought of herself with six-legs and a snout. She didn't know if the spark of the molger lived within her or if she could even transform into one. Ashira had bound Zara's monstrous hybrid form when she'd been a child, yet her aunt had never spoken of it. Nor would Zara ask. She'd rather die than confess ignorance. "Stay here. If I do not return after eight Moon Peaks, I am probably dead."

Content with her explanation, it was more than she offered most, Zara turned away, but Lukas jumped in front of her. "What? Why? I'll come with you!"

"No," she said, walking around him.

"Why not? You said we were going to help, uh, other Zara, but we don't even have a plan yet! Also, we need to come up with a name for her. We can't keep calling her 'other Zara,' or 'parasite,' though I know you're, ah, fond of that one. I think it's a bit much considering she saved both our lives and…"

Zara's attention faded as she tuned Lukas out. She'd found it the best way to deal with him. "I do not go for the parasite," she said when he paused for breath. "I go so I might finally have a moment of *peace*."

Lukas flinched, falling silent, but to her irritation still kept pace with her. Passing through the shattered remains of the main hall, he called out a greeting to the vaxion who carried out their chores as if their lives depended on it.

Zara couldn't hide her disapproval when Fatyr paused to call out "good morning." The man ducked his head at Zara's gaze, returning to sweeping.

"You don't have to glare at everyone like they owe you money," Lukas whispered.

"It is First Dawn," Zara replied, not bothering to keep her voice down. "Work should be done quickly. And *silently*."

Lukas rolled his eyes but said nothing. Zara had finished her own chores during the night when sleep eluded her.

She finally came to "her" room, though it still felt like just another sign of Ashira's guilt. Clothes homespun to fit her at nearly every age were laid out in holes carved into the rock with Ashira's own claws. A bed made with furs lay in the corner.

Zara usually slept on the floor.

She grabbed a pack, taking only a change of clothes and rations she'd hunted for herself, still unable to accept anything for free. She expected to find Lukas hovering behind her, but he was nowhere to be seen. A sigh of relief and irritation escaped her. Relief that he'd left and irritation that she hadn't heard him go—he'd clearly been practicing his shapeshifting.

She was about to leave when her conscience pricked at her. Grabbing a scrap of paper she scrawled a clumsy note—she hadn't had much need to write while under Magnus' thumb. The words "Ravenna's Breath" were practically illegible, but it should stop Ashira from charging after her.

Sun high in the sky, Zara had just stepped outside when a voice called for her to wait. Jaza practically danced up to her side, her smile as wide as Zara remembered from childhood.

"Ashira said you planned to brave Ravenna's Breath," Jaza announced, and Zara silently cursed her aunt. How had she found the note so quickly? She must have followed Zara to her room. Zara's temper flared at the thought. This—this was why she felt like an outsider among the vaxion. Even her own aunt didn't trust her!

"I have some grilled meat leftover from last night's Moon Peak," Jaza said, pushing a cloth-wrapped bundle into Zara's arms. Though the woman had taken care with her phrasing—it was taboo to openly offer a gift—Zara still planned to refuse it. But she didn't have a chance. Jaza barreled on, speaking quickly and without pause.

"I am unsure what condition Ravenna's Breath will be in—Yemena used to travel all the way to Taskir every two weeks or so to tend to it. And while she is… was a formidable *shi'ara*, she was only one woman. I imagine the maze will be in ruins, perhaps even caved-in in parts—the tunnels were made of earth not stone. I fought a pack of ripperbacks during my trials while another only had a dozen stonebreakers to deal with. My father claimed he fought a xandi during his trial but considering they're the size of a small mountain… well, he always liked his stories. Either way, anything still down there will either be dead or half-starved, so you should have little issue reaching the maze's center. You will know it by the statue of Ravenna painted in every color of the rainbow." She cheerfully waved and skipped away, calling out, "Oh, and watch your feet! I split mine open on the jaws of a long-dead whippertusk! The maze is *littered* with skeletons."

Jaza appeared to walk into the waterstone itself as the illusion that hid the entrance shuddered, then reformed—giving no hint the woman had ever been there. Befuddled by the barrage of information, Zara looked down at the bundle Jaza had given her. She was about to leave it behind, this wasn't food she'd killed, when her stomach grumbled, and she remembered her forgotten breakfast. With a furtive look over her shoulder, Zara slipped the meat into her pack and began the long trek to Taskir.

## Chapter Four

On a good day, Lukas wanted to strangle Zara twice. Today, he was up to three times, and it wasn't even Second Dawn. He'd invite her to play bones with Fatyr, go hunting with him and Himora, and even made a half-hearted attempt at meditation with Jaza, all to try to get Zara to spend some time, *any* time, with the other vaxion. She refused every time.

It was like trying to herd a cat. A very angry, depressed cat.

At the beginning, self-preservation drove Lukas to insert himself among the vaxion. He despised the falslings—they killed for no reason, had driven the molger out of the Moonvale Mountains, and were the reason that when his father fell ill, he'd had no access to life-saving medicine. He blamed them for his father's death, none more so than Ashira, and while they may not be able to shapeshift anymore, they were still vaxion as far as he was concerned. And no amount of time playing house with them would change that.

Yet mere days with the vaxion, and the boiling hatred he'd once felt faded. He watched, amused and then touched when they left anonymous gifts outside the rooms of those injured during the attack. How they quietly took over the chores of those who couldn't stop crying. How they didn't even wait a single day after the battle before putting their heads down and beginning the arduous task of repairing their home. They were stubborn, stoic, and when it came to their emotions, he could only describe them as "constipated."

But he found himself fascinated by them—bloodied Void, he even liked some of them now. Yet if he was being honest, doing chores and drinking with the vaxion hadn't changed how he felt about them.

Ashira had.

After Lukas' almost botched attempt at saving Zara—he'd transformed into a vaxion and tried to catch her midair—she'd taken Lukas outside and commanded he shift. He stripped, uncharacteristically embarrassed, but Zara's clinical gaze made it clear this wasn't a tryst in the woods (thank the Void). He fell to his knees, black fur erupting from his skin as his spine snapped and elongated. His eyes grew too large for his human skull, bulging against his eyelids. Finally the infamous vaxion coils, the source of their lightning abilities, burst from the back of his head, cascading down his back like snakes.

He blinked, comfortably on all fours, his vaxion form complete.

"Terrible," Zara announced. "Again."

He shifted back and forth over and over, the creaking hunger in his stomach growing to a painful ache. After the sixth time she finally said, "You shift like a molger. You begin with fur and spine, but your coils come first—they are your greatest weapon. And your change is as wasteful as a flat-footed cub's. The heart is where our mana sings, and we have more than the molger—you should be able to shift a dozen times, yet here you stand, already swaying."

It was the most Zara the Fury had ever said to him.

When she strode toward him, he couldn't hide his flinch—he was in vaxion form and comfortably came up to her shoulder, but in that moment he felt no bigger than a child.

"Claws," she demanded.

He unsheathed them, and her lip curled. "Tsk," was all she said, circling him. "You are a man fully grown, yet your vaxion is closer to a cub's—one who has yet to sprout his first nose hair." She batted Lukas on the snout for emphasis, and he snarled, his hackles raised.

To his surprise, Zara smiled. "I'd be impressed… if you didn't sound like a scared kitten." With one hand she undid her leather armor, the snap of buckles too loud in the quiet dawn.

**"Witness me,"** she said, fully naked. Her words carried a spark of magic that made Lukas shiver. **"For I am *death*."**

All it took was a single step. While Lukas had to focus, and at times even force parts of his body to transform, Zara shifted all at once, her flesh becoming liquid. She fell on all fours, twice his size, the coils twisting above her head already crackling with power. His breath caught at the sight of her fur, white as fresh snow.

She was beautiful. It was a thought that caught Lukas unawares and made him shift uncomfortably. Zara nodded toward the forest and took off at a blistering run, her gigantic form moving as silently as a shadow. Lukas followed, his mind flooded with memories of the last time he'd raced the "Other Zara." How they'd laughed and taunted one another. How free he'd felt. It was the first time he'd transformed into a vaxion in front of someone, and she'd looked at him with no fear—only pride and joy.

The real Zara fell back, nipping his shoulder. *Faster,* her eyes commanded. He picked up the pace, but she easily outpaced him in seconds.

***

Lukas was dead. Well, practically.

Zara had run around what felt like the entirety of the Moonvale Mountains. Twice. When the vaxion home came into view, the top of the waterstone still partially caved in, he nearly wept. The only thing stopping him from collapsing was knowing Zara would bite him.

When they finally reached the waterstone Lukas was pleased to see Zara panting. In the time it took to blink she shifted back to her human form and was snapping on her armor without a word. Lukas sprawled on the ground like a drowned starfish, one paw twitching, his tongue hanging from his mouth as he tried to convince his heart that no, it wasn't exploding.

"We will meet again tomorrow before First Dawn," Zara said. "You shift quickly—quicker than the vaxion. But not quick enough for… those with our abilities."

He was pleased she wasn't calling him a "mongrel" anymore. Guess it was tough finding out you were a mutt too.

"The molger is a second skin for you, and the vaxion must become the same if you are to survive." He raised his head in confusion. She sounded almost *worried.*

"When we rescue the parasite, I have no need of dead weight. Either keep up or stay behind," she said, walking into the waterstone without a backward glance.

Lukas sighed.

"You are not breathing," came a voice. A voice that even after all these years made Lukas want to curl up into a ball and hide. Ashira stood behind him, partially hidden by the long shadow of a tree. Her hands were stained with dirt, which told Lukas exactly how she'd spent her morning.

"When shifting, our instinct is to hold our breath. Yet when we do our mana has nowhere to flow," Ashira said, crossing her arms. She casually leaned against the tree as if she hadn't just spent the last few hours burying the dead. "Jaza explains it better than I, should you wish to ask her. Back when we… when we still had our vaxion forms, her transformation was a work of art."

Lukas nodded curtly, then shifted back to his human form as quickly as he could. He held his breath, not out of spite, but because being near Ashira had that effect on him. The woman had as good as killed his dad and hadn't even had the decency to send word when his mother died too—a victim of the plague. Jaza had to tell him over *breakfast*.

Angry now, Lukas yanked on his clothes. He couldn't leave Moonvale. Not without Zara—he was as determined as she was to save the "parasite." But seeing Ashira made him shake with a rage that promised death. He had to get away from her.

"Speak," Ashira said.

Pants on, Lukas finally met her eyes.

"Jaza claims I am as dense as stone, but even I can tell you have much to say to me."

"Nope," he said cheerily, his smile closer to a grimace. "All is peachy here. Unless you happen to have a bowl of *grobz* in your pocket? I know it stinks like a molger's armpit, but I confess it's growing on me. Speaking of, I think I'll head in and grab—"

"Banishing the molger. Your father's death. Your mother's. The blood-debt you take such care to hide," Ashira said. "You need only ask. It is your right."

Lukas froze, his hand automatically coming to the deep, angry scarring on his right forearm. Usually hidden by a bracer, it looked bright red in the light of dawn.

"You know what?" he said, smiling brightly. "There was something I wanted to ask you. You remember those 'mongrels' you used to collect? The poor bastards whose only crime was a monster they couldn't control? People like me? Like *Zara*," he said, every word filled with sing-song contempt. He waited for Ashira to flinch, but the woman just stared at him with her single eye. "When I was a kid, you had three of them under your control, thanks to a blood-debt. Now, obviously you had to kill them when the vaxion got sick. Can't have mongrels getting ideas about freedom, am I right? But I can't help but feel like you missed out on the perfect decorating opportunity. Mongrel skulls nailed to the wall really sends a message, don't you think? Here's an idea—why don't we go dig them up? Or better yet, *order me* to do it. After all, I'm just a *mutt*." By the time Lukas finished, he was breathing hard, his head screaming at him to shut up, keep your head down, and for the love of everything holy, *stop baiting her.* But it was too late.

Ashira huffed a laugh. "Your spine has turned to stone since we last met, Aerzin."

"*Lukas*," he spat. "My name is Lukas. I'm no *vaxion*, remember?"

She dipped her head. If he hadn't known better, he'd say it was an apology.

"I didn't kill those bound to me, Lukas," she said finally. "I let them go."

He blinked in shock.

Ashira almost smiled. "Once I believed those who fell to the monster within were weak. That they deserved to be dominated. Controlled. But when Zara… when I had to bind my own kin in a blood-debt to save her life, I couldn't…" She huffed, frustrated.

Lukas laughed. It was a high, hysterical laugh. "Are you telling me the mighty Ashira, the terror of Moonvale, felt *bad* for the people she'd kept as slaves for years?"

"Mock me all you like, it is the truth. I only wish it had not taken the near-death of my niece to see it."

"You think 'feeling bad' makes it okay?" Lukas snapped. "I saw you make a man eat a *metal* cup! The *shi'ara* spent days picking bits out of his intestines. And what was his crime? Trying to run away—from *you*. Do you have any idea how terrifying it is for someone to have that kind of power over you? For your life to not be your own?" Lukas' claws inched from his fingers, an anger he usually kept hidden behind a smile bursting forth.

Ashira looked at him for a long moment.

"I do not tell you this out of a desire for absolution," she said finally, her chin raised in defiance. "I seek no forgiveness. Not from you, or the molger. I know now that the plague was not their fault—it was a ploy of the Tyrant's. Zara told me that much."

"Well, why didn't you say so! I'll tell my *dead dad* it's fine. Sure, you killed a bunch of molger, then drove the rest of us out of the only home we've ever had, but it was all just a misunderstanding!"

Ashira moved like lightning, appearing in front of Lukas in a flash, her teeth bared. Up close, he'd forgotten how huge she was. "I lead the vaxion, and were I to waste time on regret, guilt, and sorrow, the few still alive would starve," she snarled. "So let me be clear, boy. Should you tell the molger the truth of us, that we have neither fang nor claw to our name, and they come knocking?" She leaned close, her breath hot on Lukas' face. He felt his own fangs grow, a burst of courage in the terror that was Ashira's wrath. "Know that I offer up my head on a spike to them in penance, *if* they let the last of the vaxion live out their days in peace. After that the waterstones, Moonvale, all of it is theirs to do with as they see fit."

Lukas was aware that his mouth had opened and shut several times, but no words, usually his specialty, came out. Was the woman known as the scourge of the vaxion offering up her own life as… as an apology to the molger? Had he really heard her just say she'd give up *Moonvale?*

He wondered if he'd died on his run with Zara, and this hallucination was his body's way of coping.

Ashira's lip twitched in a ghost of a smile, sorrow etched into every line on her face. "In my rage at our sickness, I lashed out—hurting those who had done no wrong. Now I look at the vaxion, a people once feared by the world, and see only grief and ashes. My own niece can barely look at me. Nothing I say can fix what I have done—so I will let my actions speak for themselves."

To Lukas' surprise, he felt a stab of pity for her.

"Should you have questions, I will do my best to answer them. But if that is not enough, and you seek vengeance for your father?" She raised her throat. "All I ask is that you bury my body and clean up the blood before you tell the others. I'd rather Jaza not see my guts splayed."

Lukas thought she was mocking him, but Ashira closed her eyes, staying perfectly still. She meant it. She'd let him kill her then and there as payment for what she'd done to him, to his family, and to the molger.

He thought about it. He really did. But in the end, he left her standing there, his mind a storm.

# Chapter Five

Something moved in the darkness of the forest below, too quick for the human eye.

But then, Eternity wasn't human.

**"Feel the weight of his power, and tremble,"** she intoned, opening the door between her and Gallow, the God of Judgment. She slapped her hands on the ground, forcing the power of a god into the rock. A thunderous crack sounded as it split in two, an earthquake shaped by her palms that raced down the side of the mountain to the forest below, ripping up trees like a charging xandi. It hit the forest and a chorus of screams answered—the sound high-pitched and unnatural—but she just poured more power into the stone until the very mountain shook.

She stopped when the screaming did.

Breathing hard, Eternity furtively wiped her bloodied nose. The sleeve of her dress, once a light blue, was now a deep, rusty brown.

"Four," she said, staring down at the forest. "Maybe five. I'll scout ahead—there's a chance I missed one." She made to move but a gauntleted hand reached, taking care not to touch her.

"My men might not be Gallow's Chosen, but they can handle scouting," King Najar's second-in-command said. Rhys' words were light, but his expression was anything but. Stone-faced, he gestured ahead with two fingers. Four men broke off from the twenty at his back and began picking their way carefully down the ruined avalanche Eternity had left of the mountain.

"Please, tell them to be careful," Eternity said, unable to help herself. "The monsters below are—"

"Shadow-fiends, yes," Rhys said. "Foot soldiers of the Tyrant's that are capable of killing ten men without pause. You've made that very clear, my lady."

Cheeks flushed, Eternity ducked her head. "Sorry. I am… simply worried."

Rhys' expression softened. "I know, my lady. Why don't you take some respite for now? Sightings of shadow-fiends have doubled in the last week alone. You'll have to deal with more before the day is out, I imagine."

The thought of a cup of water and a chunk of bread sounded divine to Eternity, and she was about to take Rhys up on his offer when a scream, human this time, cut through the air. Gallow's words came to her, whispering the promise of a new gift if only she had the courage to grasp it.

Eternity did.

Without a word, she ran for the cliff-edge. Taking a deep breath, she threw herself into the open air, arms outstretched. Rhys roared her name, but Eternity felt no fear. She closed her eyes as she fell, her heart steady.

**"Bless mine body, so I might better tread your path,"** she whispered, Gallow speaking the words in time with her. His power trickled along her skin, and she was suddenly soaring through the air as if carried by invisible hands.

"What in the—my lady? My lady, wait!" cried Rhys, but she was already gone, her hair whipping about her as she flew through the air, the world mere pinpricks below her.

It had been decades since she'd been graced with a new gift, but never in her wildest dreams did Eternity think she'd receive *flight*—only the very First of her name, the Eternity who'd stood alone against the Tyrant had been so blessed. But her joy at her new power quickly faded. She wasn't here to fly about without a care in the world, she sternly told herself. Her task was far… bloodier.

Eternity flew over a cluster of scarlet sunders, their lush red leaves suddenly gray, their huge trunks twisted and black. The earth fared little better, the soil ashy and gray, and Eternity's heart broke at the sight of the forest below her. A single step from the shadow-fiends was all it took to pollute this world, killing all life, and they were only the beginning. She tried to feel grateful that Calamity's servants left such obvious signs—it made them easier to track.

A flash of movement caught her eye. Eternity dropped like a stone, trusting Gallow to break her fall. She hit the ground with a boom, earth exploding outward from the force, but to Eternity it felt like landing on a soft feathered pillow. In front of her lay two corpses.

The men were scarcely dead, but their bodies resembled meat left in the blistering sun for weeks on end. Dried flesh clung to bone, and their lips and gums were so stripped back, their skulls looked like endless rows of teeth. They barely looked human anymore.

Eternity bowed her head, etching their names into her memory. They'd chosen to die rather than serve the Tyrant. It was a choice not many people made.

A moaning sound, low and unsettling, made Eternity whip around to see a monster staring at her, its head tilted to one side. Her heart leaped, adrenaline flooding her body. She hadn't heard it—hadn't even seen it until now.

The creature was tall and stick-thin, its too-long arms trailing along the ground. Ink black shadows swirled around its body, shuddering in and out of reality, its very presence an affront to this plane. At the center of its chest was a gaping hole so wide she could see straight through to the other side. It was a shadow-fiend—a monster brought to life by the Tyrant's rage, an all-encompassing fury that needed only the beating of a human heart to summon it, or so the legends said. Blades stuck out of its body, one in the leg, another in its neck, vain attempts at bringing it down.

But that wasn't what made her fists clench.

Its left hand was wrapped around a soldier's head, its long dark claws digging into his cheek. She thought the man dead, but then she saw his eyelids flutter.

"Release him at once, Tyrant," she called out. "Your fight is with *me*."

In answer, the shadow-fiend lifted the man high in the air—and shoved his head into the open wound that was its chest.

"No!" Eternity called out, but it was too late. The edges of the wound shuddered and clamped down on the man's neck, sealing him within. The soldier's limbs jerked, slapping and kicking the shadow-fiend in blind, animalistic panic, his screams dulled by the cage of flesh that trapped him.

A sharp *crack*, and the soldier's body went limp—his neck broken.

Eternity knew what was about to happen. She desperately wanted to look away, but she forced herself to watch and learn what she could—she'd be the first to see it and live in a thousand years.

It was slow at first. Inch by inch the soldier's neck and shoulders disappeared into the shadow-fiend's chest. But in seconds the man was sliding into the monster at speed, as if dragged. When his booted foot vanished, the creature bent forward, jerking as it retched. Ink black claws shot out of its back. An arm followed, then a shoulder. A new shadow-fiend dragged itself out of the first in a twisted mockery of birth.

Through it all the two shadow-fiends made a low moaning noise—their voices, one high, one low, a pain-filled symphony.

Eternity's stomach lurched. The entire process took less than a minute, but it felt like hours. *This is why we fight,* she told herself. *This is why we must stop the Tyrant—no matter the cost.* She raised her hand, feeling the weight of every Eternity who came before her. "You chose to serve the Tyrant," she said, her voice steady. "Some would shun you but not I. I cannot save you, but I can make your deaths swift and painless."

The two shadow-fiends screamed in reply and charged, heads low, claws trailing behind them.

*I will not fail,* she thought fiercely, throwing the door open to Gallow with wild abandon. Eyes as black as the Void, her hair slipped from its bun and swirled around her.

**"You have been judged. And you have been found wanting,"** she yelled, a sphere of darkness gathering at the tip of Eternity's finger.

*I cannot fail.*

The creatures leaped for her as one. She swept her arm out in an arc, a blade of dark energy erupting from her finger. It shot forward, cleaving the heads of both shadow-fiends from their shoulders. They hit the ground, the darkness that once enveloped them fading into the twilight, leaving behind two headless human corpses.

Hands on knees, Eternity focused on breathing, her heart screaming at her that she was dying. Fresh blood poured from her nose, and she knew she'd pushed herself too hard. There was a time when using Gallow's powers twice a day was foolhardy. She was up to five times today alone, and she knew it would only get more frequent the closer they got to the Tyrant's arrival.

When she was relatively sure she wasn't going to pass out, Eternity examined the bodies—one was the soldier she'd failed to save. She grimaced at the headless man, her stomach churning, and quietly asked for forgiveness.

The other body belonged to a woman. Eternity frowned when she realized the woman was a *dwarf.* It had been fifty years since Eternity had seen one in person.

They generally kept to the eastern kingdoms, far beyond the Jaded Sea. What was a dwarf doing here? Could the Tyrant have reached the east already?

Closer now, she saw the woman wore armor that even Eternity could tell was expensive. It bore no house, kingdom colors, or any other hint of her identity.

Eternity knelt, surprised at the twinge of magic she felt coming from the woman's wrist guard—or rather, a hidden slot for a blade. Eyes closed, Eternity trailed her fingers over it, feeling the remnants of a paralysis spell—a powerful one. The type a mercenary or bounty hunter would use. This only added to Eternity's confusion. If her guess was correct, what job would drag a dwarven mercenary all the way to Navaros?

Eternity sighed, knowing she would likely never learn the woman's name.

Head bowed, she whispered the eighty-first sublimation to Gallow, praying the God of Judgment would show the dwarf mercy for her weakness. When the Tyrant offered her a choice, to "serve or die," this woman had given in to her fear. Had given in to her desperate need to live and in so doing, became a monster who would murder her own mother without pause.

Eternity didn't judge anyone for choosing to serve—she knew what it meant to be afraid. Powerless. She just wished their choices didn't hurt so many innocent people.

A coughing fit made Eternity bend over, her hands on her knees. The clang of armor reached her ears. Rhys was by her side a minute later.

"It would have been *helpful* to know you could fly, Lady Eternity. You frightened the life out of my men. Myself included," he said stiffly.

"I couldn't... until that moment," she managed, a tickle burning in her throat.

He looked at her incredulously. "How is that even possible?"

"Gift... Gallow," she rasped. If she spoke anymore, she'd start coughing again.

A thousand questions flashed across Rhys' face, and she knew her cryptic answer only made him more uneasy. Then his eyes strayed to her stained sleeve and the bloody trail she knew ran from nose to chin. Eternity ducked her head, praying he wouldn't ask her the dreaded question—"Are you all right?" She wasn't. Using

Gallow's powers hurt her—every single time and asking about it only made her all the more conscious of it. But to her relief he only asked, "Any shadow-fiends left?"

Eternity closed her eyes, trying to sense a shudder in the air, the creep of the unknown—anything that could be a sign of a shadow-fiend. Sensing nothing, she shook her head.

"Mara!" Rhys called to an older woman in full-plate armor. "Prep and search the bodies. Anyone not ours, I want to know who they were and where they came from…" His voice trailed off as he approached the dwarven woman. Or rather, her head, which had rolled off to the side. Eternity kept her focus on Rhys, not wanting to meet the dead woman's eyes.

"Did you… know her?" Eternity asked, pleased the burn in her throat had lessened.

"No," Rhys said after too long a pause. It was a lie, and an obvious one, but Eternity didn't have time to wonder at the secrecy for the commander pointed at a young mage. "You there! Stop gawking and help Lady Eternity!"

The mage shot Rhys a glare but offered no argument. Eternity had dragged herself to the base of a tree and was concentrating on breathing. The young mage knelt next to her. It took her longer than she'd like to recognize him: Kilin, an old student of Gabriel's.

"Mana charge?" he offered as he pulled out a waterskin.

She drank from it eagerly, making sure to leave at least half.

"No, I'm not…" She winced, head pounding. "My magic isn't depleted."

"My affinity lies with defensive magic, but I have the basics of healing. I could—"

She shook her head, then immediately regretted it. "I'll be fine. Thank you," she hurried to add.

To her surprise, Kilin stayed next to her. Together they watched the soldiers wrap the dead in large sheets of spelled canvas meant to bind the corpse within— until they were sure the bodies were free of the Tyrant's magic, they could take no chances. Mara, a woman Eternity had last seen in the service of the Gilded Knights, took a large piece of charcoal. With a steady hand she marked the canvas of those who'd been shadow-fiends with a large "X"—she didn't even need to ask Eternity which were which. Those who swore to serve the Tyrant lay fresh and blood-filled while those who'd refused him were desiccated and skeletal.

Eternity looked away when they tied up the heads.

## Chapter Six

I couldn't see. Couldn't hear. A red-hot weight squeezed me above and below, the force slowly crushing me. My lungs shuddered, my breath a rasp that barely kept me conscious. Calamity's voice echoed in my mind.

**sERvE**

**Or diE**

Calamity was a god, but he wasn't all-powerful. He could force me, I knew. But it cost him. Cost him enough that he *needed* me to say yes. Needed me to fall in line like Valerius.

Every day he asked. And every day more of me wanted to say yes. But then I thought of Noah. Zara. Lukas. Eternity. Lenia. All the people in this world who'd helped me. Who'd suffer a thousand times over if I gave in.

*No,* I thought, but the refusal sounded weak even to me. Calm and collected, the god pulled back from my mind.

He knew it was only a matter of time.

\*\*\*

It wasn't just the vaxion who felt strange and alien to Zara the Fury. Once, there was nowhere she felt happier than the Moonvale Mountains. There were the poisonous lumbar trees with their pink flowers. Edible only once a season, they left you paralyzed the rest of the year. The trudging stonebreakers, a vicious enemy even experienced hunters struggled with—Zara took down her first at nine years of age. And a host of other deadly beasts, insects, and vegetation she'd once loved.

Running her fingers over the trunk of a lumbar tree, the ancient claw marks carved into the wood made her heart race. Palm outstretched, she held it against the scarred wood, marveling at how small the marks now looked. She'd been a child when she made them, clawing every tree in the area. A young Zara had boldly proclaimed that as future leader of the vaxion she was simply marking her territory— and if anyone took issue with that, they were welcome to challenge her. Turning away, Zara couldn't decide if she hated the loud, arrogant, brash kid she'd been, or envied her.

Hours after setting out from the waterstone Zara reached "Ravenna's Heart," a lake at the center of Moonvale. She knelt by the water, inhaling deeply. While she had her memories back, her mind still struggled to sort through them. The lies Magnus had told her—that Ashira had sold her, and that all the vaxion hated her, fought with the memories she had of the vicious, battle-hungry falslings who'd been her pride and joy as a child. It made her days with these new "vaxion" who shared their food and could no longer shapeshift all the more confusing. Sometimes she wondered if she'd wake up back in Ashfall, Magnus standing over her, asking if she'd enjoyed her "little dream"?

Zara plunged her hand into the lake, the icy sting bringing her back to the present.

*Magnus is dead. He's* dead. *And should anyone else raise a hand against you, you'll strip the meat from their very bones.*

She yanked off her armor, desperate to feel the cold against her skin, and dived into the freezing lake, breaching the surface with barely a splash.

*You faced down a god, Calamity himself, and showed no fear. You will find him, rend the parasite from his grasp, and return her to her world. Then you will owe no one. Then you will finally be free.*

She swam hard and fast underwater, crossing the length of the lake like a grit-shark on the hunt, trying to convince herself a sense of duty was the only reason she was so determined to save the parasite. On the other side of the lake, she paused to take a breath before swimming back with the same ferocity.

Bursting through the water, Zara's lungs burned, her mind swirling with thoughts of the parasite. The bite of cold air on her skin made her shiver with pleasure, and she idly wondered if Lukas was right—perhaps a name other than "parasite" was needed for the girl.

A word came to her mind, and a blush lit up her cheeks. She banished the name immediately.

Dressing quickly, Zara took note of the sinking sun. She could hike through the night, but stonebreakers were most active when the moon was high. When she was a child, they'd kept to the outskirts of falsling territory, but with the molger gone and the vaxion forced to cower in a waterstone, the huge beasts had made all of Moonvale their territory. Zara could easily kill a stonebreaker one-on-one, but if they surrounded her, she'd have no choice but to use her fire. And summoning a column of flame in a *forest* was unwise.

And so, begrudgingly, Zara dumped her pack, and set up camp. For Zara, that meant finding a dry patch of grass to sleep on—she had little time for the bedrolls Lukas loved to travel with. To celebrate her first night beneath the stars, she gathered some dried twigs and snapped her fingers.

**"Spark, so that the world may know my flame,"** she said.

The twigs burst into flames, a pleasant fire brewing. In her old life, she hadn't needed words to use her own magic. But since getting her body back such phrases had become as natural as breathing, each triggering a different facet of her magic from shapeshifting to fire. Were Zara anyone else this would have been cause for concern, but this change was so minor in the upheaval of her life that she'd barely given it a second thought.

Hands behind her head, Zara let her senses expand, taking in the nighttime whispers of Moonvale. *This is what I needed,* she decided. *Not guilt-ridden glances from Ashira, pointless babbling from Lukas, and my weight in grilled meat from Jaza.* This.

She waited, eager for a sense of peace and calm to envelop her.

*Relax. Breathe in the night air. This is who you are. This is where you belong.*

Her shoulder twinged, and she turned onto her side. That made her hip uncomfortable, so she rolled back.

*Stop fidgeting! Mind whirling, body a barrel of chattering tree-toppers, you are as bad as the parasite—*

"Shek!" Zara cursed, her mind now awash with unwelcome thoughts—the hours the parasite spent sitting in the darkness with Zara, telling her inane stories about her life. The blood on the girl's teeth when she bit into her own arm, swearing she would save Zara and the vaxion. Her sad smile when she returned Zara's body to her—telling her Calamity would never let her go, and Zara needed to forget about her. Needed to live her life.

*Stop thinking,* Zara ordered herself, hands pressed to her lids. *Stop it!*

*"You cannot, oh-ho! For your heart sings with the gut-strings of guilt and the wet-willy of sadness. You call her parasite but, oh—how your blood soars with joy when you think of her. Her sauce is special, hehe!"*

A sing-song voice echoed in Zara's mind, each word more nonsensical than the last. She spun to find herself face to face with the largest stonebreaker she'd ever seen.

It was twice her size, its shoulders double that length. Skin the color of stone and ten times as tough covered its round, heavy body—impenetrable but for the soft layer of fur it kept hidden beneath arms locked over its stomach. A second set of arms burst from its shoulders, each the length of Zara. But its rock-hard skin wasn't what had earned the beast the name "stonebreaker."

A set of fangs, gray as steel, hung from a jaw that could crush stone. The molger had the strongest bite of any falslings, clinging on even in death, but theirs paled next to a stonebreaker's. Ashira once said that a stonebreaker bite was one of the worst ways to die, for so tightly did they hold you, you would go to Ravenna's embrace with their jaws still wrapped around your skull.

For a moment neither Zara nor the stonebreaker moved. A single step from the beast, and the earth sang for miles of its coming. Why hadn't she heard it?

And then it raised its leg and brought it down—hard.

The ground erupted beneath her, splitting from the force, but Zara was already gone, leaping out of the way.

*"Big bad Zara gnashes, and trashes, and bashes! But she didn't gnash, or trash, or bash Magnus. Not for many sleeping nights and waking days. She brushed his hair. She washed his feet. She wonders... did the blood-debt make her stay or... did she like his silky hair? His stinky feet? Hehe!"*

The voice grew louder, memories flashing in Zara's mind of Magnus hitting her. His smile as she dragged a comb through his hair. The fingers he trailed along her cheek, whispering, "You love it here, don't you? Say it. Say you *love* it, Zara."

Distracted, she didn't see the stonebreaker swing at her until one of its rock-hard fists caught her in the side, sending her flying. Zara hit the dirt, skidding awkwardly on all fours.

*"Auntie Ashira's big sad eyes cut your heart, chop, chop! But the wall is too high. It grows bigger and bigger, tightened by guilty gut-strings. Need help? Slap! Need to talk? Double slap! Zara has the tummy bug of self-hatred! WEE!"*

"Shut up!" Zara hissed, her head spinning. The voice wasn't coming from the stonebreaker—they had the wit of a slapped toddler. But who was it? *What* was it? "Only the weak despise themselves!"

*"Liar, liar!"* The voice grew louder and more insistent. *"We sing-song see your mind-box, Zara! You hate, hate, hate yourself!"*

With a growl, Zara's eyes glowed like burning suns. **"Witness me,"** she hissed. **"For I am death."**

Tendrils burst from the back of her skull like fragments of bone. In the time it took to blink Zara was on four paws, each the size of the stonebreaker's skull, her vaxion form as deadly as it was breathtaking. Lightning trailed along her skin.

*Look into my mind all you like*, she thought, knowing the voice was listening. *You only delay the inevitable.* The night above turned stormy, thick black clouds blotting out the moon as Zara summoned her magic. The stonebreaker charged, dropping down to all fours as it raced forward, each step a small earthquake.

Lightning erupted from the sky, hitting the stonebreaker full force. She'd seen Ashira bring down an entire herd of them as a child with the same magic. Yet instead of falling, twitching as it burned alive, the stonebreaker barely faltered, picking up speed.

Shocked, Zara hesitated, and the stonebreaker hit her full force, unlocking the arms that protected its stomach to wrap all four around her in a crushing bear hug. They hit the ground together with a thud that echoed throughout the entire forest. Zara bit down on the beast's shoulder, a shockwave of pain reverberating in her skull when one of her fangs chipped on its skin.

*"Boring, boring!"* The voice laughed. *"Tell us the truth and tell us no lie—the squirmy-wormy girl in your head. Why do you fight so hard to save her? She's a pretty little parasite, but she belongs to the slug man! Why? Tell us. Tell us!"*

Zara's ribs cracked in answer. She tried to summon her flames, the forest be damned, but something smothered her magic, making her head feel dull and cotton filled. She could have pushed past it, her magic was far stronger, but as if sensing this, the stonebreaker tightened its grip around her.

*"Haha! 'Duty' your mindbox says. Debt. The squirmy-wormy saved you, now you must save her. But your mindbox lies, even to you!"*

Zara shook her head, her claws fighting to find the soft flesh of the stonebreaker's stomach, but its hold was too strong—she couldn't move a single paw. The voice grew in power, as if eager to hear her answer, but Zara's mind roared in refusal: *I will burn first, shek!*

Fire burst from Zara's paws, burning her and the stonebreaker both. The beast could withstand intense heat, walking through flames as if they were nothing, but they weren't invulnerable. She simply had to hold on long enough to—

The stonebreaker relaxed its grip, and she slid out of its arms like a viper, fangs bared, the scent of her burnt fur tainting the air. She waited for the stonebreaker to attack, ready to rip its arms off and feast on its soft belly, but it just stood there—swaying like a blade of grass in a gentle wind.

The voice laughed, a high tinkling sound.

*"Such a treat to meet, oh darling sweet,"* the voice sang. *"I bleed, I starve! But you are the candied meat who will end it all! Find me…"* Its last words were a whisper that trailed off into the night.

The stonebreaker shook its head, as if coming out of a trance. With a groan akin to falling rocks it lumbered away, first on its hind legs, then dropping down to four as it picked up speed.

Zara grabbed her pack, one hand cradling her tender ribs.

Were the parasite here, the girl's mouth would have moved at speed, thoughts and possibilities pouring from her like a waterfall. What just happened? Who had taken control of the stonebreaker's mind? And what did they want with Zara—daring to call her a "candied meat?"

But the parasite wasn't here. And Zara had survived this long by only dealing with what was right in front of her. Whatever controlled the stonebreaker wanted her alive. Thought of her as *meal*. As far as Zara was concerned, the plan was simple—go to Taskir and kill it before it killed her.

Yet her chest twisted, the weight of the parasite's capture weighing her down.

With a sigh, she grabbed her pack and set off at a brisk walk, knowing that what little chance of sleep she had was gone.

# Chapter Seven

"You knew Gabriel, right?" Kilin asked. He'd offered to replenish Eternity's mana twice more, and while she was grateful for the topic change, the question made her chest ache.

The dead soldiers, shadow-fiends and the dwarven woman had all been bound in spelled canvas. Rhys had everything in-hand. Nothing seemed to bother the commander, not even the desiccated husks of the people he'd once led. Before, she'd have felt sorry for him and what he must have gone through—now she admired his resilience.

"I was honored to call Gabriel friend," Eternity said, smiling sadly at the memory of the mage's furrowed brow and sharp wit—especially when he argued with Marito. The two had fought like an old married couple. "To laugh beneath the stars as Marito told ridiculous tales of their adventures with the Gilded Knights while Gabriel sat blushing, clearly pleased. I miss him… I miss them both," she said, surprised at how much she'd revealed. She hadn't spoken to anyone about their deaths. No one at the Gallowed Temple knew them, Imani and the other Champions wouldn't approve of her lingering on such things, and Lazander… well. He had enough to deal with.

"Gabriel spoke fondly of you," Eternity said, trying to distract herself from thoughts of Lazander. "He said that what little magic you didn't understand, you'd slam your head against it until you did. He was the same."

Kilin smiled. "He was usually the one I was slamming my head against, but then he's the reason I'm the mage I am today."

A horse neighed, rearing. The corpse tied to its back slid off, and it took three soldiers to stop the animal from bolting. The large "X" of a shadow-fiend stood out on the fallen body, pitch-black against cream.

"I confess I am surprised to see you here," Eternity said to Kilin, following his gaze. "Gabriel might have been Gilded Knight, but he was a palace mage first. I'm sure a student of his would be welcome to join their ranks at the Ivory Keep."

Kilin winced. "The king wants to disband the palace mages. There's talk of a mandatory term working as a battle mage in his army before we can apply to the Ivory Keep—a 'cushy position,' he called it." Kilin shook his head. "He wants to disband the knights too, not just the Gilded. That's why Mara is here." He gestured to the knight Eternity had spotted earlier. Mara took the reins from the soldiers and was patiently leading the horses to the corpses, letting them sniff each in turn. Only after did they allow the dead to be tied to their backs.

"Apparently, it doesn't matter if you're a mage or a knight—you're a soldier first and foremost, which means you do as Navaros commands," Kilin said bitterly.

For a moment Eternity was glad Marito and Gabriel were dead. The Gilded Knights had represented everything they'd stood for—honor, courage, *hope*. To see not just the Gilded disbanded, but the very knightly order they'd loved, would have broken their hearts. But then Champion Malik's words rang in her ears. Her duty was to follow Gallow. And the more people willing to stand with them against the Tyrant, the better their chances.

"Not two weeks past, no one had even heard of shadow-fiends," Eternity said after a long moment, considering her words carefully. "Now they roam Navaros, more and more appearing every day. Refugees knock on the Ivory Keep's doors with nothing but the clothes on their backs and panic in their eyes. Three hundred arrived this week alone, yet this is only the beginning."

She gestured to the forest around her, Kilin's eyes locked on hers. "According to Gallow's sages, the Tyrant will be here in months—and as we draw closer to his arrival, the veil between this world and the Void will tear. Seas will boil, mountains will turn to glass. Even the dead will rise, so polluted does this plane become by his presence."

Kilin looked at her with wide, terrified eyes, but Eternity wasn't done. "Freyley has chosen to deny all signs of the Tyrant's arrival. Evergarden has adopted a 'wait and see' approach while barricading themselves behind their walls. The only ruler on this side of the continent taking this seriously is King Najar.

"I… will not claim to agree with everything he is doing. But he is doing *something*, and that alone makes—" A coughing fit cut Eternity off, her chest burning.

"Lady Eternity, I—I don't mean to be rude, but I've seen Champions use Gallow's abilities with abandon, splitting rock and leaping incredible distances. But the more you use your powers, the more…"

Eternity hacked up a glob of blood, and to her surprise, Kilin placed a hand on her back, rubbing it in small circles. He didn't seem to realize he was doing it.

"… the more it seems to affect you," he finished awkwardly.

"Every Eternity before me has suffered backlash when channeling Gallow," she said, catching her breath.

"With respect, Lady Eternity, that's not very reassuring."

She laughed. "I simply mean that I am not the first to experience this, though… it seems to hurt me more than previous Chosen," she admitted, a sudden wave of shame washing over her. She told herself this was why she needed to work harder—why she needed to prove to Gallow she was worthy. "It is not Gallow's fault, nor is it something he can control," she hurried to clarify at Kilin's frown. "The fault lies with, well, reality. This plane is not meant for gods, which is why the role of 'Eternity' is so vital. I act as the link between Gallow and the Champions, but I am also the funnel through which the Champions exist and use their powers."

"And you have no such funnel," Kilin said, catching on immediately.

No wonder Gabriel was so proud of him, Eternity thought. "Precisely. When I use my powers, I connect with Gallow directly. And while I have served him for… a very long time, I am far from a god. So it, well, it hurts at times," she explained, trying to downplay it. "But it is a necessity. Just as the Tyrant being here twists this world, Gallow's presence would too—it is why he takes such care to work through those who serve him."

"But isn't it less 'care' and more that Gallow has to? If he doesn't want to turn this world into a pile of goo, anyway," Kilin said, rubbing his chin, his eyes narrowed. "In fact, aren't Gallow and the Tyrant very similar? They both come from the Void, use followers to do their bidding… and the Tyrant even has 'Champions' too. Look at what Valerius did to the Ivory Keep—are you telling me Malik, Imani, or Vivek couldn't do the same?"

"Do not speak of Gallow and the Tyrant in the same breath!" Eternity said sharply. "Gallow offers us a choice—the Tyrant's demands you serve or die."

Kilin raised his hands in a show of apology, but Eternity noticed he didn't look very sorry. "From what I heard, Gallow didn't exactly ask Lazander's opinion before making him a Champion. And Mara and I aren't the only ones who've noticed how much he's changed—and I'm not talking about those big new biceps he's got."

"That is different—Lazander was *dead*. Still would be if Gallow had not—"

"We've reports of twenty more shadow-fiends west," Rhys said, appearing at her side with a frown.

Eternity was grateful for the interruption, even if it was bad news. She had no idea how to explain that yes, Lazander was different now—unrecognizable, some might say. But he was out there day and night fighting to save this world. He was putting his life on the line alongside Malik and the other Champions while Kilin sat on his haunches *criticizing* them.

"You're to stay here with a contingent of ten, Lady Eternity," Rhys continued, snapping out a series of gestures. Immediately the remaining soldiers spread out, some saddling horses, others heading to the base of the mountain. "I'll send word if you're needed." At the worried look on her face, Rhys added. "We can't expect you to come to our rescue every time we're up against the Tyrant's monsters—we need to learn how to fight these shadow-fiends ourselves, so that you and the other Champions can take on his more… formidable beasts."

She knew he was thinking of the wallow-tail, the bird made of pure flames that attacked the Ivory Keep. "The king is sending out a shipment of spell-enhanced weapons," he continued. "The mages have been working night and day on them—they're stronger than dragonscale, I'm told."

"What?" Kilin interrupted. "You have mages on forgework? We should be focused on divination, not making shiny swords for fools to wave about. How else are we supposed to predict where shadow-fiends will attack?"

Eternity knew that if King Najar was here, a sharp glare and a few hours in the stocks would be his answer. Rhys was gentler.

"Speak to me like that again, and I'll have you in chains. Clear?" Rhys said, one hand on his sword, both eyes on Kilin. Well, fractionally gentler than King Najar, at least.

Kilin went pale but nodded.

Eternity sighed, feeling exhausted. She forced herself to her feet despite Rhys' protests and held out her forearm. Kilin stared at her in confusion, but Eternity said nothing—she simply waited.

Less than a minute later the dark spot circling the sky grew larger, hurtling toward the earth. The feathered edges of a hawk took shape, and Merrin waited until she'd reached the treetops to snap out her wings, the wind dragging her to a sharp, elegant stop as she landed on Eternity's outstretched arm.

"Stylish as always, brave Merrin," Eternity said with a smile. She saw Kilin's eyes go wide at the sight of Lazander's hawk, and she cut him off before he could say anything. "I want you to go with *Rhys*, all right? *Rhys*," she said, gesturing to the commander.

Rhys raised an eyebrow, looking bemused. Merrin chirped sadly, pressing her head against Eternity's in open affection. After a moment, she flapped her wings, landing lightly on Rhys' shoulder.

"She'll find me quicker than any messenger," Eternity said. "But should Gallow order me to you, I'll be there immediately."

Rhys surprised her by raising a hand to scratch under Merrin's beak. He hadn't struck her as an animal lover.

"It is an honor, Lady Merrin," he said formally. "Your legend precedes you—I heard you saved Lazander from an assassination attempt."

While Merrin couldn't understand Rhys, she knew Lazander's name—and she squawked happily, looking around as she searched for her old master. "Ah, forgive me," Rhys said, realizing his mistake. "I didn't mean—"

"Merrin? Merrin!" Eternity said, stepping close to Rhys. She noticed him stiffen but chose to ignore it. He hid it well, but she knew he was scared of her—most people were. She tapped Rhys' chest plate twice, and the sound calmed the hawk. With a chirp she took off, a single beat of her tremendous wings sending her high into the sky.

Rhys coughed, a hint of pink on his cheeks. "Rest up, Lady Eternity," he said awkwardly.

As if summoned, a soldier appeared at his back with the reins of a beautiful Freylen warhorse called Meadow. Eternity tried to take in every detail of the animal, from her lustrous coat to her sturdy hooves. Lazander's eyes used to light up whenever he spoke of the stud farms on the outskirts of Freley, a few hours from his home in the capital. She'd tell him all about Meadow the next time they met.

A small, treacherous part of her wondered if he still cared about such things.

Rhys and over half his soldiers wordlessly took off in a flurry of armor and hooves that was quickly swallowed by the silence of the forest. Eternity watched them, or rather watched Merrin who dutifully followed Rhys, her lazy circles becoming more and more distant. The sight made her heart ache more than Eternity expected, and her fingers tensed as she gripped the sleeves of her dress. She felt like she'd been run over by several warhorses, but she still hoped Gallow would order her to follow them.

He didn't.

With a heavy sigh she turned on her heel and started the long trek back through the forest and up the side of the mountain to where they'd camped—a blissfully short distance when Gallow lent her the power of flight that now looked impossible. Particularly when her lungs had only recently decided they were happy to stay inside her body.

"Let me help," Kilin said, holding out his arm.

Eternity smiled too brightly in response. "No need," she said, passing him. She'd tried to comfort him about King Najar and the war, and in return he'd suggested that Gallow and the Tyrant were the same. Yes, his points about Lazander were… correct, but he didn't understand. He didn't know, couldn't know, how much they sacrificed so people like him could live in blissful ignorance. She understood Gallow's insistence on secrecy, it was for their protection after all, but it frustrated her. And if she was being honest, it made her feel even more isolated from the world.

She shook her head, banishing the resentment in her heart. Gallow was the only one who could save them from the Tyrant—and if that meant feeling a little lonely, well, that was a small price to pay.

Several soldiers followed her at a distance, their heads low as they whispered, but their furtive glances in her direction told her all she needed to know.

Maybe Champion Malik was right, she begrudgingly admitted. Maybe deep down, all humans were the same.

## Chapter Eight

"**B**end to his might, break before his Judgment."
Lazander drove his fist into the floor. The wooden boards shattered; splinters he couldn't feel embedding themselves in his bare knuckles.

"I'd answer him," Malik said, trailing a casual finger over the grimy surface of the bar. "The next won't miss."

The two Champions stood in a bar in the dredges of the Freylen capital, the worn paint outside reading "The Giggle Worm." Lazander entered first, stooping low to avoid clipping his head against the doorway—he was still getting used to his new height. Malik followed, the short man barely grazing Lazander's elbow. A handful of patrons as grimy as the bar raised their heads when Malik clicked his tongue for attention. One look at the Champions and their pitch-black armor, and every customer stood to attention like naughty children summoned to the top of the class. Malik jerked his head at the door, and they fled, one muttering an apology on the way out.

The bartender wasn't so lucky.

"Well?" Malik asked the man who cowered beneath Lazander, half an inch from where the Champion's fist split the floor. The bartender was a pale, ruddy-cheeked shrimp of a man with a wisp of a goatee and a pot belly.

"I don't know! I swear on Gallow's name I don't—"

Lazander gripped the man's neck, cutting him off with a squeak. Careful of his new strength, Lazander spread out his fingers, trying his best to be gentle.

"I wouldn't go invoking the God of Judgment, friend." Malik smiled, teeth glinting in the dim light. "My friend here is a touch sensitive."

Terrified blue eyes locked onto Lazander.

"Forgive me, sir. I—I didn't mean nothing by it. It's just—I was only the middleman. I hadn't even heard of this Ravenna gal 'til Grim came knocking."

The man's hot breath hit Lazander in the face, and he had to fight to keep his expression neutral. The bartender stank of gazzy, a "beer" that smelled like horse urine and tasted much the same. His father had let him take a sip when he'd been a kid, slapping his knee with laughter when Lazander spat it out.

"Grim?" Malik asked, gray eyes wide. "Tall man? With a scar?"

"That's the one!" The bartender nodded eagerly. "This place was my da's, but when he died he left me more than the Giggle Worm. I was drowning in debt and a bad week from closing for good when Grim showed up—offered to buy my debt and let me pay it back at my leisure. All I had to do was let some folk hide in my basement every now and then."

"Who were they? How many? How often?" Malik snapped, stepping closer.

Lazander made a show of yanking the man up and into the air—keeping him away from Malik.

"I dunno, I never saw their faces but—but I kept a ledger," he gasped, small legs kicking. "Loose floorboard by the wine. There might have been nights I missed—Grim had a key, but I've been a light sleeper ever since my wife died."

Malik leaped over the bar. Lazander gently set the bartender down, covering the movement by stomping hard on the wooden floor. The man stared at him in confusion but didn't dare move, or even adjust his shirt, which had ridden halfway up his stomach.

"Got it," Malik called, appearing so suddenly it looked like he'd materialized out of thin air. The bartender let out a cry of surprise, but the Champion ignored him, waving a slim red notebook at Lazander. "One step closer, brother," he said with a fierce grin, slipping the notebook inside his armor as he left the bar.

Lazander waited until Malik was out of sight. "You've helped many people today, sir," he said softly to the bartender. "Thank you."

The bartender stared hard at the floor, a hand shamefully covering his crotch. It was only then that Lazander noticed the dark stain blossoming from the man's groin, all the way down the side of his trouser leg. Horrified, the Champion was about to apologize when something moved out of the corner of his eye.

A small boy watched him. Though the child was blurry, his features nothing more than a shimmer of light and darkness, Lazander could feel the boy's disapproval.

"Lazander, we've talked about this," Malik called from outside.

The red-haired Champion left, ducking lower than necessary through the open doors, and tried to focus on their goal, repeating their mission to himself.

*Stop Grim and Ravenna—before they kill again.*

* * *

"You think I don't know what you're doing? Handling that bartender as if he were made of glass. Bowing your head like you're in the wrong when he's in cahoots with *terrorists.*" Malik shook his head. "That bleeding heart of yours is gonna be your ruin, Zander, you mark my words."

The two Champions meandered through the streets of Freyley. It was midday, and the sun was shining high and hot on the broken cobbles of Gazzy Lane—so named for the perpetual stink of horse urine and beer. Though it was noon, the bars were fit to bursting as locals knocked back a beer or seven during their lunch before returning to their eighteen-hour shifts at the slaughterhouse. Lazander didn't blame them. He remembered his father working there while his mother slaved for coppers, training to become a doctor who specialized in animals.

A ramshackle three-story house with a collapsed roof caught his eye. Rot clung to the walls, and he knew it was weeks if not days before the entire thing came down on itself. He frowned—he remembered the house being so much bigger. Six families had been crammed into it, including Lazander's, but that hadn't mattered to his mother— "We live in the biggest house on Gazzy Lane," she'd say with a wink. "That practically makes us royalty, don't you think?"

He didn't bother relaying this to Malik or the dozens of other memories that came alive with every step he took through his childhood city. He knew the Champion wouldn't approve.

"You hear me, Zander?" Malik probed, sharper this time.

"I've bled in Gallow's name," Lazander said, staring straight ahead. "Fought. Killed."

"Aye, I'm not questioning—"

"I know that if Ravenna had had her way, Grim would have poisoned Evergarden's wells, and half the city would be dead, their lives offered up in tribute to the Tyrant," Lazander said, cutting him off. "It is only because of you, because of *Gallow*, that all those people were saved. Yes, I find Gallow's cryptic orders, and lack of transparency... difficult. But I've seen the good he does. Just as I've seen the cruelty Ravenna will inflict if we allow her. I'll do whatever it takes to stop her. You know I will."

Malik said nothing, perhaps wisely sensing Lazander wasn't done. "But unless Gallow explicitly orders me, I will not hurt, kill, or maim anyone, Malik. Especially not a bartender whose only crimes are debt, a dead wife, and getting taken advantage of. We have a name now. 'Grim.' One we could have gotten without making the poor man *piss* himself."

The older Champion's eyes widened at Lazander's profanity—the man's words were usually cleaner than a nun's bloomers. Malik dragged a thoughtful hand through this beard, his hand resting on the tiny silver bead at the end.

"We could've spent time convincing him to give us Grim's name and the ledger, that's true," Malik conceded. "But when it comes to words, humans lie—it's their nature. Fear, however, well... I've always found it the quickest way to the truth. But let's say we'd done it your way. Do you think a man whose *entire* livelihood rests in the hands of Grim would give his benefactor up? Just like that? We'd have wasted hours, days even, trying to get him to trust us—and it might have been for nothing. My way, however, took what?" He made a show of squinting at the sun. "Twenty minutes? Tops?"

"We could have tried, Malik. People are worth the effort."

"Not when we have months before the Tyrant shows up, Zander. And no—it's not a matter of 'if' he arrives, it's *when*. He's already fired the first shot—the Ivory Keep would be ash if not for Gallow."

Lazander resisted the urge to say it was Eternity who'd saved the Keep from the wallow-tail, but it was the same difference to Malik. Instead Lazander changed tactic. "Then shouldn't we be defending people from wallow-tails, shadow-fiends, or whatever horrors await us as the Tyrant inches closer? Or better yet, tracking down Valerius? Last I checked he took out half the Ivory Keep—by *himself*. We're the only ones who can put him down." While Lazander had started out calm and reasonable, by the end his words were laced with fury. Images of Valerius flashed in Lazander's mind—in one memory he drank with the Gilded, quiet and taciturn, in the next he murdered Gabriel and Marito in cold blood, his teeth bared in a mockery of a smile.

Valerius had tried to kill the Gilded Knights, and he'd succeeded—Gabriel, Marito, and even Lazander lay dead. But Gallow had chosen to save Lazander, making him a warrior of the God of Judgment, a Champion of legend, and Lazander believed he'd done so for one reason—to stop Valerius.

The red-haired Champion clenched his fists, fighting the rage that made his muscles tremble.

Malik placed a steadying hand on Lazander. After a long moment, the new Champion sighed. "I know—Gallow wants us to hunt down Ravenna first. But I think Valerius—"

"This isn't the Gilded Knights, Zander," Malik said gently. "We can't run to every fire, hoping a sword and a cheeky catchphrase is enough to put it out. Gallow will send us to Valerius when the time is right. For now, our job is finding the bastard who tried to poison a bunch of men, women, and children—Grim. Our job is to *do*, Zander, not think."

The older man sighed. "That said… I know life as a Champion has been tough on you, so I'll tell you what. Next time you take point, and I'll give you the same time you gave me—twenty minutes. If that doesn't work, we do things my way. Deal?"

Lazander begrudgingly nodded. Malik was the most flexible of the Champions—Imani would have beaten the bartender bloody while Vivek would have set fire to the Giggle Worm as "encouragement." He should take what concessions he could.

"Deal."

"Now then," Malik said, rolling his shoulders. "What say you and I crack open this ledger and see if we can't find our dear old friend Grim?"

# Chapter Nine

Zara hiked through the night, keeping a lookout for stonebreakers that remained suspiciously absent while she rummaged in her memories for what she knew of Ravenna, the so-called "birth mother" of the vaxion and molger. As a child she hadn't been the most attentive student, preferring to brawl with her fellow cubs. When that became too easy, she shifted into her vaxion form and taunted the gigantic two-legged xandi just outside Moonvale's borders, competing with the older kids to see who would flinch first when the beasts brought a colossal hoof down. Yemena's many lectures and devotions to Ravenna were just white noise to Zara now, and to her embarrassment, the only thing she could recall was a children's story one of the den guardians loved telling.

"Vaxion and molger were not born falslings. They were humans once—a small, isolated tribe on the outskirts of the world," a man said, his voice warm and rich. Children crowded around, eager to listen.

While Zara was only six-years old at the time, she pushed the other kids out of the way, taking a spot at the very front. She was one of the youngest, only Fatyr was the same age as her. But they all let her pass, knowing to fear the claws she could already summon.

Zara sat cross-legged before the den guardian—the closest thing the kids had to a parent at that age. Vaxion children only learned the names of their birth parents when they hunted and killed a predator at the age of ten—usually a ripperback. Before that they were all raised together by a chosen group of vaxion. It allowed the children to quickly learn the pecking order of society, and the parents were spared the grief of spending years raising a child only for them to die during a hunt—a common occurrence.

"The Tyrant ripped open the skies with one mighty claw and stepped down upon the earth—almost breaking it in two," the den guardian continued. "People tried to fight back at first, but the Tyrant bore the skin of a stonebreaker and fangs the length of Moonvale. In days, tribes from the east to the west lay down their weapons, throwing themselves at the Tyrant's mercy."

"But why did the Tyrant come here? What did he want?" Fatyr asked.

Zara remembered she'd been annoyed—it was a stupid question.

"Who knows? Perhaps he saw in us what we see in mongrels—beasts who are only fit to be leashed," the den guardian replied.

The children booed, none louder than Zara. The man raised his hands, placating them. "I said 'perhaps.' Others think we angered the Tyrant in some way, and he sought retribution. The *shi'ara* says it is simply in his nature, the way it is in ours to hunt, feast, and fight."

"What does it matter?" Zara asked. "Would goober-pigs be happier if they knew we eat them because they're delicious? No."

"A fair point, little star," the den guardian said.

Zara stumbled on the memory—she'd thought only Ashira called her by that ridiculous pet name. The man's face sharpened in her mind, adding dark stubble along his chin and large eyes that shined like molten lava when the light caught them. "All that matters is that we were outmatched. Humans and gods alike fell to the Tyrant. In the end only one god stood—Ravenna, the Goddess of Truth."

Zara's nose had wrinkled in disgust. She'd hoped Ravenna would be the goddess of war, or death—something *impressive*. The thought of their patron being something as pathetic as "truth" was embarrassing. The guardian saw Zara's face and laughed.

"Patience, Zara. 'Truth' is important to this story. For the whole world was conquered until all that remained was a single pocket of light. A lone band of humans with nothing more than bows and spears stood against the Tyrant—*us*. But when the dark god appeared, half of us were struck down with a single step. The rest lay broken and dying, unable to move."

The children leaned forward, quiet now. They'd always thought the vaxion had sent the Tyrant running with his tail between his legs. "Everyone that is, but for one girl. Smaller than the rest, and barely older than a cub, she stood tall before the Tyrant, arms raised, a snarl upon her face."

The guardian dropped his voice. "And what, fair cubs, do you think she said?"

"I REFUSE!" the children cried, nearly collapsing over one another to yell it the loudest. "I REFUSE DEATH!" Zara joined in, fighting to yell louder than all the other kids combined.

The guardian clapped, whooping loudly. "Were the Tyrant here, he would flee! Alas, the young girl stood bloodied and alone. And so the Tyrant raised his foot—and brought it down upon her."

"What happened to her? Did she die?" Zara asked, unable to stop herself.

"Yes. And no. He struck the earth, but the girl was *gone*. The sky darkened, and our ancestors found their bones now healed. Fur and claw burst from their bodies as we swelled and grew. And suddenly the Tyrant no longer faced *humans*." The den guardian raised his hands, claws inching from his fingers as a fine layer of dark fur sprang from his skin. In seconds, he fully transformed his right arm, the dark and deadly claws of a vaxion stretching outward. "He faced the *vaxion*."

The children cheered, almost missing his addition of, "… and the molger."

"What happened to the girl?" Fatyr interrupted.

"Remember I said Ravenna was the goddess of 'truth'? Well, her worship was simple—the more bone-cutting truths you admitted, the greater the praise. When the girl proclaimed, 'I refuse death,' it was more than a battle cry. Had there been the slightest hesitation in her heart, Ravenna would not have heard her. But so furious was her cry, so radical her truth, that she became our first witch—our *shi'ara*."

Zara stopped at the memory, almost tripping over her own feet. The cold of night vanished from her skin in vapors as the sun rose. The story smacked of the usual vaxion arrogance—she doubted more than a kernel of it was true. But that wasn't what made her pause. She'd heard a tale just like it before, or a version of it, at least. Except in it, the girl's name was "Eternity" and the god who saved her was "Gallow," the towering God of Judgment that humans were so fond of worshipping. She knew stories changed the longer they were told, but it was odd that two gods had such a similar origin.

A whisper tugged at her—the faint sound of a laughing woman.

Zara snarled, "Shut up or show yourself."

The forest fell silent.

Zara's fists clenched, her heart hardening. Gallow, Calamity, Ravenna—their names didn't matter. They treated mortals like toys, content to play with them until they broke. Maybe Eternity and Gallow saved the humans while Ravenna rescued the vaxion and molger. Maybe neither of them did, and both stories were bald-faced lies—Zara didn't care. She had a job to do—rescue the parasite. And if Ravenna tried to trick, refuse, or bind Zara in any way, well… that just meant she had one more god to kill.

*\*\**

"Every date Grim hid out in the Giggle Worm matches up with the arrival of a shipment of mana crystals from the merchant Untis Gap," Lazander said. "Best guess says they hole up in the pub the night before, slip in as the ship docks, and are out before the sun rises." Lazander stretched, relishing the feel of his loose tunic and trousers. He'd swapped out his armor for something less intimidating, despite Malik's protests.

The docks of Freyley's oldest port looked much the same as he'd remembered—private sloops and the odd commercial schooner bobbed in steady waters, each as battered as the last. Redwind port served two kinds of people: those too cheap to pay the city center's docking fees and those who wanted their… business transactions kept quiet.

Lazander guessed Untis Gap was both.

"Mana crystals? That doesn't make a lick of sense. What would Grim want with mana crystals? Bloody things are huge and cost a fortune," Malik asked, arms crossed, sticking out like a sore thumb in his armor. He'd refused to change into "common" clothes, and so Lazander had moved among the dock workers alone, a bottle of gazzy in his back pocket for show, a smile on his face.

"The cost would explain why he's *stealing* them," Lazander said, trying and failing to keep his voice neutral. "As for why, who knows? He has at least one teleportation mage with him, and that's no lightweight magic. Depending on how often she's moving them around, she might be using the mana crystals to keep herself topped up."

"Hell of a lot of risk to take for a single mage," Malik said, shaking his head. "This stinks of a dead end."

"I thought the same until the foreman showed me this," Lazander said, pulling out a dark cloak. It was long, well worn, and smelled faintly of dust and earth. "Recognize it?"

Malik snatched it, giving it a sniff, his eyes going wide. "Grim was wearing something like it in Evergarden."

"One of the thieves left it behind just last week."

Malik narrowed his eyes. "I find it odd this foreman was so eager to spill the beans."

"It turns out he's my father's old drinking buddy," Lazander said, smiling sadly. "He thought I was still with the Gilded. Told me he's been begging the dockmaster to hire extra security, but his boss refused—said if there's a single crystal missing from the next shipment, he's fired."

Guilt tugged at Lazander. He thought of how eager the foreman was to tell him everything, thinking the Gilded Knights were here to help with the robberies. While Lazander hadn't *explicitly* lied to the man, he hadn't corrected him either. He told himself if he stopped Grim, then the thefts would stop too, and the foreman would keep his job. It helped quieten his conscience.

"This is all very fascinating," Malik said. "But Gallow ordered us to find Grim, not his shopping list."

Surprised at Malik's sharpness, the man seemed determined to take issue with everything Lazander said, he hurried to explain his reasoning. "The crates are important because they're warded with both light and divination spells. If a blood-assigned mage doesn't deactivate them within six hours, all of Navaros will know where they are. Which means..." He pulled out the map of Freyley the foreman had given him, laying it on a section of the docks he was relatively sure wasn't going to collapse. "They must have a base within six hours of Freyley—that's when the wards are set to go off."

"They have a *teleportation* mage, Zander," Malik said. "All she'd have to do is port them underground, and they're as good as gone."

"Teleportation has *very* strict weight and mass limitations—otherwise they wouldn't need the Giggle Worm, nor would they need to move the crystals by hand. Plus, only an incredibly powerful mage with an affinity for divination could deactivate the wards," Lazander countered. "And it just so happens that two such mages live within the six-hours." He gestured at the map, and two circles just north of Freyley's border

"This foreman is an expert in wards and mages too, is he?" Malik said, though Lazander could tell he was wavering.

"He's a good man, Malik. One who's terrified of losing his job," Lazander said, carefully folding the map. "He's done all the legwork for us—he just needed someone to believe him."

Malik stared at him for a long moment, then nodded, looking sour. "Lead on, brother."

## Chapter Ten

The parasite knelt, her forehead pressed into the floor as if an invisible force held her there. "You... you shouldn't be here," the girl said, every word threaded with pain.

Zara blinked in surprise, heart pounding when she realized where she was. The pitch-black darkness was a familiar sight—it had been her prison back when the parasite was in control of Zara's body.

The girl hissed in pain, and Zara bit her tongue. Asking if she was all right was as stupid as it was pointless—she clearly wasn't. "Does Calamity know you're here?" Zara asked instead.

"Sent me. Can't pull you out of your, *argh,* your body. Not like before. Yemena... did something."

Zara nodded, remembering the *shi'ara's* claim that she had "loosened" Calamity's hold. She silently thanked the dead witch—Yemena had been useful in the end, it seemed. "He's brought you here to tug at my heartstrings in the hopes I give you back control, granting him dominion over us again, correct?"

The girl nodded weakly. She opened her mouth to speak, then shut it tightly, her skin undulating as if something slithered beneath it. Hands in her dark curls, she dug her fingers into her skull, gasping in pain. "Stop, I'll tell her! I'll tell her! Just stop *screaming.*"

Collapsing onto her side the girl lay still, breathing hard, a trickle of sweat trailing down her cheek. Zara desperately wanted to help her up but didn't dare. A single touch might be all it took for Calamity to lock them both away.

"I take it the slug has something to say to me?" Zara asked quietly, doing her best to hide how much the girl's pain twisted a blade into her heart.

"He does. He wants to offer you a deal. If you give your body up, and I do as he says, he'll give the vaxion back their powers. When Magnus 'cured' the vaxion of Calamity's plague, he severed their connection to Ravenna—locking away their ability to shapeshift. But Calamity can restore it. He can make it so Moonvale is full of lightning once more. If you refuse..." the parasite's lips pulled back in a tired smile. "If you refuse, he'll kill me, he says." The girl didn't sound afraid at this proclamation. Quite the opposite—she sounded hopeful, as if death would be preferable to whatever the slug was doing to her in the Void.

A cold rage settled in Zara's heart.

The girl forced herself up onto one elbow, locking eyes with Zara, gold meeting hazel. Taking a deep breath, she spoke rapidly, as if every word was her last. "But he's lying. He *needs* his players to release him. He's running out of—"

The girl screamed, a horrible shrieking sound. Blood poured from her nose and ears, and Zara leaped backward, claws unsheathed.

"Stop it, foul beast!" she roared, the girl's screams nearly drowning her out. "Stop, or I will feast on your innards, Calamity!" But the darkness didn't reply, and Zara was forced to pace as the girl screamed, rolling on the ground like she was on fire. The sound of it, and how helpless Zara felt, made her want to rip her own skin off.

But then Calamity knew that. It was why he was doing it.

After what felt like hours, Zara couldn't take it anymore. "Take it. Take back control, *Teema*," she said fiercely, the name slipping out. "We defied him once, and we'll do it again."

Teema raised her head at Zara's new name for her but threw herself back at the Fury's outstretched hand.

"Don't!" Teema hissed. "I'll end up like Valerius—I'll do what he says, when he says it. I'm not... I'm not strong enough to say no. Not anymore." She raised her head, blood and tears smeared all over her cheeks. "Don't offer again, Zara. I'll... I'll say yes."

Zara's eyes snapped open, Teema's words echoing in her ears. The sun was high in the sky, the heat of noon doing little to rid Zara of the chill that drilled into her bones. She leaned against the trunk of a pink-flowered lumbar tree, her food half-eaten in her lap. She must have dozed off.

That wasn't like her.

On her feet, Zara ran tired hands over tired eyes. Calamity's "deal," Teema's screams, the girl's words on repeat in her mind.

"I'll say yes."

"I'll say yes."

"I'll—"

Zara drove a fist into the tree, splinters of bark digging into her knuckles. She punched it again and again, pink flowers floating around her like soft rain. She punched until she stopped thinking about what Calamity was doing to Teema. Until she stopped wondering why her heart was being torn in two—and for a girl she'd once called enemy, no less.

Anger flowed through her, washing away her embarrassment at choosing the word "Teema" for the parasite. Zara had to get to Calamity. But *how?*

*"Teema's mindbox is custard, slop, slop! Calamity makes it squishy, but he takes care not to break her—his spindly fingers need her! Needs you!"* the singing voice whispered. Light fingers brushed Zara's cheek. *"Will you help the sluggy boy? Will you give it all up for your 'Teema'? Or will you eat frogs and kick the moon, hehe!"*

In answer to the voice's nonsense, Zara snarled, **"Witness me. For I am death."**

She picked up her pack in her vaxion jaws, her lunch abandoned, and raced on four paws for Taskir.

***

Ravenna's Breath was dark and miserable—and therefore the most Yemena way of "honoring" the goddess that Zara could imagine.

Six statues of the same long-haired woman were arranged in a ring. In some she held out a gentle hand, a smile on her face, in others she swiped at an invisible enemy. What all the statues shared, however, be they smiling or glaring, was an imperious look—as if you should be grateful to be in her presence. Or perhaps that was just Zara's interpretation of the goddess. Either way she had to fight not to spit at the goddess' feet.

"You and I need to speak, Ravenna," she snarled at the closest statue—this one holding her arms out, as if waiting for an embrace. "*Now.*"

The goddess didn't answer. Zara sighed. Could nothing be easy?

Zara circled the statues, remembering their past splendor. Yemena used to sit for hours painting Ravenna's ridiculous cloak in garish colors, a pointless waste of time Zara thought, even as a child. Polished to perfection, any hint of creeping moss was ripped out at the very root. But that was a long time ago. Now, Ravenna was missing an arm here, a leg there. One was even headless, her stony body reminding Zara of a corpse stuck to a pike in warning. The vaxion frowned at the grime, muck, and moss that littered the shrine entrance. Hadn't Yemena been making the trek out here to tend to it? If so, the *shi'ara* had clearly forgotten how to use a scrubbing cloth.

Zara ran a finger along the edge of one of the statues, noting the claw marks. A vaxion had broken it, she knew. It didn't take much to guess why—Ravenna had sat back and done nothing while her precious vaxion were ravaged by Calamity's plague. She wondered what killed the vaxion who did this—the sickness, or Yemena's fury when she found her shrine desecrated.

But the grubby statues meant little to Zara—she hadn't hiked all this way to look at a bunch of stone. Walking past them, she got as close as she dared to the edge of the gigantic, perfectly spherical hole the statues circled. She leaned over, staring into the thick impenetrable darkness. Darkness that shouldn't exist when the sun burned hot in the sky. Frowning, she picked up a twig.

**"Spark, so that the world may know my flame."**

The wood burst into flames, and she tossed it into the hole. The unnatural darkness swallowed it instantly, denying her any hint of how deep it was, or what lay below.

"Spelled," Zara announced. "Your doing, Ravenna, or a leftover from when Yemena licked your boots?"

Silence.

Zara stared into the darkness, remembering the stories of Ravenna's Breath she'd heard as a child. A vaxion earned the right to the names of their birth parents when they slew a predator at age ten. However, to be named true vaxion, you had to master the ability to shapeshift and present it to Ravenna—and what better way than by combat?

Unlike a child's first hunt in which you were tossed into the fray and expected to sink or swim, this was no battle of instinct. To earn Ravenna's pleasure you were required to fight in your vaxion skin with the ease of your human, shift at least a dozen times without pause, and be able to replenish your mana within the hour. The last was especially important. It was why most vaxion spent their teenage years meditating when not fighting or feasting. Though Jaza hadn't shifted in over a decade, she still spent hours in the freezing cold streams of the undergrotto practicing her breathing.

Zara had missed out on the years of preparation needed for Ravenna's Breath—she'd been a child when Magnus had taken her. But even if she'd spent her teenage years among the vaxion, she doubted she would have taken to what she dubbed "fancy breathing." She could never sit still, nor did she have any interest in learning about the "heart as a mana focus," and "mana pathways." Instead she relied on the sheer wealth of mana she possessed. The little she remembered from lessons with Yemena she'd passed on to Lukas.

However, as she stared into the darkness below, Zara briefly regretted not being a more attentive student.

What lay within Ravenna's Breath varied. Jaza's claim that she'd fought ripperbacks while another vaxion faced down stonebreakers matched up with what Zara had heard. Ravenna tailored each trial to the individual. One vaxion might be five transformations deep when a starving ripperback horde descended while another could spend their trial chasing whippertusks through tunnels thick and thin, shifting through endless obstacles. But while that was the official story, there were rumors. Stories of mongrels Ashira had no use for who prowled the tunnels, trapped in a monstrous collision of molger and vaxion body parts, unable to think. Unable to feel anything but bloodlust and rage. A shiver ran through Zara. In another life, she might have been one of the mongrels dumped in Ravenna's tunnels—fodder for true vaxion to sharpen their claws on.

Yet despite the horrors of Ravenna's Breath, it was extremely rare for a vaxion to die. "Ravenna wishes to challenge you, to see you use your gifts to the fullest," Yemena always said. "She does not wish to harm you. You will not be given any task or battle that you cannot conquer."

Zara's fists clenched. If the vaxion's safety was so dear to her, where had Ravenna been all these years her "children" were dying? Where was she when Valerius and Magnus showed up? When Yemena, her most devout servant, had her head cut off by Magnus?

She'd been here—*hiding*. And it was past time someone dragged her out.

Zara spat into the hole. "When I find you, and I *will* find you, Ravenna, you will weep with delight at the thought of aiding me. Or Gallow will be the only god left alive in this wretched world. Do you hear me?"

The darkness didn't answer.

Foot raised, Zara was about to drop down when the hairs on the back of her neck rose—someone was watching her. She made a show of tensing, as if she was about to leap, then charged for a cluster of trees off to her right.

**"I am death's mistress, bow before me,"** she hissed. Claws erupted from her fingertips and toes, as sharp as they were deadly. Fearless, Zara drove headfirst into the undergrowth, only to slam into Lukas. She pinned him by the throat before he could blink.

"Zara, it's me! *Zara*!" he yelped, hands raised in surrender.

"What are you doing here, cub? I told you to *stay*," she growled, claws still pressed to his neck.

"A couple of things, Zara. One—we're the same age, stop calling me cub. And two—only one lady gets to yank my leash, and she's busy getting her head kicked in by a *god*." He raised his right forearm, shifting his bracer to reveal the edge of his blood-debt, dark red and angry. "Yes, she's my friend, and yes, I'd cut off my leg to save her. But that doesn't change the fact that I have to pay this back *somehow* or die a horribly painful death. Until then I'm your problem and you're mine. Now, I'm not kink-shaming, but can you kindly stop choking me, so we can help… spirit lady, other Zara—you know who I mean!"

"I came here for *peace*, not for Teema," Zara snarled, irritation making her contrary.

Lukas grimaced. "I know I've skin like a baby's backside, but I wasn't born yesterday. This is obviously—wait, what did you say? Teema? Is that… is that your new name for her?" His eyes grew large when he saw Zara's face. "Are you *blushing?*

Ah, I mean, I'm just surprised you chose 'Teema.' I knew she meant a lot to me—she saved my life, after all. But I didn't know you felt like *that*."

Zara released Lukas, turning away abruptly. "It is a name, nothing more."

"I didn't really study vaxion script, but doesn't teema mean—"

"It means *nothing*. Now are you here to help or not?" Zara said briskly, striding away. Lukas jogged to catch up, a large, stupid grin on his face. Zara growled, but he only smiled harder.

"I like Teema. It suits her," Lukas said. "You know, she worried about you all the time. We'd be nearly ripped to shreds during one of Calamity's ridiculous quests, but as we fell asleep, she'd be excited to tell you what happened. Even the weeks you didn't say a word to her, she still looked forward to seeing you. You scared her, but... she admired you. Told me you were the strongest person she'd ever met."

Zara wanted to tell Lukas to shut up but found her heart was twisting with a heavy emotion she couldn't name. They came to the edge of Ravenna's Breath, the darkness before them beckoning.

"Keep talking, cub," she said, stepping into the open air. "It makes you excellent bait." She dropped like a stone into the shadows below, knowing Lukas was only a step behind her.

## Chapter Eleven

Valerius felt *amazing*.

All this time he thought serving Calamity was a punishment. A trial he had to suffer through, whining all the while—why him? What did he do to deserve this? Now as he bit down on the soft throat of a passing stranger, blood filling his mouth like sweet wine, Valerius saw the truth. It didn't matter what was real—this world with its arcade game characters or his life back on Earth with screaming fights between his parents and the brothers he didn't remember. All that mattered was *Calamity*.

The man in his arms twitched, his final words lost to a gurgle. Valerius dumped the body on the ground and waited. Wiping blood from his mouth, he smiled when the man's flesh twitched, shadows crawling up his skin. The man had chosen wisely.

He'd chosen Calamity.

In seconds, the darkness stretched over the man to form the beautiful, elegant form of a shadow-fiend. With a jerk the creature rose on its skeleton-like feet, born anew thanks to their master. Valerius pointed at the curl of smoke in the distance, nearly lost to the noonday sun. The monster turned, and lurched toward the village, picking up speed as it grew used to its powerful body. In the space of an hour everyone in that village would be either dead or freshly born shadow-fiends. And with every beast born, another five followed. Soon all of Navaros would be overrun, and from there Freyley, Evergarden... no, the entire *world* would fall.

It was almost too easy.

Gratitude warmed Valerius' heart like a fire in the depths of winter. Calamity could have turned him into a mindless shadow-fiend, but the god had given Valerius chance after chance instead, offering him endless gifts while Valerius stamped his foot like a child throwing a tantrum. Calamity was patient. Calamity was *kind*.

"Thank you," he whispered aloud, knowing the god could hear him. "Thank you for choosing me." As if in answer ice frosted the tips of his fingers, and his sword arm twitched in anticipation—the heady power of the game versions of Magnus and Valerius coursing through him. He was powerful. *Unstoppable.* He was— a stabbing pain shot through his skull, grating like steel against steel.

*Breathe. One. Two.*

*Breathe. Three. Four.*

His left hand shook violently. Grabbing it with his free hand, he tried to force the tremors to calm.

*I am the first. The first strong enough to cage two souls—one a hero, the other a villain. Calamity chose me. I will not fail him. I will not!*

It was only when he bit his lip hard enough to bleed that his body calmed, the souls of the real Magnus and Valerius fading into the shadows. He took a steadying breath, sweat dripping from his brow, his mind his own—for now, at least. But this couldn't continue. If he had an "episode" in the middle of a fight, as he'd taken to calling the random, painful attacks, it could be the end of him. But Calamity's voice whispered in his ears, and Valerius smiled.

Calamity had a plan. He always did.

Back on Earth, Valerius was just a child—when fate conspired against him, all he could do was cry and pray the "adults" would protect him. But they never did. In this world, he'd worn the mask of Valerius, but failure dogged his footsteps as he tried to live in two worlds—the hero Valerius in one, servant of Calamity in the other. Now, after all this time, he finally knew who he really was.

A player—one who served Calamity. And since the idiot who wore Magnus' skin came first, and the rebel who'd turned on Calamity third, his new name only made sense.

Player Two.

\*\*\*

"Now this one right here is a *beauty*. Lean in a bit, sonny, don't be shy." The old man proudly held up the ugliest ceramic frog Lazander had ever seen, which was impressive, considering he'd been shown about twenty of them in the last ten minutes.

"It's… lovely," he managed at last.

Emeret Grouse smiled toothily. His robes, once the deep purple of Navaros' palace mages, were now gray and moth-eaten. Lazander and Malik sat in a rundown cottage just outside Freyley's border where chickens, pigs, and sheep ran amok outside. A goat the size of a wolfhound sat in the cottage next to Lazander, chewing on a lump of straw with lazy contentment. Lazander had tried to ask why a goat was in the house, but two minutes with Emeret Grouse had proven that getting a straight answer out of him was like trying to catch water in a sieve.

Emeret shuffled toward Malik, the ugly ceramic frog cupped in his hands. The Champion leaned against the door, wearing a look that could crack stone. "Would you like to meet my frog, sonny? This one is called Wilbert," Emeret said, unaware he was seconds from death.

"Mage crystals!" Lazander said quickly, darting in front of the old man. "We were talking about mage crystals, remember? You used to spell them for the merchant Untis Gap, right?"

Emeret frowned but nodded. "Yes, yes that's right. I left when he tried to cut my fees, claiming he could get a fella from Evergarden for half the price. 'Go ahead!' I told him. 'How many people can say they have an Ivory Keep mage working for them? Eh?' Untis was real rude about it too. Told me I should've returned my robes when the Keep gave me the boot—and all because I like the odd bit to drink!" Emeret shot Lazander a panicked look, clutching his worn robes. "Wait—are you here for my robes? You can't have them, you hear! They're mine!"

"Of course they're yours, Emeret," Lazander said kindly. "I would never take them."

"Good, that's good. Have you met Wilbert?" he asked, holding up his ceramic frog for the third time. Lazander heard the whisper of a blade leaving its sheath and knew he had seconds before Malik took over.

"Grim," Lazander said, throwing caution to the wind. Every question he'd asked, Emeret either hadn't known or gotten distracted within seconds of answering. It was time to be honest. "We're looking for a man called Grim. Tall, scar over his eye—"

"—from Evergarden," Emeret finished. "I know him. Why?"

Lazander heard Malik's blade ease back into the sheath slightly.

"He tried to poison the wells of Evergarden. If we hadn't stopped him, he would have killed a lot of people," Lazander said, deciding on the truth. "We're trying to find him before he hurts anyone else."

Emeret shook his head, looking distressed. "No, that ain't right. Grim… Grim ain't like that. He wouldn't hurt a fly."

"It's true, old man," Malik said, barreling past Lazander. "And you can either tell us where he is, or I'll strip you naked and burn your robes to ash."

Emeret clutched his palace robes, dropping his frog. It hit the stone and shattered instantly. The old man gasped, shaky hands reaching for the pieces. "Wilbert! Oh, Wilbert, I'm so sorry."

"Let me help," Lazander said, shooting a glare at Malik as he picked up the pieces. "Malik, why don't you step outside and let me handle this?"

In response, the Champion crossed his arms. Lazander bit back his irritation.

"Wilbert…" the old man said softly.

Lazander led him to a chair and gently took Emeret's hand in his, aware of how parchment thin the old man's hands were.

"Mr. Grouse," Lazander began. "Grim is… in danger."

"He is?"

Lazander nodded, hating the lie. "And we need to find him, so we can protect him."

"Does that mean you're one of Ravenna's boys?"

"That's right," Lazander said, holding his smile in place.

"Oh, why didn't you say so?" Emeret reached into his robes and started patting them down. "Bloodied Void, can never find anything in these…"

Malik moved to grab a chair but Lazander held out a hand, shooting him a warning look. If they disturbed Emeret now, he might forget what he was doing. To Lazander's surprise, Malik backed up.

"Ah, here it is! They told me to keep it for emergencies," Emeret said, holding up… another ceramic frog. This one was dark red with bright yellow eyes. Its mouth was open slightly, a pitch-black tongue just visible within.

Malik threw his hands in the air and stormed out of the cottage, slamming the door behind him.

"Who's that? Is someone there?" Emeret asked, looking worried.

"Did Grim give you this?" Lazander asked, pointing at the frog.

"Benjamin? No."

Lazander sighed, ready to thank Emeret for his time, but the mage tapped the frog twice on the head. Its black tongue shot out and twisted away—pointing toward the door.

"Grim only gave me the spell—I chose the vessel. And Benjamin here nearly hopped himself to death, he was so eager for the job! Grim and his lot move about constantly, but he said if I ever ran into trouble, I was to use this to find them."

Lazander had to fight not to reach out and snatch the frog. This was it. Weeks of searching, and they'd finally *got* him.

"I know your... frogs are precious to you," Lazander said. "But I really, really need to find Grim. Can I borrow it—"

"Benjamin."

"Can I borrow Benjamin for a while? I'll bring it back to you after, I swear it on—" He almost said Gallow but realized that although he'd promised to serve the God of Judgment, that wasn't what was most sacred to him. "I swear it on my mother's life," he said finally.

Emeret stared at him for a long moment, then nodded. "Grim told me not to give Benjamin to anyone else, but you've got eyes like Grim. Kind eyes. I don't think he'd mind if you borrowed Benjamin for a little while." He handed the frog to Lazander as if it were made of gold, and Lazander took it with the same reverence, making a show of wrapping it in cloth before putting it away.

"Thank you, Emeret," Lazander said. "You've saved a lot of people today."

Emeret's eyes glazed over, and he looked up at Lazander with a frown. "Who are you? What are you doing in my house?"

*\*\*\**

Lazander found Malik pacing the dirt road leading to the ancient cottage. He'd only been outside for a few minutes, but he'd already worn a path in the dirt, Gallow's gifts lending him speed. Chickens and pigs trotted by him, making sure to give him a wide berth.

Lazander didn't blame them.

"What a colossal waste of time," Malik snapped. "Juliet Withers knew *nothing*, and Emeret is a doddering fool. 'Only two mages within six hours' my eye. *This* is why we do things my way. This is why we—"

Lazander held out the crimson frog. Malik's eye twitched, and he looked ready to smash it into the ground when the frog's tongue moved, pointing south.

"It'll lead us to Grim. I'm not sure if it's spelled to find him specifically, or just his hideout, but we're on the right track," Lazander said, taking care to keep his voice even.

"Well, color me surprised. Well done, brother." Malik smiled, anger evaporating too quickly. He gave Lazander a friendly slap on the shoulder. "That took a bit more time than I would have liked, but I'm glad I let you take point on this one. Now, why don't I take it from here?"

He held out a hand, and Lazander had the sudden urge to put the frog back in his pocket—a ridiculous sensation he quashed, giving the makeshift compass to Malik.

Lazander took a moment to look back at Emeret's rundown cottage before they left, silently apologizing to the mage for the deception.

*It's for a good cause, I swear it. I'll not kill or hurt anyone I don't have to, and I'll have Benjamin back to you before you know it.*

He sped after Malik, tendrils of guilt squeezing his heart.

# Chapter Twelve

Eternity sat bolt upright in bed, Gallow's voice booming in her ears.

**"SOUTH."**

It was one word, but that was all she needed. Outside it was still dark—the birds had just begun their morning chorus, but Eternity leaped out of her bedroll immediately. Moving quickly, she grabbed a bag, shoving the bare essentials inside. She'd served Gallow for over a century, yet in all that time she'd either traveled by carriage, in which case all her things were packed for her, or she was being held in a dungeon, tower, or temple by whoever held dominion over her—in which case possessions were the last thing on her mind. Either way, she'd never needed to pack her own things.

Which meant when Gallow first ordered her to track down the shadowfiends, she'd shown up with two trunks—one of which was entirely filled with books. After a few weeks traveling with soldiers, and some gentle instruction from Mara, a simple satchel was now all she needed.

Outside her tent, Mara and Kilin stood watch. Well Mara did, with her back straight, one hand resting on her sword. Kilin was fast asleep, a line of drool trailing down his chin.

"My lady?" Mara asked. "Is everything all right?"

"Gallow summoned me."

"I'll rouse the men, just give me a—"

**"LEAVE THEM."**

"No," Eternity said, sharper than she intended. "Now, I… I am to head south alone."

"Whatever for, my lady?"

Eternity considered dodging the question until she realized the knight's frown was one of concern. Mara wasn't like the other soldiers—she'd worked closely with the Gilded, and through them, Eternity. She wasn't as intimidated by Gallow's Chosen as most people were.

Kilin's own snore jerked him awake. "Washappenin'?" he asked.

"I… do not know what Gallow needs of me," Eternity said, looking at Mara. "We rarely do."

Mara frowned. "Begging your pardon, my lady, but in my experience, a mission where most are kept in the dark rarely succeeds."

Eternity bristled. "The God of Judgment provides. Kindly send my apologies to Commander Rhys. Gallow willing, I'll return at speed."

With that she ran for the cliff edge, leaving Kilin blinking owlishly and Mara's brow furrowed. Cold air whipped about her face when she leaped into the air, and she let herself freefall for a moment, taking in the red and orange bursts of dawn.

**"Bless mine body, so I might better tread your path."**

Light as a feather Eternity shot into the air, arms wide. She couldn't help the laugh that escaped her. Gallow could be a difficult taskmaster, but the rewards? She spun in the air, imagining this must be how Merrin felt when she flew—joyful and free.

As she soared, however, the reality of her situation settled in. Gallow's orders were never exactly informative, but having nothing but a direction was unusual. Had the wallow-tail reappeared? Had another of the Tyrant's servants broken free? She sped up, fearful of what she would find but also selfishly hoping Lazander would be there.

It had been too long.

\*\*\*

Zara hit the ground almost immediately, surprise making her land awkwardly. She looked up to see that the "hole" that served as the entrance to the trials of Ravenna's Breath was barely ten feet deep. From above, it looked endless. Lukas landed next to her—with half her grace and twice the noise.

"Ah, my backside isn't made of stone, Ravenna!" he yelped, grimacing.

Zara barely heard him, she was too busy examining the bizarre room they'd found themselves in. Every story and account she'd heard of Ravenna's Breath described it as a simple earthen maze. If anything was alive, she'd expected to find the beasts crowded around the entrance—a stonebreaker or two perhaps or a particularly stubborn whippertusk who refused to be a good little piggie and die in the dark. What she hadn't expected was a gigantic room made of *metal*.

Zara frowned in confusion, staring first at the walls and ceiling, which seemed to glow from within, lighting the entire room, then down at her feet. Kneeling, she ran her fingers over the wavy lines and curved symbols. With growing unease, she realized that every inch of the metal cavern, from floor to ceiling, was engraved by hand with strange glyphs. The script looked painfully familiar, but she couldn't place where she'd seen it. However, she understood a handful of words— "hidden," "contain," and for some reason "mana" written over and over again.

What was this place?

Zara scanned the room to find they stood at a crossroads. Tunnels spiraled out like the points of a star, all lined with the same strange metal and glyphs. The room was spotlessly clean, and dust-free—suspiciously so. A memory tickled the back of Zara's mind. She'd never laid eyes on the maze before, but it reminded her of something. Something important.

*"Starry-eyed, starry bride!"* The voice returned at full blast, making Zara jump. The memory slipped away, forgotten. *"The cage rattles, the screen cracks, the arcade lingers!"* it cried, more gleeful and irritating than before. Zara didn't know what an "arcade" was but resolved to break it the moment she found it. She glanced at Lukas to see him muttering as he dusted himself down but gave no sign he'd heard the voice.

Zara's fists clenched. The thought of the voice tormenting her alone made her guts twist. She'd spent so long under Magnus' influence, she despised the thought of someone, or *something,* taking up his mantle.

*"Games, games!"* the voice cried. *"Joystick left, attack, roll—too slow, too quick!"*

"Are you all right?" Lukas asked her. Zara belatedly realized she'd been growling.

"Yes," she said quickly. "Just… trying to remember what I know of Ravenna's Breath. This is not what I expected."

"Same. I thought it'd be the usual storybook stuff: monsters, a maze that challenges our 'friendship,' and Ravenna swooping in at the end to give us a big wet kiss, or something. I didn't think her shrine was the glorified inside of a helmet."

"Hm," was Zara's only answer, suspicion digging its talons into her mind. Taking a breath she let her senses expand. A surprising scent of cleanliness, almost surgical, met her nose, carrying none of the usual decay that came with being underground. Then an acrid scent hit her, making her stomach flip.

"Do you smell that?" Zara asked Lukas, not trusting her senses.

"Oh gods, it's like a drunk's underwear after a binge. Urgh, why can I *taste* it?"

Pleased that the scent wasn't a trick of the voice, Zara chose the tunnel where it was strongest, walking toward it.

"Why are we going *toward* the vomit-inducing smell?"

"Ravenna!" Zara called out, her voice reverberating down the tunnel, becoming louder and louder. "I seek to kill Calamity. Will you aid me or end up another corpse in my wake?"

Silence.

"That's why."

"That literally answered nothing. Zara? Zara!" Lukas gave a loud, dramatic sigh but begrudgingly chased after her.

\*\*\*

Hours later, Lukas realized something was wrong with Zara—aside from her usual rage and inability to handle any emotion other than said rage. She was walking at a blistering pace and kept jerking her head to one side, then shaking it off with a frown.

It was unnerving. He almost preferred it when she was snapping at him.

They passed countless other metal rooms, much like the one they'd first entered. Zara would take one long sniff, then head for the tunnel that smelled like feces after a week in a hot attic. He kept pace with her, waiting for the walls to turn to stone or earth at any moment, but they never did. Every inch of the maze-like tunnels was covered with the same strange metal. The sheer *cost* of such a structure was mindboggling. Where had the vaxion managed to find this much steel? For a people who shunned weapons and preferred leather for armor, how had they scrounged up the money for something like this? Even a simple sword cost a couple of gold.

And then realization struck Lukas like a blow to the head.

"The vaxion didn't build this," he said aloud. "They couldn't have—the time, materials, expertise... there's just no way."

"That much is obvious, yes."

"And you didn't think to share that with the class?"

"I did not, for the same reason I felt no need to tell you that the sky is blue," Zara replied.

Sighing, Lukas chose to ignore that one. "Then who..." His voice trailed off when he spotted rust-brown stains on the wall, smeared in places. He tentatively scratched at one with his finger, surprised when it flecked off easily.

"Blood," Zara and Lukas said at the same time.

The trail continued, the blood stains growing in number and size, smeared against the wall and ground. Yet the halls remained free of bodies.

Zara groaned, pressing her hand against her skull. "Shut up!" she yelled. "Enough of your riddles!"

Lukas looked around, suddenly very aware he was alone underground with a woman known as "the Fury."

"Are you... talking to me?" he asked gently, unsure what he wanted the answer to be.

"No, I trade blows with a coward!" she snarled, head whipping around. "One who seeks to torment me rather than speak clearly." Whatever she heard made her angrier. "'Save game'? 'Calamity System'? Each word is more nonsensical than the last!"

"Wait!" Lukas said, a memory surfacing. "Teema mentioned the Calamity System. She said that was how her boss spoke to her—how she spoke to you too. Is *Calamity* speaking to you?" he asked, voice dropping to a low whisper.

"No. I know the slug's voice—it is not him. But I have a feeling I know who it is." She gestured with a flick of her chin down the hall, and for a long moment Lukas only saw more smears of blood turned dark over the years. But as he moved closer, he could make out the rough sketch of a figure painted in blood. At the person's feet people knelt, pulling their chests open with their bare hands, revealing bloodied hearts. The faces were a swirl of scribbles, each messier than the last. Only the hearts were drawn in any real detail, or as much detail as a finger dipped in blood was capable of.

Lukas had seen his fair share of gruesome sights in his time, from dead bodies to ripped off limbs. But none of them had made his skin crawl like the mural did.

"What is this thing?" he asked, at a loss for words for once.

"Do you not find it interesting," Zara said, trailing a claw over the figure at the center. "That everything we've been taught about Ravenna's maze is a lie? I see no earthen walls nor the desiccated remains of the hundreds, nay, thousands of monsters the vaxion killed down here, all in Ravenna's name."

"Maybe that's part of it," Lukas said with a shrug. "You learn and prepare for one thing, and the super fun bit is that all that work was for nothing. That would be *very* vaxion."

"Perhaps, but Jaza spewed everything she knew of Ravenna's Breath at me. She is wracked by the same guilt as Ashira over what happened to me—she would not lie, nor would a lie serve any purpose. Without Yemena overseeing the trials, Ravenna cannot pass her blessing on to us, marking us vaxion true."

Lukas realized she was right. Plus, the more he thought of it, the more insane it was that neither of them had heard of a gigantic metal maze that ran under half of Moonvale. Probably more, seeing as they hadn't explored most of the tunnels. The vaxion kept their secrets close, but no one drank like they did. Surely someone would have spilled the beans, especially when every *single* vaxion had to come down here at some point.

"Wait, why is it so bright?" Lukas asked, pointing upward. "We're hundreds of feet underground, but it's as warm and cheery as the noonday sun. Do you see any torches? Or mage-fire lanterns?"

"I wondered when you would notice," she said.

A stab of disappointment hit Lukas. What else had she figured out but hadn't bothered to tell him?

"Magnus claimed to be one of the most talented mages in Navaros," Zara continued, trailing a hand over a clean patch of the wall, "but not even he could make the walls glow like a sun. I have never seen anything like this."

"I don't like this place, Zara," Lukas confessed, knowing she was probably going to yell at him for it. "Something feels... wrong."

"Or right," Zara said, surprising him. "Can you not feel it? The walls, the ceiling, the very floor hums with magic. *Our* magic. Or should I say—*her* magic." She tapped a claw against the bloodied figure in the center of the mural.

"Ravenna," he whispered. Somehow knowing that it was the vaxion goddess made it even more disturbing. He shuddered, covering it with a shrug, "I feel like you're trying to get at something, but let's both pretend I'm too stupid to figure it out and skip to the bit where you explain it to me."

Zara sighed. "Let us go with your theory—that the stories we were reared on of Ravenna's Breath were a lie designed to throw us off the truth of the trials. That does not explain why neither Ashira nor Jaza mentioned a metal colossus. Unless..." she trailed off as she dragged a claw through the bloodied figure of Ravenna.

"Unless..." Lukas echoed, the dark look in Zara's eyes making him more nervous.

"My time with Magnus taught me one thing," she said, unusually quietly. "That thought is malleable, and memories but a stream that can be directed."

"You think... you think someone messed with the vaxion's memories? Every *single* one of them?"

"A far-fetched idea I admit, but why else have we never heard of this place?"

Lukas tried to think of any other theory, he really did—but beyond someone spiking all of the vaxion's drinks after they did the trials, he had nothing. He shook his head. "But why would someone do that?"

Zara's claw split Ravenna's body in half. "Not why—who? Who told us stories of Ravenna's Breath? Who ran the trials? And who alone visited this place long after the vaxion fell to the plague, braving wild stonebreakers to 'tend' to a defunct shrine?"

"Yemena, obviously—she was the *shi'ara*. 'Was' being the operative word."

Abruptly Zara slashed at the wall, rendering the mural an incomprehensible, flaky mess. Lukas' eyes widened when Zara slashed at it again and again, then stepped back with a gesture. He frowned and realized what she was trying to show him—despite her claws being hard enough to break stone and steel, she hadn't left a scratch on the wall itself.

"Calamity is not the only god with secrets," Zara said, every word laced with anger. "There is a voice here, a *presence,* that calls out to me. And I would bet my left claw that Yemena heard it too."

\*\*\*

Lazander turned the ceramic frog left, then right, but the creature's tongue kept pointing downward.

"This can't be it, can it?" Malik asked. He pressed his hand to the soil, running his fingers over the meadow's soft grass—the kind Lazander's horse, Mabel, loved to eat. Thoughts of Mabel summoned Galora and her rumbling chuckle. She was the first dragon Lazander saw laugh. Merrin's soft chirp followed, a sound she made when she was falling asleep. It was the only thing that had made him feel safe when he was a boy.

Lazander's gaze grew hazy, lost in a memory that vanished as quickly as it appeared, his left hand suddenly ice-cold.

"What do you reckon, brother?" Malik pressed.

"That you were right," Lazander replied, shaking his head—what had he been thinking about? He slipped the frog—Benjamin—he corrected himself, into his pocket. "We're only a day's ride from the Freyley border and a stone's throw from Moonvale. All Grim would have to do is get the boxes to Emeret, have him disable the wards, then haul them here, or rather…" he tapped the ground with his foot. "…underground. The question is, where is the—"

Malik drove a fist into the dirt, splitting soil and rock with a single punch.

Lazander leaped back, but Malik kept going, gritting his teeth, the earth exploding outward with every punch, quicker than any shovel. Several feet deep, he straightened, hands on his hips.

"Oh, that's tough on the old back. You take over."

"Malik, you're destroying half the meadow," Lazander snapped, gesturing at the mounds of earth and half-buried flowers. "There must be an entrance somewhere nearby."

"I know you're a tree-hugger, brother, but we'd spend all day looking for the damned thing. They're right below us, and we know that for a fact."

"For *now*. I imagine they heard your fists in Freyley," Lazander said, his mouth a thin line.

"Then you best get thumping, eh?" Malik grinned. "Can't have them giving us the slip, now can we?"

Lazander sighed but leaped into the rough hole, his fists raised.

# Chapter Thirteen

Valerius, Prince of Navaros, leader of the Gilded Knights, was losing his mind.

He didn't drink. Didn't eat. He hadn't slept in what felt like weeks. Yet he continued to live and breathe in the strange impenetrable darkness that was his prison. Thick chains wound around his neck and wrists, but they had no lock or keyhole. The links that ran from his bindings simply disappeared behind him into the endless dark.

He was alone, as he had been for most of his imprisonment. Valerius had been captured once by a rival kingdom, and while it had been far from a pleasant experience, it had taught him what to expect. Threats, beatings, perhaps even a cut-off finger or two to be sent for ransom—he steeled his heart, trying to ready himself.

Yet when his captor appeared out of thin air, Valerius' jaw dropped, his grand, valiant speech about how Navaros dealt with villains all but forgotten.

Valerius' captor had dark hair, sharp cheekbones, and a jawline his mother teased was a sculpture's dream. His captor didn't just look like Valerius—his captor *was* Valerius. Every detail was perfect, from the tiny scar above the left eyebrow caused by a stray dagger, to the dimple in the right cheek. It was like looking in a mirror.

A doppelganger. He'd been captured by, of all things, a doppelganger. Valerius had read about the shape-stealers in fables as a child but thought them creatures of myth and legend. Yet there the doppelganger stood—staring at Valerius with a mix of awe and fear, as if the prince was the imposter and not him.

What followed was bizarre, and even weeks later, Valerius still had no idea what any of it meant.

The doppelganger sat opposite him and began speaking rapidly, nearly tripping over his words as he told Valerius his story. He claimed this entire world was an "arcade game," that Valerius was just a character, and that for a "player" to get home, he had to complete the "Operator's quests" and reach the "endgame."

What few words Valerius understood were nonsense.

Despite his doppelganger's obvious insanity, Valerius tried to reason with him. The Gilded Knights were vital to the safety of Navaros, and without Valerius, only two members were active—Marito and Gabriel. They'd spent months scouting for new knights to join their ranks, and Valerius had heard promising stories of a soldier called Lazander, but the boy wasn't ready—not for a year or two at least. The doppelganger risked hundreds if not thousands of lives by keeping Valerius captive, the prince argued, and if he agreed to let Valerius go, he swore the creature would suffer no repercussions.

But the doppelganger kept shaking his head, looking terrified, and so Valerius tried a different tactic. He was alive, which meant the creature must want *something*. He offered gold, pardons, even a small patch of land to do with as he saw fit.

But the creature refused, saying the same thing over and over again— "I have to do what the Operator says."

Eventually the doppelganger stopped visiting, but Valerius never gave up. He fought his chains every moment he had the strength, but as the days went by, the darkness started to play with his mind. In the shadows he saw flashes of a vaxion woman, Magnus of Ashfall, and a strange red desert. For some reason, the images terrified Valerius, making him shake with a fear he didn't understand. Whenever this happened, he used a tried-and-true trick to calm his mind—he focused on the last thing he remembered, walking through every scent and smell as if he were still there.

The Gilded were tracking the Brothers of Blood, a group of bandits who were attacking Navaros' borders, striking smaller towns and burning them to the ground. The queen's mysterious spymaster sent word as he always did, through one of his spies known as "shadows." The Brothers of Blood were headed straight for Ashfall—home of Magnus, a reclusive ice mage with a… penchant for vaxion. While Magnus' skill was renowned, even more so than his eccentricities, he was only one man against an army of bandits. The Gilded raced for the castle, praying they weren't too late.

But they hadn't known. Hadn't known that the stories of Zara the Fury and the fire she wielded weren't just true—they paled in comparison to the woman herself.

Valerius watched Zara call down fire from the sky, trapping the bandits in a narrow valley. One by one over eighty men fell to her flames. They screamed as they burned and she along with them—though hers were screams of joy.

And then an agony he'd never known exploded in his mind. Falling from his horse, the world went white. He barely felt it when he hit the ground. The last thing he remembered was Gabriel and Marito. The giant of a knight scooped him up easily, one hand around his shoulders as he roared, "I am here, my prince! What ails you? Speak, good ser!"

"Mari, I don't think he can talk *and* scream at the same time. Now, move your bloody hands out of the way!" Gabriel called, laying a hand on Valerius' forehead.

And then the prince was gone—Marito and Gabriel an afterimage against his eyelids.

When next he opened his eyes the Gilded Knights—his friends and brothers—were gone, and he knelt chained and alone in this strange darkness. He didn't know where he was, how he'd gotten there, or how long it had been. But he did know one thing—none of this made *any* sense. Who was the doppelganger? Why was he holding Valerius captive? And why had no one come for him? It had taken Marito and Gabriel only a few days to find and rescue him last time, but it had been weeks now, maybe even months. What was taking them so long?

"Let me die," a low, pitiful voice whispered. "If you have any mercy, just let me *die*."

Valerius blinked to find a man with lustrous blond hair and silken red robes kneeling before him, a chain around his neck and wrists—a mirror image of Valerius' stance.

"Magnus? Magnus of Ashfall?" Valerius asked, the joy of seeing another person after so long overriding his shock.

The mage raised his head. Purple shadows made crescents under his eyes, and while he looked the same as the knight remembered, there was a deep pain to Magnus' expression that disturbed Valerius.

"Two? Is he *insane?* He bound two of us to a single host?" The mage rattled his chains, panicked. "If we are not eaten by his madness, we will be swept up in it. Damn it all, why not just kill me, Tyrant?"

"The *Tyrant?* As in… the evil god Gallow fought against?" Valerius asked, grasping the only thing he'd understood from the mage's ramblings.

Whatever Magnus was about to say was cut off when a dull glow lit up the darkness, and someone appeared between them, materializing as if by magic. He wore heavy full-plate armor that shined like a lantern in the night, and strapped to his back was a wicked looking sword that made Valerius recoil. Even without magic he could sense the evil embedded in the blade.

"It's been a while, Valerius. Gone mad yet? Or is the goodly prince made of sterner stuff?" the golden warrior asked.

Valerius raised his eyes to find it was him—the doppelganger, the strange man who wore Valerius' face as his own. But there was something different about him. He didn't apologize or bend his head meekly, eyes filled with regret. Instead there was a vicious twist to his lips, and the eyes that stared at Valerius were two dark stones at the bottom of a well, whispering a promise of madness.

In answer, Valerius straightened, his chin raised high.

"Ever the stalwart knight, I see," the doppelganger said, mockingly. "My master bid I check on you. Well, his precise words were *Torment Valerius,* but that's splitting hairs. You've been very naughty—pushing at your chains, making my head hurt. That's not very nice, you know." The man smiled, but it didn't reach his eyes.

Valerius looked at him in utter confusion.

"Oh dear, I thought you were doing it on purpose, but you're staring at me like a goober-pig at a blackboard!" The doppelganger let out a forced laugh. "When I first arrived, I kept you locked down tight—didn't want you seeing or hearing a *peep*. Pathetic, I know, but guilt makes one do pathetic things. But I was sure, nay, *positive* that the Gilded's finest would have figured it out by now."

Valerius' heart pounded, but he kept his expression still. The doppelganger's grin widened, teeth glinting like knives. "Tell me—how long have you been here? Have a guess. Go *wild.*"

"If your little speech is supposed to impress me, I suggest you—"

"Three years," the man said. "You've been trapped in here for three years."

"What?" Valerius said, paling. "That's—that's impossible."

"Also, quick update. Marito? Dead. Gabriel. Dead. Lazander—also dead. Technically, anyway. He did end up joining the Gilded Knights by the way, but he only lasted a year." The doppelganger raised his fingers as if checking off a list. "The spymaster? Dead. He was a nasty little beast called a zindor—gave me quite the run for my money. Oh, and the queen…" He paused dramatically. Valerius' stomach twisted so violently, he thought he was going to be sick.

"… the queen is still alive. Not kicking, per se, but she's around. Bedridden these days, but worry not, our daddy dearest has taken the reins. He's put *quite* the tidy sum on our head, even sent a bounty hunter after us! You should see the stage he's built in the center of the Ivory Keep. When he gives us the chop, he wants *everyone* to have a bird's eye view of the infamous Prince Valerius Najar—traitor extraordinaire." The doppelganger gestured at himself, grinning like a grit-shark. "You've had a busy three years, my prince."

Valerius was drowning. A tidal wave of confusion and dread struck him, and in his panic, he latched onto memories of Marito and Gabriel like a life buoy. The knight thought of his friends—camping beneath the stars, drinking in far-off cities, and the countless fights they'd survived. Marito and Gabriel were formidable alone, but together? They were unstoppable. A single doppelganger couldn't kill them, the very thought was laughable! And if that was a lie, the rest was too.

Calm again, Valerius chuckled at the creature's obvious ploy: appeal to the prince's pity by spouting nonsense about "games" and "characters" and when that didn't work, torment him with lies. It was pathetic.

"If you think tall tales are all it takes to break a Gilded, think again," Valerius said, straining against his chains. "Marito and Gabriel would *never* fall to such a coward."

"Ha. Haha!" The doppelganger laughed, almost hysterical. "I thought Master came up with those corny lines for the game, but you really sound like that." He wiped a tear from his eye. "I can't believe I wanted to be you when I grew up."

"Enough. I am Prince Valerius Najar and you will release me or face the full wrath of Navaros!"

"You hear that Magnus? Aren't you happy to be housed with *royalty?*" The doppelganger gave Magnus a vicious kick, catching him in the knee. The mage cringed, head bowed, and Valerius frowned, expecting him to spit out a slew of obscenities as he was known to do. But this quiet man was nothing like the Magnus he'd met—one who got rip roaringly drunk at parties and told everyone uncomfortable stories about Zara the Fury.

"Since the prince doesn't believe me, why don't you bring him up to speed, hm? I know Player One made you watch. I could see it when I ate you, little man." The doppelganger leaned forward, trailing a finger down Magnus' cheeks. The mage's body went rigid with terror. "And you were so very delicious."

Magnus turned as pale as the full moon, his hands trembling. Abruptly the doppelganger straightened, his head cocked to one side. "Ah, Master wants me to get Bala, is it? Hmm. Would have thought he'd start with Gaj, but Master knows best." The doppelganger smiled down at Valerius, his teeth knives in the dark. "I might be Player Two, but I'm the favorite for good reason—I follow orders. And the sooner you sit on your haunches like a good pup and do what you're told, the easier this will be. I speak from experience."

He vanished, his light extinguishing like a candlelit flame, and the darkness closed in on Magnus and Valerius once more.

"Player Two? Bala? What in the Bloodied Void is he talking about, Magnus? It's—it's all a lie, isn't it—about Marito, Gabriel, and the others? ... Magnus? Damn it, man, answer me!" Valerius roared, his ironclad mask slipping for the first time.

Magnus shook his head, eyes squeezed tightly in pain. "It's true. Every word is true, and worse than you can imagine, Prince Valerius. Ten years. Ten years they've held me. The things they've made me do. I can't... I can't..." His voice trailed off, and Valerius knew he had seconds before he lost the man.

"Magnus, look at me. I've fought despots, tamed dragons, and charged through the ice valleys of the Jaded Sea without fear. They sealed their fates by housing us together, you understand? We *will* figure out how to escape—together."

At the word "escape" Magnus opened his eyes ever so slightly.

"But you need to tell me everything," Valerius said. "Where we are, who holds us captive, and how they brought us here. Leave *nothing* out."

Magnus winced. "You need to look. It's the only way I understood. But know that I am... deeply sorry for what you're about to see."

He raised his hand, pointing to the darkness. Valerius frowned, unable to see what Magnus was gesturing at. Slowly images began to flash—a glint of a sword here, a shock of red there. Instinctively he looked away.

"Don't. If you want to see, you have to look. Let your mind drift while your body stays."

Valerius did as Magnus said, feeling as if he were floating.

And then his entire world came crashing down.

***

Valerius stood in flames, the remnants of what looked like a small village collapsing around him. Clad in gold armor, the wicked blade he'd seen on Player Two's back was in his hands. But he couldn't move. Couldn't so much as blink. He could only watch as a woman scrambled in the dirt, backing away from him like he was a ripperback on the prowl.

"Please, don't! Please, Gallow, help me!"

Valerius' body moved of its own volition, and he drove a vicious knee into the woman's neck, pinning her to the ground. Her nails dragged harmlessly against his leg, spittle falling from her lips as she screamed.

"There you are," Player Two said aloud. "Took you long enough to get here." Valerius was shocked to find his lips moving, but it wasn't him. He wasn't speaking!

He watched in horror as he flipped the dark sword, grasped it tightly in one hand and casually drove it deep into the woman's chest. *"Fester,"* Player Two whispered.

The blade lit up, tendrils of malachite creeping down the blade and into the woman. She jerked, foaming at the mouth. Valerius fought to look away, but Player Two's gaze never strayed from the woman's.

Valerius saw the light die in her eyes, the word "please" on her lips.

"Release whatever spell you have over my body at once!" Valerius ordered, proud his voice didn't shake. "Is it gold you want? A title? Name it, and I will see that my mother, the queen—"

"Didn't you hear what I said? You're not a prince anymore, 'Val'—not really. You're enemy number one as far as mummy and daddy are concerned. Even if I gave you back your body, you're screwed. *You* killed the Gilded. *You* betrayed Navaros. You have nothing, Valerius. You are *nothing*."

The full weight of what was happening hit Valerius so hard, he almost passed out. Had he his own legs to stand on, he would have fallen to his knees.

"There we go. I knew you'd catch on. But I'm afraid we're not done yet. Have a look," Player Two said, gesturing with his sword. Flames ravaged the few buildings left standing, greedily inhaling wood and straw. Bodies were strewn on the ground, blood and gore mixed with dirt. A dog lay curled atop a dead man, both felled by the same blow, while the head of a cow was nearly lost among a pile of limbs in the village's center. At first, Valerius thought the dead had fallen where they stood, but then his captor dragged the woman he'd just murdered to the pile, arranging her on top like a candle upon a name day cake.

"Why… why are you doing this?" was all Valerius could say. If he voiced the truth of his impossible, fantastical situation aloud, he would start screaming.

And never stop.

"Because I've been chosen. Like Gallow chose Eternity, and she her faithful Champions, Calamity chose me. And you are blessed to be my main character—both in the game *Knights of Eternity*, and here."

Player Two sheathed his blade, rolling his shoulders. He casually strolled to the pile of bodies, pulling out a ruby the size of his palm from his pocket. "This wasn't even my quest, you know. It was supposed to be Player Three's—she was right in the middle of freeing Calamity's servants, even if she didn't know it. But alas, she is… indisposed."

Player Two drove the hand that held the ruby into the pile of corpses, the wet, sliding sound making Valerius' stomach churn. He stepped back, not even bothering to wipe the blood off.

"That's why we're here—Calamity can hardly conquer the world without his lieutenants, can he? Bala was the first to fall. His soul was sent to the Void where it was chained to a sun, and he's spent the last thousand years burning to the very precipice of death, unable to die. His body, on the other hand, was locked away here in a *ruby*, of all things. In time the gem was lost—humans are so careless when they get complacent. But about a year ago, it ended up in the hands, or rather fins, of some carnivorous fish…"

Player Two was rambling, his tone that of someone discussing the weather. Valerius strained, fighting to take back control of his body, to draw his sword and skewer them both—anything to stop this.

"… Gaj on the other hand, is much trickier. But she's next on our list. And I figured if my quest is to torment you, what better way than to take you along for the ride? To show you exactly what you've been up to for the last few years?"

At some unseen signal the corpses began to shiver, fingers and tongues twitching.

Player Two snapped his fingers, and the bodies exploded, shooting upward in a tower of blood and gore.

## Chapter Fourteen

Eternity didn't know what to expect when Gallow summoned her south and directed her to a small cluster of trees by the coastline. As she touched down, Imani and Vivek appeared from the shadows, their dark armor rendering them almost invisible. Imani looked as she always did—tall and imposing, her hair shaved to the quick. Vivek's silver hair was pulled back in its customary tight plait, the Champion's pale eyes almost translucent with anticipation. The two Champions offered neither greeting nor explanation to Eternity. They simply stood, eyes locked on the horizon, the silence shifting from awkward to tense as the minutes turned to hours.

Eternity knew better than to ask what they were doing here—the God of Judgment would tell her what she needed to know, and nothing more. He spoke little at the best of times—reaching out to her from the Void took immense energy, and Gallow had to take care with every single word. Eternity knew this. She accepted it. Never questioned it.

Until the sky opened as if split. In the distance a roiling tower of blood and death shot up into the air with an explosive boom. Terrified, Eternity looked to Imani and Vivek, her gorge rising as she desperately wished Gallow had told her something, *anything*, about what was happening. Surely they were as scared as she was? But the Champions looked calm, even *eager*.

"That's the signal," Imani said, cracking her knuckles, her white smile a crescent moon in the dark.

"Kindly keep the bodies to a minimum," Champion Vivek said. "I'd rather not spend my entire night cleaning up after you. *Again*."

"The only bodies will be the ones the little prince left behind," Imani replied. "And his, once I'm done with it." She vanished, a blurred afterimage the only sign she'd even been there as she took off at supernatural speed, Gallow's power flowing through her.

*Little prince?* Eternity thought, stung that once again the Champions seemed to know more than she did. Once she'd arrived, Gallow had told her to follow Imani and Vivek—that was it. Would he ever trust her as he did them? "Are we to fight Valerius? Is he the source of that monstrous tower?" she asked Vivek.

The Champion scoffed, running a hand over the two blades belted to his hip. "Keep close and to the skies," he replied without looking at her. He vanished as quickly as Imani, and once more Eternity found herself alone. It was the most Vivek had said to her in weeks.

It had been like this ever since Eternity had thrown herself in harm's way to save the queen. She'd done so without Gallow's orders, which was akin to spitting in the God of Judgment's face according to the Champions. Since then they'd kept her at arm's length, conversations lulling to an awkward pause whenever she spoke, or even outright ignoring her. But today Eternity would fight alongside them on the battlefield, no longer kept locked away in a tower—a parcel to be passed between kingdoms. They needed her. *Gallow* needed her.

Her nails dug into her palms, determination settling in her heart. This was her chance to prove herself.

Rising several feet off the ground, Eternity shot forward, moving slower than Vivek and Imani. But where they had speed, she had distance. She glided upward, a snowdrop in the wind, her blonde hair whipping about her. The cold, pleasant breeze of the nearby sea was tainted with the coppery tang of blood.

Cautiously, Eternity glided toward the tower of blood—a twisting, pulsating mass that swirled like a tornado. While it was hard to tell from here, it looked like it had come from a small coastal village—one she doubted even appeared on a map. At the tornado's head a rift as thick as a river cut the sky in two, a jagged line of darkness that would have been invisible but for the stars it blotted out.

Eternity had seen it once before in the memory of the very First Eternity, the woman who had stood alone against the Tyrant—it was a gate, a portal from this world to the Void. It was how the Tyrant had come through to this world, but it couldn't be him, Eternity told herself—it was too soon! But if it wasn't the Tyrant… then who could it be?

All at once the sparse trees and craggy rocks below gave way to a small, ruined village. Two figures battled only a few feet from where the tornado touched the earth, sending the soil churning. Eternity scanned for survivors among the still-burning ruins, hoping they weren't too late. She saw no hint of life, nor did she see any corpses. Praying the villagers had fled, she silently asked Gallow to guide them to safety.

A grunt of pain called Eternity's attention back to the fight. Her eyes widened when she saw a man in gold armor dart forward, almost lazily dodging Imani's strikes. He wore a dark blade on his back but made no move to draw it, instead swinging at Imani with a vicious left hook. She ducked and drove her fist upward with a roar, catching him full force in the chin.

Eternity almost cheered—the man might be fast, but Imani hit like a charging xandi. There was no way... The thought trailed off when the man didn't so much as stumble. He drove his head forward, slamming it into Imani's nose. The Champion hit the ground with a resounding thud, her limbs splayed—unconscious.

As if sensing Eternity's gaze, the man looked skyward, and her heart leaped when dark eyes met hers.

"Valerius," she said in disbelief. Covered in blood, his cheeks were gaunt, his dark hair long and tangled around his ears—she barely recognized him. Eternity glanced at Imani, who groaned, turning onto her side. How was this possible? The last time Imani and Valerius fought, the Champion beat him with a *single* punch. How was Valerius not only matching Imani's blows, but winning?

And then Eternity saw it. Draped around Valerius' body like the finest of silks was a gigantic slug. It squirmed, twisting and sliding, its head coming to rest by his ear. A split formed, and it opened a mouth to reveal rows of teeth as pale as sharpened moonlight.

"Gallow have mercy," Eternity whispered, a hand coming to her mouth. What *was* that thing?

Valerius smiled, keeping his eyes on her as he raised a booted foot, ready to drive it into Imani's skull, but Vivek appeared behind him in a blinding flash of light, his eyes aglow. *Guided Strike*—a gift from Gallow, it allowed Vivek to attack undetected. In his hands were blades of pure dragonscale, their iridescent sheen deadly.

Vivek drove both swords into Valerius, the tips punching through the front of his armor, cutting through the prince like a blade through cream.

Eternity let out a deep breath, relief flooding through her.

It was over—Valerius was dead. And while the thought made her sadder than she'd expected, it was for the best, she knew. He'd hurt so many—Gabriel, Marito, Lazander, the queen, the spymaster… it was past time he paid for his crimes. "You have done some truly terrible things, Valerius," she whispered. "But in a time not long past, you were a hero to this land. I pray that in death Gallow has mercy upon you and through him you find the redemption you so desperately need."

She turned away, having no desire to watch Valerius choke and splutter as he died, and focused on the obvious reason Gallow had called her here—the tower of blood. Any moment now he would order her to dismantle the portal, and while she'd never cast the spell before, she knew the theory—it was easiest right before a portal's zenith, when the mana within stabilized. Eternity frowned, staring at the tornado in confusion. Was it her imagination, or was something moving *inside* it? There, just for a second—

A whisper of cold on her skin saved her. She turned to see a wall of ice racing toward her, growing in size and speed. Dropping like a stone, Eternity twisted out of the way, ice shattering a ruined barn and several trees as it shot toward her.

**"Feel the weight of his power, and tremble!"** she shouted, palms up. The ice wall struck her, freezing her hands, but Gallow's power was stronger. A crack formed in the wall, and then it exploded, chunks of ice raining down in a deadly shower of hail. Hands burning from the cold, Eternity allowed herself a single breath before flying in the direction the spell had been cast.

*Imani, Vivek—please be all right. Blessed Gallow, please be all right,* she thought, cursing herself for looking away from the fight. For not being willing to watch someone die.

She scanned the ruins, eyes flitting from ruined cottages to a still standing barn, but she couldn't see the Champions, or Valerius. The only sign of the fight was Vivek's dragonscale blades stuck in the dirt, standing upright and foreboding. Eternity landed awkwardly, wiping her sleeve against her nose. It came away bloody. Where were Imani and Vivek? Did Valerius flee?

"Flight? How adorable," Valerius said, materializing in front of her, his fist following. Next thing Eternity knew she was on her back, stars in her eyes, her nose exploding with pain.

"Poor little Eternity. She tries so hard but she's never enough. Gallow will always keep his prized peacock on a tight leash." Valerius smiled with too many teeth. "The 'God of Judgment' doesn't trust you with the truth. He feeds you lies. Builds himself up to be a hero, when he was only one traitor among many. I have to give it to him though—he was smart enough to steal all the glory."

**"Kneel. Cry. *Beg*,"** Eternity managed, forcing herself onto one forearm, her free hand outstretched, **"for you are not worthy."** A dark sphere gathered at the tip of her finger, and she pointed it at Valerius—aiming for his heart.

A beam of pure mana the size of a fist shot out, her aim true.

Grinning maniacally, Valerius raised his hands, catching the blast head on. Dirt churned as he was forced back, a colossal boom sounding when he hit a barn—and kept going. Wood and stone collapsed on him, burying him beneath. Eternity shakily got to her feet, clutching her still bleeding nose.

That spell was enough to take down the wallow-tail—at least briefly. But she knew that whatever Calamity had done to Valerius, he was now stronger than the bird of flame. She wasn't powerful enough to kill the prince.

Not anymore.

But there was more to it than the slug-like creature that now wound around him. He spoke and acted like a completely different person. Even his voice sounded strange, his usual rich timbre now grating to her ear.

Above her the column of blood spun, flexing and pulsating. Mana slipped from it like water through splayed fingers, and every breath made Eternity's lungs burn. Something flickered within, whispering to her, a dark bolt of lightning within the bloodied storm.

It was only then she saw the faces.

Inside the tornado corpses spun, their mouths open in horror. Cattle, canine, and human alike whirled inside, trapped in an endless scream. Eternity gasped, and the tornado grew, swelling as it leaned toward her. All at once the enormity of what was happening hit her.

The Tyrant, no—*Calamity* was coming. A god who could rip holes through the very fabric of reality, who could crush her with a single flick of his finger. Who was she to stand against him? A woman, a child really, whose own Champions barely spoke to her. Whose only friends were a horse, a hawk, a dragon, and Zara the Fury—a woman she'd known for mere hours.

A woman who was off having wonderful adventures and probably never thought of Eternity. Not once.

Eternity fell to her knees, and the blood-spun tornado inched closer to her. Her breath came in short, sharp gasps, wisps of her hair lifting as she was dragged into it. She was dead. The Champions were dead. And it was her fault for not being good enough, for not—

A slap brought Eternity back. She blinked in surprise, and the tornado snapped back, swaying in place as if it hadn't been about to drag her in among the dead. Imani stood over Eternity, bleeding heavily from a wound in her neck, hand raised for a second slap.

"Imani! Imani, are you all right?" Eternity asked, the horror of what she'd thought, how close she'd come to giving in, vanishing at the sight of the injured Champion.

"Where is he? Where's Valerius?" Imani snarled, falling to one knee with a groan. Eternity rushed to her side, clamping a hand on the torrents of blood pouring from Imani's neck in a steady stream. Every drop that slipped through Eternity's fingers hovered in the air for a moment, then whipped toward the tornado, sucked up by the horrors within.

Taking a deep breath, Eternity blasted a tidal wave of magic into the wound in one solid burst. To her relief it began to close—no one healed quicker than Champions, but Imani stepped away, breaking the connection.

"Did Gallow command you to heal me?" she demanded.

"Bloodied Void, Imani!" Eternity swore. "I used my own magic, not Gallow's. Now come here before you bleed to death!"

Perhaps it was the tone Eternity had taken, or the fact that she'd sworn aloud—the first time in over thirty years. But Imani knelt, allowing Eternity to continue. The Champion had wasted much of Eternity's mana by stepping away, but the Chosen still had some to spare. Using what little she had left, Eternity breathed a sigh of relief when the wound closed like a tightly stitched seam.

"Vivek!" Imani roared the second she was healed. "Get up! If I'm not dead, you better not be."

The sound of wood shifting came from their right amidst the ruins of a house. With a thunderous burst it exploded outward, making Eternity jump. Stone and wood fell from the sky like rain, and at the center stood Vivek, weaponless and bleeding from the forehead, but very much alive.

"I'm going to kill him," he said, mouth twisted in a snarl.

"Get in line," Imani replied. "I couldn't even get an ability off before he downed me. I've never seen anyone get that strong that quickly, not even a Champion."

"Nor have I seen a Champion survive being run through. Twice," Vivek added. "Whatever the Tyrant has done to him is nothing short of unholy."

Eternity was about to mention the slug she'd seen when Vivek pointed at Imani. "We can't rush him headlong—not again. Imani, you're up front, but do not engage unless you have to—I just want his focus on you for now. Lady Eternity, have you enough magic to resume your flight?"

"I do."

"Good," he said, and Eternity felt a thrill at being included, despite their dire circumstances. "I need you to attack from the air. I'll circle from the back. At my signal, we—"

His words were cut off when Valerius appeared behind Vivek in a supernatural blur. Eternity watched it all as if in slow motion. Vivek's eyes widening almost comically, Imani charging forward, a fist raised—too slow. Valerius' smile as deadly as the dark sword in his hands.

And then Vivek's head was sailing through the air, his white hair shorn from where Valerius' blade had sliced through. It hit the ground, rolling to one side, the Champion's eyes permanently wide in death.

## Chapter Fifteen

Imani roared, **"at the final hour, all will kneel before his might!"** A horrible grating sound of bone against bone began as her body doubled, then tripled in size, dark armor rapidly expanding. The veins in her neck bulged, her expression twisted in a vicious snarl.

Valerius leaped back in surprise, but Imani was quicker. Her huge, monstrous form darted forward, grabbed him by the ankle and threw him bodily over her shoulder, smashing him into the ground. Valerius' breath left him in a *whoosh*, his sword falling from his hands as Imani flung Valerius to one side—his body hitting the dirt like a skipping stone.

*Now,* Eternity thought, eyes turning dark with the Void as she threw open the door between her and Gallow, ignoring Vivek's lifeless corpse as it collapsed next to her. She raised her hands, aiming a pointed finger carefully at Valerius.

**"CLOSE THE GATE."**

Gallow's command came through, loud and certain. Eternity hesitated, her eyes flickering between the swirling tornado and Imani, who skidded backward, a bolt the size of a harpoon sticking out of her shoulder. Valerius' hands glowed as he got to his feet, a familiar hammer appearing in his hands.

"Let me help her first," Eternity pleaded. "Vivek… Vivek is dead, and—"

**"CLOSE THE GATE,"** Gallow repeated.

Eternity screwed her eyes shut and turned her back on Imani even as her heart begged her not to. Hands raised, Eternity let her anger, both rare and potent, fuel her.

**"This world is his domain, go back to the Void whence you came!"** she cried, eyes dark with power. She shook, fresh blood pouring from her nose as her body and mind were flooded with the God of Judgment's presence. Grinding her teeth, she held her ground. Eternity had almost fallen to the *Tyrant's Despair,* a spell that wove a feeling of loss and hopelessness in all who heard it. It was so powerful, it allowed the dark god to conquer half the world without him having to lift a finger. She wouldn't be so weak again, she told herself. She'd close the gate, *and* help Imani. She just needed a few minutes.

Inch by inch the tornado slowed its devastating spin, the dark lightning at its core flickering. The corpses within became more visible, and Eternity tried to focus on the rift above. *It's closing. I can do this, I can!*

Something white shimmered before Eternity's eyes, and a tremendous boom sounded right by her ear. Imani cried out in pain, and Eternity bit her lip to stop from breaking the spell and turning around.

And then lips were against her ear like a lover. "Impressive," Valerius whispered. "Calamity was sure you wouldn't be able to close it, not even with your Champions at your back. You've grown, Eternity."

Eternity's hands shook, fear and anger threatening to overwhelm her. She waited for Gallow to order her to help Imani, to strike Valerius—anything but "close the gate." But the God of Judgment said nothing, and so Eternity didn't move. Didn't even acknowledge Valerius, though she trembled, waiting for him to raise his sword and drive it through her.

"Hah! I take it back." Valerius laughed. "What happened to the girl who threw herself at my feet to save a queen she owed no allegiance to? Hmm?" The prince stepped around her, his golden armor stained with blood. Too much blood for one person to lose and survive.

*Close the gate, close the gate, close the gate.* Eternity repeated Gallow's order over and over, trusting that he had a plan. The tornado shrank further, the rift above now the size of a small pond instead of the ocean it had been minutes ago.

"Imani is right behind you, you know. Poor thing is bleeding out. Now, I won't lie to you and say you can save her—even you aren't that good. But wouldn't you like to say goodbye?" Valerius goaded, and Eternity almost turned around, unable to bear the thought.

Then it hit her. Why wasn't Valerius attacking her? If Imani was down, or worse, and Eternity was stuck closing the rift, it would be child's play for him to kill them both. It was only then she noticed the pearly-white shimmer that enveloped her, almost invisible to the naked eye.

A shield. *Imani's* shield

A hand clasped around Eternity's ankle, almost breaking her concentration, and she looked down to see the Champion. Curled up on her side, tracks led from where she'd dragged herself to Eternity, a hand curled around her stomach.

**"Your heart is… worthy, your soul divine. Bask in his… protection,"** Imani grunted, every word laced with pain. The shield grew brighter, enveloping them both, and Eternity's heart leaped. Gallow had a plan! How foolish she was to doubt, how—

The shield shrunk until it only covered Eternity.

"Imani? Imani, what are you doing?" Eternity said, panicking when Valerius stepped forward, making a show of slowly drawing his sword.

"She almost had me, you know," Valerius said. "Even with a bolt in her. But when I fired one at you, she shielded you—leaving herself wide open. You didn't even look at her. But this time… well, this time you will."

"Imani, expand the shield!" Eternity cried. Valerius was steps away.

"Gallow ordered me… to save you, and only you," Imani whispered, her words punctured by the blood that dribbled from her lips. "Shield is stronger… on one."

"Damn it, expand it, Imani!"

Tears formed in Eternity's eyes when Valerius reached them. With one hand, he grabbed Imani by the ankle, as she had to him mere minutes ago, and threw her far from Eternity, a smile on his face. Imani hit the dirt—boneless. Valerius walked toward her, casually resting his sword on one shoulder.

"Time to make a choice, Eternity," he called, straddling Imani. The Champion swiped at him feebly. Valerius didn't even bother blocking it. He took the blow, then struck her—hard. Blood burst from her nose, the whites of her eyes showing.

Eternity's head whipped between the tornado, now the size of a house, and the rift above it, a tenth the size it once was. She only needed a few more seconds. *Gallow, save Imani, please,* she prayed fervently. *Do not make me—*

"Time's up," Valerius called, flipping his sword and driving it one-handed into Imani's chest. The Champion gasped, her back arched. Valerius leaned in, whispering something. Dark green threads ran up Imani's neck like creeping fingers.

Imani started to jerk and flail, foam at her lips. Tears in her eyes, Eternity looked away.

With a rush of power, the bloody tornado folded in on itself, the rift above vanishing as Eternity finally closed it. The stars brightened once more, and the air was suddenly clear and easy to breathe. Only the scent of blood and charred wood tainted the silence.

"I have to thank you, you know," Valerius said, his sword and cheeks stained with blood. "Calamity is usually pretty strict in his quests, but this one was an exception. I had to either release Bala or kill whatever Champions showed up." He shrugged. "Being the tryhard I am, I wanted to do both, but I guess we can't win them all, can we?"

He cocked his head, frowning slightly. "Haha, the little prince did *not* like that. You should hear Valerius yelling at me! He's not… oh, he is. He's actually ordering me to get away from you. If this wasn't all so pathetic it would be adorable."

"Why?" Was all Eternity managed to say, though she didn't expect an answer—the man was clearly insane. But she needed to know. Needed to understand, as if it would make the sea of bodies any easier to bear. "Why are you doing this, Valerius? What did we ever do to you?"

"Valerius? Oh, that name is dead and gone," he said, leaning down so he was eye-level with Eternity. "The prince of Navaros who was so loved and adored is no more. I am who he was fated to become, his destiny—I am Player Two." His lips twisted in a half smile, eyes alight with madness. Eternity's heart nearly stopped at the sight. "Do you remember that night at Magnus' castle? How *Zara the Fury* rushed to your aid?" He said the woman's name as if it was a joke, trailing a finger over the shield that still covered Eternity. The skin on his hand started to peel away, but he didn't even flinch. "She thinks of you often, you know. But I wonder… what would the Fury say if she saw you now? Would she help you? Or would she finally see you for what you are—a girl with the power of a god who is somehow still completely and utterly *useless*. Do the world a favor, Eternity—give up. It'll be the most helpful thing you ever do."

With a sigh, he stood, a strange silver key appearing between two fingers. "Gaj is next on my list, and if you thought Bala's blood tornado was something…" He gave a low whistle. "Well, let's just say you're in for a treat with Gaj."

He strolled off with a wave. Eternity fell to her knees, her hands in her hair. And screamed.

## Chapter Sixteen

Lazander and Malik felt it at the same time—a shard of ice in their chests that spread like a deadly flower, threatening to consume them. Gallow's voice boomed in their heads.

"DEAD.

"DO NOT FAIL."

Lazander stumbled, hand sliding in the loose soil of the cavernous hole he and Malik dug. Malik stared down at Lazander, a look of fear on the older Champion's face that Lazander had never seen before. Images flooded Lazander's mind, too many to process. He saw jagged cliffs off the coast of Navaros where a horrifying, blood-soaked tornado reached up into the sky. The silhouette of a man in gaudy gold armor. Eternity—her eyes wide with terror.

"Eternity!" Lazander started. "Something's happened to her—we have to go, Malik. Now!" The very thought of Eternity being scared, hurt, or worse filled Lazander with a dread so powerful, he knew he would run to the very end of the world to keep her safe. Surprised at the intensity of the feeling, he told himself it was because he didn't want anyone else to die.

"Eternity is fine, brother," Malik said, a strange expression on his face. "Gallow's message wasn't about her." He looked away, his voice devoid of emotion. "It was about Imani and Vivek. They're dead."

Lazander's relief at Eternity being all right was immediately overridden by horror. He'd seen Imani and Vivek fight. The pair were unbeatable, soldiers and mages falling to them like flies as they tore through their enemies. "Who, Malik? Who did this?"

The look on the Champion's face told him everything he needed to know.

With a burst of strength Lazander leaped out of the hole and landed next to a fallen log where his dark armor was carefully laid out. "We have to go after Valerius," Lazander said, snapping it on haphazardly, the buckles catching in spots. "He can't get away with this, I won't let him."

Malik caught Lazander's forearm, gripping it tightly. "Did Gallow order us?"

"You can't be serious. He killed Imani and Vivek. You've fought with Imani for what, nigh on twenty years, and Vivek twice that!" Lazander said, aghast. When Gabriel and Marito were killed by Valerius, he'd felt like his soul had been split in two, and he'd known them less than half that time. "Malik, this isn't about Gallow and the Tyrant. It's about our comrades. Our *friends*. How can you just stand there and take it?"

"Did Gallow order us?" Malik repeated through gritted teeth.

Lazander shook the man's arm off. "This is ridiculous. I've been a soldier, a knight, and now a Champion. I know how to follow orders, but we can't just blindly do everything we're told. Without thought. Without *question*."

"You think there aren't times I want to flip Gallow off and do as I damn well please?"

Lazander blinked in shock. Malik had never expressed anything but undying loyalty to Gallow. "Then why don't we? We have a way to find Grim whenever we like. I recognized the cliffs in Gallow's vision—we're just a few hours from Valerius. This could be my chance to—"

"Aye, there it is," Malik drawled. "'My chance.' This isn't about Imani and Vivek. You just want the prince's guts for garters."

"After what he's done? Of course I do! And I know you feel the same."

"No, I don't," Malik said, suddenly quiet. "If Imani and Vivek are dead, then this was either part of Gallow's plan, or they failed him. Either way, they're no longer my concern."

"You—you can't mean that," Lazander said, slack-jawed.

"You know I do," Malik said, head high. "Am I surprised they went down so easily? Of course. But I have faith in Gallow. A faith you seem to be sorely lacking, even after all the gifts he's given you." He jabbed a finger into Lazander's stomach like a blade. "This isn't about your petty squabble with Valerius. This is about saving the world, Zander. So, get your head out of your backside, and *do as you're damn told*."

Lazander knew Malik's anger wasn't about him, not entirely. Despite Malik's words, he grieved Imani and Vivek—he could see it in the Champion's eyes.

But that didn't mean Malik could talk to him like a dog who wouldn't behave. He opened his mouth to say just that when a small icy hand slipped into his. Lazander looked down to see a young boy by his side, his outline blurred and unfocused like a rough sketch.

Gallow.

Gallow appeared to all the Champions, albeit in different forms. As time wore on, the boy had shown up less and less, apparently happy to remain a shadow in the back of Lazander's mind. But now Gallow gripped Lazander's hand, and he felt his anger deflate, a renewed sense of purpose flowing through him.

If the Champions rushed to kill Valerius now, they might tip the scales in favor of the Tyrant. Lazander had to stay his hand and stop Ravenna and Grim first. He *had* to—even if the thought made Lazander's heart shrivel in his chest.

With a heavy sigh, Lazander nimbly slid down the near vertical sides of the hole they'd made. "Better," Malik muttered under his breath, and it took every shred of Lazander's control not to jump back up and punch Malik in the face.

**"Bend to his might, break before his Judgment,"** Lazander intoned, supernatural strength flowing through his body alongside a vicious bout of rage. He punched the ground, earth flying into the air, losing himself to the task. Minutes later his fist struck something hard, his teeth rattling from the force.

"What in the Void? You all right, Zander?" Malik asked, the mask of the "concerned uncle" firmly in place once more. Having seen how quickly Malik could take it on and off, Lazander found his lip curling in disgust.

"Not sure," he said, making a show of kneeling down while he got his expression under control. "Whatever it was, it's harder than stone." He wiped away the dirt, surprised when he saw something shiny and gray peeking through.

Malik landed like a cat next to him. The ground beneath them was metal with strange sigils engraved on every inch. A feeling of déjà vu overcame him. He was sure he'd never seen this script before, so why did it look so familiar?

"Clever bastards," Malik muttered.

"You know what this is?"

"Aye, trouble," Malik said evasively, stomping on the steel with his heel. Lazander belatedly realized it didn't have so much as a scratch on it despite him pummeling it at full strength. "This thing is gonna need the two of us to get through. Ready?"

Malik grinned at Lazander as if their argument had never happened. Unease settled in Lazander's chest, but then visions of the Tyrant finding Eternity and ripping her apart flashed in his mind, and he shivered—suddenly freezing cold. He had to do this, he told himself. For the world. For *Eternity*.

As one the two Champions raised their fists, hammering the impossibly strong steel. Lazander's knuckles popped, his fingers going numb with pain, but he hit it with everything he had. Malik punched through first, the metal cutting deep into his forearm. Without batting an eye, he gripped the metal from the other side and pulled—ripping it open.

Malik stood, hands on hips, the gushing wound in his arm closing in seconds. The gap he'd made was narrow, and barely big enough for one of them. Within the hole lay a heavy darkness that seemed to pull all light into its depths. It was impossible to guess how deep it was.

Lazander was about to ask Malik if he had a torch when the Champion grinned at him. "Suck the gut in," he said with a wink, patting his own stomach as he fearlessly jumped. Lazander waited to hear the Champion hit the ground.

And waited.

And waited.

Hearing nothing, he turned to his right where the childlike form of Gallow still stood, impassive. "We won't fail," he said softly to the boy. The child just looked at him, his strange featureless face as unreadable as always.

Lazander took a breath and stepped into the darkness below, his cape whipping behind him like the single wing of an injured bird.

\*\*\*

It was only when Zara and Lukas reached the "heart" of the maze, where a rainbow-colored statue of Ravenna was supposed to be, that Zara realized what the strange metal tunnels reminded her of.

Every step after the bloodied mural was laced with foreboding. Zara's instincts screamed at her to leave, but she forced herself forward. Two hours later, and they'd come to a large room, much like the first they'd landed in but for one key difference.

"Look at those things," Lukas whispered. Instead of a charming rainbow statue at the maze's center, twisted black sculptures were laid out in a circle. They were huge, each reaching toward the ceiling like fingertips. All harsh lines and edges, there was something disturbing about them.

"Why do they all look like women getting tortured?" Lukas asked, taking a half step back.

Zara realized he was right. The pointed edges resembled knees and elbows, a long sheet of metal at the back the flowing hair of Ravenna. But Zara had never seen the goddess depicted as anything but powerful and imposing or disgustingly welcoming with big doe eyes.

"*See, see!*" the voice yelped with delight, loud enough for Zara to jump. "*Come see! We need the sugar heart, the sugar rush!*"

"What's the voice saying?" Lukas asked quietly, but Zara shook her head, her feet moving of their own volition toward the room's center.

"*Sugar heart, sugar heart!*" the voice sang, excited now.

Zara's feet were too loud on the metal floor, each step echoing until the whole maze felt like it was humming in anticipation. Her skin crawled when she passed the sculptures, as if someone was watching her, and she was surprised to see they circled something—an empty pool lined with metal. Empty, that is, but for a slug the size of a cat curled up like a withered apple peel.

"Urgh," Lukas said, appearing at her side. "So that's the thing that's been stinking up the maze? It looks like my chamber pot after a double-helping of spike-hog stew and mushi herbs."

The slug twitched, a soft mewling sound escaping the slit at the top of its head. Lukas yelped, grabbing Zara's arm. "It's alive! What in the Bloodied Void is that thing?"

"If I'm right," Zara said, shrugging him off as she knelt, tracing a hand over the sigil-etched floor, so like Calamity's prison, "that is the goddess we traveled the breadth of Moonvale for in the hopes she would help us save Teema." She looked at Lukas with a sigh when he frowned.

"No way that's… you mean it's…"

"The Goddess of Truth," Zara said, her tone mocking. "Hero to the vaxion, and birth mother of all falslings—the mighty *Ravenna*."

## Chapter Seventeen

Lazander fell for several seconds before he hit the ground, one knee resting on the hard metal floor. It was pitch black. He couldn't see or hear a thing.

"Malik?" he called, but when he opened his mouth, no sound came out. He tried again, shouting this time, but nothing happened. Taking a calming breath, he stretched out his hands, trying to reach a wall, a door, anything that would help him get his bearings.

*"No salty boys, only sweet!"* a voice shrieked in his head, sharp and indignant. *"Get out, get out, get out!"*

Lazander's sword was drawn, and he was crouched in a defensive position when Malik chuckled.

"Sorry, brother—should have warned you," Malik said, his words nearly drowned out by the voice who continued to scream at them to get out. "Didn't think she'd sense us so quickly."

"Who? Where *are* we?"

"First things first, let's get your eyes sorted. Kneel down—you're too damn tall for this."

Lazander did as he was told, knowing better than to ask Malik what he planned to do. The Champion never gave any more information than he was willing to give, no matter how often Lazander asked. He heard Malik remove his gloves with his mouth, and then the man pressed rough calloused hands over Lazander's eyes.

**"Pierce the illusion, so we might better see your truth,"** he said, power thrumming with every word. Lazander blinked owlishly as the room lit up like the sun. The voice vanished, cutting off mid-curse as it called him a "salty boy" again—whatever that meant.

"Vivek isn't… wasn't the only one with gifted eyes," Malik said, trying and failing to smile. "Gallow's gifts allow me to cloak myself in the guise of another, but they also give me some control over illusive magic. And this place right here…" He gestured at the smooth metal walls, all engraved with the same bizarre symbols. "…

is cloaked to the Void and back against 'intruders' such as ourselves. For a so-called Goddess of Truth, she's damn good at hiding."

"What is this place?" Lazander asked, staring around in wonder. While Evergarden was the most technologically advanced city he'd ever seen, there was something about the smooth curve of the wall and the perfectly symmetrical tunnels that was… unsettling. The size, shape, and design were so perfect, it looked almost inhuman.

"Somewhere I'd only ever heard of," Malik said, clicking his tongue. "This right here is where Ravenna fled when the Tyrant attacked. She locked down the doors while the other gods and her followers hammered outside, then offered every one of them up to the Tyrant as tribute." He shook his head in disgust.

Lazander waited for him to say more, but Malik cocked his head, staring down one of the tunnels off to the right. A gust of something acrid hit Lazander's nose, and he had to fight not to cough, his eyes watering.

He heard it a second before he saw it. It started as a low growl, Lazander's chest vibrating from the force. Sparks flashed in the tunnel up ahead where the smell was strongest, and it took Lazander a minute to realize it was the effect of claws skittering against the metal floor.

A lot of claws.

"That'll be the welcoming committee," Malik said, pulling his gigantic hammer from his back. "Save your strength for when you need it. You've been run ragged today with the trip from Freyley and then punching the living daylights out of Ravenna's hidey hole."

Lazander gripped his sword tightly. While he couldn't hear the voice anymore, he knew it was still there, yelling at him to leave. A deep sense of foreboding filled him.

"Steady," Malik said, flashing him a smile. "Gallow sent us here because he knows we can handle it, all right?"

Lazander wanted to ask if Imani and Vivek felt the same way before they died, but he bit his tongue.

A heavy paw emerged from the darkness, then another, followed by a short crimson beak and a long neck. Scales lined the creature's throat, a shower of iridescent colors that blinded Lazander if he looked too closely. A hard, shell-like back came after, wide and flat like a platform. The beast was huge, almost as big as a dragon, with a beak that looked just as sharp as their fangs.

A reptizoid Lazander realized, shocked. They lived in the eastern kingdoms, close to the dwarven territories where they were used as guardians and mineral transporters. The only reason he even knew what they were was because of the hours he'd spent as a child reading his mother's journals, back when she was studying animal medicine.

What was it doing here? *How* was it even here?

It took Lazander a minute to realize a man sat cross-legged on the reptizoid's back, his hands resting on his knees in quiet contemplation. His hood was down, but Lazander knew who it was even before he saw the vicious scar that tore his face in half.

"Howdy, Grim," Malik called cheerfully. "We were in the neighborhood for some mana crystals. You wouldn't have any lying about, would you?"

Grim didn't answer. He leisurely got to his feet, eyes burning with hate.

"Why won't you leave us alone?" he asked, his rich baritone carrying easily across the room. "We're not hurting you, or anyone else."

"Tell that to the people of Evergarden," Lazander said. "If you'd had your way, half of them would be *dead*."

Grim frowned in surprise. "What are you talking—"

Whatever he said was lost when Malik leaped forward, hammer raised. Grim didn't even flinch. He clapped his hands together, the sound echoing loudly in the chamber. Malik charged, covering half the distance between him and Grim in seconds. As he reached the center of the room, a sigil on the floor lit up, turning crimson. The Champion realized his mistake too late and tried to back up, but the trap was sprung. Blood red lines whirled around Malik, spinning to create a cage around the Champion—trapping him within.

Lazander rushed forward, relieved when he saw Malik swinging his hammer against the vein-like walls, looking furious but unharmed. A flash of silver caught Lazander's eye, and he ducked as an arrow zipped past him.

Then another. And another.

Thirty or so people came pouring out of the tunnel behind Grim, their cloaks torn and ragged. Almost every one of them had a bow in their hands. Lazander's eyes darted between them, searching for the mage whose magic bound Malik.

"Ready," Grim called, pointing at Lazander from the top of his reptizoid like a general on the battlefield. His soldiers knelt in two lines, the front line nocking their bows while those at the back drew their bowstrings, arrows at the ready.

"Loose!" Grim shouted. A barrage of arrows shot at Lazander, and while some flew wide, most of the archers fired with deadly aim. When he was still a Gilded Knight, Lazander would have thrown himself to the side in a tight roll, hoping to dodge out of harm's way.

But he wasn't a Gilded anymore.

Lazander ran forward, weaving in and out of the arrows like fish in a stream. The front line stood when the back line knelt to nock, loosing their arrows at Grim's command, but Lazander barely slowed, his sword deflecting the few he couldn't dodge.

Sixty feet from Grim. Fifty.

"Ket?" Grim called, a thread of worry in his authoritative voice.

"Working on it!" a woman answered, a flash of red light coming from somewhere behind Grim. Lazander darted behind the blood cage that contained Malik, taking care not to touch it as a barrage of arrows struck it, turning to ash.

"What are you *doing*?" Malik hissed, swinging his axe at the swirling cage. Despite how many times he hit it, the blood that flowed around him hadn't so much as wavered.

"Getting you out!" Lazander replied, fighting to keep his tone level. "Blood magic can only be broken by the caster—who is currently hiding behind a crowd of archers—or an overwhelming force. You're not strong enough alone, but if we work together, we might—"

"Your job is to kill these bastards and pin Grim to the bloody wall!" Malik said viciously. "Ravenna is locked away somewhere down here. This is our chance to kill her, once and for all!"

"She's *here?*" Lazander asked, shocked. Even Gallow couldn't set foot in this world, not without doing immeasurable harm to it. "As in, *physically?*"

"Yes! Now stop bloody standing there and do your job."

There was a pause as the archers stopped firing, a tense silence creeping in. "I didn't know Gallow's dogs loved hiding so much," Grim called, his words such obvious bait.

Lazander didn't bother answering. Instead he nodded at Malik, drawing his bow. It was a beautiful, curved weapon inlaid with dragonscale—a remnant from his time with the Gilded. Grim was trying to keep Lazander at a distance while Ket, the blood mage he guessed, wrought whatever magic she needed, but that was a mistake. Lazander was a hunter first and foremost—he was happiest with a bow in his hands, his target in sight.

Lazander closed his eyes, visualizing the layout of the cavern. Grim—left, fifty feet away. Twelve archers at the front, a foot between each. Twelve archers behind. People clustered behind them, and at least one mage—but he couldn't get to her without taking care of those up front. Eyes still closed, Lazander stood, his back as close to the blood cage as he dared. Even from here, he could hear the whisper of the archers' steadying breaths, the air tense as both sides waited for the other to move.

Lazander nocked and drew, stepping out from behind the cage at speed and letting an arrow fly, his natural strength as a Champion making it blast through the air like a comet. It hit an archer in the shoulder, sending the man flying from the sheer force. The fallen archer collided with the man behind him, causing chaos as they both hit the ground. A flash of red moved behind them, but the mage was already gone, darting out of sight.

*Fine,* Lazander thought. *Grim it is, then.*

The Champion loosed two more arrows before the archers could raise their bows. His arrows found their targets, shouts erupting.

"Steady, steady!" Grim called, but it was too late. Grim's soldiers clearly had some training, but how tightly they bunched together told Lazander they lacked experience. And nothing threw the inexperienced like chaos.

Three men screamed in pain, arrows jabbed through shoulders and shins while people fell over themselves to pull the injured back. Grim was shouting orders, but Lazander was already running.

Forty feet. Thirty. Twenty. The reptizoid hissed when Lazander drew his blade, seconds from closing the gap to Grim. The beast's head snaked forward, her razor-sharp beak aiming for his neck. Lazander brought up his sword, deflecting her with the flat of his blade, unwilling to kill the creature.

But a blast of magic hit him in the side, and Lazander realized too late he'd left himself wide open.

## Chapter Eighteen

Dead. *Dead.* DEAD.

Zara. Lukas. Noah. Their bodies lay still and lifeless—their eyes locked on mine.

*And it was all my fault.*

I tried to look away, but Calamity forced my eyes open.

Zara—throat slit. Lukas—limbs torn off. And Noah... oh God, Noah...

**loOK**

My eyes itched but the tears wouldn't come. They couldn't—I was too thirsty. Too hungry. Too broken.

**tHIS iS tHE COst oF yOuR DIosbeDIEnCE**

**mORE wILL dIe iF yOU dO NOt SuBMit**

I wanted to beg for forgiveness—to throw myself at Calamity's mercy. To say the words the god so desperately wanted to hear. And then I remembered Zara's golden eyes. Her strength and ferocity. Her *courage*.

"I..."

\*\*\*

"You're telling me the creepy slug thing is... Ravenna. A goddess. A magical, omnipotent being who's been worshipped by the vaxion for over a thousand years. Who gave us our ability to shapeshift. *That* Ravenna is... a slug goddess? That slug, specifically," Lukas said, pointing at the twitching creature with a grimace.

"I was not sure until now," Zara confessed, fingers tracing the sigils beneath her feet. "The voice first spoke to me on the trek here when it set a stonebreaker on me. It knew... things about me. Things only someone with the power to peel back the layers of my mind would know. Magnus had complete control over me, even tampered with my memories, but not even he had such abilities. Calamity, on the other hand, does."

"Who is... also a slug?"

"Yes."

"*What?*" Lukas yelped, hands in his hair. "You forgot to mention that, Zara!"

"I did not see the need. Be Calamity slug, beast, or behemoth, I will cut the godling down," Zara said, walking forward.

"Oh, you are *not* going to—"

Zara stepped into the open air, landing beside the slug, beside *Ravenna*, with a thump.

"There's not enough gold in the world for me to go in there," Lukas called.

Zara knelt by the slug, head cocked to one side as she examined it. The long curve of its body and the row of teeth at its head were the same as Calamity's, but it was smaller, its skin parchment-thin and flaky. It mewled again, a strange crying sound, but gave no sign it knew she was there.

"What if it isn't Ravenna?" Lukas asked. "What if it's Calamity's long lost twin brother or something?"

"While it was endlessly irritating, the voice wanted me to come here. I nearly killed Calamity last we met—I doubt the godling is eager to see me again," Zara replied. "Think of the mural we saw. In it every man and woman bore their beating heart to Ravenna. And the heart is…" She couldn't help but raise an eyebrow at Lukas, wondering if he'd been listening during their shapeshifting lessons.

"The source of our vaxion forms—our mana," he said, frowning.

At the word "mana," the slug twitched, its teeth gnashing as it writhed, hungrily snapping at the air.

Lukas backed up, but Zara stood her ground, her teeth bared in a snarl. "There it is. The truth of what our beloved birth mother wants. This is why Yemena trekked across Moonvale, despite there being no trials. Her master needed a little *snack*. It is why the vaxion know nothing of this metal maze—you wipe their minds after you feast on them, *slug*, don't you? Does it feel good to have spent a thousand years in your grandly named 'Ravenna's Breath'?" Zara laughed with bitter realization. "Oh, I see it now. The joke. The *jest*. For what air is to us, mana is to you, is it not? We are nothing but *sustenance*."

It wasn't enough that Calamity made her and her people playthings in his conquest. Their own goddess, the one who was supposed to protect them, had done the same thing. And she'd done it from the very beginning. "You *abandoned* us when Calamity's plague ravaged us and again as the vaxion lay declawed, helpless, and practically extinct!"

The slug mewled, and the voice returned at full volume, excited and joyous. *"Sugar heart! Please, oh please! A taste, a whisper! We cannot breathe, cannot think!"*

Lukas gasped, his hand coming to his head, and Zara knew he'd heard Ravenna's plea. "You beg for my heart's mana, even after everything you have done? After all the lies you have wrought?" Zara said, raising her foot to stamp on the slug's head. "Have some dignity, slug."

*"Teema! The pretty parasite, Calamity's toy, we help her! Feed us the sugar heart, and we help, please, please, please!"*

Had Zara been alone, she would have brought her heel down on Ravenna's head. But Lukas yelled, "wait!" and to Zara's own surprise, she pulled back.

"Can you do it? Can you help Teema?" Lukas asked, leaning over the edge.

*"Yes, yes! She screams now, screams as he cuts her. As he breaks her!"*

"Lukas," Zara said, her voice a growl of warning. "It is a lie. She only seeks to drain us of mana, so she might survive until her next victim."

"Teema is stuck in Calamity's prison, and unless you have Eternity hidden in your back pocket, we don't know anyone else with a connection to the Void." He took a deep breath, then hopped down into the metal pool, cringing when the slug turned toward him, mewling. "Look, I also don't want to feed the carnivorous slug monster my mana, or heart, or whatever it bloody wants, but let's think about this *before* we kill it."

"Only one of us has met a so-called 'god,' cub, and it bound me, enslaved Teema, and tortures her as we speak."

"Exactly," Lukas countered. "You couldn't kill Calamity, and Ravenna feels like the next best thing. I get it, I do!" He raised his hands. "But—"

*"Salty boys!"* Ravenna hissed, curling in on herself, her voice low and terrified. *"Salty boys come. They gnash. They trash. They bash. Listen, listen!"*

Despite herself, Zara cocked her head, letting her senses expand. A huge *boom* sounded, followed by silence.

"What was that?" Lukas began, but Zara was already moving, jumping up and out of the pool.

**"I am death's mistress, bow before me,"** she hissed, her claws inching from her fingernails as she scanned the room of twisted sculptures. Nothing moved, but she felt a change in the air, the hair on the back of her neck raising like a threatened cat.

"We are not alone, Lukas," she hissed.

*\*\*\**

Lazander was knocked back by the blast of magic, instinct alone keeping him on his feet. Lashes of what looked like blood-filled arteries appeared, snapping around his arms, legs, and neck—threatening to choke him. The archers parted, a woman with a strange wound that split her face in two taking a shaking step toward him, her face contorted in concentration. She raised two fingers, pressed them against her bleeding skin, then pulled them back as if to strike.

"Wait, Ket," Grim called.

"*What?* I have him, Grim!" the blood mage answered. Instead of lowering her hands she brought them to her chest where her fingers moved constantly at strange, unnatural angles. Unlike the trap that held Malik, which had been prepared using a sigil, this spell needed constant casting, Lazander realized. He could use that.

"No, something is different about this one," Grim said. "He—"

**"Bend to his might, break before his Judgment,"** Lazander roared, Gallow's strength flowing through him. He flung his arms outward, the arteries that bound him snapping like worn string. The mage cried out, clutching her head from the mana backlash of a broken spell. By the time she hit the ground, Lazander was free.

His vision turned dark at the edges, and Lazander knew he was one ability away from ending up like the mage, groaning on the floor in pain. And while one mage and three archers were down, over twenty still stood, their arrows trained on him. Lazander made a show of cocking his head as if he didn't have a care in the world, his bow at his side, a hand on his sword.

He was ten feet from Grim, and until he could use his strength again, there was only one thing he could do—stall.

"Tell me," Lazander began, "why mana crystals? That's the one thing I haven't been able to figure out. Was it for the teleportation mage? The amount of magic she'd need to teleport all of you in and out of these tunnels is phenomenal, but she'd have to leave the mana crystals behind—they're too heavy." He snapped his fingers loudly, as if something had just occurred to him. "No, silly me—they're for the blood mage, right? I mean with ten stolen mana crystals you could bring a city to its knees. Who was next on your list, Grim? Back to Evergarden, or have you set your sights on Freyley? Or perhaps…"

Lazander trailed off in surprise when the reptizoid sniffed the air, her huge body moving toward him. He gripped his blade, but her steel-gray eyes were so wide and inquisitive, it was obvious she wasn't going to attack. This close he could see where her iridescent scales turned to pink flesh around her delicate eyes and the gray feathers at the sides that marked her as female. Hot air burst from her nostrils, and she let out a soft cry of delight when she sniffed his chest, butting her head gently against him. He was so shocked he stumbled.

"Beatrice likes you," Grim said softly, a smile on his face, still seated comfortably atop the beast. "Which says a lot considering you just tried to kill me."

"I wasn't, ah—"

The beast pressed her cheek to his, rubbing against him. Instinctively his hand came up to pet her, and the reptizoid's throat rumbled in a heavy purr. The archers shot confused looks at Grim, their bows dipping.

"Stop petting the damn bird and *kill them*, Zander! Grim is the only one we need alive!" Malik roared with a fury Lazander didn't understand.

"At ease," Grim called, and his soldiers immediately lowered their weapons. He raised his hands. "I'm going to get down from Beatrice now, is that all right?"

Lazander nodded while trying to gently hold the reptizoid back—she was trying to stick her tongue in his ear and was slobbering all over in the process.

"Easy girl, easy." Lazander laughed. "You're worse than Mabel."

Beatrice cooed in reply, chewing on Lazander's hair, just like his horse did.

"My name is Grimwald Flint," Grim said, holding out his hand. "But you can call me Grim, most people do."

Up close the man was as large as Lazander remembered—he was only an inch or two shorter than the Champion. Scars lined his neck and hands, but it was Grim's eyes that struck Lazander—even though they'd been trying to kill each other only seconds ago, there was a warmth and a kindness to them that disarmed Lazander.

The situation was so surreal—he was being licked by a reptizoid while Malik roared from a blood cage, and the man who'd tried to poison half of Evergarden introduced himself—that Lazander found himself shaking Grim's hand.

"Lazander Evercroft of Freyley," he replied. "While I appreciate you ordering your men to stand down, I cannot sheathe my weapon. You're, ah!" Beatrice nipped his ear, and Grim laughed as he gently shoved her away. While the man was large, he was older than Lazander, unarmed, and lacked a Champion's gifts. At this distance it would be child's play to knock him unconscious and be halfway out of the maze with Grim over his shoulder before the archers could blink. But the clear love in Grim's eyes when he petted Beatrice made Lazander hesitate.

"Down Betty. Not everyone likes getting covered in reptizoid spit, hm?" he said.

Beatrice huffed but pulled her neck back.

"I told my blood mage to wait because I have something to ask you, Lazander. Tell me—why didn't you kill Betty? Or my men?" Grim gestured to his fallen soldiers, who'd been dragged out of the line of fire. Arrows jutted from shins and shoulders, but they were alive.

Glaring at Lazander, but very much alive.

"You lead these people, correct? In Ravenna's name?" Lazander asked.

"I do."

"Do you lead all of Ravenna's forces or just this small band?"

Grim chuckled. "Forces is a dramatic word—this is all that is left of us thanks to Gallow and his Champions. But yes, I do."

"Then you're the only one I need. Once your blood mage is up, you will order her to disable the cage that holds my partner. In the meantime, please turn around. I'm going to bind your wrists. Cooperate, and none of your men will be hurt."

Grim smiled, the crow's feet around his eyes crinkling. "I notice you didn't say *I* won't be hurt."

Lazander wanted to lie but deceiving the poor elderly mage into giving up his ceramic frog still sat poorly with his conscience. "You tried to poison the wells of Evergarden at Ravenna's behest," he said, trying to keep his voice soft and free of the anger he felt at all the innocent lives almost lost. "That is not a crime that can go unpunished."

"Zander, enough of this!" Malik screamed, grabbing at the swirling bars of the blood cage with his bare hands. "Knock the bastard out, or I'll slit his throat, and every one of his men, too! You hear me?"

"Don't you find it interesting…" Grim began, staring at Malik with open hatred. "… that your so-called 'partner' interrupts every single time Evergarden is mentioned? Almost as if he doesn't want you to ask me about it?"

Lazander half-turned, keeping an eye on Grim while he signaled Malik. The Gilded Knights had an entire dictionary of code words and gestures, and while he'd never practiced anything like that with the Champions, he chanced laying his palm flat, and then holding up his index and middle-finger.

*Wait. Two minutes.*

Malik glowered but said nothing. Lazander turned back to Grim, trying to hide his confusion at Malik's anger. He might not have been a Champion for long, but he wasn't an idiot. All he needed was a few more minutes, then he could take down the entire room without killing anyone. He could keep his oath to serve Gallow *and* keep the bloodshed to a minimum—the best-case scenario in his book.

"I'll make you a deal," Grim said, surprising him. "Walk a circuit of this room with me, then we can go right back to killing each other."

"I'd rather you came quietly."

"Even if I do, your partner will kill every one of my men."

Lazander wanted to tell Grim that wasn't true, but he knew it was—Malik was out for blood.

"We do a circuit, I tie you up, and you order your people to flee down the tunnels," Lazander decided, knowing Malik would be furious but not seeing any other way to end this peacefully. "When your blood mage is at the periphery of her spell, she releases Malik."

Grim paused, considering the offer. "Malik is quick on his feet. He killed Hanna, my bodyguard, in the time it took to blink." Grim's tone was light, but Lazander noticed his fists clench. The image of Malik's axe cutting through Hanna, splitting the hand-painted image of Ravenna on her shield in half, flashed in Lazander's mind. Malik cut the woman's head off seconds later.

"If you cooperate with us, and tell us where to find Ravenna… I'll stop him if he tries," Lazander said finally.

Grim blinked in surprise. "Were you any other Champion I would laugh in your face, but you mean that, don't you?"

"I do. Unless Gallow *directly* orders me to kill your men, I won't do it. Not unless I have to."

A pause. Grim's eyes were locked on Lazander's, boring into his very soul.

Lazander stared back unflinching.

"Deal," Grim said finally, clasping his hands behind his back and setting off to the right at a leisurely pace. Lazander followed a few steps behind, half an eye on the archers in case this turned out to be a trap. Other than the tunnel they'd entered through, there were four more leading off from this room, all lined with the same strange metal. As they approached one Lazander was about to tell Grim to stop, but the man meandered gently to the left.

He meant it. He really was doing a circuit of the room.

"You were wrong by the way," Grim said casually, staring straight ahead. "The mana crystals weren't for the 'teleportation mage' as you called her. Nor were they for Ket, the blood mage. She's sworn herself to Ravenna and is the first of the goddess' witches who wasn't a vaxion—it's a title she holds proudly." He nodded to the blood mage, who was slowly getting to her feet, a hand clutching what Lazander guessed was a very sore head. "It didn't have the effect we'd hoped—Ravenna has... specific needs that we've struggled to fill. But still, I'm proud of Ket."

Lazander was about to correct Grim and say magic-users were called "mages" not "witches" but stopped himself. What did it matter? The man was just rambling.

"The mana crystals were for Ravenna," Grim said in the silence.

"What does a god need mana crystals for?" Lazander replied, unable to stop himself. He was still wrapping his mind around the fact that Ravenna was apparently *here*, in this world, and not in the Void.

"Because," Grim said softly, grief threaded through his voice, "Ravenna is *dying*."

# Chapter Nineteen

Lazander almost stumbled at Grim's revelation but collected himself. "I know most of the gods died when the Tyrant descended, but I didn't think anything but a god could kill another," he said.

"Come now, Lazander." Grim smiled. "Call him Calamity. He doesn't deserve to hide behind a moniker."

"I... most people don't know his true name."

"Most people don't serve a god who fought back. Ravenna is no friend of Calamity, regardless of what Malik told you."

Lazander nodded, keeping his expression neutral. The poor man was more brainwashed than he'd thought.

"But you're half-right—it's difficult to kill a god," Grim continued. "Weakening one, however, is far easier. Calamity's followers cut Ravenna off from her worshippers a decade past, leaving her without the only magic that allowed her to live and breathe on this plane. She's been a... shell ever since. Can you imagine that? Starving to death over ten long years?"

Grim looked so distraught that Lazander felt the bizarre need to comfort him. Everything Grim said was clearly a lie, but it was one the man believed.

"That sounds horrible," Lazander said, nodding in false sympathy.

"The mana crystals have kept her sustained somewhat, as has Yemena, but since she vanished... well. We're out of time, I'm afraid."

"Is that why you're in this strange bunker?" Lazander asked, trying to coax more information out of him. "You're feeding mana crystals to Ravenna?"

"You think I'm talking nonsense," Grim said, smiling sadly.

"I've seen what Calamity can do, how he can twist a man's mind until up is down and left is right," Lazander said softly, remembering Valerius and the look in his leader's eyes when he killed his own men. "I don't know what Ravenna told or did to you, but I don't think you're a bad person for believing her, Grim. And I mean that."

"Says the man who thinks I tried to kill half of Evergarden. Did Gallow tell you that? Or was it Malik?" Grim asked, sharper now.

"I saw the vial of poison—*Ravenna's Dying Breath*. And the map on your bodyguard... on Hanna with the location of every well in Evergarden. It was obvious what you were trying to do."

Grim reached out a hand to stop Lazander, and the Champion went to draw his sword, but the man just stared at him—looking utterly baffled.

"Oh. Oh, he didn't. Ha. Haha!" He laughed a proper belly laugh. "I knew Malik was a lying bastard, but that is a new low!" He wiped an eye, staring at Lazander. He made a show of opening his robe slowly, reaching a hand inside while Lazander watched him carefully. He pulled out a half-empty vial, the contents dark as night—just like the one Lazander saw in Evergarden. Grim gave it a shake, and the insides swirled to a metallic silver. There was no doubt about it, it was the same poison.

Lazander shot back, sword unsheathed, but Grim held up a hand. "You recognize it—that's good. It took us weeks to find someone who could make us another. I don't like to waste 10,000 gold, but if you don't believe me, well, we're all dead anyway."

He popped the cap, and before Lazander could stop him, he drained it dry. Grim flinched at the taste but held out his hands, gesturing to himself. "If it's poison, why am I still breathing?"

Lazander stared at Grim and the vial, thoughts racing through his head. "I saw the note, Grim. You can't drink your way out of that," he began. But the man was shaking his head before Lazander finished speaking.

"I don't know a damn thing about a note, but there's no such thing as *Ravenna's Dying Breath*, Lazander. This?" he held up the vial, "is called a *Kingkiller* potion. Why? Because a mage developed this to increase his own mana, and it worked—too well. His body, unused to the sheer volume of mana he could now produce, exploded—killing not only himself but the very king he'd sworn to protect. If a mage can drink this without dying, he briefly has the power of fifty mages high on mana. Entire wars have been won with this thing. I emptied what was left of my family's vaults to buy this for Ravenna, hoping it would encourage her own body to begin producing mana again." He looked at the empty bottle sadly. "She barely twitched. We knew there wasn't much chance it would work with a god's physiology, but we'd tried everything else—this was our last shot." He sighed so deeply, Lazander could feel it in his bones. "We failed."

"You're lying. And before you try to pin this on Malik, *I* found the note on Hanna's body."

"Did Malik tell you to search her?"

Lazander frowned, trying to remember. "He… he did. But what does that—"

"I bet you found the note exactly where he said it would be."

Lazander was about to say that wasn't true, he'd found it in a secret pocket on the inside of Hanna's tunic, but then he realized *why* he'd searched there. He and Malik had killed followers of Ravenna earlier that day, and Malik had found the vial in just such a pocket on one of the dead. It wouldn't have dawned on Lazander to check there if he hadn't seen the older Champion do the same.

"Lazander!" Malik called, slamming on the blood cage. "Whatever he's saying, don't listen to a damn word of it, boy! This is what Ravenna does. She pulls you in with lies and makes you doubt yourself." The blood cage sizzled, Malik's skin burning where he slammed his fist against it. "This is why I told you to take him out, boy. Do it now, before he gets any further into that thick skull of yours!"

"Does Malik still have it?" Grim asked. "This so-called *Ravenna's Dying Breath*? If he does, I'll drink it right in front of you."

"I…" Lazander started, glancing between Malik and Grim.

"Ravenna isn't a threat, Lazander. No matter how many mana crystals we feed her, she revives only briefly before fading. *Kingkiller* was our last gamble. I'd gladly let her drain me dry, but she needs a… specific kind of mana. One I can't give her." Grim took a step toward Lazander. Instinctively the Champion backed up.

"Ravenna saved me. Years ago I ended up half dead in Moonvale, and she wasted some of her precious magic to breathe life into me anew. Me—a human. And all she asked in return was that I save someone else's life when I had the chance." Grim lowered his head. "I wanted hers to be that life, but I failed. Gallow is too late—Ravenna is as good as dead. She… she isn't even in her right mind anymore. Let her die in peace, Lazander. She deserves that at least."

Lazander gripped his blade, running through everything both Grim and Malik had said to him, weighing the unease he felt at how quick the Champions were to take a human life while remembering the feel of the note in his hand—the most damning piece of evidence against Ravenna. Could Malik have planted it? No, that was impossible. Lazander had pointed a sword at Malik and told him to stay put while he searched the dead bodyguard. There was no way he could have darted to the corpse, planted the note, and then laid back down without Lazander seeing it.

But then he thought of his fight against Valerius. He'd only been a Champion for a few weeks, and his body was so new and alien. Valerius had thrown a fireball at Lazander, and Malik had pushed him out of the way—saving his life. Lazander hadn't even seen him move.

Malik. From the vial being poison, to who Ravenna was and what she had stood for had come from Malik. Any other followers of Ravenna they'd met since hadn't had the chance to speak—they'd killed them immediately. Was Grim telling the truth? Had Lazander been slaughtering innocent people this whole time? No. No, that couldn't be true. Even if there were times Lazander had… issues with how Malik did things, Eternity served Gallow. And there was no one in this world he trusted more than Eternity.

Wait, Eternity.

"If all you wish to do is live in peace," Lazander said, raising his sword, "then why, with her dying breath, did your bodyguard threaten to cut off Eternity's head?"

"Ah," Grim said, smiling. "I wish you'd led with that." Flames burst from Grim's fingertips, an inferno circling Lazander. It swept around him, pulling the breath from his lungs and melting the metal floor beneath his feet.

## **Chapter Twenty**

Eyes closed, Zara could hear it—the sounds of battle. Who was it? And what were they *doing* here under Moonvale?

"Get it off, oh gods, get it off!" Lukas yelped.

She whirled to find Lukas on his back, the slug on his chest, Ravenna's body writhing as she tried to burrow into his heart.

Zara snarled, diving for Ravenna, not caring if she snapped her neck when she hit the ground. Claws bared, she swiped at the slug—

And vanished.

\*\*\*

"For what it's worth, Lazander, I didn't lie to you," Grim's voice called from outside the inferno.

The heat was intense, and Lazander screwed his eyes shut as if that would help ward off the flames that blistered his skin. "Ravenna *is* dying, and we were in Evergarden to pick up that *Kingkiller*, not to hurt anyone—certainly not to poison anyone. But I'm afraid we have no interest in peace. Not while Gallow still rules."

The flames inched closer, and Lazander could feel himself beginning to boil within his armor, the metal now hot to the touch.

"Gallow isn't the god he says he is. He wants to *feast* on Calamity to grow in power—the very thing he's been trying to do to Ravenna for years. You're not here to kill Ravenna, Lazander. You're here to serve her up to Gallow on a silver platter."

Lazander held his breath, the air in his lungs burning him. Pieces of his hair caught fire, turning to ash. Underneath the crackle of flames, Lazander heard Grim wheeze as if in pain.

"It's dumb luck I didn't blow up when I drank that *Kingkiller*. I figured if it killed me, I'd at least take you with me. But damn, if it doesn't *hurt*," Grim groaned, and Lazander heard the unmistakable thud of a knee hitting the metal floor. "You're a good man, Lazander. I don't trust people, but I trust Betty. And that grumpy reptizoid hasn't liked anyone but me in years. I wanted to give you a shot, to see if there was any human left in you. But Gallow has his claws in too deep. I'm sorry, Lazander—I really am."

The fire closed in around Lazander, his flesh peeling from bone as Gallow grew in his mind.

**"DO YOU DOUBT?"**

*No,* Lazander thought, barely able to think through the pain. *Grim was lying. He lied the whole time, and I was a fool to listen.*

**"WILL YOU HESITATE?"**

*No. Never again, I swear it.*

Lazander fell to his knees, barely conscious.

**"MY POWER IS PRECIOUS,**

**"A SINGLE DROP THE DIFFERENCE BETWEEN VICTORY OR DEFEAT.**

**"BUT I REWARD THOSE LOYAL TO ME.**

**"SPEAK."**

**"His touch is stone, his body eternal,"** Lazander whispered, his words whipped away by the flames. **"Let my own speak true."**

Gallow's power flooded Lazander, and the flames suddenly felt cool to the touch. He opened his eyes, instinctively shutting them when he saw the flames still whirled around him, though they no longer burned. Realizing he could breathe again, he looked down at his hands to find his skin as gray as stone.

He clenched his fists, hearing a slight crack. He wasn't "gray as stone," he *was* stone. Grinning, Lazander stepped through the flames to where Grim knelt, the mage's eyes going wide with fear.

\*\*\*

"Woah, *woah*! What's happening? Where are we? Zara!" Lukas yelped. The scent of old magic, coppery yet sweet reached Zara's nose. She waited a beat before opening her eyes.

No red sand slid beneath her feet, nor did twin suns hang in the sky. Instead she was kneeling on stone, wet and cool to the touch. A waterfall thundered a few feet from her, the sound low and comforting like a heartbeat. They were in a cave of deep purple rock. Patches of it glowed lilac, adding a soft light to damp dark.

Zara growled, coming to stand in front of Lukas, her back to him.

"What is it? What's wrong?" Lukas asked, sticking his head around her like a cautious turtle. At the cave entrance a waterfall fell in a solid sheet, the land beyond a blur of red and gold. But the strange alien landscape it hinted at wasn't what made Zara tense.

A young girl stood before them. Her blonde hair fell to her waist in luscious curls while her arms and legs were thin as sticks. She looked eleven years old at most but could have been as young as nine. Blood stained the lips she pressed her small fingers against.

*"Ravenna,"* Zara snarled.

"Esmia Ravenna, ane ilto kara!" the girl said. Her eyes were huge, pupils almost eclipsing her emerald-green irises. "Lesi—oh, whoops!" she giggled.

*Giggled.*

"Hehe, wrong language. Oh dear, it's been so long since I drank the sweet mana of the vaxion, that I feel quite… *dizzy*. I'm terribly sorry, but I—I think I need to sit down."

"You feast on a cub's heart blood, a cub under *my* protection, and ask for forgiveness? I will rip you apart, slug!" Zara hissed, her body shuddering with the need to transform and rip Ravenna to pieces, but the cave was too small. She'd get to Ravenna but crush Lukas in the process.

"One—cub, really?" Lukas interjected. "Two—that was actually very sweet, Zara."

Zara ignored both him and the stab of embarrassment she felt. **"I am death's mistress, bow before me."**

Claws unsheathed, she ran at Ravenna with a growl, aiming for her throat. Swaying slightly, the goddess made no move to dodge—she simply snapped her fingers. Stone shot out from the walls like liquid, wrapping around Zara's hands and feet, freezing her in place. A sliver of rock crept up her neck, and Zara struggled against it, thinking Ravenna meant to strangle her. But it wrapped around her mouth instead, muzzling her.

Furious, Zara screamed a slew of curses, each more incomprehensible than the last, but other than jerking her shoulders and nearly wrenching them out of their sockets, she couldn't move.

"Zara, please—I know you're angry, I would be too, but you have to understand, I'm not…" Ravenna winced, touching her head. With a shaky hand, she steadied herself against the wall. After several deep breaths, she grimaced. "I would much prefer it if we didn't have this conversation while the room spins like the clutzaped nebula, but we don't have time to wait it out." With what looked like supreme effort she straightened up, brushing down the front of her emerald-green dress. "As introductions go this is probably one of my most awkward, which is… impressive, considering my history. But first thing's first—Lukas, I owe you an apology."

"You do?" came Lukas' nervous voice from somewhere behind Zara.

She didn't look at Lukas—couldn't even if she'd wanted to. Ravenna's stone bindings kept her staring straight at the goddess, so she settled for glaring with every ounce of rage she had.

"I do," Ravenna said with a small smile. "I've spent years on the brink of starvation, and along the way my mind… fell away. I was half-mad with hunger, and while my memories from that time are hazy at best, I know I fed on you without your permission. I wish to apologize."

She paused, looking expectantly at Lukas.

"Ah… no worries, boss," he said, going for jovial but sounding like someone had a knife to his throat.

"That's very good of you, Lukas. Thank you." The girl had a high, sweet voice but the look in her eyes was ancient. It made the hair on the back of Zara's neck stand on end, her instincts screaming at her to run.

"I used half the mana I stole from Lukas to bring us here—to the in-between," Ravenna said, either oblivious to or ignoring Zara's discomfort. "It's not the Void—setting foot there would be a death sentence for me and disastrous for your world, but we're safe here for now. It then took almost a third of what was left to bind you Zara—something I didn't want to do."

Zara glared at Ravenna with a ferocity that would have made even Ashira flinch.

"What I mean to say," Ravenna said quickly, hands wringing nervously, "is that I have ten thousand years of regrets to explain but lack the mana to keep us here and do the tale justice. The less we argue, the quicker this will end, and then you may do with me what you wish—you have my word."

*"Hek hu!"* Zara roared, her curse muffled by the stone muzzle.

"She means go ahead," Lukas said.

Zara shot him a look, and he shrugged as if to say, *"You can argue with the powerful slug god if you want, but I'm not that stupid."*

"As you guessed," the girl said, "one of my many names is Ravenna. I've also been called the birth mother of falslings, and the Goddess of Truth, but none of those reflect who… or rather *what* I am. Not that I need to tell you that—you've seen my true form." Ravenna looked down, and if Zara hadn't known better, she'd say the girl was ashamed. "You were also right about the maze and its trials. Making it to the center *did* help the vaxion—connecting with me gives you a twenty-five percent increase in transformation speed and a boost to your Essence stat, which gives on average a ten percent increase in mana."

Both Lukas and Zara simply stared at Ravenna in utter confusion—neither had a clue what she'd just said.

"But," Ravenna said, plowing on, "the benefits to the vaxion were just a bonus. The maze's true purpose was to feed me. Without System access, falsling mana is the only… food source I can survive on in your world."

Zara threw a slew of mumbled curses at Ravenna, the words "I knew it" and "shekkin gods" were almost intelligible.

"It wasn't a choice I made, nor was it one I refused," Ravenna said hurriedly. "I stripped myself of both Void Mana and my status as a System Operator—I didn't trust myself not to be tempted by its power. Not after what it had done to my family… Wait, sorry, I'm getting ahead of myself. Or is it behind? Time is… a difficult concept."

"Let's start easy then, shall we?" Lukas said casually, stepping in front of Zara despite her growl of warning. His stance was casual, his words easy, but Zara could tell by the tightness in his shoulders he was terrified. "Why are you *here*, and by here I mean in our world? I thought gods could only exist in the Void, otherwise chickens became dogs, and trees became chocolate, or something?"

Zara cocked an eyebrow at him in surprise, torn between wanting to strangle him for speaking and shocked he'd known such a thing—she hadn't. He shrugged at her. "I got a disciple of Gallow drunk once and picked their brain. You'd be amazed at what people say after a few drinks."

"People think you talk too much, Lukas, but they forget you listen more than you speak," Ravenna said with a smile.

Lukas' expression froze in a look Zara recognized as *'Why does the crazy lady know that? Is this the bit where I die screaming?"*

"What I mean to say is that you're right, Lukas. Gods can't step foot in your world without harming it. But then, I'm not a god anymore… not really. I gave up my 'godhood' nearly a thousand years ago—my *Void Mana*."

She pulled the top of her emerald-green dress down slightly, revealing a large hole where her heart should be, its edges black and necrotic. No one should be able to survive a wound like that, and for some reason this disturbed Zara more than seeing Ravenna in her slug form.

"Void Mana is the key to the impossible: from conquering planets, to pulling a human from another world and giving her control of a young vaxion's body." Ravenna looked pointedly at Zara, who glared in return. "However, once you've used it up, it's *gone*. There are… ways to replenish your Void Mana, but I chose not to. I won't bore you with why—it's a long and pathetic story that boils down to a life of greed and hunger, followed by bottomless regret." She dropped her eyes, a look of shame painted on her face.

Zara growled, furious the slug would try to make her feel sorry for it.

"It's why in the end, I used all my Void Mana, every last drop…" Ravenna raised her hands, palms up, and gestured to Zara and Lukas. "… on you. Or rather, your fangs, fur, and claws."

"Wait," said Lukas, eyes wide. "Does that mean you're really…"

"Your creator?" Ravenna said with a smile. "Yes. Yes, I am."

## Chapter Twenty-One

"While I might be your creator, calling you my creations isn't right," Ravenna said, her smile dropping slightly. "You were my... penance. A paltry one, considering the thousands if not hundreds of thousands of lives I've taken. But I wanted so badly for things to be different. I convinced my siblings to try—told them that if we stopped fighting, maybe the pain and death would stop too. And we were close... so close. But then it all went wrong." Her eyes welled with tears. "I couldn't stand it anymore—*refused* to be part of it—so I used all my Void Mana to help what humans I could. To give you the tools to fight back, should anyone else try to take your world. I'm only sorry I could help so few of you."

A hundred thoughts ran through Zara's mind—that if Ravenna was telling the truth, every vaxion tale she'd heard of their origins was a lie. If the slug had more "siblings" than just Calamity, how many of these wretched creatures roamed the world? But what cut through the clutter of her thoughts was her irritation at Lukas—and the wonder in his eyes as he stared at Ravenna.

"I knew giving up all my Void Mana would kill me—and it would hurt. In truth... I hoped it would," Ravenna said softly, "but as I lay dying one of my newly born vaxion found me. I thought she'd recoil in horror when she saw my cold, clammy form... but she picked me up. Cradled me in her arms." Ravenna smiled, and despite Zara's distrust, even she couldn't deny the love she saw in the goddess' eyes. "To this day, I don't know how she knew what I needed, but she placed me against her heart... and I *fed*. I came alive in an adrenaline rush of pure mana, much like I did just now."

She coughed, looking embarrassed. "The vaxion who saved me became your first witch, a *shi'ara*, and they've carried on this tradition ever since, bearing the brunt of the burden by binding their vaxion forms, giving me enough mana to survive on for years."

Zara snarled, remembering the lies the den guardians fed her of Ravenna and the fantastical tales of the *shi'ara* who were "sworn to protect" the vaxion and carry out the goddess' will. Anger swelled in her—how many of the vaxion had known? Had she been wrong, and Ashira was in on it this entire time? The thought made her entire body tense—she didn't think she could take it if her aunt knew.

While she couldn't speak, Ravenna must have seen the question in her eyes. "No one but the *shi'ara* knew, Zara. It's why Yemena and the other witches were so brutal when they trained you for the trials. The more mana you had and the more seamless your shapeshifting, the less I had to take." The girl paused, clearly not wanting to continue her confession. "Yet all the lies and deception were for naught—without you all I… I starved."

Zara felt a particular rush of anger at Yemena—while she had never liked the zealous witch, the fact that she'd known the truth about Ravenna and had hidden it from her own people, had used them as glorified *livestock* for this slug, was beyond betrayal to Zara. She wished she could bring the witch back to life, just so she could have the pleasure of killing her all over again.

"So you gave us the ability to transform into massive beasts—without asking us by the way—and in return we became your permanent snacks?" Lukas asked, mouth in a thin line.

Zara felt a rush of pride—perhaps he wasn't a complete idiot.

"It's not as parasitic as you make it sound, but… yes," Ravenna said, looking ancient and sad. "I didn't choose to be saved, but I chose to live—I let the *shi'ara* keep my secrets from you. I let them fool you all into keeping me alive. But I'd be lying if I said I regretted it. It was only in your world, free of Void Mana, my siblings, and the System that I finally felt… *alive*."

Her eyes shone, and she wiped away unshed tears. "For a thousand years I've watched each and every one of you. I've laughed alongside you: loved, cried, and grieved. I never planned to reveal myself, but now that it's happened, I have so much to tell you and no time to say it. So this will have to do."

To Zara's surprise, Ravenna got on her knees and bowed until her head touched the floor. "Thank you—thank you for teaching me what it means to feel. To be human."

Lukas looked from Ravenna to Zara, and she could see his resolve wavering. It was hard not to—love and sincerity flowed from Ravenna in waves, and had Zara not been picturing the bloodied mural in the maze, she might have fallen for the goddess' words. But Ravenna could pretty herself up in all the beautiful dresses and child-like curls she wanted—Zara knew the truth. The goddess was nothing but a slug, and Zara refused to be manipulated again.

"*Ural!*" she yelled into her stone muzzle, furious at how hard it was to say the word. "*Ural!*"

"Ah," Lukas said with a frown. "Zara wants to know who painted the mural in, ah, blood that shows you feeding on a bunch of people's hearts? Or rather mana, which is… so much better."

Ravenna's head was still pressed to the ground, but her entire body flinched as if struck.

"When the vaxion fell to a mysterious plague," she said, not looking at them, "I was as helpless as a babe. Without Void Mana, I'm barely more powerful than a *shi'ara,* and I could only watch—useless and terrified for you. When Magnus appeared promising a cure, I encouraged Yemena to take it. I was so desperate to save you all, I thought the world of man and magic might be your only hope. I didn't… I didn't know the plague came from Calamity."

She raised her head. Thick tears rolled down Ravenna's cheeks, her grief raw and open.

"When you leaped from your beds, hale and hearty once more, I was overjoyed. By the time I realized what Magnus had done it was too late. You… you were gone."

"What do you mean 'gone'?" Lukas asked.

"You were my night sky, each of you a star that shined as brightly as the sun," she said, her soft smile at odds with her tears. "But with every one of you he cured, you vanished from that sky—severing the connection between us. Severing the… magic I gave you."

"Is *that* why the vaxion can't transform anymore?" Lukas asked, horror in his voice.

Ravenna nodded. "And why the two of you can—you were never cursed with Magnus' cure."

"*Ural!*" Zara said, louder this time.

Ravenna dipped her head, needing no translation from Lukas this time.

"You saw me," Ravenna said, her hands bunched in her dress. She spoke rapidly, her shoulders so high they nearly touched her ears. "You saw the… half-mad creature I'd become—but that was nothing compared to what happened when Calamity was done with me. With half the vaxion dead and the few still breathing cut off from me, I lost myself to a haze of pain and confusion. By the time I'd dragged myself out of it, it was too late. There was… so little of them left. I hardly recognized their bodies." She put her face in her hands, forcing each word out between gritted teeth. "Enera, Trix, Midra, and Gok."

A memory drifted to Zara of several older vaxion, each at the very front of the crowd whenever the *shi'ara* delivered a sermon about Ravenna. They'd been almost as devout in their worship as the witch.

"They went looking for me," Ravenna said, face hidden. "I don't know if it was to curse me for the sickness that nearly wiped them out or to wrongfully thank me for 'saving' them, but I… I…"

"You killed them," Lukas said, and Zara was pleased at the fear and disgust in his eyes. She *knew* it—Ravenna was no different to Calamity.

"I did. Trix painted the mural after I'd… taken her legs. The *shi'ara* wanted to scrub the walls clean, but I insisted she leave it. I'd hidden behind lies for too long. I decided that if people found me again, they should know the truth. And if you kill me for it… well, that's the least I deserve."

Silence stretched between them, tense and filled with a sadness that made Zara want to rip her own skin off. On the one hand, Ravenna's story filled her with rage—the "goddess" had just admitted to murdering her own people and to lying and using them as food for centuries. But in the same breath she'd bore her soul to them, claiming they could kill her once she'd said her piece. Zara had met Calamity, and the slug had no concept of things like "love" or "grief"—yet they radiated from Ravenna, alongside her clear remorse and pain.

*No.* Zara shook her head, furious at the weak thoughts that gathered there. She was here for one thing and one thing only—and she refused to let a slug's sob story change that.

*"Eema,"* Zara barked.

"Zara, didn't you hear what she just said? This is *huge*. Don't you think we should—" Lukas began, but Zara pulled against her stone manacles, her shoulder cracking painfully. When she yanked again, harder this time, Lukas raised his hands, speaking quickly, "Ravenna, hi, sorry to cut in after that, well, truly horrifying story if I'm being honest, but we're not here to seek vengeance or anything like that. We're here for Teema. You said you could help her? Right around the time I stopped Zara from stomping you to death, I believe."

Ravenna raised her head, looking confused. "I said that? Ah, it's true!" Ravenna hurried to add at Zara's threatening look. "I can get to Teema and return her to your world, but I can't get her home. She's still bound to the System—Calamity's version of it, at least, and without Operator privileges there's only so much I can do."

Zara did what she always did when she didn't understand something—she glared. Ravenna tentatively stepped toward her. "Zara, I want to speak to you as an equal, not as someone I have to bind and gag. If I release you, you must swear you won't attack. I don't have the mana to stop you again *and* return us to your world. And there are... things happening there I can't protect us from."

Zara hesitated, not believing a word Ravenna said but knowing that if she refused, she wouldn't have another chance to strike. She nodded, but as the stone slid back, freeing her, Lukas pointedly stepped in front of her. Annoyed, she realized he'd known she'd planned to attack. Since when had the cub been able to read her so well?

"I know we're here for Teema," Lukas said to Zara, hands raised. "But this might be our only chance to get some answers about us, the vaxion, Calamity—everything. Let me speak to Ravenna for a minute. *Please*."

Zara's immediate reaction was to push past him, but she'd never seen him look so serious. With a sigh, she nodded. Let him ask his questions—it didn't matter what Ravenna said, so long as she helped them save Teema.

"A couple of things, first—this is insane," Lukas began, hands clasped, a winning smile aimed at Ravenna. "Second, I have so many questions, but let's start simple—what the hell, Ravenna?" He shifted his bracer, revealing the edge of the blood-debt on his forearm. While usually red and angry, it was more muted now and looked like it had shrunk slightly. "When you made us, did you mean for some of us to shift into uncontrollable rage-monsters? I don't mean to criticize, but that's a *bit* of a design flaw."

Ravenna winced. "No—that isn't a fate I'd wish on any of you, but that doesn't mean it wasn't my fault. Before your world, I'd only ever used the System to feast and destroy—yours was the first where I'd tried to *create*. Of the planets my siblings and I had already ingested, I chose several beasts for you to inhabit using the System. Unfortunately when I chose the third beast, I miscalculated the essence needed when I assigned your base stats, which caused—"

She rambled on; every word nonsense that only made Zara angrier.

Lukas shot Zara a glance, then spoke quickly. "We're an accident—got it. Now, what is this 'System' thing we keep hearing about? Teema mentioned it too."

"I… hah," Ravenna laughed softly. "Forgive me. That's a good question but it's like being asked why is water wet, or what is the color blue."

Zara growled.

"Imagine you had the rulebook for the entire universe at your fingertips," Ravenna hurriedly began, "and all you needed to bend reality to your will was access to the System as an Operator. The greater the task, the greater the power needed. Now—you could technically use simple mana to accomplish what you desired, but you would need trillions of points to do… well, what I did to the vaxion and molger. *But,*" she raised her finger, "Void Mana is different. It's the single most rare and powerful substance in the universe—what we call our 'godhood.' While granting you fur and fangs would take endless magic, it only took me a hundred points of Void Mana."

Lukas pressed a finger to his lips, and Zara wondered if he was as lost as she was, or if he was simply a better actor than her—the latter she guessed. "Let me get this straight. It's not your powers that make you and Calamity 'gods'… it's the fact that you are, *were* in your case, System Operators with access to Void Mana. Is that correct?"

Ravenna nodded while Zara tried not to be annoyed Lukas had understood while she hadn't.

"Wait, does that mean Gallow is also…" Lukas asked.

"My... brother is an Operator too. Every god is—though I don't know how many of my siblings are still alive. I can't see without Operator access."

"Then what is the 'Calamity System'? Ah, it's the version..."

"... of the System Calamity holds dominion over, correct," Ravenna said, looking pleased at how quickly Lukas was picking it up. "As an Operator we can mold the System to our will, creating unique rules and guidelines as we see fit. We are of course limited by how much Void Mana we have access to. We could wait centuries to build up enough mana to accomplish what a single VM point can do, but that's—"

"Enough! You've had your questions, Lukas," Zara barked, knowing an endless conversation when she saw one. "Teema. How do we save her?"

"Zara, did you hear a word she just said? Ingesting planets? Beasts from other worlds? A System that lets anyone be a *god?*" Lukas asked, uncharacteristically awestruck. "We haven't even asked her about Calamity, or what the hell happened when he invaded our world!"

"None of that matters," Zara said, taking a step forward. "We could spend a lifetime figuring out the past, or we can take charge of the future. Now, slug—tell me how to save Teema, or you will dearly wish you'd left me muzzled."

Ravenna sighed, her long blonde hair falling in front of her like a waterfall. Zara was struck by how small she looked—no doubt Ravenna's intention, she told herself.

"I'm a shadow of a 'god,' an imposter dealt a power I abused in favor of my own greed." Ravenna raised her head, a glint of steel in her eyes. "And though I didn't choose this life, I can choose my death."

"Why do I not like the sound of that?" Lukas said, looking from Ravenna to Zara.

"You're called the Fury for good reason," Ravenna said, emerald eyes locked on Zara's. "I watched you as a child. And while my kind don't experience things like 'love', I felt something close to it seeing you come into your power. But there is a collar around your neck. The System that brought Teema to this world is both a blessing and a curse—it allows her access to powers and abilities far beyond her ken, but it is entirely at the Operator's, at *Calamity's* discretion. And while you are no player, Calamity holds sway over Teema, and through her, you. I suggest we change that."

Zara smiled. "Now we're talking, slug."

## Chapter Twenty-Two

A single blink and Lukas and Zara were back. While Zara stood, claws out, eyes sharp, Lukas had his hands on his knees and was doing his best not to vomit all over his trousers. Fun new fact about himself he'd just discovered—inter-plane travel made him nauseous.

"Damn it," he said. "There's still so much we don't know, and what we *do* know is crazy! Did you miss the bit where our molger and vaxion forms *come from another planet?* Like, up in the sky there are entire worlds, Zara! Just swimming around or something."

"We live on stolen time, Lukas." Zara said, not looking at him. "Without Teema, you and I would be dead—you by your own people, me by Magnus when he either grew tired of me or became a little too enthusiastic with his 'punishments.' We have one shot at saving Teema, and we owe it to her to grasp it with everything we have."

Ravenna lay between them in her slug form once more, now the size of a mouse. Her skin was still thin and flaking, but there was a new alertness to the way she tilted her head toward Zara—the goddess was awake, aware, and listening.

"I know, I *know*, but we don't have to do it now!" Lukas said, finally able to stand without his stomach flipping. "Ravenna was *there* when Calamity attacked. He's her... brother, or something. If you're serious about killing Calamity, anything we learn about him might help us. Let's grab Ravenna and get out of here—Grim can do the ceremony in a few days, right?" Lukas looked down at the goddess, his heart sinking when she shook her head.

"You heard the slug," Zara said. "We are not the only ones who hunt Ravenna. We need to find Grim, and—

A rush of flames blasted over the metal pool they stood in. Lukas ducked, but hands were already pulling him close. Zara threw herself over him and Ravenna, protecting them both.

A hiss, and the flames dissipated. Lukas could hear shouting from above where two men were yelling for the other to stand down. He was about to ask Zara if she was all right, but then he saw her face—she was smiling, a wide grin that lit up her eyes like stars.

"Too long I have sat on my haunches, my claws and flames useless. Now is the time to take back control," she said. She picked Ravenna up with surprising gentleness, then tucked the slug inside her armor, right by her heart. "Feast, slug. I have mana to spare."

"You're absolutely insane, Zara," Lukas said with a smile, "and I mean that as a compliment."

"And you are a timorous whelp who cowers in the face of your own *immense* power," Zara said, deadpan. "You hide behind smiles and humor while fearing your own claws and the monster locked within. I need the beast at my back, Lukas—not the cub." She moved to leave the little safety they had in the pool, then paused. "I did not mean that as a compliment."

"No, I got it, Zara. *Thanks,*" Lukas said, sighing heavily. But she was gone, disappearing over the rim of the pool and into the fray.

He looked down at his claws, mind whirling. They'd met a *god*, who was a *slug*, and everything was so absurd that he didn't know if he wanted to laugh or cry. Yet Zara had taken it all in her stride, not even flinching when Ravenna told her what she'd planned. And here he was, hiding.

Zara was right he realized, though he'd go to his grave before telling her that. Teema had gone out of her way to make sure he never had to fight, but he couldn't hide behind her anymore. He had to either embrace the monster within or give in to it—but he couldn't live in fear. Not anymore.

With a growl, he fell to all fours—fur bursting from his back.

\*\*\*

When Zara jumped headfirst into the fight, she hadn't known what to expect. Two things hit her at once: one, a man made of what looked like stone was fighting who she assumed was Grim, based on Ravenna's description—and the mage was *flying*. Flames abandoned, Grim raised his hands, slapping them together. Although they were deep underground, a cold wind whipped around her, stinging her skin. It picked up, and what was a cutting wind became a deadly hurricane, tearing through the room like a blunt axe. Arms raised, the stone man slid back but stayed on his feet.

Zara wasn't so lucky.

She flew backward, claws dragging along the steel floor, unable to puncture it. She was about to be thrown back into the pool when she collided with something warm and solid. Coarse fur dug into the back of her bare arms like dull needles. With a grin, Zara turned to find a huge molger behind her. Thick brown fur covered his body while six legs, each as wide as a tree-trunk, barely had to dig into the ground to hold them both in place.

"About time I saw your teeth, Lukas," she said. "I cannot transform—Ravenna will have nowhere to hide if I do. The stone man is yours. I will handle Grim."

He nodded, breath from his wide snout coming out like wisps of smoke while his small eyes and smaller ears twitched in agreement.

The hurricane died, but Grim wasn't done. He landed on his feet, panting slightly. He hadn't even noticed Zara and Lukas yet—his eyes were firmly locked on the stone man.

"Stop this!" Grim called. "Gallow is *lying* to you. He's as power-hungry as Calamity! What do you think will happen when Ravenna and the Tyrant are gone, and he's the only god left in control? Do you think he'll just let us go?"

"How *dare* you accuse Gallow of lies when you have done nothing but twist the truth!" The stone man lowered his guard slightly but kept his fists high. "I could have killed you and your men, but I chose not to! I stuck my neck out for you, defying Malik to give you a chance. And what do you do? String me along and try to *burn me alive.*" As he spoke, Zara saw his face clearly for the first time. A memory flashed in her mind of a young red-haired knight on a glittering dragon, diving through the air to save Teema and Eternity. Gray skin aside, he was different now—taller, broader, his eyes dark and haunted, but there was no doubt about it—it was *Lazander*. "Malik warned me. He told me my bleeding heart would be my ruin, and he was right!"

Grim dug his hands into the metal floor, and to Zara's shock his fleshy human fingers punched through it. Veins bulging in his neck, Grim threw his hands skyward, *tearing* the metal floor apart, revealing the russet brown rock beneath. With a jerk, he slapped palm to stone. A huge column of rock burst forth, twisting through the air like a ferocious snake.

"Impossible," Zara whispered, watching Lazander throw himself to the side in a tight roll, the strange stone snake striking where he'd been only a second before. Sparks flew as it dragged along the metal, ripping a new hole in the floor with a shriek that made Lukas wince. The stone snake twisted back on itself at speed, body creaking as it flew toward Lazander with deadly accuracy. "Grim used flame, wind, metal, and now *stone* in the same breath. Magnus could manipulate other elements when pressed, but even he could not control them all like this."

*"Something—something's wrong with Grim,"* Ravenna said in Zara's mind. She squirmed over Zara's heart, and the Fury felt a sharp prick when the slug bit down, feasting on her mana. *"I'm calling out to him, but he either can't hear me, or is refusing to answer—which isn't like him."*

"Then we will make him answer," Zara said, dipping into a crouch. "Lukas... *now.*"

She charged forward, muscles flaring to life as she ran at full tilt for Grim. On the other side of the cavern, half the metal had been ripped from the walls and floors, and from each tear another stone snake burst forth, chasing after Lazander—who showed no signs of slowing down.

Zara forced herself to look away from Lazander, trusting Lukas to take care of it. Hands deep in the stone beneath his feet, Grim swayed, falling heavily to one knee. "I don't care, Ket," he said aloud, panting hard. "Get them out. I'll grab Ravenna, and... Ket? Ket, can you hear me?"

"I have Ravenna," Zara said, skidding to a halt in front of him. Grim swung for her, fire bursting from his hands, but she ducked, driving a fist into his stomach. He doubled over with a gasp, bile spewing from his lips. "She's been trying to speak to you. Now stop being an idiot and *listen.*"

"I'll rip your—" Grim's face went blank. To Zara's surprise, tears filled his eyes. "Ravenna? I... I heard you, but I thought it was the potion driving me mad. No, don't—don't worry about that, how are you here? And *speaking?* I tried everything. I even went looking for the molger to see if their mana would help feed you, but I couldn't—"

A massive boom cut Grim off. Lazander had stopped trying to dodge and was now driving his fists into Grim's stone monsters. They lasted only a strike or two before shattering into useless, inert rubble. His strength was immense, but Zara refused to linger on it—if she did, the battle would already be lost. Lukas stood mere paces from Lazander, his head low, feet wide. He growled, a rumble that filled the entire cavern with a simple threat.

*Run. Or die.*

Zara felt a twinge of pride.

"We have no time for heartfelt reunions. Tell Grim what to do, Ravenna," Zara said, eyes trained on the fight. When the last of the stone snakes fell, Lazander charged, and Lukas answered in kind, his massive molger form thundering across the room. As Lazander raised his stone fist, Lukas' flesh turned liquid, and he slid under the shocked Lazander easily, the nut-brown of Lukas' human skin visible for a split second before coils burst from the back of his skull. By the time Lazander turned, a pitch-black vaxion had its jaws on his stone neck, pinning the knight to the floor.

"Still sloppy," Zara said, already collating the notes she would give Lukas after the fight. "But better."

"No, Ravenna! I just—*we* just got you back," Grim said, staring at the tiny slug-like head that poked its head above Zara's armor. "Look at what only a drop of mana from Zara and Lukas can do for you. This can work—they can feed you."

Zara resented Grim offering her up like a buffet but said nothing, feeling Ravenna squirm uncomfortably over her heart. Whatever the slug said in return, Zara wasn't privy to it. "I don't care if it isn't enough," Grim protested. "We'll figure it out. Please, Ravenna, don't... don't do this."

The man's clear anguish took Zara by surprise. He was tall, and the scar that tore his face in two clearly wasn't his first judging by the raised flesh that disappeared down his collar. Grim had been in his share of battles and won—no simple feat for a breakable human. Yet he looked at Ravenna with such love and despair, it made Zara suspicious.

*A spell of yours, Ravenna?* she asked mentally, knowing the slug would hear her. *It must be helpful to command such devotion.*

"*You shouldn't be so quick to judge, didn't Teema tell you that?*" Ravenna asked, a barrage of images flooding Zara's mind. Grim, half-dead at a stonebreaker's hands when he threw himself into Ravenna's maze, praying the fall would kill him. The days Ravenna spent, a year without vaxion mana at that point, pouring everything she had into his wounds, her sanity slipping with every drop. "*Grim and you are the same. He fought to save me to repay a debt, and in time it turned to true loyalty and affection.*"

Zara bristled, and Ravenna chuckled. "*I see who you are, Zara. And I hope someday you let Teema, Lukas, and Ashira see it too. You've got fangs sharper than anyone I've met, but your heart is true. And that is more precious than Void Mana.*"

"Fine," Grim said, head bowed, every word laced with grief. "If that's what you want and not something you're being *forced* to do." He glared at Zara, and she realized Ravenna must have kept the two conversations going at once. "Then fine, I'll do it. But if we're going to breach the Void, *and* pull this Teema person out of it, I'm going to need time—a few hours at least."

"*I'm afraid we don't have the luxury of time,*" Ravenna said for both their ears. "*We'll just have to make do. And while I know this isn't a comfort, I want you to know I'm happy it's going to be you. I… well, I couldn't ask for a better death.*"

Grim nodded, brushing a rough hand over his face. The veins in both of his eyes had exploded, blood pooling around them, and he was breathing hard. "The *Kingkiller* potion is wearing off. My mana is… all but gone. How long can Lukas hold him?"

A whine sounded, and Lukas' massive form hit the ground, skidding halfway across the cavern. A myriad of wounds covered his vaxion body, and several of his teeth were missing. By the way he moved, Zara could tell he'd broken some ribs, but Lukas didn't even look back at them. He shook his head, and planted himself firmly in front of them as Lazander casually strode toward them.

"Zara the Fury?" Lazander called, head creaking to one side. "I thought you were dead."

## Chapter Twenty-Three

"When Valerius threw you from my dragon, we presumed you dead. I reported it to the queen and demanded Valerius face consequences. You were innocent, I claimed. A woman forced to do a sick man's bidding," Lazander called. "Eternity fought harder for you than anyone. The queen received a missive from her every single day arguing that Valerius was wrong—that you weren't Magnus' puppet." His stone features twisted. "I see now she was mistaken. Was I a fool for believing you and every other sob story I've heard?"

He glanced bitterly at the mess that was the cavern. The twisted sculptures that circled the room's center were nothing but scrap while almost half the metal that lined the walls and floor had been ripped away. "Let's get this over with. Where is Magnus? What hole is he hiding in while he pulls your strings from afar?"

"He's dead," Zara said, her voice calm and detached. "I punched my fist through his spine."

Lazander looked surprised but nodded. "If you're not lying, know I offer this for Eternity's sake—step away from Grim and leave." He raised his chin. "I won't ask again."

*What happens if we do the ritual without preparation?* Zara asked Ravenna silently. *Can Grim still pull Teema in from the Void?*

*"Using System calculations, there is a 93.7 percent chance it will kill her,"* Ravenna replied.

Zara thought furiously. If she gave the slug to Grim and told him and Lukas to run, she could transform and keep Lazander busy. But while Grim had agreed to the plan, one look told her he was a love-sick fool. With Lukas injured, she didn't trust the mage not to grab Ravenna and escape—and that was the last thing she needed.

*"I don't have Operator privileges anymore, but I know the System inside and out, including its backdoors. Gallow is Lazander's Operator, though it looks like he's hidden all stats and menus from his players. How odd."*

*Ravenna, I thought you only spewed nonsense when starving,* Zara said mentally, measuring the distance between her and Lazander. *Either help or shut up.*

"Sorry, sorry! *Let me see—he's stronger than you, but I think you can best him without your vaxion form. Keep him busy while I pull up his stats,*"Ravenna said. Zara had the strange sensation of the slug drawing away from her and curling up in the shadows of her mind.

"Lazander, you helped… *me*, back at Magnus' castle," Zara began tentatively. Teema had been in control for only a few hours back then, and Zara hadn't yet figured out how to see the world through Teema's eyes. She only had the girl's stories of her rescue of Eternity and her escape from Magnus' castle to go on. "You know who Valerius is, then?"

"If you speak of the traitor and his service to the Tyrant, then yes—I know." There was a creak as his stone fists clenched. "If you serve the dark god too, then I will have no choice but to put you down."

"Quite the opposite—I seek to kill Calamity." Zara smiled at Lazander's shock. "He took someone… important to me. I will get her back, and then I will *rip* his head off. However, I need Grim to rescue her. Let me have him, just for a few hours. Whatever follows is none of my concern."

Grim recoiled at her side, taking a step back, and she fought not to roll her eyes—if he couldn't tell she was lying, there was a chance Lazander couldn't either. She waited for the slug to bristle at her favorite servant being dangled like a lure, but whatever Ravenna was doing had her full focus.

A long pause followed Zara's proclamation, Lazander's eyes boring into hers. She met his gaze calmly, her hands loose and relaxed at her side. *Take it,* she wanted to say. *Take the bait.*

"Do you plan to leave this maze?" he finally asked.

Her heart soared, but she kept her face neutral. "I do not."

"Then…" Lazander flinched, eyes darting left as he stared at an empty space, shivering despite the sweat that trailed down Zara's neck. For a split second his eyes glazed over, and then it was gone—so quick Zara wasn't even sure she'd seen it. He raised his sword, pointing it straight at her. "You have my admiration, Zara the Fury," he called. "Both for breaking free of your master and for your quest to kill the dark god. But neither of us can stop Calamity—only Gallow can. And it will take everything—including Gallow's life—to rid this world of his tyranny once and for all. Now," he took a heavy step toward them, "get away from Grim."

*Shek,* thought Zara. She'd hoped to keep him distracted a while longer.

*"I have it,"* Ravenna said. Sheets with numbers flashed in front of Zara's eyes, each as confusing as the last.

|  | Current: |  |
|---|---|---|
|  | Stamina | 100/1700 |
|  | Hit Points | 800/1600 |
|  | Mana | 30/210 |

*"The ability he's using is called* Stone Skin, *it renders the user's body invulnerable. Duration is tied to his strength stat, and has a… goodness, a twenty-four-hour cooldown,"* Ravenna said.

*Ravenna, you have five seconds to get these numbers out of my face and explain to me what is going on before I shove you down Lukas' gullet and send him running.*

*"Oh, ah, looking at his base stats and mana, he can maintain his* Stone Skin *for another sixty seconds!"* she said, almost breathless. Zara could tell she desperately wanted to explain more, but that was all the Fury needed.

"Good," Zara said, widening her stance.

Lazander frowned, but Zara was already moving, a blur of speed and fury. **"If the world will not yield, I will break it,"** she roared, driving a fist into Lazander's gut as strength rocketed through her body. She'd punched stone before in fits of temper, but hitting the knight made her bones rattle. Two of her knuckles popped.

Lazander skidded back but stayed on his feet—Zara had hoped to send him flying.

"For Eternity's sake, I am sorry," he said, darting toward her. Despite the extra weight of his stone form, the man moved with speed. His leg snapped out, trying to sweep Zara's legs out from under her, but she was already in the air, spinning gracefully. The back of her heel connected with his temple, red-hot agony shooting down her leg as her bones cracked, breaking from the force. Zara winced—her foot screaming in pain, but Lazander's head shot back, buying her a few precious seconds. She landed awkwardly, stumbling on her broken foot.

*"His base stats are higher than yours, but once* Stone Skin *fades, you have the advantage with your claws,"* Ravenna said, her voice tight with worry. *"Forty seconds. Just hold on, Zara."*

"Lukas! Take Grim and *run* back to where we started!" Zara yelled, Lazander's fist grazing her cheek. She slapped a hand on his forearm.

**"My fury is but a whisper of the flames to come!"** she roared, flames bursting forth, wrapping around him. He walked through them as if they were nothing, as she knew he would—her fight with the stonebreaker had taught her that much. But she wasn't trying to hurt him. She was trying to distract him.

*"Twenty seconds,"* Ravenna whispered.

Ducking under his guard, Zara slapped a palm over his eyes. Flames shot out of her hand into the one part of Lazander not covered in stone. The knight finally yelled in pain, stumbling backward.

Zara heard the unmistakable sound of claws scraping on the metal floor as Lukas ran but didn't dare look.

*"Ten seconds!"* Ravenna said, breathless.

Lazander flailed, struggling to stay on his feet. Zara slipped behind him, planning to jam her knee into his kidney, but her injured foot collapsed under her without warning. She followed it, falling to one side at speed like a stone dropped into a pond.

**"Bend to his might, break before his Judgment,"** Lazander roared, spinning to face Zara, his fist raised as the stone peeled away from his skin, revealing bright green eyes and hair the color of fire.

*"Now!"* Ravenna called, her voice high-pitched. *"Use your* Claws of Fury, *it—"*

Whatever Ravenna was about to say was lost as Lazander drove a fist downward, aiming for Zara's chest—where Ravenna lay curled up. Zara snarled, bringing her guard up to divert the blow, her forearm clipping his. He missed her heart.

And drove his fist in her throat instead.

She rocketed back, slamming into the ground with a colossal boom, the stone at her back splitting. Her body leaped off the ground, and by the time she fell back down, she was grasping for her throat.

She couldn't breathe.

A rock the size of a mountain seemed to be lodged in her throat, burning like molten lava. The pain alone nearly made her pass out.

"No," Lazander said, eyes wide as the last of the stone fell from his skin. "I… I didn't mean…"

A painful gurgle filled the air. Zara was horrified to realize it came from her.

*"Zara! Zara, do you have any* Healing Void *potions? Spells? Anything? Zara!"* Ravenna's words tumbled over one another in her panic.

Lazander stared down at Zara, who was slowly choking to death, her throat collapsed from the blow. Teeth gritted, he looked away. "This… this isn't my fault. I gave you a chance, damn it! You—you *forced* my hand."

He took off at a run, his steps echoing down the same corridor Lukas and Grim had disappeared down less than a minute before.

*"Yes, you have a* Healing Void! *Wait, why can't I… no, no! Your Inventory is locked because you're not the System user."* Zara felt something slither up the side of her neck, surprisingly warm to the touch. *"Zara, stay with me. Grim is still in range of my telepathy, let me—"*

*No…* Zara spoke mentally, but every word took as much effort as if she'd tried to say it aloud. Black spots dotted her vision. *Lazander… kill… Lukas. Run… have to… run.*

Ravenna shuddered, and Zara's mind was suddenly awash with images. She saw a Void, dark as night, and then a singular star. As planets and other life winked into existence, the star shuddered—pulling everything toward in an endless tide. Whatever was dragged into its light vanished, and the star grew, and grew. It became so large, it filled all of Zara's vision.

Suddenly the star contracted in on itself and exploded—bursting outward in a ripple of light that shook the very universe. Hundreds of stars poured outward, some large, some small, all moving at speed.

*What… what is…* Zara asked, her eyes shuddering closed. Her throat had stopped hurting. In fact, everything had stopped hurting. A part of her realized this wasn't a good thing, but she couldn't figure out why.

*"It's a Void-star. It's how I was 'born,'"* Ravenna said softly.

Something crawled along Zara's neck.

*"There were so many of us—thousands born at the same time. We could have made something beautiful. Something meaningful. Instead… we fought. We feasted. We ate one another until we grew fat and powerful with* Void Mana*—for only by eating the flesh of our own kin can we replenish our 'godhood.'"*

Even barely conscious, Zara could hear the disgust in Ravenna's voice.

*"And then one day as I chewed on my sister, her blood bursting in my mouth, I realized what I was. What my* godhood *had brought me. Teema was never the parasite, Zara—we were."*

Ravenna slid over Zara's cheek.

*"My brother and sister stood by my side. We were going to stop this mindless slaughter, we were going to end the cycle and live together in p5yge eace. But… greed, selfishness, or perhaps our very nature ruined it. We don't deserve the power we have, Zara."*

Ravenna's voice was a whisper in a dream. Memories flashed in Zara's mind, a confusing cacophony she didn't understand—a rift in the sky, three slugs bunched together and writhing, a piece of glass in the shape of a flower, glowing with crimson light.

*"I need you to remember one name—Thaddeus. He was a servant for the Queen of Navaros when last we spoke. You need to find him, Zara, and keep him from Calamity at all costs."*

Ravenna slid into Zara's mouth, but the world was slipping away, the edges turning dark.

*"For what it's worth… I am sorry,"* the slug whispered. A jolt of what felt like lightning made Zara bite down—and her entire world changed.

## Chapter Twenty-Four

Lukas ran slower than he would have liked considering he was running on six legs and could usually outpace a vaxion, but two things were slowing him down—the broken ribs that *loved* him shapeshifting from vaxion, to human, and then molger again. And the man on his back who wouldn't stop shouting.

"Go back! We have to go back!" Grim shouted. "We left Ravenna!"

*Actually, we left Zara* and *Ravenna, thank you very much,* Lukas thought, wishing he could speak, or even better, use Ravenna's telepathic abilities. But he had to make do with an eyeroll and a *harumph,* hoping Grim would get the message.

He didn't.

As they rounded the corner, Lukas skidded to a stop. They were in yet another metal cavern from which *another* series of tunnels spawned. It looked exactly the same as the last cavern. And the one before that.

*Shek.* They were lost.

Growling, Lukas spun around. Why did every room look the damn same? They'd been able to find Ravenna because of her smell, but now he had nothing to guide him out.

Grim used his hesitation to jump off his back and start running… back down the tunnel they'd just come from.

*No! You idiot!*

Lukas caught up with Grim easily, gently shoving the man with his shoulder—and sent him flying into the opposing wall with a *thunk.*

*Oh, shek, sorry! I forget how fragile humans are. Listen, Zara has it all under control. She'll deal with Lazander, we'll meet up at the entrance, and then unless Lazander wants to deal with a very angry Ashira, we'll be able to—*Lukas continued his argument, which came out as a series of growls, head shakes, and even an ear flick or two. Grim looked at him in utter confusion.

"Please, sir," Grim began, which amused Lukas endlessly. No one had ever called him "sir." "Ravenna has no Void Mana, nothing but the few scraps left in her flesh—which she can't even use to defend herself, not without a ritual to draw it out. I know... I know she wants to help you, and I thought I could do it, but I can't lose her. Not again."

Lukas huffed, jerking his head in what he fervently hoped was the exit. When Grim stared at him in confusion, Lukas sighed and shifted. His fur sucked back into his skin, teeth dulling and becoming flat as he halved in size then halved again.

"Ow, ow, *ow!*" Lukas said, human again as he clutched his ribs. "Oh, it's burning. Why is it burning?"

"How did you... I've never seen..."

"Yes, yes, I shift quickly—the benefit of being a mutt. Listen, I know you want to charge in and save your girl like the knights of old, but Lazander isn't the one you need to be afraid of—Zara is. Once she's done wiping the floor with the Gilded, we can—"

His reassurances were cut off when Lazander appeared next to them, materializing as if from thin air. All Lukas saw was a shock of red hair, and then Lazander had Grim by the throat, and was slamming him into the wall. "Where is she? *Where's Ravenna?*" the knight roared.

Lukas snarled, coils bursting from the back of his skull as he started to shift into his vaxion form, but Lazander backhanded him without even looking—breaking Lukas' jaw instantly.

One of Zara's lessons came to him as he hit the ground. "Once you start shifting, cub, do *not* lose focus—because if you do?" Lukas' concentration vanished as what felt like half his face shattered. An explosion of pain in his skull followed a split second later, rendering him blind for several seconds—backlash from the interrupted transformation.

"You've lost, Grim," Lazander said, panting.

Lukas stared at him through a cracked eyelid, watching as the knight sagged against the wall, slapping his left hand against it for support. He was clearly exhausted and could barely stand, but he kept his right hand wrapped around Grim's throat.

"Ravenna's gone," Grim said, smiling despite his gasps of pain, the whites of his eyes lost to the crimson of burst blood vessels. "Gallow will never... find her."

"Malik will be out of the blood cage by now," Lazander said. "Your soldiers are dead, as is Zara, your attack dog."

Lukas froze, the world suddenly murky and difficult to focus on, like he was looking at it through a filthy mirror. Zara? Dead? No—she couldn't be.

"Where. Is. Ravenna?" Lazander hissed.

"I... was wrong, Lazander." Grim eyes fluttered closed. "There is no... human left in you."

With a roar, Lazander slammed Grim into the floor. "We're saving the world, damn it, as well as you, and every other ungrateful bastard in it. I have fought, bled, and even *died* for you, yet you stamp your feet like ungrateful children!" He kicked Grim in the side, ignoring the crack of bones as he kicked again and again. "We're the heroes! We're the ones risking everything for you! Why can't you see that?"

Lukas was on one elbow now, his blood pounding, his body lighting up with pain.

"We. Are. The. Heroes!" Lazander roared again. His voice was ragged with anger and grief, but he kept kicking.

Lukas stared in horror at the blood and gore at Lazander's feet. "Ee's de—argh, mah muff," Lukas groaned, every word rocks in his shattered jaw. "Ee's ded! Ahzanda!"

Lukas knew what he'd said was barely human, but it was enough. Lazander froze, looking down at the bloodied corpse at his feet. He'd killed Grim after the third kick, his foot connecting with the mage's chin—breaking his neck.

Lazander stumbled back, ghostly white and shaking. Lukas knew he hadn't even realized he'd killed the man. He'd been too far gone. The knight's back hit the wall, and he slid down, landing on the floor with a *thunk*, his eyes locked on the gristled remains of Grim.

For once, Lukas was glad he couldn't really speak.

"Ara... Ara... ded?" he mumbled, trying and failing to say Zara's name.

Lazander didn't look at him. He buried his face in his hands.

"Who's the stiff?" a male voice called, low and rich.

Lukas shifted his head enough to see a short broad man approach. He had a long, dark beard that was tied off at the end with a delicate silver bead. Laughter lines dotted eyes that nestled in a kind face. He would have looked like a cheery uncle come to stop by for tea but for the blood that covered him from head to toe, a huge, equally blood-stained axe resting on his shoulder.

The man approached the dead body, gingerly kicking it. "Ah," he said. "I recognize the shirt. That'd be our boy Grim, right?"

Lazander nodded.

"Did he tell you where Ravenna was in this damned maze?"

Lazander shook his head.

"Hey, kid," the man said, acknowledging Lukas for the first time.

As his eyes locked onto Lukas, a chill ran through him. The man might have had a kind face, but he had the eyes of a corpse—cold and dead.

"You can call me Malik. Now, I'm sure you thought running with Grim and Ravenna was a good idea, but as you can see, that didn't work out so well for you lot." He jabbed a thumb in Grim's direction. "Unfortunately, I just killed everyone in the other room, reptile-bird thing included, because I thought Zander here would keep it together." He cast an eye at Lazander, who sat still as a statue.

"But I've had temper tantrums myself, so I can hardly blame the man." Malik leaned forward, and Lukas cringed.

Between the fight with Lazander and the run here, he'd shifted seven times, not including his botched transformation. The most he'd ever managed in practice with Zara was eight, and that was without broken bones that felt like burning metal ripping his insides apart. Even if he did manage to change, it'd be slow. Too slow. And one look at Malik told him this man wouldn't hesitate.

The cold realization he was about to die hit Lukas, and he closed his eyes.

"Now, now, I need you to look at me," Malik said, slapping Lukas in the face.

Lukas gasped in pain, collapsing onto his side.

"... broke his jaw," Lazander said, his voice almost a whisper.

"You did? Damn. When you stop messing about, you stop messing about, brother," Malik said, standing up. "But that gives me something to work with." He pressed a booted foot against Lukas' cheek. His heel barely grazed Lukas, but it felt like wildfire. He hissed, tears springing to his eyes.

"Luckily, I don't need you to speak. I just need you to *point*." Malik pressed down, and Lukas nearly passed out from the pain. "Which way is Ravenna, boy? You can point, can't—"

The pressure on Lukas' cheek vanished, and he blinked, tears blurring his vision.

Malik was gone.

Lazander got to his feet with a gasp, but he wasn't looking at Lukas. He was staring down the tunnel, his eyes wide, his breathing ragged.

*Thump. Thump. Thump.*

Lukas managed to shift his head minutely—and saw a monster.

It was huge, bigger than the largest molger he'd ever seen. Its shoulders grazed the edges of the tunnel, white fur shining like a full moon in the night sky. As it padded leisurely toward them, the tunnel widened, revealing a long tail that whipped lazily behind it, a needlepoint the size and length of a spear decorating the tip. Fur covered the monster's four legs but stopped at its ribs where glittering scales lined it from shoulder to hip. Lukas frowned when the scales shifted in time with the sway of the beast.

Not scales, he realized. *Wings.*

His eyes came to the creature's shoulders where a thick silver mane ringed a cat-like face. Scales lined its golden eyes, and Lukas froze. He knew those eyes.

"*Ara?*" he asked, grimacing in pain.

In answer, she unhinged her jaw. He thought she was going to roar, but instead a rich violet glow began at the back of her throat. A heartbeat passed, the glow brightening, and then a beam as bright as the sun shot out of her mouth at blinding speed, hitting Lazander square in the chest. He flew backward, passed the tunnel exit, the edge of the cavern, and came to a tumbling stop in the next room with a heavy *thunk*. Beside him, Malik groaned, only just getting to his feet—a huge hole in his chest plate, the skin underneath as red and raw as mince.

Lazander lay unmoving. Lukas dearly wished he was dead, the ferocity of the thought surprising him—but he couldn't bring himself to regret it.

The monster padded toward Lukas, bowing her head to sniff him gently. She growled, glaring at Lazander and Malik, and Lukas almost laughed.

If the eyes hadn't given it away, the glare would have. It was really her—it was *Zara*.

"Ah… okuh!" he mumbled, trying to reassure her that he was okay. He wished he could tell her that even though she had temper tantrums like a spike-hog in heat and annoyed the hell out of him, when he thought she was dead his heart almost stopped. But all he could do was reach up a hand and press it against her snout. It was wet and cold to the touch.

Zara closed her eyes, leaning into it. *"I heard that, cub,"* she said, her words and throaty laugh reverberating in his mind, *"and I… was not happy to see you beneath that shek's heel."*

*Not a cub, also you can* hear me? Lukas thought, feeling a heady mix of outrage and embarrassment.

*"Apparently. Another gift from Ravenna. I will explain in time. The effects are… potent. But I am steady enough to deal with…"* She suddenly growled, charging forward so quickly she was a white blur. She ran into the next cavern, stopping in its center. Sniffing the air, she spun, eyes roving.

"Gone! Maggot-riddled cowards! I'll rip your tongues from your throats and feast on them. You hear me, Lazander? Teema may remember you amidst a field of rose petals, but I see you for what you are!" She threw her head back and roared, the sound making the very ground shake. "A sad, pathetic, spineless sack of meat whose head I will see on a spike! Do you hear me?"

*Zara, Zara! It's okay… it's… okay…*

Lukas' eyes were heavy as stone, and he couldn't keep them open a second longer. The last thing he saw was Zara running for him, her cat-like face creased in worry while the bloodied corpse of Grim stared at him, a single eye remaining in his caved in skull.

## Chapter Twenty-Five

"**N**ORTH."

Gallow's command was clear, but Eternity screwed her eyes shut, bringing her face over her hands.

She couldn't do it. Not today.

When dawn broke on the coastal village, Player Two's destruction was laid bare. Eternity lay where Player Two had left her, her throat hoarse from screaming. She hadn't slept, eaten, or taken so much as a sip of water. Instead she'd spent the whole night staring at what was left of Imani and Vivek, replaying their deaths over and over in her head. Vivek's wide eyes when Player Two cut off his head. Imani's sad smile when she shielded Eternity, knowing she was about to die.

The Champion hadn't even cried out when Player Two killed her.

It was this memory that made Eternity get to her feet. She'd never dug a grave before—that day she dug twenty.

More than that had died, she knew. But so little remained of some of the villagers that she'd been forced to match up what she could. She worked until the sun began to set, and only two corpses still lay in front of her—Vivek and Imani. It took time for Eternity to find enough stone, longer to find two pieces that were both large and flat. She had little experience with stone masonry, but Eternity stacked the rocks as best she could until she'd formed two cone-shaped graves. Using her magic, she carefully lifted Imani and Vivek, setting Vivek down in the first grave, Imani in the second. Flat stone followed, forming the lids of the makeshift cairns.

Eternity briefly hesitated, then opened the door to the Void, not caring if anyone took issue with her "misuse" of Gallow's powers. Her index finger burned like a hot poker, and she pressed it into the lid of Vivek's grave, engraving:

"Vivek Heathfred: a Champion of Gallow whose swords were as sharp as his wit. He gave his life to save this world from the Tyrant."

Imani's took more time. Her smile kept haunting Eternity, and suddenly the makeshift tombs she'd spent hours building looked small—pathetic even. When Gilded Knights died, statues and mausoleums were built in their honor. Gallow's

Champions, on the other hand, got nothing. Not even a plaque in the temple of the god they served.

They were expected to die in service, after all.

Hands shaking, Eternity pressed a finger to Imani's grave. "Imani Clanbrook," she said aloud, her voice trembling, "a Champion of Gallow with fists of stone and a courage that burned brighter than the sun. She gave her life to save another with a smile."

Hands flat on the tombs, she poured Gallow's magic into the stone, slipping it between the gaps of the cairns, sealing the lids shut. Nothing, save the Tyrant, could despoil their graves now. Eternity knew the other Champions, her fellow disciples, and even Imani and Vivek themselves wouldn't approve of her using Gallow's powers like this. But for the first time in her life, Eternity didn't care. No one else might honor Imani and Vivek, but she would.

It was the least they deserved.

Two days had passed since Player Two had tried to release Bala, and Eternity still hadn't left the village. Her every waking moment was spent kneeling before Imani and Vivek's graves, her palms and forehead touching the soil as she prayed.

The second sublimation—the world is nothing without Gallow. Give everything unto him. Hold nothing back.

The third mercy—Gallow chose to save us. We repay him with our obedience. Our dedication. And we pray that when the time comes, we are worthy of his mercies.

By the time Eternity reached the fourth penance, she could list every way she'd failed Gallow, Imani, and Vivek by rote. She wasn't strong enough. Fast enough. Brave enough. Gallow had given her the tools she needed, and she'd still failed. She said it again and again, waiting for the sinking feeling in her chest that told her this was her fault. That Imani and Vivek died because of her.

It never came.

Instead treacherous thoughts filled her mind. Why didn't Gallow tell Imani and Vivek that Valerius... that Player Two was so much stronger now? Why did Gallow sentence Imani to death when her shield might have protected both her and

Eternity? Did their lives mean so little that he refused to spare the power it would take to warn them? To protect them?

Eternity had always been told she had to stay alive at any cost. That if she died, the Champions would die too. It was why she'd accepted being locked away in towers, dungeons, and temples for most of her life. She had to survive.

Now Player Two's words rang in her ears—"the 'God of Judgment' doesn't trust you with the truth. He feeds you lies, builds himself up to be a hero when he was only one traitor among many." What did that mean? Did others fight back against Calamity too? The thought was treacherous, it went against everything she'd been taught, but what followed was worse—if it was true... if Gallow wasn't the only god who fought against Calamity, then what else was he hiding from her?

On instinct she whispered the words to the fourth mercy, praying for forgiveness for her ungrateful thoughts, but the memory of Player Two kept making her stumble. "No," she said aloud, eyes squeezed shut, fingers clenched in the soil. "Stop it. This is what Calamity wants. He wants you to doubt. He wants you to question everything. You cannot let him win."

Eternity prayed, looking for answers to questions she'd never asked before. Eventually exhaustion won and she fell asleep, desperately hoping Gallow would speak to her. That he would give her something—a single word, a sign, *anything*, to show that all this pain had a purpose. That in the end, it would all be worth it.

The next morning, she got her one word.

**"NORTH."**

Eternity considered lying there and ignoring the command, a thought that would have horrified her days before. But her body was moving of its own volition, forcing her to shaky feet. Her stomach rumbled, famished after two days without food, and when she yawned her lips cracked, blood beading on her skin. But the thought of the rations and waterskin in her pack made her nauseous.

**"Bless mine body, so I might better tread your path,"** she whispered, half-expecting her doubts to weigh her down. But her feet lifted from the ground, and she was soaring through the air. As she flew, Eternity didn't look back at the ruins left in her wake.

She didn't have the strength to.

\*\*\*

"Keep those eyes open, brother, we're almost there," Malik said, panting slightly.

Lazander knew he was sliding off the Champion's back, his head jostling painfully against Malik's shoulder blades, but he couldn't move. Wait, why was he on Malik's back?

The Champion paused for a second to heft Lazander higher, and Lazander hissed at the pain that burst in his chest.

"Sorry, Zander. Sorry," Malik said, panicked. "Just hold on!"

Lazander's eyes kept drifting closed, and he tried to focus on the beautiful blue of the sky. The sun was high and warmed his cheek. As his vision blurred, his last thought was—"what a perfect day."

\*\*\*

Lazander leans against a shovel, the muscles in his back warm from clearing out the stables. He's not wearing his famous golden armor, a gift from Marito and Gabriel on his first day as a Gilded Knight. Instead he wears a simple tunic and trousers, the back soaked through with sweat, but he's smiling—it's finally time.

"Ready, girl?" he asks Mabel, saddling her. She neighs impatiently, pawing the ground. He smiles, opening the bond between them. At once he feels what she feels—a heady mix of excitement, anticipation, and irritation at how long Lazander is taking. He laughs, letting his horse feel his own excitement. "I'll take that as a yes!"

One foot in the stirrup, he smoothly mounts her. He doesn't click his tongue or kick her in the sides—there's no need. With the bond open Mabel knows exactly what to do. She takes off at a blistering pace, her hooves echoing through the Ivory Keep in a challenge. A guard yells in warning and the gates start to open—too slow. Mabel doesn't flinch and neither does Lazander. She charges forward, the huge metal doors grazing Lazander's thighs as they slip out of the Keep. "Sorry!" he calls out, a hand raised in apology, but no one hears him. He and Mabel are already gone, disappearing over the stone bridge and into the forest beyond.

It isn't long before an image of Marito, Gabriel, and Valerius flashes in his mind, the three of them packed and ready for their next mission. Lazander smiles, looking upward to see a tiny dot circling the sky—Merrin. He feels her through the bond as she sends the image again, wondering if he's setting off with the Gilded Knights. He sends her a picture of a grassy bank and a rushing river, smiling when she dives for him, chirping in excitement.

They were off to her favorite place, after all.

Merrin swoops past them in a blur of feathers, startling Mabel. The hawk opens her wings at the last second, snapping back at the drag. With a tilt of her wings, she twists around the horse, making Mabel's ears flicker in irritation. Lazander sends an image of a fallen tree just by the river to Merrin while he sends a feeling of joy and determination to Mabel. Though hawk and horse communicate differently through the bond, they both understand what Lazander is saying.

*Race you there?*

Then they're off, Mabel's hooves churning the earth, Merrin flapping wildly for their go-to spot on a perfect day like this—the Sweetdawn river.

A roar comes from overhead, and a huge shadow eclipses the sun. A voice rumbles in his mind. *"Ators, ki?"*—the unmistakable cadence of Draconic. Lazander smiles, happy to see the golden-scaled dragon.

*"Blakith net,"* he answers. His words lack the growling undertone of the language, but Galora understands him just fine, snapping her wings as she speeds up. It's one of the things he loves about the bond. Each animal uses the magic in a different way—one with images, another emotion, while the third speaks an entirely new language. But it doesn't matter—they all understand one another, and it is the greatest gift Lazander has ever been given.

"What do you think, girl?" Lazander asks Mabel. "Think you can beat Galora to the river too?" Mabel snorts in response and leaps over a boulder with such grace, Lazander whoops in joy.

Dragon, hawk, and horse all come to a skidding stop at the Sweetdawn river, and Lazander declares it a draw, despite Mabel's unhappy neigh. Lazander chews on a bread roll with lazy contentment while Mabel trots through the water. Galora is splayed out on her back like a cat, her huge body taking up almost the entirety of the soft grass. Mabel passes her, accidentally kicking water all over the basking dragon. Incensed, Galora sweeps her tails through the river with a snort, soaking Mabel in a tidal wave.

Horse and dragon square up to each other, Mabel pawing the ground while Galora dips her head, both ready to charge. The sight of horse and dragon, little and large, sizing one another up like knights about to duel makes Lazander burst out laughing. When the two look at him, incredulous, he laughs harder.

Which is how Mabel's teeth end up around his collar, dragging him to the river. He tries to shimmy out of his tunic and almost manages to escape, but Galora is ready for him. As he slips free, she shoves him in the back with the flat of her head, sending him face-first into the freezing river.

Mabel whinnies, Merrin shrieks in delight, and Galora lets out a low rumble of a laugh that sounds like rocks being smashed together. He feels joy through the bond from Mabel, Merrin sends pictures of mice—her favorite snack and how she communicates happiness, while Galora says three words.

*"Takka mit kre,"* which roughly translates from Draconic to, "you deserved that."

It's one of the best days of his life. But all too soon the scene shifts, the edges becoming hazy and distorted as his mind pulls him back into the darkness.

Mabel. Merrin. Galora. He hadn't thought about them in so long. When was the last time he'd spent the day with them? Wait. When was the last time he'd *seen* them? With a sinking heart, he realized it had been weeks. For Galora this wasn't uncommon—the dragon had her own hunting grounds a few hours from the Ivory Keep. But he'd raised Mabel since was a foal, and Merrin…

His heart broke at the thought of the hawk. They hadn't spent more than a day apart since he was eight years old. They couldn't speak so easily anymore, not since he'd lost the bond when he became a Champion, but they were still his friends. His *family*. How could he have left them behind like that? Like they were nothing?

\*\*\*

"Steady there, Zander, try not to move too much, all right?" came Malik's voice.

Lazander's eyes snapped open, his heart pounding with wild abandon. He wasn't in the Ivory Keep, wasn't even in Navaros, judging by the greenish stone of the cave walls. His nose wrinkled at the musty scent of rotten food and droppings—they were in a bear's winter den. His mind took all this information in at speed before he realized he had absolutely no idea how he'd gotten here.

*Focus,* he chided himself. *Focus on Merrin, Mabel, and Galora.*

"I have to go," Lazander said, pushing himself up on his elbows, every muscle screaming in pain. He looked down to see he was shirtless and stripped down to underclothes that barely reached his thigh. Despite how little he was wearing, Lazander was sweating. "What happened?" he asked, staring down in confusion at himself. "Why am I…" his voice trailed off when the cave walls spun.

"Woah, what did I say, Zander? Steady. That beastie gave you a hell of a beating. Me too, if I'm being honest. Wonder how long Ravenna had that monster up her sleeve, eh?" Malik said, trying to smile, but the tightness around his eyes betrayed his worry. The man pressed a gentle hand to Lazander's chest, and he fell back onto his makeshift bed—a deep navy cloak and a bundle of bright blue cloth that served as a pillow. Neither were Malik's. He was about to ask where the Champion had found them when a chill made his body clench as tightly as a fist. He was hot, cold, sweating, and freezing all at the same time.

"Where are you getting to in such a hurry anyway?" Malik asked, grabbing a waterskin and holding it to Lazander's lips. "You got a date you didn't tell me about?"

"No, I have to…" But as he spoke, Lazander realized he couldn't remember. All he had was the desperate feeling that someone, somewhere, needed him. But who? And why?

"Your job right now is to lie there and not move, brother," Malik said with a sigh. He was still dressed in the dark armor of the Champions, but something about his chest plate caught Lazander's eye. It looked different to the rest of his armor—

brighter and more polished. Almost new. "Now drink up. Gallow's working overtime to keep you alive, and you need to make it as easy as possible for him."

Lazander realized he wasn't just thirsty, he was *starving*—he hadn't been hungry since becoming a Champion. He'd thought it was because of his new body, but as his stomach gnawed at him from the inside, he realized his lack of hunger and thirst was a magical effect—one Gallow must have been constantly maintaining.

"Ah, here she comes. About damn time. I'll grab more water, Zander, you'll be drinking like a fish for a while I reckon," Malik said, tipping two fingers to Lazander in a salute as he ducked out of the cave. Lazander was about to ask who he was talking about when Eternity stepped in, smiling gently.

Malik passed her without a word.

"Good," she said softly, "you're awake."

Lazander stared at her, unable to keep the shock off his face. What in the Void had happened to her?

## Chapter Twenty-Six

If someone walked into the cave and was asked to guess who'd been seriously injured, Lazander would have bet money they'd point at Eternity. Her long blonde hair, usually neatly brushed and plaited, was a bird's nest haphazardly tied off her face. Her dress was torn and spattered with blood, and Lazander knew from experience that more than one person had bled on her. Cheeks hollow, her dress hung loose around her waist and arms—she'd lost a shocking amount of weight. But none of that scared him as much as the look in her eyes—empty and dull, without the usual spark that lit up the room.

"When I saw you laid out like that I... well, I feared the worst," Eternity said, a tremble in her voice. "Thankfully, your body... Gallow's magic," she quickly corrected herself, "has done most of the work. You were simply exhausted by the time I got here."

She dropped her head, eyes downcast as she walked toward him. His heart leaped when he thought she was going to sit next to him, but she strode past him, a small basket in her arms. "I'm no hunter, but I remembered what you told me about Freylen mushrooms, so I picked what I could."

"Eternity..."

"Please check them before you eat them. When it comes to mushrooms, I trust your judgment... your *opinion* more than mine," she said, trying to cover the stumble with a weak laugh.

"Eternity?"

"Gallow has orders for us. Gaj, another of Calamity's servants, is being summoned, but Malik agreed to wait a few hours until you can—"

"Eternity!" Lazander barked. "Why won't you look at me?"

She froze, her back to him. Shaking, she bent her head, her shoulders hunched. "I cannot," she said softly. "If I do, I will weep until I cannot stand. And I have no such luxury."

"Eternity," Lazander said, his chest aching at how small and scared she looked. The sight cut through the fog that gripped his mind, and he focused on her.

"What is it? What happened? Don't turn away from me, please. Not after everything we've been through."

She started to turn, but Malik strode into the cave, triumphantly holding up two waterskins in his hands. "Pack up, kids!" he said with forced cheer. "Lazander, I imagine that pesky hunger will fade in an hour or so now that you're up and about. Eternity, those mushrooms are enough for you, right? Good," Malik said without waiting for her to answer. He pointed at Lazander's thick black armor. It had been carefully folded and placed on a smooth piece of stone—Eternity's work, he knew.

"Gallow's armor saved us from having gaping holes in our chests—a good thing too. I don't think the shadow-fiend look would suit us," Malik said with a grin as he grabbed the armor, tossing it to Lazander. The simple act of catching it left Lazander bent over double and wheezing. It was only then he remembered the gigantic white monster with the wings of a dragon and the tail of a scorpion. A monster who shot what felt like a beam of concentrated *fire* out of her mouth. He touched his chest, remembering the feel of his ribs shattering and the trail of heat that burned him from the inside out.

A red scar in the rough shape of a star stood out on his chest—the edges raised like a brand.

"I've got one too," Malik said. "Gallow, in his grace, repaired our armor, but we'll both know to dodge next time. Anyway, get kitted out, I'm sure Lady Eternity is sick of seeing you half-naked," he said, every jovial word ringing false. Malik hadn't looked at Eternity once since he'd walked into the room, not even when she turned to face them, wiping a hand over her eyes.

"I am not some maiden who will faint at the sight of a man's chest, Malik," she said tightly. "Besides, I thought we agreed to wait a few hours before traveling?"

"No, you suggested it, and I said, 'We'll see.'" He shrugged. "And I say it's time to move."

"Did Gallow order us to move right this instant?" she asked.

Malik paused, watching Eternity closely, and Lazander knew the Champion was trying to guess what Gallow had told her. Had he revealed more to Malik about their next mission, or Eternity? Who was in the know this time?

"... no," Malik said finally.

"He would have if it was needed," Eternity said, hands folded primly in front of her.

"Ah," Malik said, crossing his arms, a smile Lazander didn't like on his face. "*Now* you know how to follow orders, is it?"

Instead of looking cowed, however, Eternity strode toward Malik with an anger Lazander had never seen. "Enough!" she said, index finger raised. "I have been ignored, dismissed, and treated like an unwanted stain ever since I saved the queen's life. No. More." Eternity raised her chin, a hint of her old spark in her eyes. "I am Gallow's Chosen, and while you may not care for me, Malik, you *will* respect me."

Lazander fought not to smile, proud she'd stood up for herself, even while his gaze flitted to Malik, wondering how the Champion would respond.

Emotions flitted across Malik's face like he was flipping through a scrapbook, trying to choose the perfect one. "Sorry, Lady Eternity," Malik said after a long tense pause. "I got a bit sharp with you there, and I shouldn't have. It's just… well, Imani and Vivek's deaths are hitting me harder than I thought."

Eternity looked aghast. "I am sorry too. It is at times like this we need to be kind to one another, not fall to pointless arguments."

"Well said as always, Lady Eternity. But since we're talking about Imani and Vivek, there's something I've been meaning to ask."

Eternity's shoulders tensed almost imperceptibly, but she nodded.

Grief in his eyes, Malik asked, "Were they… were they in pain when Player Two murdered them?"

Lazander was about to ask who Player Two was but couldn't. Not when he saw the light die in Eternity's eyes. "Vivek felt no pain. He did not have a chance to. But Imani… he hurt Imani."

"And there was nothing you could do, right?" Malik asked, his voice low. "You did everything you could to save them?"

"I… I mean of course I tried to, but Player Two was so strong, and *fast*, and—"

"I didn't ask if you tried," Malik said, leaning closer to Eternity. "I asked if you did everything you could."

Doubt flashed across Eternity's face, and Malik pounced. "Imani and Vivek served Gallow for almost a hundred years between them, and they'd *never* lost a fight. Not once. Not until they fought with you. Did you disobey Gallow again? Did you put their lives in danger?"

"No, no, I did everything Gallow asked! I even begged him to let me help Imani," Eternity said, eyes welling with fresh tears. "But he ordered me to close the gate. They died right in front of me, and he said nothing. Not a single word!"

"So you're blaming Gallow now, is it? You know the cost of doubt, don't you, girl?"

"I… I…"

Lazander appeared in front of Eternity in a blur, his back to her. He heard her gasp in surprise and without turning held his hand out behind him. Eternity slipped her hand into his, her fingers barely covering the width of his palm. He held her loosely so she could pull away if she wanted to, but she gripped his hand tightly—and he squeezed in return.

"Take a walk, Malik," Lazander said quietly, staring at a spot on the cave wall behind the Champion.

"What was that, Zander?" Malik asked, stepping closer—a move that would have been intimidating if he could reach beyond Lazander's elbow. Lazander looked down at Malik's smug, condescending expression, anger cutting through the glaze of his memories. He remembered how often he'd tried to go back to visit Merrin, Galora, and Mabel, and how Malik always insisted they couldn't spare the time. How he'd promise they would call in on the way home, but that never seemed to happen. And somewhere along the way Lazander stopped asking… stopped even *thinking* about his family.

He had to fight to make his right hand relax. If he didn't, he'd break Eternity's fingers.

"Take. A. Walk," Lazander said, each word a promise of what would happen if the Champion was stupid enough to stay. He waited for Malik's usual smile to snap back into place, for him to raise his hands and make a joke of it. But the Champion glared at Lazander with a cold rage.

Malik strode out of the cave, and Eternity let out a sigh of relief that Lazander echoed.

"Are you all right?" he started to ask, but Eternity flung her arms around him, sobbing. The top of her head brushed painfully against the fresh scar on his chest, but he didn't care. He held her close, one hand on her back, the other gently stroking her hair. In that moment he would have done anything, given anything to take away her grief and pain.

"Malik is right," Eternity said, her words barely audible between her sobs. "I doubted Gallow, I *blamed* him for Imani and Vivek's deaths, but it is my fault. I could have done more. I could have saved them."

"Don't you dare," Lazander said fiercely. "Malik is an ass. He's been an ass since the first day we met. He's just better at hiding it than Vivek was."

*"Lazander,"* Eternity said, pulling back in surprise.

"It's true," he said, giving word to the weight in his chest that grew every moment he spent with Malik. "I know you, Eternity. You're smart, stubborn, and braver than anyone I know." She looked down, but Lazander put a finger under her chin, lifting it. Her blue eyes locked onto his, bright and beautiful, despite the tears that filled them. "The other Champions were angry you saved the queen, but I couldn't have been prouder. You did the right thing. And now you're telling me someone who threw themselves at the mercy of a madman's hammer wouldn't have done everything she could to save Imani and Vivek?"

Eternity frowned, eyes distant.

"Don't," he said softly. "You're running through the fight again—I can tell. After Gabriel and Marito died, I did the same, and… well, when I say it will drive you insane, trust that I speak from experience."

"There's… there's something else, Lazander," she whispered, squeezing her eyes shut. "I have served Gallow for over a century and not once have I questioned him, even when I did not understand him. But now… it is all I can think about. I see death where we might be merciful, pain where we might have helped others. I keep asking myself why—why is Gallow doing this? Why does he force us to keep secrets, even from one another? And why… why does he never *explain* anything to us?" She covered her face with her hands. "I'm a failure. A failure of a Chosen."

Lazander felt the overwhelming urge to tell her to trust in Gallow. To understand that while we may not know what the God of Judgment was doing, it was vital we followed his orders—there was no other way to defeat the Tyrant.

He blinked. That wasn't like him. The overzealous, blind faith was Malik's style. Lazander had promised to follow Gallow, but he'd also sworn to stick to his principles—he wouldn't kill unless ordered to, he wouldn't harm anyone unnecessarily, he wouldn't—

And just like that, he heard the sound of Grim's skull crunching beneath his boot. He was back, back in the maze, where he kicked the man until there was nothing left but ruined flesh. He remembered the heady rush he felt when he promised Gallow he would never again doubt the god, never hesitate. The righteous fury he felt when he fought Grim, enraged the man dared stand against Gallow.

And Zara. Gods, *Zara*.

He'd crushed her windpipe and just... left her there, choking to death. Why? Why would he do something like that?

"Lazander?" Eternity said. "Lazander, what is it? What is the matter?"

And Malik's *lies*—about Evergarden, poisoning the wells, Grim... Lazander stumbled back, his mind a whirlpool. As a Gilded, he'd have pinned Malik to the wall and kept him there until he'd explained himself. Yet he hadn't even questioned it.

Something was wrong with him. Deeply wrong. He took a breath and tried to tell Eternity—tried to tell her that he was forgetting about Mabel and the others. That he was losing himself to a blind devotion that he didn't... a small icy cold hand pressed into his thigh, freezing the words in his throat.

He looked down in horror to see the blurry outline of a young boy, his small fingers digging painfully into Lazander. Malik had always preached the importance of Gallow appearing to him, as he did to each of his Champions—he did this to guide them, Malik claimed. To soothe their hearts and strengthen their resolve. Now, as a fog descended behind Lazander's eyes, stealing away all his doubt and fear, Lazander had one final moment of clarity.

Gallow only appeared when Lazander doubted the God of Judgment. The boy never showed up for long, but he didn't need to—all it took was a single touch for Gallow to slip into Lazander's mind and strip away everything he cared about. Strip away everything until all that remained was *Gallow*.

"Lazander, you're scaring me," Eternity said, reaching up on her tiptoes to touch his face. "Are you all right? Can you hear me?"

"Sorry, Eternity," Lazander said, shaking his head as he tried to remember what he was saying. "That last fight is catching up to me."

"Oh goodness, I am so sorry. You must be exhausted, and here I am crying my eyes out. Here, sit down, please." She guided him back to his makeshift bed, and Lazander was shocked at how exhausted he felt. And his *head*—it was pounding like thunder in a storm.

"I remember now," Lazander said as he lay down, trying not to wince. "You're not a failure as a Chosen, Eternity. Please never say that."

Eternity's smile didn't reach her eyes. "Ignore everything I said, Lazander. I am perfectly fine."

"No, I'm trying to tell you I understand," he said, taking her hand. With every word he spoke, the pain in his skull faded. "I didn't get it until the maze. Malik warned me about Grim, but I didn't listen to him. I tried to talk to the man, to make him see reason—and I nearly died for it. If not for Gallow…"

## Chapter Twenty-Seven

"*Z*ara, *Zara!*" Lukas yelled, his hands gripping her mane for dear life. She ignored him, continuing her charge for the cliff edge.

"Zara, you don't even know if you can fly!"

*"Then what better way to find out, cub?"* she asked, grinning as the winding river of Ravenna's Heart came into view, twisting off into the distance at the base of the cliff. Though her paws were the size of tree trunks, her new body felt light and graceful. She tentatively stretched out her wings, laughing when the wind caught them, making her stumble. She could do it, she knew. She could *fly*.

"No, no, no!" Lukas yelped.

*"Yes, yes, yes."* Zara laughed, leaping into the air. Her wings snapped out, and she instinctively lowered her tail to act like a rudder. She roared with joy, the wind rustling her silver mane. For a brief second she was floating midair, a whole new world opening up to her. Where would she go? How far could she fly?

And then she started to fall.

*"Shek,"* Zara cursed.

"What do you mean, 'shek'? Zara stop it, this isn't funnnnny!" Lukas screamed as they plummeted toward the river.

Zara fumbled with her wings, trying to unfurl them, but the wind was too strong. It pushed them closed, jamming them against her ribs.

With a growl, she got one free, the wind catching the delicate membrane of her wing, making them spin. Lukas was screaming something about throwing up, and Zara was concentrating on getting her other wing open when they hit the water with a boom.

\*\*\*

"Never again," Lukas announced, flopping onto the bank. He was soaked to the skin, his blond curls now a mousy brown plastered to his face. Zara was still in the river, her claws struggling to grip the crumbling soil and pull her massive body out.

"It doesn't matter what you say—Lukas, don't touch the poisonous spider. Lukas, drink this if you don't want to die from touching the poisonous spider—I'm not listening to you. Ever again," he announced.

Zara landed with a wet, clumsy *thunk* next to him. She'd never admit it, but perhaps he was right—she should get used to her new form before trying something so ambitious again.

*"We are alive, are we not?"* she said, shaking her mane vigorously. *"And we are almost home, despite only setting out an hour or so ago."*

Lukas stared at her stone-faced as she shook harder, covering him in a second, then a third shower of water.

"Do. You. *Mind?*" he asked, gesturing to his freshly soaked self.

Zara ignored him as she licked her coat, wondering if it would be as quick to dry as her vaxion form. She doubted it—her new fur was thick and dense while her mane reached all the way down to her powerful shoulders. Her claws became tangled in it when she tried to pat it down—how was she supposed to clean it?

Lukas sighed and pulled his shirt off, grimacing when he wrung out what looked like half the river. After a few minutes of silence, he awkwardly gestured to his head. "Has… she said anything since?"

*"Nothing,"* Zara replied. *"It is strange. I know Ravenna is dead. I felt her die when I bit down on her flesh. But she is still… there. Not like with Teema. More…"* Words failed her, and she trailed off, frustrated. She considered changing the subject, but Lazander showed no sign of impatience, other than with the trousers he now twisted in his hands.

*"More like she left a piece of herself behind,"* Zara managed, unable to describe the gentle cadence that thrummed through her mind. In a strange way, it was comforting.

"Did she tell you anything about…" Lukas gestured vaguely to Zara's new form.

She grinned, flicking her scorpion-like tail. *"The voidbeast? Do you ask out of curiosity or because a part of you wonders if you have such a creature within you too?"*

"You know, you're a lot more insightful than you let on, Zara."

*"And your face reveals more than you know, cub. But… I would wonder the same, had it been you the slug chose to feed herself to."*

Lukas shuddered. "I can't believe you *ate* a god."

*"She was surprisingly sweet, like honey fresh from the comb."* She laughed at the horrified look on his face. *"As for your question, I do not think the voidbeast was a kindhearted gift from Ravenna to me. Rather, I think it was a…* correction.*"*

"Well, that's not ominous."

Zara lay down, crossing her paws and resting her head on them. It was a pose that felt comfortable in her vaxion form, and she was happy it was the same for her voidbeast. *"Ravenna admitted it was her fault that you and I were cursed with monstrous forms."*

"Well, she said it was her fault, and then she said a bunch of words like 'base stats' that I didn't understand."

With his clothes laid out on a warm rock to dry, Lukas sat on the ground, resting his back against the rock. Zara noticed how much more comfortable he was with her after just a few days traveling, but what surprised her was how pleased that made her. The feeling was mutual, after all.

*"Teema sealed your monster, Ashira mine. But you feel it, can you not? In your nightmares you are a monster once more. And when you first wake, you have a moment when you know not what skin you wear."*

Lukas' eyes widened in surprise—they'd never spoken about their time trapped in the bodies of inhuman beasts. After a long moment, he nodded.

*"Mine is gone,"* Zara said.

Lukas sat up sharply.

*"Ravenna had no Void Mana left, but her flesh contained remnants of it—it is why Gallow was so keen to feast on her. When her 'godhood' fell to me, it… corrected whatever mistake she made during our creation. I do not know if all vaxion and molger have the voidbeast, or if it is only those cursed to be 'mongrels.' But this body, this* voidbeast, *is who you and I were meant to be, Lukas."*

Lukas looked at Zara with wonder. "So this Void Mana stuff is key to me transforming into *that?*" He gestured at her, and she was bemused by his refusal to name the beast. "Or maybe... it could get rid of the blood-debt?" he asked, hand drifting to his scarred forearm.

*"I know not. But if it is in my power, then I will see you freed,"* Zara said, choosing that moment to stare at a particularly large lumbar tree in the distance.

"Zara..." Lukas said softly.

She shifted, uncomfortable with the raw emotion in his voice. *"After we rescue Teema, of course."*

"Of course," Lukas said. She risked a glance at him.

He was grinning.

*"Stop that."*

"Stop what?"

Zara flicked her tail in annoyance.

Lukas' smile widened. "See? Being nice to people isn't so bad, is it?"

*"Perhaps I will turn you into a goober-pig instead,"* she shot back, and Lukas laughed, startling some witterflies that fluttered angrily away.

"You'll have to figure out the System first. Do you still see all those wiggly lines and numbers?"

*"Every time I close my eyes,"* Zara said, instinctively doing so. *"Had Ravenna not shown me, I would have thought myself mad."* On cue, strange lines and numbers appeared.

| | |
|---|---|
| Name: Zara the Fury | |
| Access: Limited. **Unassigned System User.** | |
| Current Status: Transformed | Transformation: Voidbeast<br><br>Transformations available: Human, Molger, Vaxion |
| Stamina | 2300/2500 |
| Hit Points | 3000/3000 |

| | |
|---|---|
| Mana | 1200/1200 |

Some of it she understood: this particular page of the System was about her. While she didn't know what "Hit Points" were, she was able to guess based on the two words she did understand—Stamina and Mana. This was a summation of her, one she immediately resented. Who had decided she could be narrowed down to simple numbers? The System? A glorified magical book she could neither read nor use?

It was infuriating. She tried again to make it *do* something. She thought of "Teema," commanding the magical book to either bring her here or take Zara to Calamity's prison, but nothing happened.

Zara was about to open her eyes when she realized some of the letters were darker than the others—**Unassigned System User.** She focused on those. As if sensing her thoughts, the lines and letters shimmered, changing to something new.

| | |
|---|---|
| User: SYSTEM ERROR. Aliases: Teema, Player Three, parasite, girl-child, Other Zara, crazy spirit lady. | |
| Current Status: UNAVAILABLE | |
| Stamina | UNKNOWN |
| Hit Points | UNKNOWN |
| Mana | UNKNOWN |

The excitement Zara felt at the changing page faded. It was about Teema, but it told her nothing about the girl other than her ridiculous monikers (what did "crazy spirit lady" even mean? Or "Player Three" for that matter?).

Zara thought back to Ravenna's plan—Grim would extract drops of Void Mana from her slug form and use it to steal Teema away from right under Calamity's nose. It would kill Ravenna in the process, something Grim was vehemently against, but Ravenna had insisted, claiming Gallow would find and feast on her sooner or later. If she was to die, she'd rather do it on her own terms.

It was the slug's only redeeming quality, in Zara's opinion.

*Void Mana,* Zara tried thinking. *I want to use my Void Mana.*

**VOID MANA DETECTED.**
**9/9999**
**WOULD YOU LIKE TO USE VOID MANA TO EXECUTE A GOD FUNCTION?**

Zara gasped, equal parts joy and confusion. *Teema!* she thought, hurling every shred of her concentration on it. *Take me to Teema!*

**GOD FUNCTION ACTIVATED.**
**TELEPORTING NOW…**

"*Lukas,*" Zara said calmly, not willing to open her eyes in case it broke whatever spell the System was weaving. "*Lukas, I am about to disappear. I will be back shortly with Teema.*"

"Jokes need a punchline, Zara," Lukas said, a smile in his voice. "The only way you're 'disappearing' is if I grab a xandi, enough butter to drown in, and a really big—"

Whatever Lukas was about to say was lost as Zara started to fall. She opened her eyes, hot air making them sting as she plummeted through the air from a dizzying height.

Zara snapped out her wings with every ounce of her strength, feeling a rush of joy when they shook but held. The drag made her jerk upward, her left wing threatening to crumple, but it held, her muscles shaking from the force. Heart pounding, she waited until she was sure she could maintain a slow glide before taking in her surroundings.

It was a landscape she'd seen countless times in daydreams where she ripped Calamity to shreds and in nightmares where Teema lay dead and gone. Red sand stretched endlessly in all directions, twin suns hanging in a sky that burned so hot, her lungs felt like they were being scraped raw with every breath. Only now one of the suns differed from her memory. It was cracked, a deep black line splitting it in two, but otherwise there was no doubting it—she'd done it. She was in the *Void*.

"*I am coming, Teema,*" she said, sending the thought out into the desert, hoping the girl could hear her. She tried to bank left, planning to circle the landscape to get a better look, but she bent her wings too sharply—nearly dropping out of the sky.

"*Shek,*" she hissed, straightening up. Gently, ever so gently, she tilted to one side. Her efforts were rewarded as she began a painfully slow spiral, her descent almost lazy, but she didn't dare sharpen the turn.

Zara's eyes fixed on the desert below. Sand. Dune. Sand. Dune. The horizon was the same in all directions, and she caught neither sight nor sound of Teema. Casting her mind back to her battle with Calamity, she tried to remember the landscape. It had been… sand. Dune. Sand. Dune.

Zara was almost level with the desert floor, and suddenly her spiral didn't seem so slow anymore. With no idea how to land, she stuck out all four paws and hit the sand at speed, stumbling.

Panting, she gave herself no time to pat herself on the back for miraculously staying upright. "*Teema!*" she called out mentally, wishing she could speak aloud. Who knew what Calamity had done to Teema? Maybe she couldn't even hear her anymore? "*Teema, it's Zara! Say my name in your mind, and I will come for you!*"

The sand burned Zara's paws, and she hissed when ink-black symbols crawled up her legs. It hurt less in this form, but it still *hurt*. "*Teema!*" she tried again, "*I am here. Just say my name!*"

Silence.

Zara cursed and spun in place, ignoring the pain when the symbols reached her stomach, digging into her soft flesh.

*Think. If you go charging into the desert, you will become hopelessly lost. There are no landmarks, and the stink of the slug overpowers everything, so you cannot track her by scent. There must be a way to find her. Just think!*

"*Za... ra?*" came a voice in her mind so soft, she almost missed it.

# Chapter Twenty-Eight

"*Teema!*" Zara cried, scanning the horizon. She couldn't see the girl, but she could hear her—that meant they had a chance. "*Listen close, can you hear this?*" Zara roared as loud as she could, not caring if Calamity heard her. She'd nearly killed the slug in her vaxion form—let him try and tangle with a voidbeast.

"*Is that... is that you? You sound...* big," Teema's words were slurred, as if she was drunk. But she'd heard Zara, which meant she was close.

"*It is me. Though you may not recognize me. Tell me when I am loudest,*" Zara said, picking a direction at random and running full tilt for thirty seconds. Skidding to a halt, she roared again, her throat straining from the force.

"*Quiet... quieter,*" Teema whispered, her voice fading slightly.

And this was how Zara tracked Teema, playing a game of prey and predator as she had as a child. With every roar, Zara prayed her voice would hold, and that Teema would stay conscious. If she didn't, Zara had no way to find her.

"*Loud... loudest,*" Teema said weakly.

Zara had ended up only minutes from where she'd started. Instead of sand dunes clustered like old men sheltering from the wind, the desert here was as smooth and flat as glass. She could see for miles in any direction, but no matter where she turned, she couldn't see any sign of the girl.

"*Tell me what you see,*" Zara commanded, trying to stay calm. Where *was* Teema?

"*Eyes won't... open... Hot,*" the girl managed, the last word barely audible.

Panic made Zara almost dance on her feet as she paced back and forth.

"*... Heavy.*"

Wait, *heavy?*

Zara looked down at the sand in horror. She dug her paws in, flinging painful sand into the air, not caring when it rained down on her. The hole widened, sand slipping in from the sides and filling it again, but Zara just growled, digging faster. Her skin was on fire, her paws pitch black and blistering. She told herself she didn't feel it.

*Clang.*

Zara's claws hit something hard and metal. She growled, then moved around it until she found a gap and could dig again.

*"Teema, can you hear me? I'm coming!"* Zara called.

The girl didn't answer.

The strange metal sections hidden deep in the sand guided Zara, narrowing in on a space she could barely fit into. Balanced precariously on her hind legs, she lowered the top half of her body into the narrow hole. Soon the space was so small, she was frantically digging with one paw. A pit of what felt like lava sat in her chest, spreading its painful tendrils outward, and Zara knew the sand had found its way inside her body.

And then she felt it—something soft, buried in the very depths of the sand. She couldn't see it, could barely even touch it, but it was there. She tried to flip her paw under it and pull it out, but it rolled out of her grasp.

Cursing, she unsheathed her claws and carefully pressed into the softness, trying to hook it. It *whimpered*.

*"Teema!"*

Zara growled, calming only when she pictured biting into Calamity's body and ripping him apart. The slug had buried the girl so deep in his desert that neither light nor water could reach her—content to let her rot until she gave in to him. Zara assessed the dark narrow pit Teema was trapped in—she'd need both hands to drag her out of it, but she couldn't fit in this form. She could transform back into her human self, but she'd been avoiding it for good reason—she had no idea if she'd be able to change in the Void, and if she did, would Calamity be able to trap her in her human form with his Void Mana? If so, they were as good as dead.

From the darkness Teema groaned—making Zara's decision for her.

The Fury's skin shifted like water, and suddenly she was stepping into the darkness, human feet first. The hole was about six feet deep, and she landed in a wide stance, hoping to avoid stepping on Teema.

She failed.

*"Argh!"* came a grunt of pain just under her.

"I am here," Zara said in reply, her eyes lighting up as they adjusted to the dark. Beneath her Teema was wrapped in something heavy and... *sticky*. Zara grimaced but picked the girl up easily, throwing her over one shoulder.

Taking a breath, she leaped straight upward, pulling them both out with a single arm. Above her, the ridges of the strange metal she'd unearthed poked out of the sand like uneven steps. She picked the largest one and jumped for it, wiping stray sand off the floor as she set Teema down.

The girl was wrapped in what looked like layers and layers of cobwebs.

**"I am death's mistress, bow before me,"** Zara hissed, barely waiting for her claws to lengthen before carefully cutting away the web around Teema's face.

The girl's small face appeared, eyes closed as if she was sleeping.

"Teema?"

Zara slapped her. When that didn't work, she slapped her again. Harder.

"Ah!" Teema yelped, hazel eyes shooting open. "I'm sorry. I'm sorry, I won't do it again. Please don't hurt me, I'm sorry!" She wept, rolling onto her side.

"It is *me*, Teema," Zara said, making quick work of the rest of the cobwebs. She was furious to find Teema not only terrified out of her wits, but also naked—the slug-god had stripped her until she had nothing but her own skin to shield her from his wrath. The thought made her blood boil.

"Not real," Teema said, wrapping her arms around herself. "Zara. Dead. Lukas. Dead. Killed them. Killed everyone."

**cURIoUS**

**wHErE iS raVENNa?**

Calamity's voice boomed throughout the desert. Teema whimpered. Zara made a show of smiling while her eyes roamed the sand, looking for the slug. "Dead. As you soon will be."

Her smile turned feral, eager for the slug's shock and outrage at her proclamation, but Calamity said nothing. Annoyed she pushed harder, ignoring the drops of blood that fell from her nose. "I am surprised you did not eat her yourself—she was so very *tasty!*"

Something in the desert shifted in anticipation, and the hair on Zara's neck rose.

Calamity *laughed.*

**a DIffERenT pATH**

**NO mATtER**

**iT eNDs ThE SAmE**

**yOu wiLL aLL BOw tO Me**

Zara bared her teeth. "I will burn first, slug."

**aS YOU wiSH**

The desert shook. Sand cascaded down on top of them, threatening to bury her and Teema. The girl lay rigid with terror, hands over her face. Zara cradled the girl against her chest as she ran, stumbling and falling in the sliding sand.

**yOU ArE a CHiLD wItH ThE POwER oF A GoD**

**yOU kNOw NoT WHaT yOU wIEld**

Something wet slid out of Zara's ear, but she finally made it onto level ground, panting hard. In the distance the sand began to undulate, a wave forming beneath the surface. Teema trembled in Zara's arms, but the Fury raised her head, yelling at the sky. "It will help me kill you, *slug*—that is all I need to know!"

**tHREe GoDs CoULD NOt sTOP ME**

**oNlY SlOW mE**

**wHAT cHANcE dO MORtalS HaVE?**

Zara filed away what he said—three gods had stood against him, not just Gallow—but she had no chance to linger on it. A tidal wave of sand grew rapidly, the top of it touching the sky itself as it charged toward them at speed. Zara tried not to roll her eyes—did slug know no other tricks?

She pulled up the System, knowing she should leave immediately, but she couldn't resist driving the blade in one final time. "I'll make you a promise, Calamity."

In the distance the wave of sand slowed.

## VOID MANA DETECTED.
## 8/9999
### WOULD YOU LIKE TO EXECUTE A GOD FUNCTION?

"An oath in blood," Zara whispered, feeling the desert hold its breath.

## GOD FUNCTION ACTIVATED.
## TELEPORTING NOW…

"You will die impaled on my fangs, your sweet nectar on my *lips*." Zara grinned, vanishing as the deadly sand struck the ground where she'd stood, Teema clutched tightly in her arms.

\*\*\*

Calamity slowed the wave of sand, ensuring Player Three and Zara would escape unharmed as the vaxion fumbled with what little Void Mana she had. When they disappeared, the slug slid through the crystalized fragments of its skin until it came to the spot where Zara had stood, the scent of her still lingering in the air.

It pulled up its own System. It could have spent precious points of Void Mana forcing the girl and the vaxion to do its bidding, it would have in centuries gone by, but it was old. Old enough to know there were better ways to use its power.

The Void faded away, the god's mind expanding as the System opened—showing it the potential and possibilities of the world. It was costly, and something it did only when absolutely necessary, but Zara the Fury had done the unexpected—she'd come to the Void instead of Ravenna. It was not the first time the threads had woven a surprising fate—the god had orchestrated Lazander, Malik, and Grim's meeting back in Evergarden, hoping Ravenna's followers would end up dead, leaving the goddess defenseless. But while those threads had shifted and changed, they never unraveled. It saw its future, saw it was still tightly woven and secure, and closed the System feeling something akin to pleasure.

It was all going as planned.

# Chapter Twenty-Nine

"Stop it," Magnus said quietly. The blond mage sat cross-legged in the darkness, his chains rattling as he sighed. "You'll drive yourself mad if you keep watching."

Valerius knew the mage was right, but he couldn't stop. Magnus turned away, leaving the prince sitting in the dark, helpless as he watched Player Two slaughter men, women, and children like diseased cattle. Blood soaked the soil, and while Valerius knew he had no control, it was still his hand, his *body*, that committed these atrocities. The Prince of Navaros was not a man inclined to prayer, but in that moment, he prayed someone would stop this madness. Stop *him*.

When Imani and Vivek appeared, Valerius' heart fluttered with hope. He'd never met the Champions of Gallow, but he'd heard stories of their god-like powers. Imani grinned, charging head-first for Player Two, and Valerius felt no fear—only the shudder of relief that this nightmare would soon be over.

"Kill me," Valerius whispered. "Kill me and end this monster, I beg of you."

*"Oh, I'm not going anywhere, prince."* Player Two laughed, easily dodging Imani's fist and smashing her into the ground. *"Watch. Watch and see how the world will remember you—not as the Gilded Knight who fought for the 'good of the people' but as the traitor who sold his soul to the Tyrant."*

Vivek fell to Player Two's blade, and Imani followed, Valerius' hope dying with them. The gate to Bala's prison shuddered closed, and the bloodied tornado dissipated—leaving Lady Eternity on her knees, tears rolling down her face. Player Two strolled toward her, babbling like a drunk on a stage, a smile on his face.

"I'll kill you," Valerius hissed, hate and anger bubbling in his chest until he thought he would explode. "I'll kill you for what you have done to these people. Cease this pointless slaughter and get away from her. That is an *order*."

"Why?" Eternity whispered, tears falling from her eyes. "Why are you doing this, Valerius? What did we ever do to you?"

Valerius' heart broke anew at the pain and grief in her voice.

"It's not me!" he roared, though no one but Player Two could hear him. "It's not me, Lady Eternity, I swear it!"

Player Two left her there as she screamed like an animal in pain, the sound cutting Valerius deeper than a blade. He wanted to go back, to beg her for forgiveness, but Player Two walked away, whistling a cheery tune—smiling the whole time.

\*\*\*

Player Two didn't stop, and neither did Valerius. On and on the body-stealer went, killing any innocent who was unfortunate enough to cross his path, calling forth shadow-fiend after shadow-fiend. Ten. Twenty. Fifty. A hundred. And with every shadow-fiend he made, the monsters gave birth to ten more. Player Two was building an army, and Valerius could only watch as the world he knew and loved fell apart.

With every step shadow-fiends polluted Navaros. The trees turned gray, their trunks twisting like broken spines, rotten to the core. Animals collapsed, their flesh withered to the bone. Birds fell from the sky. But soon it wasn't just the shadow-fiends who left a trail of death in their wake.

Player Two came to a wide rushing river several horse-lengths long. The current was strong, too strong for a man to swim across, especially one weighed down by weapons and armor. Valerius watched through Player Two's eyes as the man looked up and down the length of the river.

"Walk in," Valerius taunted. "If you're worthy, Calamity will save you from drowning, won't he?"

It had been days since the failed summoning of Bala, but Player Two hadn't slept, eaten, or even stopped to relieve himself. When not carrying out Calamity's will he spent his time telling Valerius in painful, aching detail, everything he'd done while wearing the prince's body. He meant to break Valerius, the prince knew. To strip him of all hope of ever getting his body back—because if by some miracle he did, there was no one in Navaros who wouldn't attack him on sight.

But instead of losing himself to grief or madness, as most people would, Valerius hardened his heart. His life was gone—that was true. But that just meant he had nothing left to lose. And if Player Two was going to torment him, it was only fair he returned the favor.

"Player Three wouldn't hesitate," Valerius said when Player Two tensed, eyes searching for a bridge. "That's why Calamity chose Zara the Fury for her, while you got me—a lowly prince with no magic to speak of. Three is his *favorite*."

Hissing in rage, Player Two strode into the water, where Valerius prayed the current would drag them both down. But as his captor's head disappeared under the waterline, eyes stubbornly open, air bubbles began to appear. Small at first, they grew in size, floating up to the surface.

Not from air Valerius realized—bubbles from heat. The river was *boiling*.

Player Two wasn't even halfway across when the waterline started to drop. Valerius realized with horror that the man was being boiled alive, but he didn't make a sound. By the time he reached the other side of the bank the rushing river was gone, the mud beneath his feet dry and cracked. Fish and frogs littered the ground behind him, their flesh cooked through.

Player Two smiled. The very landscape turned gray, dying with his every step. "I am his Chosen. I am his *favorite*."

Valerius took a breath and imagined what it felt like to grip the dark blade in his hands, to feel the earth beneath his feet.

"Player Three turned away from him—him and Zara the Fury. They spurned him, *hurt* him. But not me," Player Two said.

Valerius flexed his fingers in the darkness, fighting to relax Player Two's hand—to drop the sword.

"I will follow him to the end, I will—"

Player Two fell to his knees, gripping the wrist that held his blade so hard, his nails left bloody crescents. The prince could only feel an echo of what his captor felt, but that was enough to tell him that whatever was happening, it *hurt*. Valerius was doing it—he was fighting *back*. *Keep pushing*, he thought, his teeth gritted. *It is your body, not his. Take back control. Take—*

Red hot agony burst in Valerius' skull, blasting apart the tenuous connection he'd fought so hard for. Player Two swayed, then got to his feet—smiling broadly.

"Ha, haha!" Player Two laughed. "Nasty little prince, you took me by surprise! But it won't happen again. Calamity won't let you…"

He babbled on, exalting the dark god and mocking Valerius in the same breath until the prince pulled away, exhausted. Back in the darkness, the weight of the chains on his wrists and neck felt unbearable.

"I warned you," Magnus said softly. "In the beginning Player One was much like Player Two. He visited me, sobbing and apologizing, claiming that if he reached the 'endgame' we could both go home. In time he visited less. And then the games began." The mage's entire body tensed, his jaw clenching. "He took… great pleasure in forcing me to watch through his eyes. Around year three, he thought me as a figment of his imagination. Started to believe that *he* was the real Magnus. By the time he died, I don't think he even knew I was there."

Valerius said nothing. Player Two had been in control for three years.

"It will be quicker for Player Two," Magnus continued. "One is enough to drive a person to madness, but holding the two of us… You've noticed it already, I presume?"

Valerius nodded. "He grows easily confused and more child-like by the day. I convinced him to walk into a rushing river just by suggesting he wasn't Calamity's favorite."

"Since we aren't dead, I take it that didn't work?"

Valerius' sigh was answer enough.

On his knees, Magnus shuffled toward Valerius as much as he could. The two had tested the boundaries of their chains and found they could come within inches of each other, but couldn't touch, no matter the knots they twisted themselves into. "I am grateful to you, Valerius. Your determination and hope have given me back a shred of my sanity. But you have spent days trying to trick Player Two into ending his own life, and us with him."

"It can work," Valerius insisted. "He might be in control, but it's still my body—and I'm far from immortal. Perhaps if you were to look through his eyes, you might see something I missed?"

"No," Magnus said sharply, a haunted look in his eyes. "I spent years watching Player One torture Zara the Fury in *my* name. She was just a *child* when he first dragged her to Ashfall, but the things he did to her... the things *I* did to her—"

"We've been through this, Magnus," Valerius said softly, wishing he could grip the man by the shoulder. "Player One did that—not you. It's *not* your fault."

"You didn't see her," Magnus said, his voice distant, his eyes downcast. "You didn't see how Zara looked at me, the *hate* in her eyes. She drove a fist through my spine, and I deserved it. I only wish I'd died along with Player One."

Valerius wanted to tell the pale shaking man he shouldn't say such things—that as long as they were both alive, they still had hope but then he remembered something Player Two had said.

"Player Three... she's in control of Zara the Fury, correct?" Valerius asked.

Magnus frowned. "We've been over this, Valerius. Player One took control of my body, Player Two yours, and Player Three Zara's."

"But there were times when Zara *herself* was in control, correct? Not Player Three?"

Magnus was about to say no, when he stopped. "They seemed to take turns—it's why Player Three was able to kill me. She wasn't bound to the blood-debt like Zara the Fury was. Do you have a question, or is this a history lesson?"

Valerius ignored the mage's frustrated tone. He knew it was aimed at their hopeless situation and not him.

"I've been wondering why Calamity ordered Player Two to 'torment' me. It seems pointless—I was sitting here in perfect ignorance, and Player Two was free to do as he pleased with my body. But he mentioned that Player Three and Zara the Fury turned against Calamity, that they managed to *hurt* him."

Magnus stared at him in shock. "They hurt the dark god? Is such a thing possible?"

"It seems so. And it must have scared Calamity—why else would he send Player Two after me? Why else would he try to break me like this? He wants to make sure Player Two and I never come together or try to fight back."

Valerius was on his feet, pacing back and forth as much as his chains allowed. "In truth, were the man not sick in the mind, I would consider it, but that ship has long since left port. But Calamity's paranoia might yet be his undoing."

"You have an idea," Magnus said, trying and failing to keep the hope out of his voice.

Valerius' fists clenched, and he smiled. "I do."

## Chapter Thirty

One moment Zara was standing in front of Lukas, her silver voidbeast mane drenched from the river. The next she was gone.

"Zara?" Lukas called, scrambling to his feet. "Zara, now is not the time for hide-and-seek!" He spun, expecting to see her leap out of the bushes and pin him to the ground—her idea of a "joke," but other than the soft gurgle of the river, Moonvale was silent.

A soft pop sounded, and suddenly Zara was back—a voidbeast no more. She knelt in the dirt, arms empty and outstretched, her eyes welling with tears he'd never seen before.

"Zara! What is it? What's wrong?" Lukas said, her tears scaring him far more than her disappearance.

"I had her... I had her in my arms," she whispered, sounding so lost Lukas had to fight not to pull her into a hug. She'd *definitely* bite him.

"You mean you did it?" he asked, understanding dawning. "You made it to the Void?"

Zara closed her eyes, and he watched her fight to steady herself. "I found Teema. I pulled her from that wretched slug's clutches. But instead of fleeing with her, I mocked the godling. *Taunted* him. And now she's gone. Stupid. Stupid. *Stupid!*" She struck herself with every word, her fist closed.

"Woah, hold on, don't *hit* yourself! What if—" Whatever Lukas was about to say was cut off when Zara punched the ground, leaving a sizeable hole.

"I have to go back. *Now*," Zara growled, getting to her feet.

"Right, well, I'm glad you stopped hitting yourself. And that you didn't hit me," Lukas began with a cautious smile. He'd never seen Zara so upset, but he knew if he tried to calm her down, she'd probably take his head off. He tried another tactic. "But let's think about this for a second. Teema just vanished, right? Calamity didn't snatch her out of your hands or anything?"

Eyes narrowed, Zara nodded.

"What if that's part of it? What if she was never meant to come here?"

"*What?* You think she is bound to the slug for life? Do not say such things!" Zara whirled on him, eyes alight with rage. "After all your talk!"

Well, this was the opposite of what he was going for.

"No, no! I think Teema isn't here because she *can't* be," he said calmly, ignoring the claws that inched from Zara's fingers. "Her mind was in this world, but her body wasn't. She had to use yours, right?"

Zara frowned, and Lukas could see the gears turning in her mind. After a long moment she took a breath, her nails shrinking. "You think... you think if I go to sleep, I will find Teema in the darkness? As she found me?"

"I mean, I'm no all-powerful slug-god thing, but if that's how you saw each other before, then that would be my guess, yes," he said gently, trying not to sound too relieved. "And it *has* been a while since you slept. You only caught an hour or two when we left the maze."

He pointedly walked to their camp where his bedroll and the remnants of a small fire lay—(Zara still slept on the cold hard ground, despite his insistence). He pulled a small kettle from his never-ending pack and began the slow, methodical process of making tea—starting the fire, prepping the leaves, and boiling the water.

Tea in hand, he placed a cup in front of her, saying nothing. If he offered it to her openly, she'd refuse it—unable to break the vaxion habits of her childhood.

He hid his smile when she picked it up, cautiously sniffing it. Her lip curled in disgust.

"Graggle leaves," he said, "they're good for sleep. I used to make it for Teema."

At the mention of Teema, Zara sipped it, grimacing. "Did she like it?"

"Nope. Said it tasted like week-old bathwater, but it did help her sleep," he said, pointedly downing his cup. Zara followed suit, then lay on her back. She squeezed her eyes shut like a little kid willing sleep to come. Lukas couldn't help his smile.

He was still nervous around her—always would be, he guessed. But he wasn't scared of her anymore. He thought her sharpness with Ashira and the other vaxion came from coldness, or disgust at how much the vaxion had changed, but the past few days together had taught him it was much simpler.

Zara didn't know how to talk to people. She was awkward, clumsy even, and relied on anger to get her through most situations. But she was also brave and loyal. Suicidally so, but still. He'd seen it when she'd charged Lazander and Malik. In how she'd thrown herself between him and Ravenna, calling him a cub under her protection.

Hands behind his head, he listened to Zara roll onto her side, her back, then her side again. He'd always been confused at how much Teema used to look forward to speaking to Zara, but now?

He smiled. Now, he got it.

***

Zara waited for sleep to come.

And waited.

And waited.

Growling in irritation, she scrunched up her eyes. As a child, she'd hated sleeping—why sleep when she could be doing something useful? Like hunting or *killing?* Her feelings hadn't changed as an adult.

"When we couldn't sleep," Lukas said, his eyes closed. "Teema and I used to tell stories. She of her world, me of the Gilded Knights. She loved hearing about them."

"I am not a child who needs a bedside story," Zara growled.

"Then let's skip the stories, and get to the good stuff," Lukas said. He took a deep, steadying breath and let it out slowly.

Zara instinctively matched her breathing to his, her muscles relaxing with every exhale.

"I didn't trust Teema when I first met her," he began. "Now in my defense, I thought she was you, and the last time I saw you, you were busy setting fire to half of Moonvale. Now in *your* defense, that's because you were turning into a slobbering murder-monster you couldn't control, but I didn't know that. I thought you were a crazy vaxion who liked burning things."

Zara grunted in reply. He wasn't *entirely* wrong—she did enjoy burning things.

"To be even more honest, not only did I not trust Teema—I also didn't like her," he said.

Zara felt herself nodding. The girl could be quite annoying.

"She was so quiet, even timid at times," Lukas continued. "Half the molger buried her in gifts for saving me, the rest just glared at her—and she seemed to prefer that. It meant she didn't have to talk to them." He chuckled. "When I finally got the courage to track her down and deal with this stupid blood-debt, I was… nervous. And when I'm nervous, I talk a lot. Some would call me over the top."

"I cannot imagine," Zara said drily and couldn't help but smile when Lukas burst out laughing.

"Oh, if you think I'm bad *now*, you should have seen me—I kept yelling about mushrooms. Anyway, I was babbling a mile a minute for hours, convinced that any second now she was going to order me to kneel and lick her feet. Then I told a joke—a terrible one about why you don't go near a spike-hog in heat."

A heavy, expectant pause followed. With a supreme amount of effort, Zara said, deadpan, "Why don't you go near a spike-hog in heat?"

"Because they're *prickly*."

Zara sighed.

"See, that's the reaction I expected, but Teema *giggled*. Not some mature, elegant chuckle. A full-on giggle, which made her snort. That made me laugh, which made her laugh even harder, and then we were gripping our knees, crying with laughter."

Eyes closed, Zara could hear the smile in Lukas' voice.

"At the beginning," he continued, "I kept looking for ways to 'test' Teema and tried to get her to show her 'true face.' I shifted into my vaxion form, thinking she might mention some casual plans to make me eat babies or something. But when she saw me, she looked so… happy. So *proud*. My dad's the only one who's ever looked at me like that." His voice caught, and Lukas coughed to cover it up.

Zara pretended not to notice.

"I still kept my guard up and painted a stupid smile on my face—I planned to make myself indispensable to her, you see, until I figured out the blood-debt. And then little things started happening. She'd lay out my bedroll facing the setting sun because she'd noticed that's how I liked it. I mentioned I loved goober-pig, and she ended up wrestling one off a cliff, trying to catch it for me. I kept waiting for the act to drop and for her to treat me like a dog. Treat me like Ashira treated her 'mongrels.'" His breath hitched, and Zara's did too. They'd both come so close to having their lives and freedom snatched away, like so many others before them.

"She never did," Lukas said softly. "She treated me like a friend—and I... didn't return the favor. Because I was too scared to trust her."

"Does this meandering have a point?" Zara asked, though not unkindly. She had a feeling she knew where this was going, and she didn't like it.

"I know when Teema went from enemy to friend," Lukas said. "It happened somewhere between the snort-laugh and her falling off a cliff, a massive pig in her arms. My question is this—when did it happen for you?"

Zara considered not answering. Walking away was how she dealt with difficult topics, but she had nowhere to go and nothing to do but wait for sleep to come. She told herself that was why she tried to be honest.

"I was raised to eat only what my claws killed. To trust nothing I could not see with my own eyes. To believe no one but myself," Zara said. "It was Ashira's way—which meant it was the vaxion way. Magnus encouraged it. The vaxion hated me, he told me. The molger. Humans. Everyone and everything hated and feared me—I was a 'crazy vaxion who liked burning things,'" she said ruefully.

Lukas shifted uncomfortably.

"The world hated me, and I hated it right back. Every hand offered in aid was a viper, every kind word a ploy to find a weakness."

She paused, and to her surprise, Lukas seemed content with the silence. His breathing deepened and hers did the same. "And then I awoke to find a creature, a *parasite,* in control of my body. At first I thought it an elaborate punishment concocted by Magnus—it was not beyond him to use a pawn. An insipid, idiotic pawn—but a pawn nonetheless."

Lukas chuckled.

"Like you, I watched for lies, sure her every word was laced with them. I treated every question like an accusation—as Ashira taught, Magnus enforced, and I had lived." The memories were coming back to her, flipping past her like the pages of a book. "But she never asked for more than I was willing to give. Yet still I refused her. In the battle against Valerius and Magnus, I was ready to let us both die rather than accept her help."

"Ominous. What changed the mighty Fury's mind?"

Only a week ago his words would have annoyed her, but now she recognized his attempt at "humor."

"I asked Teema why she was so determined to save me from Magnus, sure she was doing it out of pity." Zara's teeth flashed in a half-grin, half-snarl. "She looked me in the eye and said, 'No. I'm helping you because Magnus is a *bastard*.'"

A shocked silence followed, and then Lukas burst out laughing. "That is the most Zara reason for friendship I've ever heard."

"You miss the point, cub, as I did," Zara said softly, her body almost melting into the grass beneath her. Suddenly the feelings she'd had at the lake, the desperate need to save Teema, and the joy and relief in her heart when she found the girl in the Void all made sense. "It was only when she was gone that I realized she fought so hard because she thought me *worth* saving, and in so doing... made me want to live again."

For once Lukas was silent, but Zara should have known it wouldn't last long.

"You can just say she's your friend and you care about her."

"Do not push it, cub."

"That wasn't a no..."

Zara didn't answer. Her breathing slowed as she drifted off into a deep, restful sleep.

## Chapter Thirty-One

The queen shook, though not from fear. She sat in the Ivory Keep in the private chambers she shared with the king, though it had been weeks since his side of the bed had been anything but stone cold.

Before Valerius' attack, her every waking moment was spent in the throne room with Thaddeus by her side, the wet nose of her spymaster never more than a comforting pat away. The King and Queen of Navaros prided themselves on their division of duties, joking that Leon was the sword, Firanta the shield. She'd become something of a legend at the negotiating table, stamping out threats of war with a raised eyebrow or the well-timed stroke of her quill. Her list of tasks was never-ending—from soothing the egos of wounded nobles to entertaining foreign ambassadors. On one notable occasion a dwarven dignitary had shown up with a 300-stanza poem dedicated to her and a full orchestra. By the end of the evening, she'd convinced him that he'd never had any interest in her *and* negotiated a ten percent cut in dwarven import tax.

It was a dance she knew—a dance that exhausted her. She used to long for the luxury of boredom, of *peace*.

Now she detested it.

By day she stared out the window, by night up at the ceiling. Leon had ordered no visitors, claiming she needed to focus on resting—something she was admittedly terrible at. But she'd barely seen her husband since she'd left the healing wards. She knew he was stretched to the brink with the rising attacks in the north and east—shadow-fiends were tearing through villages like parchment. And the wallow-tail had taken to appearing above the Navarin army by night, raining down fire and killing dozens every time. Refugees, a weekly occurrence when the attacks began, now showed up to the Ivory Keep in the hundreds.

Then there were the letters. She'd gotten her hands on them, despite Leon's attempts to hide them away. Three distant cousins, a nephew, and an uncle she'd been sure was dead were all vying for the throne.

"… cannot control their own son, let alone a nation…"

"… the blood of those who died at the Ivory Keep is on their hands as much as Valerius'…"

"… wouldn't be surprised if the Tyrant's arrival is all a smokescreen…"

And through all of this, Leon was left to weather it alone. She should help him, she knew. But every time she tried to leave her chambers, she froze, her hand clamped on the doorknob. Her mind kept replaying the same scene over and over—Thaddeus bleeding out on her lap. Valerius appearing as if from nowhere, blade in hand, a smile on his face.

A single strike, and her right hand and leg were gone, her body a mess of shock and pain that nearly killed her. She could still smell her own flesh burning as Eternity frantically cauterized her wounds, Thaddeus' corpse lying next to her, his head cleaved from his shoulders.

Her autolimbs groaned as she turned away from the door, heart hammering. Her new limbs had been built rapidly and with little focus on aesthetics. A childhood illness had left the queen unable to walk without support since she was twelve years old, and while she'd cursed it at times, it ended up a blessing. Years of practice with a cane meant she was adapting far quicker to her magical limbs than most people.

Her new leg stiffened, and she had to catch herself on a bedpost to stop from falling. With a sigh she tapped her copper knee, activating the mobility spell within as the mages had taught her. Once her leg jerked to life, she sat down heavily on crinkled silk sheets, ready for another day staring out the window.

And then she saw it.

It was a simple wooden box—old, battered, and filthy. It sat on her dressing table, taking up almost a third of it. It hadn't been there when she'd gone to sleep the night before. Her single eye darted around her chambers, her *locked* chambers, searching for any sign of an intruder. Nothing beyond the box was out of place.

Heart in her throat, Firanta approached it. Up close she saw the image of a pawprint engraved on the lid. A pawprint she'd know until the day she died. The queen trembled. Thaddeus. The box was from *Thaddeus*.

The musty smell of earth suggested the box had only recently been dug up. She brushed away what dirt she could, the memory of Thaddeus and the feel of his head on her knee so strong, she looked down to see if he was there.

Thaddeus was *dead*, she chided herself. Who sent the box in his stead? And why now, weeks after his murder?

There was no lock, only a simple metal latch. She should call a guard, and a palace mage for good measure, she knew. This could be a trap, or even an assassination attempt. But Firanta found her finger flicking the latch open while her mechanical pincer awkwardly grasped the lid, lifting it. The inside of the box was mainly empty space but for a single amethyst the size of her palm. Curious, she picked it up.

"Hello, my queen. It's good to see you."

She dropped the gem at the sound of Thaddeus' voice, stumbling backward. Her autolimb locked at the sudden movement, and her good leg went out from under her. The queen hit the stone floor with a loud thud.

"My queen? Are you all right?" came a worried call from one of the guards outside her chambers.

"I'm fine!" she said, not knowing why she'd lied. "I'm fine, don't come in!"

She heard a shuffle and a low mutter and knew the guards were debating coming in anyway. That made her teeth clench—she was the queen, damn it! "Set foot in here and I'll have you thrown in the stocks!" she yelled. "I want no one in here, not even the king, is that understood?"

A beat of silence, and then, "Yes, my queen."

The clack of armor let her know they'd resumed their posts. Breathing a sigh of relief, Firanta began the long process of getting up. Steady once more, she reached out, pressing a single finger to the amethyst.

"Forgive me, my queen. I should have guessed that would startle you," came Thaddeus' lilting accent. Firanta closed her eyes, her heart pounding. The crystal grew warm at her touch.

"Am I going insane?" she asked calmly. "Or do your talents lie beyond the grave, Thaddeus?"

The hound chuckled. "Neither. If you have the memory crystal, that means I am gone. This is merely an impression of myself. Yati was under orders to deliver it to you in the case of my death."

Firanta frowned at the mention of Yati. She'd been Thaddeus' pick for spymaster, though the king had dissolved the role along with the Gilded Knights. Looking at the box, the queen realized where the woman must have been all this time.

"I take it this isn't a sentimental visit?" Firanta asked, summoning the part of her that could stare down an army with nothing but an arched brow.

"No, my queen. It would be cruel to torment you like that," Thaddeus said quietly, his voice echoing in her mind. "I don't know what killed me—this impression was made some years ago, but I can tell by your voice that... that it was bad. Does it have something to do with your missing limbs?"

The queen nodded stiffly, not trusting herself to speak.

While Firanta couldn't see Thaddeus, she swore she could feel him bend his head, a comforting paw on her knee. "Then I must beg your forgiveness. As your spymaster, I failed to see the coming threat. And as your friend, I failed to protect you."

"Thaddeus. Don't," Firanta said softly, fighting tears.

The ghostly voice of her dearest friend was silent for a long moment. "I'll get straight to business then. It's what we always did best, wasn't it?"

Firanta couldn't help but smile. "It was."

"First things first—I know this will be painful, but I need you to tell me how I died. It may change how much I need to explain and the urgency behind it."

The Firanta who'd spent the last few weeks lying in bed wouldn't have had the strength to tell such a tale, but hearing Thaddeus after so long made her back straighten and her heart harden. "It's a long story, I'm afraid. It began when Gabriel and Marito were murdered and Lazander left gravely injured. You suspected it was Valerius..."

*\*\**

What felt like hours later the queen finished her sordid tale and to her surprise found it hadn't hurt nearly as much as she'd thought it would. There had been a rhythm to her speech, an ease as she broke down the most traumatizing events of her life into cold hard facts. It was how she and Thaddeus had dealt with every threat.

"This is worse than I imagined," Thaddeus finally said.

"You said that when Evergarden was threatening to blow us into the Void with their war machines," Firanta replied. "But we had them backing down by nightfall, their tails between their legs."

"That we did," Thaddeus said. "But I'm afraid this goes beyond the world of men. You remember how we met?"

A pause. "You tell me."

Thaddeus huffed a laugh. "You still need proof it's really me? Good. You haven't lost your edge." He cleared his throat. "A nine-year-old girl with a limp found a 'demon' trapped in ice. She figured out how to break his bindings with nothing but the power of her wits and then demanded a lifetime of servitude in exchange for said demon's release."

It was Firanta's turn to laugh. "I'd feel sorry for you, but I released you from that contract years ago."

"I know. I stayed because you showed me another way. A way Ravenna tried to explain to me, but I listened too late. Had I the courage back then that I do now, things might have been different."

Firanta frowned at the name Ravenna—it sounded familiar, but she couldn't place where she'd heard it. Then it hit her. "The Goddess of Truth?" she asked.

"Yes, and no," Thaddeus said, sighing heavily. "While I still lived, I was honest with you about my past, my queen—I once followed the Tyrant's call, but Ravenna made me see the truth. Made me see that the cycle of blood and death the *rakna* were trapped in only ended one way—with the entire universe bereft of all life. I chose to stand with her and her siblings against the Tyrant when he tried to conquer this world—a decision I've never once regretted. The ice you found me in was the punishment of men. They saw my true form and assumed me the evil god's servant." He chuckled darkly. "I don't blame them."

Firanta said nothing. She'd known most of this already, but she'd never heard about Ravenna, her siblings, or these "rakna." But she asked no questions—she knew Thaddeus would get to it in time.

"But the plan went wrong—I'm not sure how or why. All I know is that Gallow was the last god left standing and named himself protector of this world," Thaddeus continued. "I would be lying if I said that, knowing his past, I didn't take issue with this, but I set my feelings aside. I'd taken on a new name and a new life—should Gallow not be allowed the same? I watched him gift his followers with impossible powers, reassured when he made no effort to cross into this world or harm it. I foolishly thought Gallow would be enough. That he and his Champions would stop the Tyrant, should he ever return."

"And now you think otherwise?" the queen asked quietly.

"I do. He can't stop the Tyrant, not if the dark god is strong enough to gift your son… to gift Valerius with the power to kill me. More than one rakna has tried to kill me, yet he triumphed where they failed."

The queen took all of this in, her keen mind running through all possibilities. While she trusted Thaddeus with her life, she wasn't a fool—there was a chance this was all an elaborate ploy. Thaddeus might have known the truth of how they'd met—a tale not even Leon had heard. Not the whole story, at least. But that didn't mean the spymaster hadn't turned traitor. Or that there wasn't some mage out there powerful enough to see her memories and mimic him. Yet all possibilities ended the same—with her needing more information.

"Where do I fit into this?" the queen asked, aware she'd been silent for several minutes. But Thaddeus had been content to wait. He knew her as well as she knew him, after all.

He took a deep breath. "First, I need to know… where's my body?"

## Chapter Thirty-Two

When Zara opened her eyes and saw a darkness so complete it threatened madness, she knew she'd fallen asleep.

Lying on her back, all she had to do was turn her head to see if Lukas was right. To see if all her efforts to save Teema hadn't been for naught. But her neck refused to obey, her body as tense and unyielding as stone.

"Dead," a small voice whispered, her words frantic. "Zara's dead. Calamity killed her. This isn't real. It's not real, damn it!"

Zara finally looked into the darkness, and her heart broke at the sight.

Teema's knees were tucked up to her chest, her hands wrapped tightly around herself. No chains bound her like they had when Zara was a prisoner, yet the girl trembled. Zara had seen Teema in her true form—standing tall and defiant, her arm bloody as she swore to take Magnus down. But the girl before her was small and thin, the bones in her shoulders and elbows threatening to poke through her own skin. Teema dug her fingers into her forearms, leaving angry red marks as she fought to stop shaking. The only saving grace was that the girl was clothed this time, though they were strange garments Zara had never seen before.

As always, the first thing the Fury felt was anger.

"Do I look dead to you, parasite?" Zara said, her tone harsh. Her touch, however, was gentle as she brushed dark curls from the girl's sweat-soaked forehead.

Teema finally looked at her, eyes welling with tears. "Are you… are you real?"

"I am. Or do you think me so weak I'd fall to a slug?" she said, giving a wolfish grin.

Zara expected Teema to have a million questions, as she often did—how did you get here? Is Lukas all right? What happened to Ashira and the other vaxion? The answers to which were: with difficulty, yes, and they are fine, respectively. But Teema said nothing. She just flung her arms around Zara's waist and buried her head in her stomach.

"Ah…" Zara stammered, hands hovering awkwardly. She'd been prepared for many reactions, but not this. This was new territory.

"You're here. You're *really* here," Teema said, her words muffled.

"I am," Zara said, gingerly patting the girl's head. When it became clear she wasn't going to let go anytime soon, Zara tentatively placed her hands on Teema's shoulders. It was the closest thing to a hug she could manage.

Teema pulled back slightly but kept her arms around Zara as if afraid she would disappear. "When I refused to help him, Calamity told me he'd killed you. He showed me your body. Lukas'. The vaxion. My nephew Noah, I thought… I was sure…"

"Shh, Teema. The slug cannot hurt you anymore. I will not let him," Zara said fiercely.

This seemed to calm the girl somewhat, but then her brow furrowed. "Teema… you called me that before. What does it mean?"

Zara felt her cheeks warm. She suddenly found a patch of darkness off to the side extremely interesting.

"Zara?"

"It is an old word in vytrex. There's no translation for it, not directly, but it means…" Zara trailed off, then chastised herself for being a coward. "It means bloodsworn. The one you trust above all others. The one you would impale yourself on your own claws to save," she said hurriedly, trying and failing for nonchalance.

Teema stiffened, and Zara had to fight not to flee, embarrassed at how much she'd revealed.

"I love it," the girl said with a broad smile. "Thank you, Zara."

To Zara's relief a hint of color had returned to Teema's cheeks.

Teema dropped her arms and Zara jumped back, running a nervous hand through her hair, something she never did. "I take no thanks for what was earned."

"You seem… different, Zara. Happier. I'm glad to see it."

Zara grunted in reply.

A light was coming back to Teema's eyes, and she brushed herself down with a heavy sigh. "I'm not going to tell you that I'm all right—because that's a complete and total lie, but I know that if I don't ask now, I never will." She took a deep steadying breath. "What did I miss?"

***

Lukas was woken by someone trying to strangle him. At least that was what he thought was happening. He was fast asleep, dreaming about a pint of hot glok (a liver-murdering molger booze usually taken in a shot, but he needed a lot more than that after the last few weeks), when arms wrapped around him. He jerked awake, and it took him a second to realize he wasn't being strangled—Zara the Fury was *hugging* him. This, however, made him panic more.

"By the Void, are you sick? Dying? Am *I* dying?" he asked.

"No. I'm just happy to see you," she murmured.

Lukas' heart soared. The Fury could be held captive by a demon, tortured to the brink of death, and look up to find Lukas there to rescue her in the nick of time—and she'd *still* never say she was happy to see him.

"Teema?" Lukas gasped, returning the hug fiercely. "Thank the Void you're back. I thought I was going to be stuck with Zara the Psychopath forever."

Teema laughed. "She can still hear you, you know."

"In that case, when are you leaving because I can't wait to have Zara the Fury, my favorite person in the whole world, back again," he quickly added.

Teema burst out laughing, and Lukas was struck by how different a single person could look and act when the driver changed. Now that he knew both of them, he was shocked he ever thought Teema and Zara were the same person. Everything about the woman in front of him screamed Teema—the relaxed slope of her shoulders, the easy smile on her face, even the slight tilt to her head. There was an ease to her that Zara lacked. Who was he kidding—murderous ripperbacks were more at ease than the Fury.

"Zara told me you chased after her when she left you behind. You're going to have to start charging me for all these rescues," Teema said.

"Oh, don't you worry, I have been. This blood-debt isn't going to…" his voice trailed off when he looked down at his forearm. His bracer was in place, as always, but usually the edge of the scar was visible. Now he only saw clear skin.

He ripped it off to find his arm free of the angry red scar of his nightmares. He gasped, running his hands up and down now soft skin—he'd done it. He'd actually done it. He'd paid off the blood-debt.

"I guess saving me from an evil god goes a long way." Teema smiled.

"I mean, that was all Zara, but I do pride myself on providing excellent emotional support," Lukas joked, trying to stifle the hope in his chest. The blood-debt was paid, but he was still bound to Teema. The old Lukas—the cynical man who'd planned to stab Teema in the neck if it turned out she was as cruel a master as Ashira—spoke up. *What if Teema never lets you go? What if she can't? What if—*

Teema took his hand in hers, squeezing it. "I'm not sure how this works but… Lukas Van Fyodin—I release you from the blood-debt."

A shiver ran through Lukas, and he fell back, a weight lifted from his shoulders—he felt lighter than he had in months. He felt like *himself* again.

"Order me to do something," he whispered.

"Stand up!" Teema said loudly and with authority. "Raise your hand! Ah, jump up and down!"

Nothing happened.

"Suck it, boss," Lukas said, pulling her into another hug as he hid his face in her shoulder, fighting to get his expression under control. He was *free*. He was finally free. "Thank you for being such a kind and generous tyrannical overlord," he said when he trusted himself to speak.

"I'd say anytime," she laughed, "but we're *never* doing that again."

"Agreed. But…" he shifted, suddenly serious. "You know that even with the blood-debt gone, I'm not going anywhere. I'm sticking with you until you're back in your own world safe and sound—that's a promise."

Teema's smile faded. "About that," she said. And just like that her warmth vanished, replaced by a furrowed brow and feet that paced back and forth, her back a wall of tension. "We know Calamity is coming."

"That has been a theme, yes. But that's what Eternity and her band of zealots are for."

"Two of them are dead—murdered by Valerius. Though he goes by the name Player Two these days."

"An... odd title. He always struck me as a man who couldn't stand coming second, but I don't see what any of this has to do with us."

Teema's pacing quickened. "Back on Earth, there's a game called *Knights of Eternity*. At first I thought this place was just that—a game made real. But only a few days here and it was obvious this world was as real as mine. But that doesn't explain the game—how and why is it on Earth? And why use it to kidnap people from my planet?"

"If it helps, I am mostly following."

"I thought Calamity created *Knights of Eternity* just to find potential servants. He pulled surface information from this world, slapped it together with Void Mana, and hid it in plain sight on Earth. He wanted people with a certain... disposition, and what better way to find them than with a game? Something people use to escape their own lives? But it's worse, Lukas. *Knights of Eternity* isn't just a trap—it's how he'll conquer both our worlds."

"I am no longer following."

"It's a *portal*," she said. "A way to invade both this world and Earth at the same time—and where is the only remaining copy of *Knights of Eternity*? In my hometown, Lukas."

He blanched, not liking where this was going. "But—but Calamity isn't showing up anytime soon! It could be months, maybe even years! Eternity might find half a dozen Champions in the meantime. This is, and say it with me, *not our problem*."

"He's not coming in years, or even months, Lukas," she said finally, meeting his eyes. "He'll be here in days."

\*\*\*

Lukas and Zara were the only reason I wasn't screaming.

It was strange being back in the "real" world, for what else was *Knights of Eternity* but my new reality? I didn't remember Earth anymore—not really, anyway. I didn't know if I had a mother or a father, brothers or sisters. I didn't know what I looked like or where I'd come from. I only remembered one thing—my nephew Noah. But his face was blurred, the edges smeared as if seen through distorted glass. I knew it wouldn't be long before I lost him too.

It was why I'd hugged Lukas without so much as a hello—I needed to feel something real. *Someone* real. His warmth and the thud of his heartbeat were proof I was really here—that I'd escaped Calamity's prison. Zara loomed in my mind, her presence huge and all-encompassing. Before my capture she was a distant figure who popped in and out of my consciousness like a stubborn daisy, each of us vying for control. Now she felt like a passenger in a car I was driving, a second steering wheel in front of her, ready to take control when needed.

I told myself I was safe. That Calamity couldn't hurt me anymore. But my mind was treacherous, and my thoughts threatened to drag me under—what if this was part of Calamity's plan? What if he let me go on *purpose*?

*It's too late. He's going to find me. He's going to kill me. Here comes the sand, oh God, the sand, just let me die, no, no, no!*

Zara growled, and my heart slowed to a comforting rhythm in response. Not too long ago that growl made me flinch. Now knowing she was by my side was more comforting than a child's teddy bear during a storm.

"Days?" Lukas said, his voice high and panicked. "Calamity is coming in *days?* As in I can count on my fingers number of days?"

I nodded. "If even that."

*"Let him try,"* Zara snarled. I couldn't help but grin at her ferocity.

"Look, I appreciate you're probably horribly traumatized and everything, but I really don't see why you're smiling about this," Lukas said, his voice strained.

"I wasn't smiling at *that,* it was something Zara—never mind. Look, we need to get back to Ashira. Calamity is already coming through back on Earth," I said, remembering the arcade the dark god had shown me. The body of a girl I didn't know lay on the ground, blood pouring from her chest while a paramedic and an older woman frantically tried to resuscitate her. But that wasn't what terrified me.

Behind the body of the girl lay the battered cabinet that housed *Knights of Eternity*, the screen cracking as a fist punched through from the other side. From the *Void*.

"If he breaches both our worlds, who knows how many more he'll conquer? This isn't about me getting home, Lukas—not anymore. This is about saving the whole damn universe."

## Chapter Thirty-Three

To my surprise Zara was silent at my proclamation. I waited for her to agree with Lukas. To say that this wasn't our problem or maybe direct some more murderous threats at Calamity, but she said nothing. We ran through to the vaxion's waterstone in record time, and I was surprised at how much stronger Zara's body felt. She'd always been powerful, fast, and vicious—but as I clenched my fist, I could feel a new strength there, just waiting to be used.

*"I have not been sitting idle while you were held captive,"* Zara said, pride in her voice. *"The peaks and valleys of Moonvale became my training grounds, my vaxion form the terror of all who have sense. I only wish I had the same time to master my voidbeast."*

A memory flashed in my mind of the colossal, winged beast. *Hell Zara, you were terrifying before the voidbeast. Bet you could take Ashira now.*

I meant it as a joke but was surprised at the pang of sadness I felt coming from her. It was strange—without the chains that bound us, I could sense so much more from her.

*Zara?* I asked as the waterstone came into view. *Did something happen with Ashira?*

*"No,"* she said far too quickly, a rush of embarrassment following.

Lukas wheezed at my side, his hands on his knees.

*Do you want to take control when we speak to her?* I asked, aware of the discomfort she felt at the thought of her aunt. I didn't know what was going on between them, Zara had been very practical in her recounting of events, but there was clearly some tension.

*"I… have concealed much from her,"* Zara said finally. *"Which is why it should be you."*

Surprised, I asked—*why?*

*"You fooled her before but now she has spent time with the real me. She will hear your bleeding heart, and your irritating way of speaking and know we are telling the truth."*

I rolled my eyes, quietly relieved—she might be happier and more trusting, but she was still Zara.

"How… are you… not tired?" Lukas asked, panting. "We *ran* the whole way here, and you're not even breathing hard!"

"It turns out Zara spent every waking moment training," I said.

Lukas' eyes bulged. "She's never heard of something called fun, has she?"

*"Training* is *fun,"* Zara grumbled.

I chuckled and was about to tell Lukas what she'd said when a voice called out, "Did you find what you seek, little star?" Ashira's huge form appeared as if by magic a second later, passing through the illusory door that led to the heart of the waterstone.

I jumped, surprised. How had she known we were out here?

*"I may still be Zara,"* the Fury said with a smug grin, *"but she is still Ashira."*

"I… uh…" I faltered. Zara thought the whole "two souls in one body" revelation was an "arrow that needed to be ripped out," while Lukas was convinced Ashira would cut off our heads and use them as decoration.

"Hi, Ashira," I said, giving a little wave.

Lukas put his face in his palm and sighed.

The leader of the vaxion didn't answer my awkward greeting. Her remaining golden eye examined me, and I couldn't help but do the same to her. The last time we'd met she'd been holding up half a collapsed waterstone on her shoulders, fighting to keep me alive. A missing eye and two shortened fingers were the only signs of the fight, but it didn't take away from the waves of power that rolled off her. I'd never met someone with such *command*.

*"A 'god' tried to break you and you did not falter, yet the sight of my aunt has your heart pounding like a cub on her first hunt?"* Zara asked, amused.

*Look, I just see where you get it, all right?*

Though Zara tried to hide it, I could tell she was pleased by my "compliment."

Suddenly fingers were on my chin. Ashira tilted my head up, forcing our eyes to meet. I froze.

"You," she said after a long moment. "You are the one who first came here. Who wears the face of my Zara yet is nothing like her. I thought it a fault of mine— that I no longer knew my own blood. Yet you are not the Zara who has spent these past weeks with me." In a flash her hands were on my throat, tight enough to hold me in place but not enough to hurt me.

"What have you done to my niece?" she growled.

*Zara! I think—*

*"Yes, yes,"* Zara said, not seeming the least bothered by the anger and fear in her aunt's eyes—fear for her niece, I knew. *"Give me control."*

When Zara was chained and bound in my mind, we had almost no control over who was in the "driver's seat." The only time I'd managed to pass her body back to her, I'd been frantically trying to reach out and touch her, with no idea if that would work. Now all I had to do was close my eyes and take a breath, imagine the darkness, and suddenly I was back there—a mere bystander once more.

In her body again, Zara snapped out a hand, striking Ashira's forearm with enough force to break her hold.

"My teema has done nothing to me," Zara growled. "She is my sworn—and she is the reason Magnus is dead, not I. She is the one I sought to kill a god for."

"You have… you have a teema?" Ashira asked, eye wide. She idly rubbed her arm where Zara had hit her but made no move to return the blow.

It was strange to watch the world through another's eyes. It let me pay more attention to the small things—a furrow of the brows here, a twitch there—but I don't think even Zara missed the light in Ashira's eyes at the word "teema." The slight twitch of the vaxion's lips confirmed my guess.

Ashira was *happy*.

"Come," the huge woman said, turning on her heel. "You will tell me everything. But first, a drink."

***

My time with the vaxion had been brief, but it was enough to show me how different they were to the molger. The vaxion were a people who did nothing by halves: from chores to drinking to fighting, every second was spent as if it was their last alive. They were stiff and formal and never offered anyone help, but that didn't mean they didn't care for one another fiercely—just that they were bad at showing it.

It also meant that when they bore a piece of their souls to another, they did so in the driest, most condensed way possible.

"The slug-god Calamity, you know him as the 'Tyrant,' took Teema from another planet and placed her in my body, trapping me. Teema fought against her master, freed me from Magnus, and now seeks to stop Calamity from consuming both our worlds," Zara said, knocking back her fourth cup of mead.

I watched from the darkness, slack jawed as she summarized every insane thing that had happened to us in *two lines*.

"That's it?" I asked Zara, incredulous. "You're not going to explain anything else to Ashira? What about Ravenna? That you know why the vaxion can't transform anymore? Your voidbeast? The fact that Calamity is coming in *days?*"

*"What have I told you before, 'parasite'?"* Zara said mentally, fighting not to grin. *"Your life would be much improved if you spoke less. If she has questions, she will ask them."*

"I see," was all Ashira said. She poured both Zara and Lukas another drink but waited until they'd taken a sip to pour one for herself—knocking hers back in a single gulp. I waited for her to speak, vibrating with tension—but Ashira just sat there, looking entirely at ease.

We were sitting at a freshly carved table in the main hall of the waterstone. The hole in the ceiling from Magnus' final desperate spell was covered by thick layers of canvas, bathing the room in the soft glow of dusk. It was late, past Moon Peak's final meal of the day, and the other vaxion had retired to their beds. The falslings rose and slept early, and while I'd found it tough when I lived with them, I was grateful for it now. It meant that in the busy life of the waterstone we had a rare moment of peace and quiet.

Lukas held his carved wooden cup like a shield in front of him, his eyes darting between Ashira and Zara. He used to be terrified of the vaxion leader, but I didn't see any fear in his eyes now. Instead he looked alert, curious even. I wished I had such patience.

Ashira finally nodded and said four simple words. "What do you need?"

My mouth opened and closed in surprise. I felt Zara fight not to say, *"I told you so."*

"But... but," I sputtered. "When we first got here you were sure Ashira was going to kill you, *us,* if we told her the truth. What's changed?" I asked.

I could tell Zara didn't want to, but she said aloud, "I expected you to strike me down when you discovered another could control my body."

"Let me speak to your teema," Ashira said, pouring another drink.

I was suddenly blinking and back in Zara's body. Switching that abruptly felt like being dropped from a height, and my hands jerked, spilling some of the mead from my cup. *Damn it Zara, a little warning?* I thought at her, but she said nothing. I felt her watching, coiled like a viper with a tension I didn't understand.

"It's, ah, it's me," I said awkwardly.

Ashira looked me over, then shook her head, a bemused smile on her face. "I cannot believe I ever thought you my niece. I am slipping in my old age." She sipped from her cup. "Do you swear to protect Zara with your life?" she asked.

I didn't even have to think about it. "I do," I said.

"Then that is all I need. Now we can do little planning if we have not slept. Let us meet before First Dawn. You will tell me what you need, and I will do what I can to deliver," she said, getting to her feet.

It was only then I noticed the dark circles under Ashira's eyes, and I realized why she'd seen us so quickly when we arrived—she'd been watching for Zara morning and night. She probably hadn't slept since her niece left... almost a week ago.

*"She wishes to go sleep? Absolutely not!"* Zara barked. *"If we are to kill the slug, we must—"*

"Good idea," I said, standing while Zara grumbled. Common sense told me I should let Ashira go to bed in peace—this had gone much better than I'd expected—but I could feel a yearning in Zara's heart as she stared after her aunt. I took a deep breath, not looking forward to the earful I was going to get for this from the Fury.

"Zara feels like she let you down. Like she let all the vaxion down," I called.

Ashira froze, her back to me.

"She thinks if she hadn't been a 'mongrel' you'd never have taken Magnus' deal, and you'd all still have your vaxion forms."

*"Teema! What are you doing? TEEMA!"* Zara was nearly clawing the walls but made no attempt to take back control.

"She snaps at you because she doesn't know what to say to you—but she sees how hard you're trying and is grateful," I finished.

Ashira's back was a ball of tension, her muscles clenching and unclenching. She finally turned her head, whispering softly, "How could I be anything but proud of my little star?"

The gigantic vaxion left without another word, and I braced myself for a deluge of rage from Zara. But the Fury was quiet in the darkness.

"I said it once and I'll say it again," Lukas said, swiping Ashira's unfinished mead and knocking it back, his own cup long empty. "Vaxion are so bloody weird."

# Chapter Thirty-Four

Finally asleep, I waited for the golden edges of the *Knights of Eternity* Menu, but a new pop-up appeared.

**SYSTEM USER ACKNOWLEDGED.**

**VOID MANA DETECTED.**

**OPTION TO UPGRADE TO SYSTEM OPERATOR AVAILABLE.**

"This is that System nonsense Ravenna spoke of," Zara said.

I couldn't see her, but it felt like she stood next to me—arms crossed, brow furrowed.

"Her words were a riddle, but I could glean the importance of this 'Operator.' This is what allows the slugs to treat the world like a drak-board, us as mere pieces. But there is a cost—Void Mana."

As if summoned, a black and white box appeared.

| *Void Mana* |
|---|
| *The power source of the universe. When used in conjunction with the System, it can accomplish almost any act, restricted only by the confines of the imagination. However, the greater the act, the greater the cost, and Void Mana is exceedingly rare. It can only be found in the flesh of rakna—beasts born at the dawn of the universe.* |

"Wait… rakna?" I said softly. "That's what they are—Ravenna, Calamity, even Gallow. They're not gods at all—they never were."

"I do not care what they are," Zara said sharply. "So long as they are *dead*."

"At least Gallow is trying to fight Calamity."

"Hm. You did not see Lazander's eyes." She huffed. "He had the look of a man whose will had been snuffed out. He is no more a hero than a rock at the bottom of a well. I doubt your precious Eternity is much different."

"She's not like that!" I said, mortified at the term "your precious Eternity." "In fact, she's the only reason you and I aren't still stuck in Magnus' basement."

"I doubt that was for our benefit. By having his Chosen release us, Gallow has given Calamity another target. We are pawns to them, Teema—never forget that. It is only by taking control of our own fate that we can fight back. This System and its Operators are the key."

While I still adamantly refused to believe Eternity thought of anyone as a "pawn," Gallow was an unknown. He'd gone after Ravenna—to kill or eat her, I didn't know—but if it really was for her Void Mana, I could see why. I might not agree with his methods, but I'd seen what Void Mana could do—a single drop might make all the difference in the fight against Calamity. And right now Void Mana and the System were the only weapons we had. If we wanted to stand even a small chance of surviving, we *had* to use them.

"I thought you'd say this wasn't our problem—like Lukas did," I admitted. "We're just a bunch of people caught up in a war between 'gods.' We're probably going to get squashed like bugs."

I felt Zara smile. "I am a predator first, Teema. This promises to be the hunt of a lifetime—I would be a fool to turn it down. As would you, should you refuse the role of Operator."

"We don't know what becoming an Operator will do to me. Or to you," I argued. "For all I know, I'll end up a slug rakna thing."

"Then I guess we shall see how we look with no hands and extra teeth," she said, and I couldn't help but shake my head, bemused. It didn't matter what life threw at her—a sadistic mage, a "parasite" who took over her body, a slug goddess— Zara took it all in her stride.

I on the other hand, wasn't like that—but I could take courage from it. "Then I guess there's no point in putting this off," I said, taking a deep breath. I knew what I was about to say was going to change everything—I wouldn't be a player anymore, beholden to the whims of Calamity or any other Operator. I would be the one in charge—and the thought *terrified* me. "Menu! I want to become a System Operator."

Silence followed my statement. I expected some kind of fanfare like when I completed a quest—little pixelated golden balloons, confetti, that kind of thing. Instead the screen shimmered, dissolving as it melted before my eyes.

And then the pain hit.

"Argh!" I yelled, my brain exploding in agony as symbols I didn't understand scrolled past.

"What is it? What do you see?" Zara demanded.

I couldn't answer. The strange, jagged glyphs sped across my eyes so quickly I could barely see them, let alone *read* them. I couldn't tell if it was an effect of the System, or my new role as an Operator, but I instinctively knew what they were—potential. Every symbol spoke of something I could do—a change in reality I could command, a creation I could bring forth.

This was what it meant to have Void Mana—the world was no longer something you had to suffer through, it was clay to be molded to your will. But I wasn't a god, I was just a human, one who could barely handle Calamity's voice in my mind, let alone the never-ending tide of possibilities of the System. I had only ever used Calamity's version of it, which was modeled to look like the *Knights of Eternity* Menu.

This was gibberish to me.

At the thought the glyphs vanished, and the pain receded. If I'd had knees, I'd have fallen to them, a pounding headache slamming the inside of my skull with a metal baseball bat.

"Speak Teema!" Zara demanded, her version of "concern."

"I'm okay," I lied, my eyes stinging. "Good news—I'm not a slug. Bad news—we have a problem. I don't think I can use the System. Not like this anyway."

The screen shifted, becoming pixelated, the edges shimmering as lines of gold appeared. Astonished, I watched the *Knights of Eternity* Menu solidify before my very eyes. It had all the tabs it did before—Quest, Spells, and Abilities, and so on. It looked exactly the same… but for a new tab right at the end.

"Operator," I said, breathing a sigh of relief when I realized what had happened.

The System was smarter than I was. A stray thought was all it had taken for it to adapt to my needs, pulling the overwhelming possibilities out of my mind.

**VOID MANA AVAILABLE.**
**7/9999**

**GOD FUNCTIONS AVAILABLE.**
**CLICK YES FOR SUGGESTIONS.**

"Yes," I thought, gasping at the first one that appeared. "Zara, can you see this?"

A pause.

"Now I can," she said, her voice carefully neutral.

"It only costs three points," I said when silence followed.

"Our points are limited," she replied. "Is this truly something you wish to spend them on?"

"Zara," I said, annoyed. "I might be the Operator but it's not about 'me.' We're in this *together*."

"The vaxion I was raised to be says no. Our points are precious, our weapons few in the war we wish to wage. But," she sighed, "I… I want this for them."

"I do too." I smiled. "So let's do it."

\*\*\*

Ashira didn't "sleep." She hadn't for many years. She lay on her bed of furs, one foot in the dream world, the other in the waking—ears trained for any noise, any sound that might signal a threat to her people. She'd failed them so many times already, yet she was determined to protect them—and if that meant giving up her sleep, then so be it.

But what made her eyes snap open, hours still from First Dawn, wasn't the sound of an intruder's footsteps or a scream that signaled an attack. It was a howl—a howl she hadn't heard in over a decade.

She was out of the carved hole that served as her chambers in an instant. In the hall beyond, the other vaxion stumbled from their beds, wide-eyed and staring at their hands in awe. Ashira sniffed the air, searching for the smell of blood but found none. No one was yelling. No one was screaming. People were just… staring at their hands.

Jaza followed Ashira out a moment later, yawning loudly. "What is it? What is going…" but she trailed off, her dark eyes lighting up with a silver glow. A glow Ashira had almost forgotten.

The woman looked at Ashira, a smile splitting her face. The next moment her skin turned to liquid, muscle and fur flowing around her, pulsing like a heartbeat as Jaza the human vanished. Four sleek paws hit the ground a minute later, each covered in fur as dark as night. From Jaza's head coils burst forth, crackling with the power of a storm. One by one, Ashira's people shapeshifted into who they were, who Calamity had stripped them of so long ago.

*Vaxion.*

Jaza raised her mighty head, the tilt to her eyes and razor-sharp fangs as beautiful and breathtaking as Ashira remembered. Jaza nodded to her in encouragement. The leader of the vaxion closed her eyes and allowed herself to feel hope for the first time in memory.

Her transformation was clumsier than Jaza's, her mind still reeling in shock, but soon she was on four paws, the snow-white fur of her vaxion form towering head and shoulders over the ten who crowded the hall. They stared at Ashira with wide, expectant eyes.

In that moment she didn't think. She didn't wonder why this had happened or what would become of her people. She simply threw her head back and *roared.*

Her people answered in kind, and her heart swelled with pride when the very waterstone trembled. Their voices carried the pain of a people brought to the edge of extinction, their lives stripped to a pale existence—but they would not be cowed. They'd been made whole again. And they would show the world who they were.

If vaxion had tear ducts, Ashira would have wept with joy.

A shuffle of claws on stone came as the crowd parted, and a pearly-white vaxion, the image of Ashira, stalked down the halls, her head held high. At the white beast's back came a smaller, darker form, his head bowed as he looked about, unsure.

Lukas. Which meant… Ashira bared her fangs in joy when Zara strode to the front of the crowd, her *pack,* ice-blue eyes meeting Ashira's. There had been a time when Zara's vaxion form barely came up to Ashira's shoulder. Now her niece was the same size as her, if not bigger.

Ashira's heart swelled with pride.

They couldn't speak, but there was no need for words. Ashira roared once more, then took off at a sprint, strength she'd forgotten filling her body as she ran through the waterstone. At her back her people followed, some stumbling, unused to four paws, but in time instinct took over, and together they burst into the crisp night of the Moonvale Mountains as one.

Zara ran by Ashira's side, the two leading the vaxion deep into the forest. That night, they ran and ran, and all of Moonvale, from tree-topper mouse to stonebreaker, knew one thing.

The vaxion were back.

# Chapter Thirty-Five

It was the vaxion's first hunt as a pack, but for Esia, who was three years old when the plague swept through Moonvale, it was his first time ever in vaxion form. Yet there were no snapping of jaws or growls of irritation when he fell behind. The others crowded around him, gently nudging him to his feet as they showed him how to walk, how to run, how to *roar*. When lightning sparked between his Medusa-like coils for the very first time, the others gave a rumbling cheer in congratulations. To my surprise, tears welled in my eyes.

Zara stood watching little Esia, overcome with emotion. Ashira leaned into her, rubbing her cheek against her niece's with open affection. I left when Zara returned the gesture, wanting to give her some privacy—which was easier said than done. I could see everything she saw, and feel what she felt, but if I concentrated, I could pull back enough to give her some alone time.

Which meant it was just me in the darkness. No Lukas to distract me, no Zara to chase away the fear. I tried to remember how to breathe—this wasn't about me, I told myself. Calamity was coming, and we *had* to stop him. We had Void Mana, which meant we had a chance. I couldn't mess this up. I *wouldn't* mess this up.

But my mind kept going back to the red sand of that desert. I shook, my throat scratchy and raw, my eyes dry and burning. I gagged, my mind convinced Calamity's sand and skin still coated my insides—the terror I'd fought so hard to keep at bay crashing down around me.

\*\*\*

Zara insisted I take control in the morning, despite my protests. "You gave them back their lives," she said. "You deserve to see the fruits of your labor."

I'd argued it had been the two of us, and we were leaving soon—wasn't it better for her to spend what time she could with the vaxion? But she shot me glare number three— "You're doing this whether you like it or not."

After hunting through the night, stopping only once the sky turned the rich red of dawn, the vaxion hadn't bothered with their beds. They'd collapsed in the main hall in a giant puddle of fur and limbs, curled up to one another, fast asleep in seconds. Only Zara and Ashira had stayed awake, talking long past First and Second Dawn. But even they, to my surprise, joined the others rather than return to their chambers.

Which meant I awoke, naked as the day I was born, surrounded by falslings—all of whom sported their birthday suits.

My cheeks burned as I focused on the ceiling. Zara cackled from the darkness.

*You did this on purpose.*

*"You wanted me to spend more time with them,"* she said innocently. *"And what better way than in our natural state?"*

Someone next to me turned in their sleep, throwing an arm across my stomach. Zara laughed harder. Grimacing, I picked my way out from the heart of the pile, which was very difficult when I was trying to keep my eyes skyward. A snort made me freeze, and I looked down to see Ashira flat on her back, her mouth wide open as she let out a thunderous snore.

*"She sounds like a goober-pig in heat,"* Zara commented, and I had to cover my mouth to stop from laughing. Ashira shifted but didn't wake—her face a mask of tranquility, an arm curled around Jaza.

I couldn't help but smile—I'd never seen either of them look so peaceful. I didn't know Ashira *could* look peaceful. She was always frowning or glaring—much like Zara, actually.

"Are you going to stand there like a creep or am I going to have to wade in there and get you?" a voice whispered.

I looked up to see Lukas at the edge of the group, fully-clothed, an eyebrow cocked.

"I-I wasn't—it's not what it looks like!" I stammered.

He rolled his eyes, gesturing to a pile of neatly folded dark leather on the ground—my armor. "I'll meet you outside," was all he said, throwing me a two-fingered salute as he walked off.

\*\*\*

"Well, that's a hell of a start to your new role as a 'god,'" Lukas said, handing me a bowl of warm grobz.

The fermented, chalky breakfast used to make my stomach turn, but after spending all night in vaxion form my body was famished. I shoveled it into my mouth, barely stopping to breathe.

"I'm… not… a god," I said between bites.

We sat outside the waterstone, the sun high in the sky—it was almost Twilight. Moon Peak and the day's end for the vaxion wasn't long off, though they hadn't stirred. In the glow of dusk the flowers of the poisonous lumbar trees looked fresh and pink. Witterflies, their delicate wings shades of red and white, floated past us, carried on a breeze that made me stop and inhale deeply.

"I never noticed how beautiful this place was."

"Don't get too comfy," Lukas said, hands behind his head as he stretched out. "If Calamity wasn't after you before, he is now. But I'm excited to see you go up against 'Player Two.' Think I could hire an artist to capture the look on his face when you beat him into a fine paste?"

My stomach flipped, and I set my breakfast down, no longer hungry. "I'm not any stronger than I was before," I began. "And I only have two options—train, which we have no time for, or Void Mana—which I have precious little of. Restoring the vaxion was easy—I didn't have to create them from the beginning like Ravenna did."

"And we don't exactly have a spare Ravenna lying about who'd be happy for you to munch on her," he mused.

I grimaced. "I still can't believe Ravenna did that. She didn't even know me, but she sacrificed herself to save me anyway. And what did she get for it? Grim and all the rest of her followers are dead."

"Not to put a damper on your pity-party, but it wasn't just about saving you. She didn't want Calamity or Gallow to get their paws on her. Wait, not paws—antenna? Do slugs have antenna?"

"And Lazander..." I said, ignoring Lukas. "I know he's fighting Calamity, but I can't believe he almost killed Zara—and you. He's a Gilded Knight, he's supposed to be the hero!"

"In his eyes, we're probably the evil ones. He's the one fighting for a guy who calls himself the 'God of Judgment' after all. And if there's one thing stories have taught me it's that no one ever thinks they're the villain."

"I think that's the most profound thing you've ever said."

"You haven't heard my rant on what gods and stained underwear have in common. But I digress," he said, clapping his hands together. He sat up smoothly, bits of grass sticking out from his blond hair. "Where to next, Your Godliness?"

"I'm not sure," I said lamely. "Calamity was... talkative. And while most of it was lies, I could see his chains—they're almost entirely broken. Once Gaj breaks through, Calamity will be hot on her heels."

"Gaj?"

"You know how in the stories they always say Calamity could split the earth in two with a single step?"

"Yeah—it's how Moonvale was formed. Apparently, anyway."

"That wasn't Calamity," I said, remembering the twin suns that hung in the Void and the waves of malice and hatred I felt pulsating from within. "That was Gaj."

Lukas gave a low whistle. "Then I guess we have to make sure she never shows up."

*"Or,"* Zara said, finally chiming in. *"We do as Ravenna suggested—we go to the Ivory Keep and find this servant of the queen—Thaddeus she called him. She told me to keep him from Calamity at all costs."*

"I'm sorry, who?" I said aloud. "When did Ravenna mention 'Thaddeus'? And why is this only coming up now?"

*"It is coming up now because it is relevant,"* she said, primly.

I tried not to sigh—yep, she was still Zara.

"Thaddeus?" Lukas said, looking confused. "I've heard that name in a story about Queen Firanta's dog. But that's hardly who we're after... is it? Oh no. Don't tell me the slug goddess sent us after a *mutt?*"

Back in the darkness, Zara burst out laughing. *"A dog, why not?"* she said, sounding far too amused.

"Well, our options are try to find Gaj—which without a lead will probably cost me Void Mana. Or, do as Ravenna suggested, and hope… a dog can help us," I said. I hated making decisions at the best of times, but this felt like choosing between getting eaten by a shark or a bear.

I was veering toward using some of my Void Mana—hopefully it wouldn't cost more than a point or two to figure out where Gaj was, or how she'd come through to this world, when Zara surprised me by saying, *"Thaddeus should be our goal. There must be a reason why Ravenna wants him kept from Calamity."*

Oh? I thought you'd be all gung-ho for using the System.

*"I have plans for your new System,"* she said in a tone that suddenly made me worried. *"And for it we will need to use your Void Mana sparingly. As for the mutt, well…"* she trailed off, sounding uncharacteristically unsure. *"Ravenna has spoken true thus far. Perhaps we should trust her as she trusted us."*

I blinked in surprise. Not too long ago the thought of trusting anyone would have made Zara jump in a fire.

*"I heard that,"* she said.

"Thaddeus," I said aloud. "We should try to find Thaddeus."

"Whatever you say, boss," Lukas said, cracking a shoulder. "Now we need to figure out what the hell do we do with a bunch of shapeshifting vaxion."

*\*\*\**

In the end, we didn't make any decisions about the vaxion—Ashira did.

We sat in the main hall, Moon Peak's meal spread out on the table. Lukas and I were on either side of Ashira, places of honor, while we feasted on the prickly root vegetable known as *pakina*. While it had been diced, cooked, and fried to perfection, that was the only thing to eat, which was odd—Moon Peak usually had a spread of meats. I guiltily remembered that despite being up for hours, I hadn't done any of my First Dawn chores, but as I sat listening to the vaxion laugh and tease one another, I realized I wasn't the only one—everyone had skipped out on their jobs.

Even Ashira.

Moon Peak was a time to chat and relax, but today it was different. People's eyes lit up as they talked about last night's transformation.

"Did you *see* the size of my fangs? I could have cracked a stonebreaker in two!"

"The lightning… I had forgotten what it felt like."

"We took down those goober-pigs in seconds! We're in for a feast tomorrow!"

None were louder than Esia who stood on the table and pretended to roar, cheered on by the others. I expected Ashira to bark at him to get down, but she kept her face in her cup, lips twitching in a smile.

"I will tell them it was you in time," she said to me, her voice low. "For now they believe it a gift from Ravenna. I did not want to ruin their morning with the truth—that we spent a thousand years worshipping a slug."

"You don't have to tell them, you know. If it's easier—"

"No," Ashira said sharply, "we spent too many years surviving on lies. We must face the past and the truth it holds, or this gift is worthless."

She looked at me, eyes burning like molten lava. "This is why you must go. Zara told me of your plans to stop Calamity, and what I said before stands true—I know nothing of killing gods. But war…" she grinned fiercely, "that is something I know of."

"What are you going to do?" I asked tentatively.

"Nothing you need concern yourself with," she said, returning to her plate with a gusto I'd never seen. She usually picked at her food. "But the gift you have given us will not be squandered—of this you have my word."

## Chapter Thirty-Six

Zara stood outside the waterstone, emotions she couldn't put into words weighing heavy on her shoulders. She knew some of them: anger—cold, and comforting. Fear at what her next steps would bring. And something she'd been too afraid to feel until she met Teema.

Love.

The first time she left Moonvale she was eleven years old, locked in a trunk by Magnus and hitched to the back of a horse like luggage. When she set off for Ravenna's maze, she'd been eager to get away from these new vaxion who were so different to the hard, stoic titans she'd left behind as a child. Zara's "goodbye" had been a note—the only farewell she'd been willing to give.

This time was different.

Every vaxion came outside to see her off. Fatyr's eyes were wet as he waved goodbye, smiling despite how sharply she always spoke to him. Little Esia jumped up and down, claiming Zara would "stomp the Tyrant into the ground." Jaza wrapped her strong arms around her, whispering, "We are so proud of you, our Fury."

Ashira was last. They didn't hug or speak—that wasn't their way. Instead she pressed her forehead against Zara's, and together they closed their eyes, the world stopping around them.

Lukas stood awkwardly next to Zara. He'd been jovial in his goodbyes—high-fiving Fatyr and pretending to punch Esia in the arm. But his cheerful act dropped when Ashira broke away from Zara and stepped toward him.

The vaxion gasped when Ashira dropped to one knee, her plait slipping over her shoulder as she bowed her head to Lukas. "I will right the wrongs of the past, Lukas," she said, her voice cutting through the silence like a blade. "This I swear."

She didn't wait for a response. She just disappeared into the waterstone without a backward glance, the rest of the vaxion following, leaving Zara and Lukas alone—an impossible task ahead of them.

Zara pretended not to notice Lukas turning away, one hand wiping his eyes.

"Well, time to go see a woman about a dog," he said brightly, a smile fixed on his face.

"And kill a god or two along the way," Zara replied.

They set off together, unsure if they would ever see the Moonvale Mountains or the vaxion again.

***

While Zara was in control and trekking through the mountains, Lukas at her side loudly wondering what would kill them first—Calamity or Zara's breakneck pace—I sat in the darkness. I wasn't paying attention to Zara's dropping stamina bar as she jumped impossible distances, *Monstrous Strength Activated* flashing before her eyes. The pop-ups had returned when I'd become an Operator and assigned her to my System. I also didn't bother keeping watch for gravediggers, stonebreakers, xandi, or anything else that would eat us alive. I trusted Zara to protect both myself and Lukas.

Instead I focused on one thing—the System Menu.

I opened the Inventory tab, unsurprised to find almost everything was gone—the silver key I'd found stitched into a xandi's leg, the cloak and ring I'd been "gifted" for finishing a quest. But not, for some reason, the *Healing Void*—a potion I was given for completing my very first quest, *Stop Aerzin*. It was how I'd met Lukas... and how I'd ended up binding him in a blood-debt.

Anger made my heart spike, my fingers itching to grow claws—though I couldn't in here. I didn't know why Calamity stripped me of everything but my first item. Maybe it was to mock me—a reminder I'd once served him. Or maybe it was such a minor thing to him, he hadn't bothered to take it. Part of me wanted to toss it, but it was too precious to waste. If my playthroughs in *Knights of Eternity* were anything to go by, a *Healing Void* could be the difference between life and death.

I skipped to the next tab—Spells and Abilities. My anger turned to sadness when I remembered how excited it used to make me. In neatly lined rows lay the sum total of Zara's powers, including some of the "rewards" Calamity had drip-fed me—payment for doing his dirty work and paving the way for his return. While he'd taken most of my items, he hadn't taken any of my powers—couldn't, I guessed. The temptation to kick myself for agreeing to even a single one of his ridiculous quests was strong. He'd given us cryptic missions on purpose—it was all part of his game, his precious *System*. Were we "smart" enough to figure out what he wanted but dumb enough to crave the dopamine hit we got when we did? Would we yearn to please him like the pathetic Player One, or would we be like Player Two—a coward who did whatever it took to save his own skin?

My fists clenched, the memory of the last time I'd seen him flashing in my mind: the Void, the fear in Player Two's eyes, how his body curled up in the sand, too scared to move. If we'd all fought together, maybe we could have killed Calamity then and there. Maybe none of this would have happened. But no—he was too busy *begging* for his own life.

"*Peace,*" Zara said, her voice a low grumble. "*I am here, Teema.*"

I sighed, sending a flicker of gratitude to Zara as I let my anger subside. I hated Player Two. But if I was being honest, there was more to it than my disgust at what he'd done. I knew that in another time, in another place, there was every chance I'd have ended up just like him—a sycophant eager to please Calamity. The only reason I hadn't was Zara—but not everyone was lucky enough to have the Fury in their corner.

"It ends here," I said aloud, thinking of all the other players Calamity had dragged here. Maybe it was just three, maybe it was countless others—I didn't know. Probably never would. But I knew one thing— "No more pain, no more cruelty, no more *torture*—it ends now. It ends with *me*."

The words—the vow—calmed me enough that I could return to the Menu and the Spells and Abilities tab:

| Bloodied Restoration | Skill base: Recovery |
|---|---|
| *Heal another by taking on their wounds and ailments. You can only heal one creature at a time, and the pain and suffering you experience is doubled. How rapidly you heal is tied to your Recovery stat.* ||
| **Inferno** | **Skill base: Essence** |
| *Call down a tower of flame from the sky itself. The length of this spell is directly tied to your Essence stat.* ||
| **Monstrous Strength** | **Skill base: Stamina** |
| *Base Strength is tripled. Duration is based on Stamina.* ||
| **Piercing Sight** | **Skill base: Essence** |
| *See through illusions, mirages, and other magic that uses invisibility, shadow, or any other concealment-based affinities. Success is based on your Essence stat when rolled against the stat of the caster.* ||
| **Partial Transformation** | **Skill base: Racial** |
| *Partially shapeshift one of your limbs into the appendage of an available form. These include vaxion, molger, and voidbeast.* ||
| **Tithe of Beasts** | **Skill base: Racial** |
| *Tap into your vaxion counterpart and use your enhanced sense of smell and sight. Note:* **Eyes of the Hunter** *upgrade unlocked. You can see in low-light areas for double the distance and in pitch-black areas for a third.* ||
| **Vengeful Rebuke** | **Skill base: Essence** |
| *Absorb an enemy's magic, and fire it back at them with an additional ten percent damage. Success is based on your Essence stat when rolled against the stat of the caster.* ||

The list continued, including more racial skills based on Zara's vaxion blood: *Full Transformation, Wrath's Storm,* and *Fury's Claw,* which gave her vaxion claws—plus its upgrade *Lightning Claw*. There was also *Blazing Whisper,* the fire-based combat spell, and a new one Zara must have gained through her training—*Lantern's Kiss,* a utility spell for lighting torches and starting campfires.

This wasn't the first time I'd seen this tab, but reading it now my eyes bulged. The description for *Piercing Sight* and *Vengeful Rebuke* summed up my astonishment nicely: "Success is based on your Essence stat when rolled against the stat of the caster."

I'd had no idea that was how it worked or that I was essentially rolling dice every time I used that ability. The more I explored the System as an Operator, the more I saw its true power—it reduced the world to a series of numbers and variables, and all you needed to change those numbers was Void Mana. The fact that three points and a single thought was all it took to return the vaxion's shapeshifting powers was still mind-boggling to me.

I opened my Character Sheet.

| Base Stats: | |
|---|---|
| Strength | 85 |
| Essence | 100 |
| Resistance | 50 |
| Recovery | 80 |
| Speed | 80 |
| Luck | 15 |

Essence influenced how much mana Zara could produce, Resistance how tough she was against magical attacks while Recovery referred to her ability to heal without outside influence. The rest were pretty much standard when it came to role-playing games, but what depressed me was how little the stats had changed. Only Strength and Recovery had increased, and that was by a paltry five points despite how hard I knew Zara had been training.

This only confirmed what I knew about the System—it was a shortcut, a way to cheat the limits of the body and the mind. But the question was, how best to use it? I'd expected Zara to want to pour everything into our stats and abilities, but she'd only wanted to know one thing—how much to get me back to Earth.

"What?" I'd asked, thrown by her question. "Zara, I'm not even thinking about... home right now. We should focus on getting you as strong as possible."

She'd just looked at me with a raised eyebrow until I sighed and pulled up the System.

**INTERPLANETARY PATHWAY TO EARTH PREESTABLISHED. VOID MANA COST REDUCED TO THREE POINTS.**

"That's it?" I said, shocked. I'd expected it to cost triple that at least. I knew I should be happy. I might not know what waited for me back home, but I probably I had a family. Maybe even friends? But I was also… afraid.

I stopped, surprised. What was I so scared of? Was something waiting for me back on Earth? Something I'd forgotten?

"One point," Zara said, pulling me from my musings. "That is what you will spend on our abilities. No more."

"Zara, this isn't about me. We need everything we can to beat Calamity, and—"

"I keep thinking you cannot be more irritating, yet you prove me wrong every time," she said fiercely. "You are not of this world, yet you risk everything to save it. You never think of yourself. It is *most* annoying."

I laughed. "Says the woman who ate a slug and threw herself into the Void to save me."

"You also change the topic whenever you are the subject. Which is even *more* irritating."

"Okay, no need to call me out like that, Zara."

"My *point*…" she stopped, taking a breath. Seeing her weigh every word, I quietened. "You helped me get my family back, and I will do the same for you. Whether you like it or not, Teema." She shifted uncomfortably, cheeks flushed.

"Thank you, Zara," I said, my heart full. "You're a good—"

"One point," she said, brusque and business-like. "No more."

Which was why I now sat in the darkness, scrolling through the System. Alien glyphs representing "potential" no longer overwhelmed me, but the possibilities still did. For instance, I didn't need to know that for only one hundred points I could replace all of Zara's organs with something called "starbrisk"—a near indestructible and self-regenerating material. Or for a paltry fifty I could give her an extra set of humanoid arms and legs.

"System?" I called out, still unsure how to refer to the thing. "Only show options I can afford with the Void Mana I have, please."

The Menu went from countless options to a neat row of about fifteen.

"Thank you." I was unsure of how sentient the System was, but it couldn't hurt to be polite. "What's the most efficient way to increase my stats and abilities while only spending a single point?"

**CALCULATING...**
**DUE TO STATUS AS SYSTEM OPERATOR, COST TO INCREASE OWN STATS AND ABILITIES IS HALVED.**
**CLICK YES FOR SUGGESTIONS.**

I mentally clicked yes, eyes going wide at what I saw.

I remembered Zara's account of her fight with Lazander and how angry it made her—she'd could have beaten him, she claimed, if he hadn't had *Stone Skin*. Smiling, I wondered if I could keep enough Void Mana for myself *and* make her strong enough to take on Calamity.

\*\*\*

Every moment Eternity spent with Lazander she felt as if she walked with not one, but two men. He seemed at war with himself, his eyes darting around the camp like a caged animal one moment, his head thrown back in delight as he praised Gallow the next.

It scared her.

When she tried to bring it up with Malik—Lazander didn't even mention Merrin, Galora, and Mabel anymore—the older Champion brushed her off. "He's got bigger things to worry about than some barnyard animals," he scoffed. "I suggest you follow suit."

They'd set off from the cave mere hours after Lazander had awoken, far too soon for Eternity's liking. She'd tried to question Malik on what had happened in Moonvale, but he was even more vague than usual— "Ravenna sent one of her beasts to take us down, and if it wasn't for Gallow's grace it would've killed us both. When next we see it, you will kill it on sight. Is that clear?"

He'd been adamant, not letting the topic drop until Eternity swore to do so.

Flying high in the sky, her eyes weren't fixed on Malik, or even Lazander, both Champions running at speed far below. They were focused on the land around her, her heart sinking with every passing hour.

When the shadow-fiends first appeared, they were easy to spot—she only had to look for trees bereft of life, their black and withered trunks standing out in the bountiful landscape that was Navaros. Now she had to search for splashes of green and gold in the barren land below.

Entire rivers ran dry, the desiccated corpses of fish and frogs picked clean by scavengers. Fields of crops lay withered and gray, the soil reduced to ash. They passed a farmer who knelt in the dirt, his fingers dug into the useless earth, sobbing. By the time they passed the fifth, some cursing Gallow, others staring blankly into space, even Eternity had to look away.

The sun was setting, the darkness covering the withered remains of Navaros like a mask, though Eternity barely noticed. Her eyes drooped, her fingers grazing the blackened treetops of the forest as she dipped, her mana minutes from being entirely empty.

*Have to... have to keep flying. Just... a little longer...*

A flash of pain lit up her right arm, and her eyes shot open—the ground hurtling toward her as she fell from the sky. On instinct she threw open the door to Gallow, fear making her take more power than she needed as she hit the dirt—earth exploding outward.

"Eternity!" Lazander cried.

She winced, bruised but conscious as she automatically called out, "I am well!" She lay on her back in a mid-sized hole, the tendrils of Gallow's power seeping away from where they'd broken her fall. Her nose bled heavily. Embarrassed that she'd *fallen asleep* mid-flight, she tried to force herself to sit up, but exhaustion hit her like a blow to the head.

A burst of red hair appeared above her, naked panic on Lazander's face. "Eternity! Are you all right? What happened?" He helped her to her feet, eyes darting over every inch of her, his mouth a thin line when he spotted her arm. She almost smiled—he sounded just like himself again.

"That wound looks deep," he said, taking care not to touch it.

"I believe I hit a branch or two on the way down. It is nothing, really, Lazander. I am... more embarrassed than anything."

"What in the blazes are you two doing?" Malik hissed, appearing by Lazander in a blur.

"I suggest we camp for the night, Malik," Lazander said, a protective hand on Eternity's back. "I think we could all do with the rest."

"Do you think we have *time* to—"

"Lady Eternity has not broken bread since this morning's meal, nor has she slept," Lazander said, withdrawing his hand, his voice stiff and formal once more. "I do not think Gallow would approve of us running her ragged simply because you forgot she has to do things like *sleep* and *eat*, Malik."

The older Champion tensed, eyes flickering between the two of them. On the one hand, she was grateful Lazander had stood up for her. As much as she hated to admit it, she needed the rest. On the other... she hadn't missed how he'd pulled away or the "Lady" that was in front of her name once more. What was going on with him?

"Two hours," Malik barked. "No more. I'm going to patrol."

*\*\*\**

Camp was a sad affair—no fire, a thin blanket and a handful of rations Eternity forced herself to eat before curling up on her side. Lazander sat cross-legged next to her, promising to watch over her while she slept. It wasn't as comforting a thought as it would have been weeks ago, but she closed her eyes anyway, sleep just on the edge of her subconscious.

And then she felt it.

It wasn't pain. Not really. More like the press of a cold finger against her neck or a soft pinch on the back of her arm—a discomfort. A warning.

Her eyes shot open, and she saw them—yellow eyes staring at her from the darkness. Dozens upon dozens of them.

## Chapter Thirty-Seven

"Lazander?" Eternity whispered, seized by a terror she didn't understand. "I see them, Lady Eternity." He was on his feet, sword in hand. She blinked, and more yellow eyes joined the dozens already there. Blink. Another pair. Blink. *Another.* And another.

Soon they were surrounded. Some stared at her from the trees, others low to the ground, and her heart pounded when she realized that not one of them blinked back at her.

*Skitter. Skitter.*

The noise began, softly at first—the sound of claws and paws on dry soil, sliding as they inched closer to her. She sat up, desperately wishing they'd taken the time to light a fire when the first creature stumbled toward her.

*Skitter skitter. Skitter skitter.*

It was a rat. A huge, colossal rat that in life would have been the length of her forearm, its tail double that. Now bones peeked through what little remained of its shredded flesh, and half its skull was caved in, a single lifeless eye staring up at her.

It was joined by another rat. A dormouse. A crow. A rabbit. Then an entire flock of cradits—low-lying lizards that favored rivers. They dragged themselves toward her, ignoring missing legs and wings in their eagerness to reach her.

"Bloodied Void," Lazander swore as forty, then *fifty* more appeared—all small animals or birds. All completely silent. "What magic is this?" He placed himself firmly between her and the creatures but there were so many of them.

Eternity was silent, blind terror gripping her heart. "It is too soon," she whispered. "Too soon for the dead to rise."

"The *dead?*" Lazander said, but Eternity was screaming. She yanked back her blanket to find she was covered in dead mice, their tiny claws and teeth biting through her dress and into her soft skin.

She slapped at them, panic making her movements clumsy. Small bones crunched beneath her hands. Lazander rushed to help her, but Eternity's sobs were a battle cry to the undead. A flock of birds rushed the Champion, pecking him. A single flick of his sword was all it took to cut one clean in two, but the beasts kept coming, swarming Lazander and Eternity.

Suddenly Eternity was up in the air, the breath knocked out of her as someone threw her onto their shoulder.

"Run!" Malik barked, holding Eternity tightly as he vanished into the night, Lazander hot on his heels. She watched the horde of undead waver, lost without a target, and then slowly turn to face one another—broken necks tilting.

She looked away when they began to devour one another whole.

\*\*\*

"Malik, I shall be sick!" Eternity said, nearly weeping as she bounced on Malik's hard shoulder, the edge of his armor digging painfully into her. He grunted in reply but came to an abrupt halt—Eternity's gorge rising at the sudden movement.

He set her down, and she stumbled, only staying on her feet thanks to Lazander, whose hand darted away the moment she regained her balance.

"The hell was that?" Malik barked.

She winced, thinking he was shouting at her, as usual.

But it was Lazander he squared up to, his index finger raised. "Why'd you waste time battering the things when you should have grabbed Eternity and legged it?"

"I—" He looked as surprised as Eternity. She waited for him to defend himself—to show the spine of steel he had whenever the older Champion criticized her. But he bowed his head, shame in his eyes. "They surprised me, and I panicked. It won't happen again."

Annoyed, Eternity said, "That is unfair, Malik—they caught me off-guard as well. They shouldn't even *be* here yet—the dead do not rise until the final throes of the Tyrant's arrival, which is weeks if not months away. We need to speak to the sages—something is wrong."

"We don't *need* to speak to the sages," Malik barked. "*Gallow* will tell us what to do. *Gallow* will guide us. And has he said anything about the dead?"

An uncomfortable silence followed, Eternity biting back her sharp reply. She'd taken a chance with Lazander when she'd aired her doubts about Gallow, but she couldn't do that with Malik—he'd lose what little of his temper remained. "No—he has not."

"Exactly," Malik barked. "Because a bunch of skeletal mice is the least of our worries—Gaj will be here by tomorrow, and we're still hours away. If we're to stop her, we need to *move*."

"Malik," Lazander said softly, "we might not need sleep, but Lady Eternity does. It took everything she had to close the gate and stop Bala coming through—and Gaj is infinitely more powerful. Look at her, she's barely standing."

"I'm not tired," Eternity said truthfully. Seeing a mouse bite into her, one eye hanging from its socket, had left her wide awake. "But it will be hours before my mana is replenished."

Malik gave an annoyed sigh, and Eternity felt something in her snap. "I cannot control how quickly my mana returns, Malik!"

The older man pinched the ridge of his nose. He'd always been the Champion Eternity got along best with—his soothing words a balm to Vivek's acerbic wit and Imani's temper—and she'd come to rely on him for that. No one knew better than the Champions how much it cost to serve Gallow, but Malik had always kept his humanity. Or acted like he had, anyway. And that was the key word—"acted." With every passing minute, more of Malik's mask fell away. And Eternity didn't like what she saw underneath.

Lazander stepped forward. "I'll carry Lady Eternity," he said.

She was so surprised, she asked him to repeat himself.

Holding out his arms, he gave a small bow. "It is no inconvenience, my lady. Malik and I tire, but do not need sleep. You should rest in my arms while you can."

His words made Eternity blush furiously, but Malik was too busy nodding in agreement to notice. "Good idea, Zander. Let's go!"

He was off like a shot, zipping through the blackened remnants of the once beautiful forest. Eternity couldn't face Lazander, not while her mind whirled with awkward thoughts. Was she supposed to step into his arms? Wait for him to pick her up like a damsel? Could she make the task easier for him, perhaps by jumping? No, that was a ridiculous—

Lazander appeared behind her, scooping her up with ease.

"Ready, my lady?" he asked.

She nodded, cheeks burning. Lazander kept his gaze forward, his brow furrowed as he picked up speed, taking care not to jostle her. His calm demeanor made her relax enough to realize she was quite comfortable. Though he wore armor, she could feel his warmth—a toasty fire on a cold night—and to her surprise found herself drifting off. But a stray thought made her force her eyes open.

"Malik called you 'Zander,'" she said quietly, though the older Champion was far ahead. "You told me you hate it when anyone but the queen calls you that."

Lazander frowned but kept his eyes straight ahead—they were moving at such speed, she knew that if he tripped and fell, she'd be squashed underneath him like mince under a mallet. "Did I say that?"

"You did," Eternity insisted. "On my very first night at the Ivory Keep You, Marito, Gabriel, and I all sat beneath the stars, drinking wine Marito robbed from the kitchens. Have you forgotten?" Eternity tried to sound nonchalant, but that night with the Gilded Knights was the happiest she'd felt in almost fifty years. They'd welcomed her with open arms, not caring that she was Gallow's Chosen. It was the first time she'd felt like a normal woman in a very, very long time. The thought of Lazander having no recollection of one of her most precious memories upset Eternity more than she could say.

A strange, uncertain look crossed his face, but he shook his head. "Marito stealing wine from the kitchen? Hah! I cannot say I'm surprised, but I fear I don't remember that particular evening—but if you say it is so, then it must be true," he cheerfully added. "Mind you, I take no issue with Malik calling me Zander—it's just a name, after all."

Eternity nodded in reply, upset and uneasy. The Lazander she knew took great pride in names—he'd called his hawk Merrin in honor of his mother and asked his horse to choose her own name. She'd pick "Mabel," a sweet flower and her favorite snack after Lazander's hair, which he'd insisted wasn't a suitable name.

Eternity and the Champions left the forest behind, coming to a long series of dirt roads. Instead of wide and empty like she'd expect in the middle of the night, they were filled to bursting with people. She only caught a glimpse of most of them—Lazander ran so quickly, all anyone felt was a light breeze as he sprinted past—but it was enough. Some pushed wagons, others hit stubborn donkeys laden with bags, and a shocking number carried nothing but the clothes on their backs. But every single one wore the same look of fear and desperation.

*Refugees*, she realized. When she'd left the Ivory Keep weeks ago, their arrival was a trickle, but this was a tidal wave. How had things gotten so bad so quickly?

Rhys and his soldiers had been determined to beat back the shadow-fiends, but looking at the sheer number of people fleeing to Evergarden, the closest city, she knew that even if the commander could take down twenty shadow-fiends with one hand, it wasn't enough—there were too many of the monsters now. The blackened destruction of the land was proof of that.

A whisper of what felt like fingertips brushed her cheek, and she jumped.

"Are you thinking of Malik?" Lazander asked softly, glancing down at her.

"Hmm?" she said, clutching her cheek. The feeling had vanished as quickly as it appeared.

"Are you worrying about what Malik said? Because you need not," Lazander said. He gave her arm a reassuring squeeze as he jumped over a ravine, landing so softly Eternity barely felt it. "He's hard on you, hard on both of us, because he's scared. He feels the weight of every life in this world on his shoulders, and he fears he isn't enough. That *we're* not enough."

Thrown by the topic change, she said, "I used to care deeply about what he thought of me. What the sages and disciples, Champions and Gilded thought. But no more. I am too tired. Too scared *this* might be our future." She gestured at the destruction around her. "You did not see Player Two and Bala, Lazander. What he did to all those people, I... I..."

"You're stronger than Player Two, stronger than Calamity. You're one of the strongest people I know," Lazander said, surprising her.

She flushed, embarrassed, and annoyed at herself for thinking he'd changed. Only the old Lazander would say something so—

"For Gallow's fire burns in you like the sun. This is what makes you strong. What makes you *unbeatable*," he said, interrupting her thoughts, his eyes shining with belief. "With the God of Judgment on our side, we cannot lose."

She wanted to believe him—she really did. But as she fell asleep in his arms, dreaming of yellow eyes in the darkness, and Player Two's blood-stained smile, she admitted what she couldn't say out loud.

They were losing—and the real battle hadn't even begun.

# Chapter Thirty-Eight

Even from a distance, they could hear the moans.

"They're here," Lazander said, increasing his pace. They'd run through the night, Eternity drifting in and out of asleep, the thrum of Lazander's heartbeat a soothing balm against the tornado of corpses that invaded her dreams. Though she knew how quickly the Champions could move, she was still astounded to wake to dawn's warmth, their destination stretched out before them—Freyley's northern coast. Or to be precise, Emerald village.

She had no chance to admire the liquid glass of the Jaded Sea, the lush pink sand of Freyley's famous beaches, or the small, picturesque village of Emerald that overlooked the stunning view. Dark shapes moved among low-built houses, the thrum of sick, unnatural magic sending a shiver down her spine—shadow-fiends.

Then the screaming started.

Eternity looked up at Lazander, his mouth a thin line. Though the Champions didn't need sleep like she did, dark purple shadows marked his eyes. He was exhausted—yet he would throw himself into the fight with everything he had. Determination gripped her heart.

"Throw me," Eternity said.

"My lady?"

"You move too quickly to set me down safely, and slowing down means more will die—*throw me*, Lazander. Now!"

To the Champion's credit, he didn't need to be asked a third time. He simply tossed her high into the air, vanishing in a burst of speed without a backward glance.

"**Bless mine body, so I might better tread your path,**" she cried, invisible hands sending her skyward. Eternity shot forward as quickly as she could, eyes locked on a cluster of huts and houses, details sharpening with every second—a man running, a child in his hands, a boy driving a pitchfork into a shadow-fiend's leg. The boy's small body going flying when the beast kicked him.

The back wall of a house close to Eternity exploded outward, wood and stone raining down as a shadow-fiend jumped through, a girl gripped in each claw. It straightened, the shifting darkness of its face twisting left and right, as if considering. With a twitch, it raised the girl in its left hand, her blonde hair almost sheared clean by its claws. Blood trailed from the countless cuts on her scalp, dripping into her eyes. The monstrous wound in the center of the shadow-fiend's chest undulated, opening wider, ready to clamp down on the girl's head where the Tyrant would offer her a choice—serve, or die.

The girl was sobbing, fists hammering against the claw that held her. "It's—it's me! It's Rebecca!" she shouted. "What are you—"

**"You have been judged. And you have been found wanting,"** Eternity called, darkness bursting from her hands. She remembered the soldier. Remembered his scream as the shadow-field ate him whole, the snap of his neck when he finally died. She would not fail a second time.

Gallow's magic cut through the air, quiet as whisper. The shadow-fiend didn't even look up, it was too intent on its prey. And then the shadows that served as both weapon and armor vanished, Eternity's aim true as it sliced the monster's head clean from its shoulders.

"I've got you, Rebecca," Eternity said, landing next to the bleeding girl. She looked fifteen, maybe sixteen at most. "Are you hurt? Was there anyone else in the house?"

But instead of thanking Eternity for saving her life, Rebecca looked aghast. "Monster!" she cried, pounding her fists against Eternity's chest, every strike weaker than the last. "You killed her!"

Confused, Eternity tried to calm the girl while covertly looking around, terrified her spell had hit an innocent bystander. The ground was awash with broken wood and stone. In the distance she could hear the clang of blades as Lazander and Malik fought, but she couldn't see anyone but the headless corpse, Rebecca, and the other girl—who lay unconscious. Eternity hesitated, wanting to go help the Champions, but not willing to abandon the girls.

"Mom!" Rebecca cried, throwing herself at the dead shadow-fiend. "No, Mom!"

With horror, Eternity looked at the corpse that had once been a shadow-fiend. Though the head had rolled a few feet away, she could make out blonde hair streaked with gray and skin permanently freckled from years of working outside—just like Rebecca's. The girl lay curled up on the dead woman's chest, sobbing as she cried for her mother.

"That was not your mother, Rebecca. Not anymore," Eternity said quietly, checking the unconscious girl—though she was a few years younger than Rebecca, the two of them could have been twins. Eternity focused on the girl's injuries. Unlike her sister, she only a single cut on her head, and her breathing was steady—she must have fainted when the shadow-fiend grabbed her. A cold anger raged in Eternity's chest, and she clenched her fists so hard, blood pooled in the marks left by her nails.

A family. A family who'd probably been sitting together, enjoying their breakfast when the shadow-fiends attacked. Did the mother throw herself in the monster's path? Did her daughters have to watch as she was shoved into the chest of a shadow-fiend, only to emerge covered in claw and darkness, a new servant of Calamity?

"Mom? Mom, please. Don't go. Please don't go," Rebecca whispered.

"You're not safe here—grab your sister and run," Eternity said, wishing her heart was made of stone. "I... am sorry about your mother."

Eternity didn't wait for a reply. She ran for where the screams were loudest, Gallow's power cradled in her hands.

***

Underneath piles of dried wood, twenty headless corpses lay on the beach. Several of the shadow-fiends had fled when they realized they were losing, but Eternity and the Champions had tracked them all down, dragging the remains back to the beach. Spelled canvas and mage-fire were the best way to dispose of the Tyrant's servants, but Malik had said a pyre would do—they couldn't waste Eternity's precious *mana* after all.

She'd ignored his tone.

The sun rose to its zenith. Eternity couldn't believe it was only noon. She felt like she'd aged a decade in just a few hours. Malik threw a torch on the kindling, the bone-dry wood catching fire immediately.

Crying and cursing came from behind them. The people of Emerald huddled around their doors, shooting dark looks at Eternity and Malil, but none of them dared come any closer. They'd asked to bury the shadow-fiends with their own dead—most of them had come from Emerald. They were mothers and fathers, sons and daughters, and they deserved to be laid to rest with their families, they'd argued. Malik had refused, and for once Eternity had agreed with him—anything tainted by the Tyrant's magic was too dangerous to be buried.

She just wished Malik had been kinder about it. Threatening to burn Emerald to the ground if they asked again had not ingratiated them to the villagers.

Lazander was the only reason they hadn't been run out. Of the five wooden houses and ten smaller huts, almost half the village had been damaged or even outright destroyed during the attack. The Champion was hard at work fixing doors, boarding up holes, and repairing roofs while Eternity watched the flames, ready in case any of the shadow-fiends tried to rise anew.

"Where to from here?" Eternity asked after a time, grateful for the sea breeze—it helped with the smell. Gallow's orders for her had been "Gaj" and "Emerald village," and that was all.

"This is it," Malik replied. "Valerius, Player Two, whatever that traitor is calling himself these days will summon Baj from here."

Eternity frowned, taking in the battered, but now peaceful village and the lapping waves of the Jaded Sea. Yes, there had been shadow-fiends, but that was it—she saw no signs of Player Two. "When he summoned Bala, he made no use of shadow-fiends. In fact, he was the only servant of the Tyrant there."

"Coward must have learned his lesson and sent his shadow-fiends ahead, hoping to take us down a peg or two," Malik said with a shrug.

Eternity couldn't deny that Player Two was a coward, but he'd seen her powers—there was no way he thought a bunch of shadow-fiends enough to kill her. Plus he hadn't ordered the monsters to attack her—he'd unleashed them on Emerald. The more she thought about it, the less sense it made. The ritual to bring

Gaj into this world took blood and sacrifice—how could he do that if his shadow-fiends killed everyone in the only village for miles? Something wasn't right.

When she relayed this to Malik, he looked annoyed. "Gallow sent us here, which means we're meant to be here."

"But—"

"Not another damn word. I mean it, Eternity," he said. He stood, axe unsheathed, his eyes locked on the horizon.

And stood.

And stood.

\*\*\*

Night fell on Emerald village and the Jaded Sea. An older man slipped out of his hut around dusk with several bowls of stew, silently offering them to Eternity. She took them with a grateful smile, relieved to finally eat something other than road rations.

Lazander lay beside her, breathing so slowly, she kept having to check for the rise and fall of his chest. He'd fixed the bones of two houses and a hut before she'd noticed him sagging with exhaustion and quietly guided him back to the beach.

Champions didn't need to sleep, but they did need to rest. And she was happy to see Lazander's brow, so often furrowed these days, smooth and relaxed, his lips parted ever so slightly. He looked like the old Lazander, the knight who never failed to drop in and tell her about his latest mission with the Gilded. Who'd take her out on rides with Mabel, Merrin, and Galora. Her heart swelled with a deep yearning for the man he once was—a man who never failed to make her smile. Without realizing it, her hand stretched out, ready to brush a stray curl from his forehead.

"This is definitely Emerald, right?" Malik barked, breaking Eternity out of the haze of old memories. She snatched her hand back, but the Champion wasn't even looking at her—he was pacing back and forth in the sand, axe in hand. The pyre had burned out, leaving nothing but bones and charcoal.

"It is indeed Emerald," Eternity said, "I checked with one of the fisherman last time you asked." They'd been here all day and seen nothing. No more shadow-fiends. No sign of Player Two.

And no Gaj.

Malik grumbled, his pace increasing.

"Has Gallow said anything since?" Eternity tentatively asked.

*"No."*

"Is… is it possible we should have kept moving?"

"If Gallow wanted us elsewhere, he'd say so!" Malik snapped, turning quickly on his heel, sand flying. His eyes flitted about, moving from the pyre to Emerald and back—she'd never seen him look so unsure.

Hours later, Eternity took to the skies, trying to see if she could spot any sign of Player Two or Gaj, but all looked quiet in the night. When her mana began to dip, she returned to the beach, determined to be as vigilant as Malik. But her standing guard turned to sitting. And sitting turned to drooping eyelids. She might be minutes from facing down Gaj, Calamity's most powerful lieutenant, yet here she was, struggling to stay awake. Marito had told her ridiculous stories of the Gilded Knights sleeping in trees and on the back of a whale out at sea once, and she'd never believed him.

She did now. Adrenaline could only keep her going for so long, and other than the catnaps she'd taken in Lazander's arms, it had been days since she'd slept properly.

Malik on the other hand, seemed determined to make a moat on the beach using nothing but his footsteps. The sand dipped several inches from his constant pacing, the edges of the incoming tide filling his path with water. He didn't seem to notice.

"Might I get you some more water, my lady?" Lazander asked her politely. He'd arisen spry and lively from his rest and refilled her waterskin four times in the last hour. She knew he was trying to be helpful, but if Eternity had anymore to drink, she feared she would burst.

"Ah, no—no thank you," she said, getting to her feet. "I think I shall go down by the sea and splash my face a little."

"I'll accompany you."

"No, there's no need, thank you!" she said, eager for a moment alone.

He looked so crestfallen Eternity was about to say she'd changed her mind when she caught Malik watching them. With a sigh she made her way down to the water, pointedly not looking at the older Champion.

The water wasn't cold—it was *freezing*, which was exactly what Eternity needed. She splashed her face, relishing the cold bite. She told herself she should be grateful for the down time—Gaj, Player Two, and the gate that would soon open. Who knew when she'd next have a moment to breathe? To prepare herself for the fight to come?

But no trill of determination hit her as it had when she'd flown into battle against Bala. It wasn't due to a lack of fear—she was terrified out of her mind. It was because deep in her bones, she knew there would be no battle. Not here. The feeling intensified when the villagers arose with the light of dawn, staring in confusion when they saw Eternity and the Champions still on their beach.

"Malik," Eternity said, unable to take it any longer. "Player Two is not coming."

"Not now, Eternity," he said, fingers tapping his axe-head.

"Respectfully, Malik," she began, "I—"

Her words were cut off, red-hot pain exploding in her skull. It was a pain she'd felt a thousand times before, so she managed to stay on her feet, but Malik and Lazander dropped to their knees. She knew why. They'd never felt it—never experienced Gallow's full power as it rushed them mind, body, and soul.

**"MOONVALE."**

Gallow's voice was usually somber—devoid of emotion. But now it echoed with something Eternity had never heard in her one-hundred and twenty years of service to the God of Judgment.

Panic.

**"GO NOW.**

**"HURRY."**

Several things struck Eternity at once: that Gallow had spoken more than a handful of words. And—

"*Shek,*" Malik swore, blood pouring from his nose. He cupped it with clumsy fingers, trying to stem the flow.

"Why… why did that hurt so much? What's going on?" Lazander asked, looking dazed.

"Gallow spoke to you directly," Eternity said, pleased her own nose didn't bleed for once. Using Gallow's powers so much must be helping her tolerance—or maybe she was simply used to the pain. "To my knowledge, he has never done so before. He uses me as an intermediary, so you are not hurt."

"You mean… you mean it hurts every time he speaks to you? Or to us through you?" Lazander asked, looking horrified.

Eternity rushed to reassure him. "Not when he speaks to you or when you use your powers," she said, dancing around the subject of Gallow speaking to her alone. "It is not—"

"Why are you chatting like wives at a bloody market?" Malik roared, fists buried in the sand as he tried to stand—swayed—then promptly collapsed. "We—we need to get to Moonvale, now!"

"Malik," Eternity said gently. "You need a minute."

"I do in my eye! Come on!" He forced himself upright with what Eternity knew was pure stubbornness. Watching him stumble, eyes blinking wildly, Eternity couldn't help but feel a hint of petty pride—she'd barely flinched at Gallow's voice. Feeling guilty, she quashed the feeling. Malik might be cruel, but that didn't mean she had to be.

"*Move,*" he barked as he took off, leaving uneven footprints in the sand. Lazander held out a hand to Eternity, and she gripped it, proud she barely blushed when he picked her up.

As they left the village far behind, she waited for Lazander to address the xandi in the room, but he said nothing. Unable to take it any longer, she asked, "Don't you think it's strange that Gallow ordered us to Emerald, only to then send us back to Moonvale?"

Lazander shrugged. "I am sure he had his reasons."

"But… but he was *afraid*. I have never heard him sound like that."

Lazander looked genuinely confused. "Did he? I find that hard to believe. Gods do not feel such things."

Eternity wanted to scream, to shake him and ask if he really didn't see it? Did he truly not understand what had just happened? The almighty God of Judgment had done the unthinkable.

He'd made a mistake.

## Chapter Thirty-Nine

They charged through Freyley, Malik and Lazander running faster than Eternity had ever seen, the landscape a blur of pink beaches and lush forests. And then the country turned dark, like a painter had dragged a thick black line through the scene, the soil turning gray and crumbling, the trees withered and desiccated. With a sinking heart, Eternity saw new towns and villages had been abandoned since they'd passed through only days before, the shadow-fiend sickness spreading at terrifying speed.

At this rate, the entire continent would be a wasteland in weeks.

The Champions weren't just fast—they were reckless. They only had a small pool of mana, far less than Eternity, but if they were careful they could keep it at a constant level, even while running. Malik and Lazander ignored that balance blasting through their magic at a dangerous rate. At this speed, they'd be at Moonvale in less than day. Exhausted and without mana, but they'd be there.

And then Lazander fell.

It was such a small thing. He'd gone to jump over a log just as a deer leaped in front of him. Lazander pulled Eternity against his chest, spinning midair so he hit the animal with his back—taking the full brunt of the blow. The deer made no sound but Eternity heard it—the sharp crack of bone, louder than the thud of an executioner's axe. Then Lazander hit the ground, Eternity clutched to him as they skidded through trees, rocks, and soil.

A boom sounded, like lightning splitting a tree. Eternity blinked, her head a fog of noise. Something under her groaned in pain.

"Lazander!" she said, untangling herself from the arms still wrapped around her. They'd been going so fast, it had taken crashing into a huge, blackened tree for them to stop. She squinted up at it, realizing it was the remnants of a scarlet sunder. A huge crack ran from its base to halfway up the trunk from where Lazander's head had struck it.

"Lazander, can you hear me?" she asked, gently squeezing his shoulder, too afraid to shake him.

"My… my lady, are you all right?" he asked, trying and failing to rise to an elbow. "Forgive me, I should have seen the… oh no."

They turned as one. They weren't looking at the thick scar carved into the earth from their fall or at the sheer distance they'd traveled—nearly the length of the Ivory Keep's inner courtyard. They were staring at the beautiful buck that lay on the ground, its ebony antlers twisting into the air like the veins of a river. Its neck was bent at an unnatural angle, the animal's deep, nut-brown eyes staring at them—unblinking.

"Lazander…" Eternity said, but he was already struggling to his feet and limping toward the deer.

\*\*\*

Lazander felt amazing—the best he ever had. On a rational level he knew things were dire. Imani and Vivek were dead, and the land was rotting before his very eyes. Worse still, they'd trekked halfway across the continent only to discover Gallow had sent them to the wrong place.

A sharp, ice-cold pain between his eyes made him wince. No—they hadn't been in the wrong place; how could he think such a thing? The God of Judgment sent them there on purpose—they were just needed back in Moonvale now. He had a plan. He always did. Lazander just had to have faith.

Gallow was all he could think about. His thoughts were filled with the righteous god and how important it was to please him. To prove that Gallow had been right to save him from death's clutches. He cringed when he thought of how ungrateful he'd been in those early days. Heart burning with determination, he swore he would do better—he would make it up to his master.

*Master?* he thought, shaking his head. No one was his master… right?

The only thing that interrupted his thoughts of Gallow was Eternity. As they'd sat together, watching the sun set on Emerald, he'd wanted to tell her how beautiful she was. How happy he was they'd met. That Gallow had brought them together. That if it wasn't for Gallow—

*Stop it,* a part of him whispered. *I don't want this. I don't want to serve Gallow!*

The stray thought caught him by surprise. He'd been wondering where it came from when a beautiful freylen buck leaped into his path. He saw it as if in slow motion—the dark tan of its fur, the pitch-black rings around its brown eyes. His mind screamed, unified by a single thought—protect Eternity!

He felt the buck's neck break. Knew he'd killed it even before he hit the ground, but it didn't matter. It was just a deer after all, and he'd kill man and beast alike if it meant pleasing Gallow.

But then he saw the dead buck. Saw the bone sticking out of its neck like an accusatory finger, and suddenly he remembered his oath. He'd sworn he wouldn't kill any innocents—and yet he'd broken that promise time and again. The buck was only the latest in an ever-growing list.

"Forgive me," he whispered, trailing a hand down the deer's neck. Its only crime was being in the wrong place at the wrong time—it was probably fleeing the polluted land like everyone else. Yet he'd killed it. "I am… I am so sorry."

Eternity reached out and took his hand, squeezing it gently.

The feel of her bare skin against his jolted something alive in Lazander. A rush of heat left him dizzy. Suddenly he could feel the weight of his dark armor, feel the ground beneath his knees. He was *himself* again.

"Lazander? Are you all right?" Eternity asked.

He was careful to keep quiet, eyes roving as he looked for the small, child-like form of Gallow. Had the god noticed he'd broken free? That his mind was his own again? Even if Gallow hadn't, he knew he only had seconds. He couldn't save himself, the God of Judgment was too strong, but maybe he could save Eternity. The thought calmed him—if she was safe, nothing else mattered. If she was safe, he could die happy—no matter what Gallow did to him.

"Run, Eternity," he said quickly. "Gallow is—" an icy cold hand touched his cheek. *No, no, no—*

Lazander blinked in confusion, clutching his head. "Oof," he said with a smile. "Must have hit my head harder than I thought. What was I saying?"

Eternity stared at him, something akin to fear in her eyes, and he wondered what the matter was when Malik appeared, a blur of murderous darkness.

"What in the blazes are you *doing?*" he roared. A vein throbbed in his neck. "Are you seriously abandoning your mission to pet a *dumb dead animal?*"

"Lazander protected me when we struck it. He hit his head badly enough to split a *tree,* and he needs a moment," Eternity said quickly, her eyes skirting to Lazander nervously.

The Champion's eyes darkened, and he raised his leg. For a wild moment Lazander thought he was going to *kick* Eternity, but the Champion brought it down on the deer's head. Again. And again.

"No!" Eternity screamed. "You beast, what are you *doing?*"

Malik kept stomping, cracking the buck's skull, its blood and brains spilling onto the ground. "Don't you idiots get it? Everyone in this world is about to die!" He reached down, and to Lazander's horror the man scooped up a handful of remains, thrusting them in his face. "This—this is what every human is going to look like once Calamity is done! But no—the stupid, bleeding-heart animal lover is worried about a shekkin' *deer!* Gallow should have let you die along with the muscle-head and the mage, you thick-skulled, empty-headed—"

Whatever he was about to say was lost because the Champion was thrown through the air, as if by magic.

\*\*\*

Malik's body hit a tree, then another, and another—and kept going. Eternity didn't use Gallow's power, but then she didn't need to—she'd been a prodigy as a mage long before she'd been Chosen. And it was past time Malik was reminded of that.

The Champion struck the scarlet sunder that had brought Lazander to a halt. The tree shook as an invisible force pressed him against it, cracks spiraling outward. Fist outstretched before her like a weapon, Eternity relaxed her hand.

Malik hit the ground in a boneless heap, groaning.

"Argh, are you *insane?* You shekkin—" was all he managed before he crashed into the dirt. Every time he tried to speak, she slammed him into the ground with the force of a mountain until all he could do was emit a dull rasping sound.

The old Eternity would never have done this—she'd probably have vomited at the very thought. But the fear in Lazander's eyes and the hate in Malik's had come together... and broken something in her.

"As Gallow's Chosen," she said, walking toward the Champion, a mantle of calm settling around her shoulders. "I am enacting a new rule. Henceforth you will speak to both Lazander and me with respect, or—" she clenched her fist, and the Champion was jerked upright by invisible hands, "—you and I will have a much longer chat. One involving your thick skull and the largest mountain I can find."

Malik's nostrils flared, outrage and fear battling for position. Outrage won. "This is why you're a laughingstock," he spat. "Everyone in the Gallowed Temple talks about it. How hard it is for you to wield Gallow's powers. How much you *bleed*. How you shirk your duty at the slightest—"

Eternity snapped her fingers, driving him so hard into the ground, his face was buried inches deep in the forest floor. She knew he couldn't breathe, but she still held him there. Waited until he waved a frantic hand to release him. The once proud and immaculate champion lay panting, covered from head to toe in filth. Twigs and bits of moss stuck to his beard, and the silver bead at the end was long gone. This time, he was wisely silent.

"I am the only Chosen you have," she said. "I know what is at stake, and that the odds are stacked against us. But what good is saving the world if we lose our kindness along the way? Or worse—our very humanity?"

She knew he didn't agree. There was no one he wouldn't hurt, kill, or maim to fulfil his duty. Eternity thought he sometimes went too far but felt it was Gallow's place to temper him, not hers. But if the God of Judgment wouldn't step in, then *she* would.

Malik glared at her, his entire body vibrating with rage, and she knew he was considering hitting her. Part of her hoped he would. Instead he took a long, gurgling snort and spat on the ground at her feet.

Knowing it was a sign of defeat, she chose to ignore it. "Second rule," she said, raising her finger. "Gallow has always fed us information piecemeal as a... security measure. This ends now. We will share *everything* Gallow tells us, and if the God of Judgment takes issue with that, he can speak to me himself. *Third*," a rush of pure adrenaline made her feel like she was floating. It was like another person had taken over her body—someone who was strong and brave. Someone who *liked* who she was. "If you ever, *ever*, speak poorly about Gabriel and Marito again, I will cut you down—this world be *damned*."

The words were blasphemous, but she didn't care. She'd seen a side to the Champions she didn't like. Saw how they interpreted Gallow's orders in the cruelest way possible. And worse… realized her god never stopped them.

"Are we clear, *Malik?*" Eternity said, his name a curse on her lips.

The Champion stared at her, and she knew that if Calamity didn't kill her for this, Malik would. *Let them try,* a new vicious part of her thought.

"We need to go," he said, turning away. "Lazander, are you ready?"

"Ah…" the red-haired Champion looked between the two of them like a startled lamb. His eyes settled on Eternity, and he nodded so quickly, she almost smiled. "Yes."

"Good," was all Malik said before he was gone, the whisper of his cloak the only sign he'd even been there.

Silence stretched between Lazander and Eternity. She felt the sudden urge to apologize but quashed it. "Would you mind…"

"Of course," he said, lifting her into his arms. He set off at a run, and it wasn't long before they saw Malik in the distance—who somehow made his anger known even as a blur against the horizon.

"You shouldn't have done that," Lazander said after almost an hour on the road. "He was right. I shouldn't have stopped, nor should I have gotten so upset over a deer. I'm a poor excuse for a Champion, and I owe—"

Whatever he was about to say next was cut off by the hand Eternity placed against his cheek. "You are one of the best people I have ever met, Sir Lazander Evercroft of Freley. And *I* have been a poor excuse for a Chosen, no—for a *friend*—for letting Malik treat you like that. For letting him treat either of us as lesser."

A sigh ran through Lazander's body, and he slowed slightly, the world around them a loose sketch as they raced through it at superhuman speed. He jumped over a fallen tree, whispering, "Thank you, Eternity. Thank you for seeing me."

Her heart swelled with pride, but she couldn't shake what he'd said to her by the fallen deer.

*"Run."*

## Chapter Forty

Zara the Fury lounged in the branches of a tree, one clawed foot dangling. While her posture was the image of someone calm and relaxed, the intensity with which she stared at the Ivory Keep was anything but. The center of power of the Najar, Navaros' ruling family, was a gigantic fortress nestled halfway up a mountain. Its iconic marble towers punched through the clouds, casting a long shadow on the only road that led to the Keep, a winding path several horse carts wide that took you to the equally gigantic gates.

This was not the Fury's first visit. She'd been here months ago, back when she was still a slave to Magnus and his sycophantic dedication to the Tyrant. In the dead of night she'd seen little, staying only long enough to knock Eternity unconscious and flee—the Chosen thrown over her shoulder like luggage. Now, every step Zara took toward the Keep sharpened the memory of the woman she used to be. The woman she'd still be if Teema hadn't saved her.

It was why Zara had wanted nothing more than to get in and out of the Keep as quickly as possible, Thaddeus in hand. But her plan hadn't been met with the joyous approval she'd expected.

"You cannot be serious," Lukas had said, two fingers to his temple.

"I am always serious, cub. We have no time to skulk in shadows. I say we make use of my wings, land in the very heart of the Keep, and demand Thaddeus be brought to us."

"And when they inevitably attack us?"

"We keep killing until they see sense."

Both Teema and Lukas shot the idea down. Lukas may or may not have muttered the words "suicidal" and "psychopath" more than once, but Teema was quick to say Zara had misheard. And so the Fury was left hiding in a godsforsaken tree like a common thief while Lukas went in alone. Apparently she couldn't be "trusted" not to start a fight.

Since she'd last been, the Keep had gone from an imposing monument to a damn fortress. When she'd kidnapped Eternity all that stood in her way was a sturdy but climbable gate and a handful of bored guards. Now heavily armored men and women patrolled the walls, eyes front and alert. A checkpoint manned by no less than ten guards barricaded the front gate where people were lined up in neat rows, slips of paper in hand. Those who presented passes were let in while everyone else was subject to an interrogation that usually left them dumped in the grass, their belongings scattered around them.

Zara begrudgingly admitted it was good Lukas was scouting the Keep and not her—had she been doing the talking, the guards would be left without spines.

*"They certainly look ready for war,"* Teema commented, and on the surface, Zara agreed. Trenches had been dug by the border of the outermost walls, with more in progress. Trees were cut down, their tips sharpened to deadly spikes, then hammered deep—each a deathtrap. And yet…

*The guards on the southern and eastern wall have at least three blind spots in their patrol patterns, while those at the front gates have dark shadows under their eyes. Look—one just yawned,* Zara said, sending the thought to Teema. While she felt it was ridiculous she'd been reduced to hiding in a tree, she wasn't stupid. Speaking aloud was a surefire way to be spotted.

*"You're right,"* Teema said. *"Damn, they look exhausted. Long shifts?"*

*Perhaps, or…* she narrowed her eyes when a woman returned to guard duty with wet hair and a clean uniform—she'd been gone less than an hour. With a start, Zara realized that almost none of the guards had changed since last night.

*They don't have enough people to protect the Keep.*

*"Wait, what?"* Teema said, her fear coming through like ice. *"But the Keep must be big enough to house hundreds if not thousands of people. Why don't they have enough—"*

"Thief!"

At the cry, Zara's gaze drifted to the large patch of scuffed grass that stretched between the fortress and the road. Usually empty but for a visiting market, a passing theater troupe, or even the occasional circus, it was now filled to the brim with people young and old, rich and poor—all piled atop one another.

"Thief!" a man in rags yelled again, pointing at another. "He stole my food! Guards? Guards!"

But the guards at the gate did nothing—not even when the accused drove a fist into the man's stomach and left him gasping on the ground—openly chewing the bread he'd stolen as he walked away.

"*Those poor people...*" Teema whispered, and Zara grimaced. She'd been trying not to look at them for the girl's sake.

*War costs more than lives, Teema,* Zara said. *Surely you have such things back in your world?*

"*Yes, but... but there's so many of them—that family has a single blanket between them. And that woman is sleeping standing up! On a rock!*"

*Do not lose sight of our goal, Teema,* Zara said sharply, glancing back at the road.

More people arrived every hour, the hope in their eyes dying when they saw the tents and rags and smelled the potent mix of fear and desperation. They clutched their meager belongings, and Zara didn't need to read minds to see them all wonder the same thing—what will happen to me?

The Fury turned away, eyes back on the Keep. *We are here to find a crack in Calamity's armor. You cannot concern yourself with every weeping human,* she said, trying and failing to soften her tone.

Teema fell silent. Feeling guilty, Zara was about to change the subject when a shout cut her off. Flattening herself against the trunk, she blended seamlessly with the shadows of the thick foliage, waiting for cries about a clawed woman hiding in a tree.

A scream was added to the shout. Then another. But they didn't come from outside—they came from inside the *Keep*.

"Lukas," Zara growled aloud.

"*It might not be him?*" Teema said, hopefully.

*Hmph. And the sky is not blue.*

A mighty crash came from the gates. Zara spotted no less than two helmets and shields go flying a split second before a huge beast with six legs and thick fur came charging out, knocking guards aside like wheat in the wind.

Teema sighed with relief when the trampled stirred, a mess of limbs and groans. Zara rolled her eyes. The cub had *one* job.

A quick headcount revealed that roughly twenty armed guards and four humans in purple robes were chasing Lukas—mages, Zara guessed. No one else would wear something so ridiculous. The only reason the cub hadn't been burned, frozen, or skewered by lightning was the absolute chaos he left in his wake and a significant dose of luck—neither of which would last for long.

He skidded to a halt at the edge of the refugee camp. People were screaming and running, some throwing whatever they had in their hands—Zara watched, bemused as Lukas was pelted with cheese, a wooden spoon, and what looked like a nightdress. The green was so crowded that if he kept running, he'd risk trampling the refugees or knocking them off the mountain—where a swift, brutal death awaited. With an unsure whine Lukas shuffled, struggling to turn his huge molger body around as the mob finally caught up to him. Guards surrounded him on all sides, shields up while the mages skittered the edges—their hands glowing with magic.

"Zara..." Teema asked tentatively. *"Maybe you should, I don't know,* go help him?"

The Fury sighed but swung her leg over the branch she lounged on. She landed on the balls of her feet to a host of screams—a family had been trying to hide under her tree. Zara ignored them, picking up speed as she ran through the camp, knocking aside pots and bedrolls.

*"Could you please not destroy what little these people have left?"* Teema asked, her voice strained.

Zara was about to ask what did it matter, but Teema's annoyance thrummed in her mind. With a louder, more dramatic sigh, Zara slapped a clawed hand on a cowering man, using him as momentum to leap over the crowd. There were screams and the distinct scent of urine as someone relieved themselves.

*"Please don't rip out the soldiers' spines, castrate the mages, or promise to bathe in the blood of their ancestors,"* Teema said quickly. *"Oh, and don't kill one of them as an 'example.' That's not what good guys do."*

*I had no idea there were so many rules,* Zara huffed. *No wonder Player Two and Lazander left the Gilded. Being a hero is drier than a grit-shark's spit.*

*"That's not why... right, think of this as a chance to use some of your new abilities— the non-lethal ones!"* Teema hurried to add, but Zara was already smiling fiercely.

It was Teema's turn to sigh.

## Chapter Forty-One

*Monstrous Strength Activated* flashed before Zara's eyes. With my System upgrade, we didn't have to speak to use our abilities, but I almost wished we still did. It might have given the poor mage Zara crept up on some warning. Grinning, she drove her foot in-between his legs, lifting him bodily into the air.

He didn't shout. Didn't scream. He just collapsed in a tight ball, his hands gripping his crotch like his life depended on it.

*"What?"* Zara asked, grabbing a startled guard and casually throwing the woman over her shoulder. *"You said non-lethal."*

"Could we not leave them broken and traumatized?" I asked, wincing when a guard made the mistake of charging her, his sword held high. She swung at him in a haymaker, catching him in the throat—he hit the ground so hard, I could *feel* his painful wheeze from here.

*"You have too many rules, Teema. What is the point in battle if not to enjoy it?"*

Chaos erupted as Zara knocked guards and mages aside like bowling pins.

I mentally apologized to the two she grabbed—her claws digging into the back of their helmets—and slammed together, grinning fiercely when they collapsed. Zara was enjoying this *far* too much, but it was working—she was only a few feet from Lukas now.

The sound of a horn, low and commanding, cut through the cries of the woman Zara pinned by the throat. The hair on the back of my head rose. What few guards still stood fled, some even dropping their weapons. The guard under Zara's knee squirmed, and the Fury released her, Zara's confusion matching my own when the woman ran like ripperbacks snapped at her heels. Even the mages abandoned their spells, fleeing with the rest.

"I don't like this, Zara," I whispered, my instincts cycling between fight or flee. I didn't have to ask what Zara would choose.

The Fury didn't answer. To her right a mage stumbled to his feet, a hand to his temple. When he spotted Zara staring down at him, eyebrow raised, his hands glowed with a blue light. "In the n-name of Navaros, I order you to—"

Her hand shot out, gripping his throat so hard his eyes rolled into the back of his head. "Lukas—*come here*," Zara called.

The molger stood, blinking owlishly in the sun—I'd forgotten molger eyes were meant for the dark—and gave a high-pitched bark of joy when he saw her, trundling toward her on six legs.

With a loud sigh, Zara fixed her face in a glare, but I felt her eyes scanning him, relief flooding her body when she saw he wasn't hurt. She was fonder of him than she'd ever admit—though you wouldn't guess it by the tone she took.

"Do not smile at me, cub," she snapped. The mage she held groaned, weakly raising a glowing hand. Zara headbutted him, blood bursting from his nose as he fell limp in her hands. "You had one job—get in, discover Thaddeus' whereabouts, and get out. Now all of the Keep is upon us."

Lukas bowed his head, tiny ears dropping.

"He didn't mean to," I said, wishing he could hear me. But only Zara could when I was in the darkness. "Go easy on him."

She huffed, unceremoniously dumping the mage on the ground. A creak cut through the air, the metal of the Keep's massive doors shuddering as they fully opened. The clip of hooves followed, the sound building to a threatening crescendo.

The guards who'd surrounded Lukas were clumsy and uncoordinated, tripping over each other as they fought both their own fear and the massive six-legged molger they faced. But the men and women who came charging out on horseback, their armor polished to a shine, weren't guards.

They were *soldiers*.

Lukas whined, shuffling back as they charged us, but Zara rested a hand on his shoulder—gently holding him in place. Though no order was given, the soldiers split with the deftness of a river, forming a tight circle around us. The guards from earlier had clearly been trying the same maneuver, but it was like comparing a toddler's tumble to a gymnast's backflip. They raced around us at speed, the gold and red of their armor a blur, their horses not even flinching at the gigantic beast in the center. Lukas ducked his head, trying to make himself smaller. Zara, on the other hand, stood relaxed and at ease as she wondered which of the humans would be stupid enough to attack first.

"Zara!" I said. "Stop picking spots in their armor where it would be easy to gut them. We're here to help these people, not *kill* them."

A spearman raised his weapon and threw it at Zara with deadly aim.

**Steel Skin Activated.**

Zara's flesh didn't shudder like it did when she shapeshifted. She simply had nut-brown skin one second, the next she was covered in a thick layer of metal harder than stone or blade—or so the System promised. It was the first ability I'd chosen for her using Void Mana, knowing she'd love it.

I'd been right.

Zara hadn't tried or tested *Steel Skin*, but she didn't even flinch when the spear hit her square in the chest. There was a loud crack as the wood splintered. It fell to the ground, the tip snapping off from the force.

The Fury smiled, and though the soldiers were too well-trained to show any reaction, I felt the atmosphere change, becoming electric with tension. An arrow leaped from somewhere in the blur of horses.

**Lightning Step Activated.**

Zara vanished with a crackle of lightning, appearing at Lukas' back a split second later, catching the arrow mid-flight. A second came, then a third. She caught every single one, making a show of raising them above her head—and snapping them in two.

"Zara, you're doing an amazing job of scaring the crap out of them," I said, "but I don't think this is going to endear them to us anytime soon."

*"You talk. I fight,"* was her only answer.

Another spearman raised his weapon, but he leaned too far forward—giving Zara the opening she needed.

**Lightning Step Activated.**

She appeared in front of him, one hand yanking the spear out of his grasp, the other gripping him by the forearm. His horse reared, terrified—breaking the perfect ring that circled us. Orders were barked, and reins were pulled, but Zara paid them no mind. She tossed the spearman behind her. A crack of bone sounded when he hit the dirt. The man groaned, clutching his shoulder—only to look up and see the Fury grinning down at him.

She grabbed him by the chest plate, hefting him high into the air.

At some unseen signal soldiers and horses alike came to a dead stop. Hooves pawed the ground, their hot breath turning to steam in the cold of the coming dusk. Lukas whined nervously.

"Zara..." I said.

*"Trust me, Teema, as I trust you,"* she said. I shut up, growing more nervous as I wondered what she was going to do. The spearman kicked the air, slapping at every bit of Zara he could reach—she barely felt it.

"Hostages won't work," came a woman's stern voice. A red streak marked the side of her golden helmet. It was so shiny, Zara could see her warped reflection in it. "Unhand him or risk the full wrath of Navaros."

"If I wanted you dead, your heads would be rolling on the ground, human," Zara said calmly. The spearman groaned, clutching his injured arm. From the way it hung limply, he must have dislocated it when he fell.

### *Bloodied Restoration Activated.*

There was a loud pop, and Zara hissed when her free arm shot out of its socket. The soldier gasped, lifting his once injured arm up in shock. He flexed his fingers, examining his newly healed limb with a look of fear and astonishment.

In Zara's mind, she gently released the man. What she actually did was dump him on the ground. He stumbled but wasted no time running to join his fellow soldiers. Zara gripped her now dislocated shoulder, took a breath, and slammed it back into place with a vicious twist. "I took on your man's injury, making it my own," she announced, her voice free of the pain I knew she felt. "And in so doing, healed him. I will do the same for anyone else I have hurt, though I am unsure how I will fare with the testicles I crushed. It will be... an interesting experience at least."

The woman with the red-marked helmet looked from Zara to Lukas and then back to the once-injured soldier. She whispered to him, and I saw him nod—holding up his hand and turning it in the light.

I held my breath when she flicked open her visor, blue eyes meeting Zara's. "Name?"

*Crap*, I thought. The second they heard it, they'd kill us. Zara the Fury was a known "accomplice" of Magnus.

"My name is meaningless," Zara replied, and the soldiers stiffened. That wasn't the answer they were looking for. "What matters is my purpose—for I have come here, *we* have come here," she said, gesturing to Lukas, who puffed out his chest proudly, "to put an end to the Tyrant and his machinations. Regardless of what you decide today, we will stand against the dark god. We are here to offer you the chance to do so as allies."

"Sending your beast to attack us is a strange way to suggest an alliance," the woman said, eyes on Lukas.

Zara elbowed him, and the massive falsling bent his head, his flesh turning to wet clay. I'd seen it a hundred times, but the soldiers hadn't. There were gasps as fur slipped back into skin and his spine broke, becoming human in seconds.

"Bloody skin-stealer…"

"… eat babies, my cousin swore…"

"… bring disease. That's what happened to a village out by Moonvale…"

The woman ceased the soldiers' whispers with a glare, but if I'd heard them, I knew Lukas and Zara had too. She didn't react, but as Lukas stood before them, naked and human once more, I could see him fighting to smile, one eye twitching.

"Hello!" he said with forced cheer, his hand raised in greeting. "It turns out your dogs could smell something was up with me, which meant your guards tried to question me, and I, uh, may or may not have panicked."

Zara rolled her eyes.

The leader looked from Lukas to Zara. My heart sank when she snapped her visor down. "The king's orders were clear—kill non-humans on sight. Attack!"

"Thaddeus," Lukas yelled, "we're looking for Thaddeus! We need—*shek*." A sword struck where his head had been a split second before, but he was already gone, his body elongating into the pitch-black of his vaxion form.

Zara growled, the bones in her back breaking as she prepared to shift into her voidbeast, but a voice rang out, cutting through the chaos.

"Stop!"

The soldiers froze, as did Lukas, who was in the middle of pinning a solider to the ground with his huge paws.

A woman in her late fifties stumbled forward, leaning heavily on a cane. She walked with a strange swinging motion. My eyes were drawn to the layers of copper that covered her right leg and the pincers that served as her hand on the same side. While she might have physically looked frail, the steel in her eyes could have split stone.

"My queen? My queen, you cannot be here! Someone escort Queen Firanta back to her—"

"Priscilla, I'm sure you're not ordering me about in my own kingdom, now are you?" the queen called. She was dressed in a simple navy gown, the edges not quite touching her ankles. Her hair was swept back in a rich red scarf, and she wore no jewelry or any adornment that might have hinted at the fact that she was a *queen*. A real-life queen, standing there, in the flesh. Just being near her made me want to stand up straighter.

*"This is your arena,"* Zara said. *"If it were up to me, I would take the feeble woman and use her as leverage. But I do not have to ask to know you would not approve."*

Zara blinked, but I was ready this time. One second I was staring at the world through Zara's eyes, the next I was in her body, soil shifting under my bare feet, the scent of unwashed bodies and fear making my nose flare. I belatedly realized the refugees outside weren't the only ones starving as I took in the gaunt cheeks and shadowed eyes of the soldiers.

I bowed, keeping my head low despite Zara's growl. She hated many things, but bowing to *anyone* was very high up on the list.

"I apologize for the disruption," I said. "If Etern—if Lady Eternity is here, she can vouch for me. We've traveled from Moonvale where the dark god has already harmed my people—the vaxion."

A murmur went through the crowd at this, and I glanced out of the corner of my eye to see the refugees and even some of the guards Zara had fought earlier creeping closer. I almost smiled. It didn't matter what planet I was on it seemed, all people were all the same—they *loved* a front row seat to drama.

"We're not the monsters you warn children about," I called, raising my voice, the soldier's venomous whispers fresh in my mind. "We're just people—people who want to live safe and happy lives just as much as you do. Who want to protect this world from the Tyrant—an enemy who threatens each and every one of us."

The green was silent, refugees, soldiers, and guards alike watching me. Hundreds of people hung on my every word, but I felt no fear. Before I came to this world, being the center of attention terrified me. Now it was a relief—if they were listening to me, that meant they weren't stabbing me.

"You said you were here for someone—Thaddeus," the queen called, and my heart leaped. "What need have you of my dog? If it's for a game of fetch, I fear he's six-feet under these days."

The flutter of hope I'd felt vanished—we'd come all this way for a dead dog. My mind whispered that I'd chosen wrong, that we should have gone after Ga instead, but I shoved the thought away. Zara's approach to life, while extreme, was at times helpful—deal with what's directly in front of you, and ignore the rest.

"I asked you a question young lady. Why are you looking for Thaddeus?" the queen asked, her tone sharp. While Zara was highly amused at being called a "young lady," I knew the queen wasn't going to ask again. I was about to lie, but something about the look in her eyes made me choose honesty.

"The goddess Ravenna sent us. I… I don't know why," I said, hoping and praying my gamble would pay off. "She just told us we had to keep him away from the Tyrant. From *Calamity*."

Silence. Horses pawed the ground impatiently, their riders looking at each other with bemusement—they clearly thought me insane. My heart sank.

"Bring them inside," the queen announced.

"My queen!" the female soldier protested. "The king—"

"Isn't here—I am. You—the vaxion boy," the queen said, gesturing to Lukas with her cane.

The look of panic on his vaxion face was almost funny.

"Turn human again, you're scaring the horses… and suffocating the poor woman you're standing on."

Lukas yelped, jumping back—the women at his feet coughing heavily. He bowed, wincing in apology.

"*See?*" Zara said. "*You talk. I fight.*"

We walked into the Ivory Keep flanked by no less than thirty soldiers who gripped their weapons tightly, clearly unhappy.

"Oh," the queen called, snapping her fingers. "And get the boy some pants."

## Chapter Forty-Two

It took time for Queen Firanta to find Thaddeus' body. Longer still to get everyone to stop fussing about her like clucking hens when she emerged from her bedchambers for the first time in weeks, freshly washed, cane in hand, and barking orders like she'd never left.

The king was half a day east, where shadow-fiends and the wallow-tail pressed on Navaros' borders—despite being beaten back from the south only days ago. Gaps were forming in their defenses—the king lacked the manpower to protect them on all sides, and Freyley and Evergarden were busy defending their own kingdoms. He'd left behind three hundred soldiers to defend the Keep in case of an attack, but with the bodies piling up day in, day out—the wallow-tail alone had claimed eighty of Navaros' army just this week—Firanta had ordered more and more to join Leon at the border.

She'd sent another hundred the night before, leaving the Keep stripped to the very bones, but they had no choice—if she hadn't spent all this time lying in bed feeling *sorry* for herself, she could have organized aid from the dwarves to the east or the merchants of Summertide in the south. But it was too late—neither would get to Navaros before the month was out. And if her folly meant there were nights when she herself had to patrol the walls, much to the shock of the Keep, then so be it.

But she wasn't thinking about failing borders, the refugees they didn't have the stocks to feed, or the growing pile of dead the Tyrant's forces had claimed. No, as she stood in the crypts beneath the Gallowed Temple, all she could think was—"I'm glad Leon isn't here."

If he was, she'd have slapped him.

When Leon had reassured her that he'd "hidden" Thaddeus, she'd expected to find his body in one of their many magical vaults or perhaps with the palace mages. Somewhere practical. Somewhere her former spymaster and friend would be *safe*.

Instead she was in a part of the crypts so ancient, the scent of dust and decay threatened to choke her lungs—she had to press a handkerchief over her mouth just to *breathe*. In front of her stood a freshly bricked wall that, for all intents and purposes, looked like any other repair of an older tomb. The faded plaque underneath read "King Astion of Navaros, ruler from the 11th year of the Windborn Era to the 20th year of the Crescent Hallow. A traitor and coward, his arrogance and greed were almost the ruin of Navaros."

Firanta might have been master of the barbed word, but apparently her husband could also hurl an insult when he wanted to. Leon wasn't a jealous man—except when it came to the spymaster. He'd never been fond of how much time she and Thaddeus spent together, and she knew he blamed the spymaster for her injuries. But sticking her friend in the tomb of a *traitor* was too far. When the king returned from the border, she hoped for his sake he wasn't hurt—because the tongue-lashing she was going to give him would leave him bedridden for a *week*.

She knocked her cane against the newly laid brick harder than needed as she searched for a weak spot. It would be only a matter of time before the king discovered she'd been down here, but nothing would bring him back quicker than hearing she'd cracked open the tomb to pilfer Thaddeus' corpse—he'd think her mad. But how else was she going to get to Thaddeus' body? And how could she explain even a tenth of the insane things he'd told her?

After seemingly endless stairs, Firanta made it back up to the Keep's outer courtyard, trying to ignore how often she needed to take a break now. But the clash of swords and shouts gave her a burst of speed, and she limped to the main gate where she caught flashes of red and gold armor executing a pincer formation. Despite her best efforts, she couldn't see who the soldiers surrounded, until a gap appeared—revealing a naked man and woman who should be dead.

"Thaddeus! We're looking for Thaddeus!" the man yelled.

Firanta almost smiled.

She'd never been a believer in destiny—she was the type to forge her own path. But as she locked eyes with Zara the Fury, she wondered if perhaps there wasn't something to the fickle idea of fate.

\*\*\*

As Malik, Lazander, and Eternity raced to Moonvale, a thought niggled in the back of her mind—one that kept coming up again and again. The land was a sea of death, polluted by the sickness of the shadow-fiends. But other than on a beach in Freyley they'd seen none of the Tyrant's servants. Where *were* they?

She got her answer when they crossed Freyley's border, Moonvale and its mountains a blue smudge in the distance. A writhing mass of shadows was laid out before them, stretching endlessly into the horizon, their claws twitching with anticipation—*shadow-fiends*. They'd been here all this time—waiting for her.

With a roar, Malik took out three with a single swing of his axe, diving recklessly into a pack of six. Eternity was hot on his heels, her hands thrumming with Gallow's magic.

**"You have been judged. And you have been found wanting,"** she yelled, a sphere of shadow gathering in her hands. It barely had time to form before she flung it outward, splitting two shadow-fiends in half, their bodies collapsing mere feet from Malik. But four more leaped for him, digging vicious claws into his back—the gaping holes in their chests throbbing with the need to clamp down on the Champion's head and drag him to the Void.

Malik cried out, this time in pain. Eternity gritted her teeth and decided now was not the time to be careful. Clenching her fist, she ignored the burst of fire in her skull as she called back the darkness she'd just thrown. It shuddered, then shot back toward her like a whip, slicing through shadow-fiends like a blade through cream—freeing Malik.

The Champion was on his feet in an instant, the wounds in his back already closing. He gave Eternity a grudging nod of thanks, then buried his axe in the neck of another fiend. It moaned, a low, ghastly sound of pain and promise that made Eternity shudder. They'd killed so many, but the monsters just kept *coming*.

Lazander's sword was a blur of silver as it danced around him, killing a fourth, a fifth, a *sixth* shadow-fiend before he was forced to pull back, panting hard. They must have killed over a hundred between them, but at least a hundred more remained, circling Eternity, Malik, and Lazander like wolves. The monsters darted in and out, forcing them to stand back-to-back.

And then the dark beasts froze.

They stood, swaying like leaves in an autumn wind, heads cocked as if listening. One moaned, an ungodly noise that wormed its way into the skull like an insect, and the others joined it. It took everything Eternity had not to slap her hands over her ears and scream—anything to block out the noise.

"What are they doing?" Lazander shouted, struggling to be heard.

"I know not, but whatever it is, I do not like it," Eternity replied.

Then the shadow-fiends turned… and fled. They ran in a long, undulating row of darkness, not even glancing back. Eternity froze alongside the Champions, unable to believe they were still alive.

"They had us *pinned*," Lazander said, his sword still held high. "Why let us go? Where are they—wait. By Gallow's grace, look! They're heading west. Navaros lies only hours away!"

"Never mind that," Malik barked, sheathing his axe. "Eternity—to the air. We'll be at Moonvale in the next hour if we push it!"

Eternity's eyes stayed on the fleeing shadow-fiends for only a second before she took off at speed, her eyes streaming. The plan was simple—she would go over the Moonvale Mountains while the Champions went *through* them. It was risky and left her alone and exposed, but they didn't have time. The sun dipped past the horizon, the sky a deep, foreboding orange that made Eternity's heart pound. They would stop Gaj, they had to, they—

Far off in the distance, nestled in the blue smudge of Moonvale, a spark of red light appeared. It grew and grew, washing the sky in a bloody, crimson glow.

"No!" Eternity shouted.

They were too late.

A rush of power bloomed, Gallow's presence spreading like wings as he gripped her. Her body hung mid-air, frozen, while her mind stood in the very heart of Moonvale—the beautiful, terrifying corner of Navaros the vaxion called home. Though she'd been alive for over a century, Eternity had never set foot in the reclusive falsling's domain. But she'd heard plenty of stories about the colossal floating waterstones, the pink lumbar trees, and the deep blue of the towering mountains. She'd always hoped she'd see it for herself one day.

She never would.

Moonvale split in two, the waterstones of legend crashing to the ground, all magic and life ripped from the land as a red wound in the sky greedily fed—demanding every last drop. With an explosive burst, the rift tore open... and *something* stepped through.

What followed was a flurry of images—a skull, huge and bloodied, Player Two, his head thrown back as he laughed, and then Eternity had to screw her eyes shut. She was dimly aware that she was falling, her senses and magic overwhelmed by the barrage of images. And then Lazander's arms were wrapped around her, holding her close.

In the distance red light engulfed Moonvale, swallowing it whole.

"Gaj," she whispered, tears streaming. "Player Two summoned Gaj."

Malik was by her side a second later, hands in his hair. "Shek!" he roared. *"Shek, shek, shek!"*

Teeth gritted like an animal in pain, he buried his axe in the dirt, looking deranged. Eternity waited for him to blame her—for holding them up, for wasting their time, but he said nothing. Perhaps even he knew they were never going to make it.

Because Gallow had sent them to the wrong place.

Her heart pounded at the treacherous thought, but she couldn't deny it anymore. She'd heard the panic in the god's voice when he'd ordered them back to Moonvale—the God of Judgment had made a *mistake*. A mistake that might cost them everything.

"This isn't over, brother," Lazander said, carefully setting Eternity down. "We *will* stop Gaj. Do not lose faith."

Malik fell to his knees. "We failed. We failed Gallow."

Eternity had never heard him sound so broken. To her surprise, she felt a twist of pity for the Champion, but anger was hot on its heels. He'd driven them at a breakneck pace, been nothing but cruel and spiteful the entire journey, and now he was going to give up? Just like that? No—Eternity wouldn't give him that luxury.

"Get up," she said. "The city of Freyley is closest to Moonvale. We need to stop Gaj before she reaches it."

Malik shook his head, mumbling to himself.

Eternity fought not to slap him.

"… two of us…" Malik whispered, barely coherent, "… and a Chosen who bleeds like a stuck pig!" He raised his head, eyes wide. "We can't do it… we can't kill Gaj. Don't you get it—we've *lost*. The whole damn world is *dead*."

"Why is he so afraid of Gaj?" Lazander asked quietly. There was no way Malik hadn't heard him, but the Champion wasn't listening. He knelt in the dirt, trembling.

"Do you remember how I said it was too soon for the dead to rise?" Eternity asked, fighting to keep her voice calm and factual—only her shaking hands betrayed her fear. "When the Tyrant had all but consumed the world, there were tales of armies of the dead who served his every whim. He had such power because of—"

**"GAJ.**

**"KILL GAJ."**

Malik, Lazander and Eternity froze—their eyes on the beacon of crimson that was once Moonvale. Gallow's orders could be cryptic at times, but this left no room for interpretation.

"Gaj makes the dead rise…" Eternity whispered as Malik forced himself to his feet, his skin deathly pale, his hands gripping his axe like a life buoy. "Because she *is* death."

\*\*\*

Player Two stood on top of the world—quite literally. The wind battered him, and he had to dig his fingers into Gaj's skull to stop from falling, cracking bone—but the giant didn't mind. Couldn't even if she'd wanted to. He risked a glance down, the land below so far away the trees were flecks of paint on a canvas. Clouds drifted past them, every step slow and stilted—Gaj for all her size and strength was not a woman who rushed, but Player Two didn't mind. He relished how she walked, joy bursting in his chest when she brought her foot down—the earth splitting beneath her, a giant among ants, a lion to mice. Being this close to her and feeling Calamity's power pulse through her bones was nothing short of *intoxicating*.

They were going to win. It was written in the stars, after all.

"There," Player Two called, pointing off to the right. A cluster of huts and a curl of smoke stood out against the barren landscape. Player Two grinned. His shadow-fiends had torn through the area hours ago, running to cut off Eternity and her thralls, yet someone had been stupid enough to stay behind.

Lucky him.

Gaj said nothing at his command but then she never did—you needed a tongue to speak. Her huge body creaked as she turned, a tower of death and destruction headed straight for the small village. He giggled like a child when tiny figures fled one of the mud huts, the idiots holding hands like a beautiful, blood-filled daisy chain. If they'd all split up there was a chance one, maybe two would get away.

Alas.

Player Two said nothing. He didn't need to—Gaj knew what to do.

She raised a mighty foot. It hung in the air for a long moment, shadow blotting out the sun. Player Two couldn't hear the humans from this high up, but as Gaj brought her foot down, annihilating houses, trees, flesh, and bone in a tidal wave of force, he hoped they died screaming.

With a whoop of laughter, he slapped Gaj's skull. "Beautiful as always, my dear!"

Calamity's lieutenant wordlessly turned, resuming her long, aching steps.

Player Two sat down, choosing a sharpened piece of bone to lean against as he looked out at Calamity's new kingdom. On his master's orders he'd run to the village of Emerald on the coast for Freyley. Blade drawn, shadow-fiends at his back, he'd readied himself to summon Gaj—only for Calamity to give him new orders.

Confused, Player Two followed his master's words to the letter—commanding the shadow-fiends to stand watch until they sensed Eternity's stink on the wind. It was only when Calamity gifted him an upgrade did Player Two finally understand his master's brilliance.

*Whispering Darkness* was an invisibility spell that hid the user from all magic and senses, rendering them effectively non-existent—only a powerful mage could counter it. He'd used it more than once while masquerading as the princely Valerius, though it drained his mana every time. However, the upgrade Calamity gifted him—*God's Secrecy*—changed *everything*.

Wearing *God's Secrecy* like a crown, Player Two practically skipped all the way back to Moonvale. The upgrade didn't just hide him from the eyes of man and mage—it hid him from the very gods, even Calamity himself! The thought thrilled Player Two—it was proof of how much his master trusted him now. It worked so well, he'd passed right by Lazander, Malik, and Eternity along the way—the trio running at full tilt in the wrong direction. He'd been so tickled that he couldn't help but reach out and trail his fingers along Eternity's cheek.

By the time she looked about, he was already gone.

Gaj brought her foot down, shattering what was once a small mountain. Player Two smiled. It was perfect. Everything was absolutely—he gasped, shocked to see his right hand suddenly gripping his sword, fighting to free it of its sheath. With a laugh, he slapped the offending hand—it instantly relaxed. "Naughty Valerius," he called. "Waiting until I was all lovely and relaxed to be so nasty. But it's too late. Even if you do manage to kill little old me, it will do no good."

He stared down at the ruined world, at the miles of empty death that followed Gaj's every step. With a smile, he let Valerius see exactly what the dark god had planned—grinning harder when the prince's terror lit up his mind like a Christmas tree. "You see, Calamity's already won."

# Chapter Forty-Three

I hadn't known what to expect at the Ivory Keep. The plan had been for Lukas to do some initial reconnaissance and figure out where Thaddeus was. Zara would then sneak in that night and grab him—we'd be in and out in less than a day. The plan had *not* been to sit with the queen in a cozy room lined with furs, teacup in hand, while soldiers glared at me like I was the plague.

I'd always figured queens ate things like sandwiches with the crusts cut-off, or scones with mountains of cream, but Queen Firanta was digging into a hearty bowl of stew like she hadn't seen food in weeks. Lukas followed suit, tipping his head back to slurp the dregs while I winced, wishing he would consider *chewing*. But the queen didn't bat an eyelid. Stomach grumbling, I was reminded that Zara hadn't eaten in hours. It was a bad habit of hers—she hated eating almost as much as she hated sleeping.

I dug into the stew, the tender spiced meat bursting with flavor. I couldn't help the little moan that escaped me.

"Our chef is a dwarf," the queen said, looking at me with a knowing smile. "He petitioned Navaros for safe haven after his brother tried to poison him. Our beloved chef had passed away just that week—old age and a love of butter got him in the end—and in a flight of fancy, I asked the dwarf if he could cook." She ate another spoonful, sighing in contentment. "This stew is the first thing he made. In a matter of pure coincidence, I have since written him into my will."

I nodded, unsure what to say.

*"It is a tale meant to give the illusion of humanity—a woman who 'loves' good food and takes in those who cannot protect themselves,"* Zara said with a sigh. *"Do not let yourself be taken in by her wiles, Teema. This one treats words like blades."*

Usually I'd tell Zara to be a bit more trusting, but I found myself agreeing with her. There was something about the queen's eyes that made me feel like I was standing before a judge. She arched a brow at me, and I realized my face must have revealed something. "I'm, ah, I'm grateful for the meal, but—"

"This is the best thing I've ever tasted. Can I have more pretty please?" Lukas said in a rush, his bowl hitting the table with a slap. The queen smiled, and a flick of her fingers was all it took for a servant to refill his bowl for the third time. He shoveled it into his mouth with the same vigor as his first two.

"As I was saying, thank you for the delicious meal, but we don't have time for this," I continued, trying to ignore the loud slurping sounds coming from Lukas. "The Tyrant…" I took a breath, aware I was about to drop a bombshell. "… the Tyrant will be here in days."

Instead of the gasps, cries, and maybe even the scream or two I'd expected, the queen brought her cup of tea to her lips and sipped it delicately. "Is that so?"

"Ah… yes. He's tried and failed to summon one of his lieutenants already—Bala. But if Gaj comes through from the Void, the Tyrant will only be a few hours behind her. That's why we need Thad—"

"Gallow has a temple right here in the Keep," the queen interrupted. "Head Disciple Harrow leads it, alongside countless sages—experts in everything related to the God of Judgment. They claim it is months still before the Tyrant descends and have been quick to reassure us that Lady Eternity and her Champions are well prepared. Who are you to contradict them?"

"I…" The words died in my throat as I struggled with what to tell her. That I was from another world? That I'd seen him with my own eyes? I settled for something close to the truth. "I know for a fact that he's coming sooner because the Tyrant took me captive. If not for my friends, I'd be dead."

The queen's eyes widened, and I knew I must have thrown her if she let her guard down enough for me to see it. And then like a window being wiped clean, her expression stilled.

"Is that so?" she repeated.

My heart sank—she didn't believe me. "It's why we need Thaddeus," I said, frustrated. "Well, I don't know *why*, exactly, but Ravenna was adamant we—"

The door to the throne room was flung open, revealing a man in dark robes with a ridiculous eye-patch. "Where are they? Who claims to speak for Ravenna?"

"Ah, Head Disciple Harrow," the queen said dryly. "I was *just* about to call you."

"Is it you?" he barked, a finger pointed at me like a blade.

Zara growled, and I felt my own hackles rise. One look at the man's smug, arrogant expression and I wanted to punch him.

"Are you truly misguided enough to serve a dead god who abandoned her own people? Who stood by and did nothing while the world was ravaged by the Tyrant?"

I pushed down the urge to defend Ravenna, knowing it would do little good. "I don't *serve* Ravenna, but she did send me here. Again, if you could just ask Lady Eternity, we could—"

"Do not speak of Gallow's Chosen! Have you no *shame?*" Harrow tutted at me. *Tutted.* "Whatever vision you think you've had, girl, it's mistaken—Ravenna is long dead. Only the God of Judgment survived the Tyrant's descent. The scriptures are *very* clear."

"That's not true," I said, the words slipping out.

Harrow's cheeks turned crimson. "Not true? *Not true?* I should have you hung, drawn, and quartered for such heresy!"

The queen sipped her tea. "We outlawed that years ago, Harrow," she said casually. "That said… they *did* injure four guards and a palace mage. The mage is particularly incensed, though Liddy has assured him children are still in his future, should he so desire." She leaned back, a finger on her chin. "Perhaps you're right, Harrow. Perhaps some punishment is in order."

I scrambled, trying to figure a way out that didn't involve killing everyone in the room—something Zara was very much in favor of. "Have either of you even looked outside?" I asked. "Rivers run dry. Entire forests and fields have turned to ash. Who cares what happened a thousand years ago? The Tyrant is on his way *right now.* If we want to stop him, we have to work together."

The queen's expression was unreadable. Harrow's, however, painted a very clear picture. "None but Gallow can defeat the Tyrant," he hissed. "He is the *only* one who can save us. It is written. It is spoken. It is *decided.*" He turned to the queen, head held high, "This is undoubtedly a ploy of the Tyrant's—one meant to sow chaos and discord. I demand they be placed under arrest, effective immediately."

*"We should slit his throat,"* Zara said, rage cutting through her words. *"His own people would thank us for it."*

*Having listened to him for thirty seconds, I agree,* I told her. *But do you really think a jail cell can hold you? Let's just… see where this goes. It's better than killing the people we're trying to save.*

Zara huffed but said nothing—the closest I was going to get to agreement.

"Couple of things," Lukas said, knocking back the last of his stew. "One—can we all stop calling him the 'Tyrant' like he's a bad dictator? His name is *Calamity*."

Harrow gasped. The queen's lips tugged in the barest hint of a smile.

"Two—I don't know what Gallow's story is, but if he really did take Calamity down, Ravenna was right there with him. She fought the bastard with her dying breath. I should know—I was there." Lukas stood so quickly his chair screeched. More than one soldier reached for their weapon. "And three." He bared his teeth at Harrow. "You are an arrogant, condescending, soft-spined shell of a man, and had I the time or patience, I would beat you into a fine paste and serve you on a side of *toast*."

"What did… Did you hear him… ?" Harrow sputtered.

"Mara," the queen called, tea in hand. "Arrest them, will you?"

A woman in plain leathers strode forward, one of her arms in an awkward sling. Some of the soldiers looked awkwardly from Mara to the queen.

"Ah, my queen?" one of them finally ventured. "Perhaps one of the king's soldiers, as opposed to a… former knight would be more suitable. After all, Mara is still recovering from her injury."

"Explain how you were injured, Mara," the queen said in a tone that was more a statement than a question.

"I was out in the field with Commander Rhys when a shadow-fiend bit down on my arm, my queen."

"You forgot to mention that you were alone and defending two of Rhys' soldiers—both of whom survived because of you."

"Forgive me, my queen."

"Considering she single-handedly killed a shadow-fiend—something that requires two if not three soldiers according to Rhys—I think she can handle clapping manacles on prisoners. Or would anyone else like to question my judgment?"

Silence choked the room—even Harrow kept his mouth shut.

Mara pressed her hand over her heart in a salute I recognized—it was how the Gilded greeted one another in *Knights of Eternity*.

Lukas and I were soon wearing matching manacles the length of our forearms, Mara leading the way as we were escorted from the room. Lukas stopped just long enough to swipe a bread roll and give Harrow a little finger wave. I grinned when the man stamped the ground like a giant, over-sized toddler, his face purple with rage.

***

While the Gallowed Temple kept fastidious records, there were no firsthand accounts of Calamity's descent. Most were penned a hundred or so years after, having been passed down by word of mouth. But they all said the same thing— with the aid of Gallow's power, the First Eternity and her Champions beat back the dark god and imprisoned him. Unfortunately, little to nothing was known about his lieutenants. Bala was usually depicted as forks of lightning and a swirling tornado, which had turned out to be somewhat true. But Eternity had only ever seen one drawing of Gaj. It was a painting of a hunched-over skeleton, the word "death" inked on the page over and over.

What Eternity saw was not a skeleton—that word implied something human. Something *mortal*. And what towered over, its body taller than even Moonvale's mountains, defied every law of magic and mortals she knew.

She almost wished they'd given in to Malik's cowardice and stayed behind.

"Gallow save us," Lazander whispered at her side.

"I told you," Malik hissed. "We're dead. We're all *dead*."

The monster that stalked toward them was made almost entirely of bone. But what transfixed Eternity was the skull that hung in the sky, a cursed moon that promised ruin with every step. White as fresh snow, serrated teeth hung from the top half of her jaw, but no bottom half followed. Where a chin should have been a mountain of dried muscle twisted around her spine to form a thick neck, the rest slithering around her body in sporadic bursts, like meat left out in the sun for too long. Eternity could *hear* the creaking of the giant's limbs as muscle pulled against bone, and she knew that if Gaj could feel anything, every step must be agony.

Part of her knew that, at least. The small part that wasn't crouched like an animal in the dark, frozen in terror as she prayed the monster wouldn't find her. Not even in her nightmares had she imagined something like Gaj—and if this was only a lieutenant of Gallow…

Sweat trickled down her brow as she shook so hard her teeth chattered.

And then a large hand took hers, squeezing it tightly, and she looked up to see Lazander. He was shaking as badly as she was, but he still had the strength to smile at her. To her astonishment, she found herself smiling back.

"You can do this, Eternity," he said.

Her heart swelled, and she spoke without thinking. "I am happy we met, Lazander. Happy that, even if this should be our last battle, it is you I stand beside. You… you make me feel brave."

His eyes lit up, but just as he was about to speak that dull cloud she saw back in the forest passed over his eyes. He dropped her hand like it was acidic, and a crack of rejection split Eternity's heart in two.

"Malik," Lazander said, turning to the older Champion.

Eternity shoved down her shame and embarrassment at Lazander's clear refusal and tried to focus.

"You take the right foot. I'll take the left. Lady Eternity can attack from above. If we cannot kill Gaj, we can slow her down. Even that monstrosity needs her tendons to walk."

A cold sweat trailed down Malik's temples, his eyes flicking to the horizon—he looked ready to bolt. With her jerk, he stumbled, clutching his head. "Yes, yes of course," he muttered, pale as Gaj's skull. "I would never… of course."

Eternity frowned. "Malik are you—wait. Look! She's… she's turning away from us."

The huge monstrosity shifted to the right, creaking painfully as she started moving west—*away* from Freyley and toward Navaros. There was nothing in that direction but abandoned towns and villages for hours, nothing but...

Eternity gasped. "Gaj is heading for the Ivory Keep."

## Chapter Forty-Four

"*Give me back control,*" Zara hissed. "*She is but a single woman—an injured one at that. I will not hurt her… much.*"

Mara kept Lukas and me directly in front of her, her sword drawn as she escorted us through the Keep. Unlike Magnus' castle, the King and Queen of Navaros kept their furnishings sparse and simple, and I found myself enjoying the tour even as I waited for Mara to drag us to the Keep's depths—where movies had taught me all good dungeons were kept.

*Zara, there are guards stationed at every second corridor. Even if you took her down, which you absolutely would, all she'd have to do is shout and… No Zara, we're not cutting her vocal cords. Look, if you kill her, we'll have to lug a body around or risk getting caught. Just have patience, all right?*

Zara kept grumbling while Lukas seemed entirely unbothered by our capture, whistling a jaunty tune as we walked. Mara saluted a trio of guards, their eyes lingering on me uncomfortably, but they let us pass without comment. We turned, coming to a long empty corridor—a massive ebony door at the end.

"Quickly," Mara said, sheathing her sword and jogging toward it. Lukas immediately followed, while I stood staring at them in confusion. Mara glanced furtively around, then unlocked the door with a key around her neck. Bracing her uninjured shoulder against it, she heaved—it looked heavy. Lukas went to help her, and I hurried to follow.

"Barricade the door," Mara said once we were inside, pointing to a piece of wood the length of me. "I'd do it, but I can't with this arm. Hurry."

I frowned at my shackles while Lukas rolled his eyes at me. With exaggerated motions he held up his manacles—and opened them.

"She never locked them," he said, "didn't you notice?"

I tested my own to find them the same. "But why…"

Lukas was already gone, busy barricading the door while Mara ran around the room, grabbing things from packed shelves and shoving them into two bags.

We were in what looked like a massive armory come supply room. Weapons of all kinds from swords to shields, spears to maces lined the walls while an entire section was devoted to armor. On the far side what looked like bags of rations were laid out as well as barrels labeled "water." The room smelled musty, as if it wasn't used much.

"What's happening?" I asked, feeling stupid. "Why are we in here?"

"It's a siege room," Mara said, pausing over a dagger. She grabbed one, then a second after a moment's consideration. "There are three in total. They're designed as a last holdout should the Keep be attacked. I'd have preferred to take you to the barracks, but there's no way I could get you in and out without notice."

Two waterskins followed as well as small flasks of iron that she handled gingerly.

"But what… I mean… shouldn't we be…"

"Apologies for my friend," Lukas said, patting me on the shoulder. "She's rather slow."

Mara's lips didn't so much as twitch as she handed me several folded pieces of paper. I opened one and was greeted by the most beautiful cursive I'd ever laid eyes on.

*Dear Zara,*

*Yes, I know who you are.*

*I never thought the day would come when I would risk my kingdom on a known enemy of Navaros, but I have little choice. Eternity and Lazander saw something in you—I only pray they were right.*

*Thaddeus told me what he could. I know Ravenna fought to save us in the final hour, and that Thaddeus holds something she can use against the Tyrant—but she needs his body to activate it. Get his corpse to Ravenna. She will know what to do with it.*

"Crap," I said aloud.

*Thaddeus lies in a crypt beneath the Gallowed Temple, but he is walled in. I have instructed Mara to provide you with weapons, provisions, and explosives. Should you use them to* blow out his grave, you will have minutes before the forces of the Keep are upon you, so do so as a last resort. The only advantage you have is the convoluted maze the pious saw fit to make of their crypts. Here is a map that will guide you both to his resting place and then on to safety.

*I will not be able to help you again.*

*Firanta*

The second sheet of paper was a map that looked like it had been drawn by a professional cartographer. I recognized the queen's handwriting by the tiny, detailed instructions along the margins.

"Catching on yet?" Lukas asked smugly.

"Here," Mara said, holding out two bags. "The mage-bombs should be more than enough. I also packed a week's worth of rations for you each."

Lukas was already slinging his on, and I followed. "Mara, I don't know what to say but… thank you."

"I didn't do this for you," she said sharply, "or even the queen, if I'm honest. I'm a *knight,* and while King Najar believes the best way to serve our country is by following orders, the Gilded taught me another way." She tapped her chest, hand over her heart. "I serve justice and honor, Zara the Fury. I pray you do too."

I mimicked the gesture I'd seen the animated pixels in *Knights of Eternity* do countless times and bowed deeply. "I meant what I said, Mara. We're here to stop Calamity—I swear it."

The door rattled with the unmistakable click of a key.

"We're out of time," Mara said, running to one of the water barrels. She awkwardly tried to shove it to one side, and Lukas ran to help, revealing a secret hatch right underneath. "This will lead you to the tunnels beneath the Keep. Head north, and you'll hit the crypts. Go!"

The door rattled, and I heard shouts. Lukas disappeared down the hatch.

"I said go!" Mara said, her voice a harsh whisper.

"For what it's worth…" I said, "I think you'd make a great Gilded."

She blinked in surprise. A boom sounded as something heavy hit the door, but I was already gone, sliding down the hatch's ladder and into the darkness below.

\*\*\*

"Bless you Mara, you absolute saint," Lukas cried as he struck a match, holding up one of the torches she'd packed us. With a sigh, he grimaced. "Creepy tunnels? *Again?* At least there are no bloodied murals… yet."

The tunnels beneath the Keep were clearly dug by hand and reinforced in places by thick wooden planks. While the scaffolding meant some repairs were being done, the layer of dust that coated everything told me it had been a *while* since anyone had been down here. The cynical part of me remembered how many people I'd seen in the Keep—both the inner and outer courtyard were filled with refugees, not to mention those stuck outside. I wondered if everyone would fit in here if Calamity attacked.

I doubted it.

"Right, you've gotten lost while going to the toilet—hand over the map," Lukas said, taking it from me before I could say anything.

"That was *one* time," I said, secretly relieved. I had the sense of direction of a drunken toddler.

Lukas barely glanced at the map before setting off at a confident stride, the light of his torch cutting through the darkness and dust. I followed, activating *Tithe of Beasts* as I went. The echoey nature of the tunnels meant it would be hard to tell *where* an attacker was coming from, but I could at least make sure we had some notice.

Two hours later, I seriously regretted giving Lukas the map. We'd doubled back at least twice, and it was only by using *Piercing Sight* that I found the almost invisible exit. Earth turned to stone as we left the tunnels and moved to the crypts—low ceilings becoming cavernous, the musky scent of dust replaced by a surprising hint of flowers. Holes were carved into the walls where long slabs of rock were affixed over them, copper plaques nailed to the center—each the only sign of the dead buried within.

There were no windows or natural sources of light, only spaced-out lanterns holding steady droplets of mage-fire. But from the moment I set foot in the crypts, I felt strangely at peace. The floors were clean and clearly regularly swept, and some graves even had fresh flowers—that would explain the smell—coins and what looked like bleached animal skulls. Frowning, I picked one up, turning it over in my hands—it was a bird's, I guessed.

"Gallow is usually depicted with a long narrow skull like a bird," Lukas said, sensing my question. "No idea why. If the past few weeks have taught me anything, it's that 'gods' are weird."

The stone that covered the tombs came in different colors—some a rough gray, others a smooth marble that felt like silk to the touch. It was obvious some were more expensive than others. At first I'd tried to read every single plaque we passed—kings and queens, Gilded Knights, and even soldiers who'd risked their lives to save Navaros were all buried down here. But there were too many to count.

As we got deeper into the crypts, the fresh flowers faded, and no copper coins were laid out for the dead. Every third mage-fire lantern lay cracked or broken, and the skitter of claws trailed my steps, a whisper of a rat's tail all I'd see before it vanished.

We rounded a corner, where the tomb of "Ikul the Honest—a man who let nothing stand in the way of his honor and integrity," greeted us. "Lukas, this is the *third* time we've run into our boy Ikul here," I said, whispering even though we were alone. The sense of peace I'd felt in the crypt had seeped away along with any warmth, my feet freezing on the cold stone. "We should be there by now."

"Keep your pants on," he said, turning the map under the torchlight. He hummed and took a sharp left while I tried not to groan.

"Lukas, why don't you give me..." I trailed off. All of the recent graves had been old and ancient with plaques so rusted some of the names were indecipherable. It was why the tombs in front of me caught my eye—their plaques were shiny and new.

When I saw the names, my heart stopped.

"I thought you were in a hurry," Lukas joked, coming to stand next to me. "What's the... oh no."

"Here lies Marito Dawnseeker, a Gilded Knight who gave his life in service to Navaros. He was a man who loved life, laughter, and his country with all his heart," I read aloud before turning to the next grave. "Here lies Gabriel Vulbrack, a Gilded

Knight who gave his life in service to Navaros. The first mage to ever join the heroic order, his loyalty and dedication were known throughout the kingdom."

The epitaphs, and the fact they were the same but for some keywords that had been swapped out, left a sour taste in my mouth.

"Look at the dates," Lukas said. "They only died a few weeks ago. No wonder Lazander was so, well… angry." He shook his head sadly. "I can't believe they're dead. Who killed them? And *how?* Marito and Gabriel weren't your run of the mill knights—these guys took on armies and *lived*."

"What happened a few weeks ago?" I asked, already knowing the answer. "Who finally decided to rip the mask off and show the world who he really was?" I had no proof, of course, but I'd played *Knights of Eternity* countless times. Calamity might only have taken snippets of this world and shoved them into an arcade game, but I knew that not just anyone, or anything, could kill the Gilded Knights.

Lukas stared at me in horror. "If it was Player Two, I doubt he took them aside and explained that he was only hitching a ride in Valerius' body. They… they must have died thinking their own prince killed them." For once Lukas looked deadly serious. "Considering he broke my jaw and was going to let his murder-buddy kill me, I can't believe I'm saying this but—poor Lazander."

I placed one hand on each of the graves, my head bent. I'd been to my share of funerals, and while I didn't know the customs of this world, I still felt the need to say something. "This wasn't how you were supposed to die," I whispered. "I'm sorry you got dragged into this. And I'm sorry that people from my world have caused so much pain and death here—but I'm not like them. I'm going to stop Player Two and…" My voice trailed off at a sudden, horrifying thought.

Zara was trapped in my mind when I first took over her body, but she'd been able to see through my eyes. At least three of us had been dragged here from Earth—Magnus, myself, and Player Two—but for some reason the fate of the *real* Magnus and Valerius had never occurred to me. When Magnus died, he no longer remembered he'd come from Earth… did that mean the real Magnus died too? What about the real Valerius? Had he been forced to watch as Player Two murdered Gabriel, Marito, and countless others?

I pressed my hands against the graves, furious I'd never given a second thought to them—real people whose lives lay in ruins because of Calamity.

"I don't know if the real Valerius is still alive," I said, hoping somewhere out there Marito and Gabriel could hear me. "And if he is, I don't know if I save him… but I can make sure no one else dies in his name."

"Let me see that map," I said, straightening up. Lukas said nothing as he handed it to me, and I was grateful he didn't comment on the tears I wiped from my eyes.

## Chapter Forty-Five

"Hold..." Lazander said.

Eternity crouched behind a scorched boulder, feeling like a child playing hide-and-seek. Lazander knelt in front of her, sword out, fist held high as he commanded them to wait. Gaj moved so slowly they'd managed to get ahead of her, gaining a few precious minutes to set up an ambush.

The earth trembled, and with every step the giant took, Eternity was forced to crane her neck back farther, the looming monstrosity a perversion of life and death made real. Her throat was dry, her breathing rapid—but whenever her mind taunted her, claiming this was an impossible plan, she'd think of Zara the Fury. Think of the fire in the woman's eyes. And a spark of courage would flare in her chest.

But if Eternity was scared, Malik was *terrified*. The brash, arrogant Champion was gone. In his place stood a man whose hands shook so badly, he could barely hold his axe. There was no loud proclamations that Gallow would save them, or that they had to do whatever it took to follow his orders. Apparently Malik was only brave when he thought winning was guaranteed.

Eternity would have enjoyed seeing him knocked down a peg or two if she didn't understand exactly how he felt.

"Hold..." Lazander's voice betrayed no hint of fear, and Eternity allowed herself a final shaking breath. If Lazander could do this, then so could she.

*Boom.*

Gaj's footsteps rocketed through her body, making her bones rattle.

*I will not fail.*

*Boom.*

*I refuse to fail.*

*Boom.*

"Now!" Lazander roared. Eternity shot up into the air, past Gaj's bony knees and the sharpened studs that lined her wrists and too long fingers—the acrid scent of rotting flesh so strong, she could *taste* it.

The giant began the slow, arduous process of raising her foot to take a step, giving no sign she'd noticed the woman zipping around her like a fly. Determination flared in Eternity's chest, overshadowing her fear—if Gaj was just a mindless puppet, they might have a chance.

Twisting around the bones that burst from Gaj's chest like ivory spears, she opened the door to Gallow. Cupping her hands, Eternity put everything she had into the spell—this was their only chance.

**"Kneel. Cry. *Beg*,"** Eternity said, forging the God of Judgment's power into a sharpened blade, imaging it cutting through Gaj's thick grizzled neck. **"For you are not worthy."**

The darkness in her hands expanded, and she was about to let it fly when a familiar voice called out— "You're not worthy either, little Eternity—but then, you never were."

It was the last thing she heard before the fire consumed her.

\*\*\*

Malik couldn't move.

His axe was buried deep in Gaj's ankle, the blade chipped—he'd only managed a single strike before terror froze him solid. Eyes squeezed shut, he wanted to curse Eternity and Lazander into the sun—Malik had been loyal. He'd been obedient. He'd done everything he was supposed to, yet he was stuck clinging to a walking undead—the stuff of nightmares made real.

The giant raised her foot, and he almost dropped his axe—a sudden burst of ice-cold wind tugging at his clothes and hair like spindly fingers, threatening to drag him to his death. He clung to a lump of muscle buried in Gaj's foot, ignoring the eye-watering stench as he hung on for dear life.

*I can't do this. I have to get away. I have to—*

**"COWARD."** Gallow's voice rang out, but instead of the joy and love that warmed Malik whenever his god spoke, what felt like a dagger of ice plunged into his heart.

**"STAND. FIGHT."**

"Please, I can't," he whispered. "Have mercy, please, I can't—"

***

Lazander hacked at the giant's ankle so hard, he could feel his blade dulling with every strike. Cutting through Gaj's rope-like tendons was akin to sawing through *stone*. He was making progress, but it was painfully slow, and their plan would work best if they all struck Gaj at once.

What made an impossible task even harder was that he could only attack when the foot he clung to was stationary. When the giant raised it, he had to drive his blade into the muscle and hold on with all his strength or risk being thrown off—it was only luck and Gallow's grace he hadn't been already.

A whisper of despair taunted him, but he banished it, telling himself to trust in Gallow—the god gave Lazander no task he couldn't handle. Sword raised, the Champion steadied himself, ready to resume his endless hacking, when a flash of light made him look up. A comet of pure fire streaked through the sky, heading straight for the ground. Lazander stopped, afraid it was a spell of Gaj's. But then the flames died, and he almost dropped his weapon.

It was a charred, ashen body.

"Eternity!" he roared, his voice louder, his thoughts clearer than they'd been in days. Gaj raised her foot, and Lazander clung to it, forcing himself to wait. "I'm coming! I'm coming, Eternity!" The wind whipped around him, blurring his vision, but he kept his eyes open and locked on the woman he'd face death itself for.

At the precipice of Gaj's stride, Lazander sprinted forward, dodging around ridged bones and elongated toes. **"Bend to his might, break before his Judgment,"** he yelled, Gallow's strength rippling through him as he jumped into the air, giving no thought to how he'd land or how he'd survive—all that mattered was getting to Eternity.

He soared toward her, his fingers grasping but missing her arm. Twisting midair, it was luck, fate, or the gods that let him grab a fistful of ashen sleeve and yank her toward him. Clutching her to his chest, he almost wept at the sight of her small limp body and the burns that covered her from head to toe.

"I've got you, Eternity! It's going to be all right," he whispered, not knowing if he said it for his benefit or hers. She didn't speak. Didn't so much as twitch as they fell together, the wind screaming in his ears. He realized too late that they were right in Gaj's path—her knee speeding toward them, a mountain about to collide with a pebble. Heart steady, he shielded Eternity as best as he could—praying it would be enough to save her.

Lazander had trained daily with Marito, the Gilded Knight hitting him with every bit of his legendary strength. In their first sparring match, a single blow broke several of Lazander's ribs, and it was months before he could handle a strike from Marito and stay standing.

Marito's punches felt like gentle kisses compared to the knee Gaj drove into his back. He felt a light pop as his spine snapped in two, the force sending them speeding through the air like an arrow. Lazander didn't cry out, didn't dare breathe for fear he'd drop Eternity. They hit the ground like a meteor, willpower the only thing keeping his arms wrapped around her. Gaj didn't flinch or give any sign she'd noticed him. He doubted the giant even felt it.

The Champion blinked, his head a fog of pain, and he realized he must have passed out for a few seconds. The sky darkened, a cloak of night blotting out the sun. Lazander's heart froze when he looked up, all thought and hope fleeing when he saw the giant's skeletal foot hover overhead—eclipsing all light. Eternity lay curled up on his chest. He tried to move, tried to throw her out of the way, but his body didn't so much as twitch despite his frantic commands. Lazander could only close his eyes and wish he'd been strong enough to save the woman he so desperately loved.

And then hands were gripping his armor, his body screaming as he was dragged, things rattling around inside of him that shouldn't. "I'm sorry, I'm sorry!" Malik was shouting, one arm around Lazander, the other around Eternity. "I'll never hesitate again, Gallow, I swear it. Forgive me!"

The last thing Lazander heard was the thunderous boom of Gaj's foot hitting the ground in the distance, and then he blacked out.

\*\*\*

"This is it," I said, rapping on the brick. We'd reached a part of the crypt so old, the plaques crumbled if I pressed them too hard, Thaddeus' shiny new grave standing out like a sore thumb. I fought not to cough, the musty scent of damp and decay so far up my nose, it was tickling my brain. Nothing but the grave looked as if it had been touched in decades.

"Right, let me grab some of those explosives," Lukas said, setting down his satchel. "'Mage-bombs,' Mara called them. I've never used one before, but I'm sure between the two of us, we have enough brainpower to—"

**Monstrous Strength Activated.**

I drove my fist through the wall, punching out the other side. It was several rows of brick deep, but I barely felt the blow. Unfortunately, the same didn't go for my nose and stomach, both of which were reeling from the rotting, fetid stench that ballooned in my face.

"Or we could do that," Lukas said. "What, you never smelled a corpse before?"

"We embalm them," I said, immediately regretting the breath I'd taken to speak. I shut my lips tightly and pulled out fistfuls of brick as quickly as I could, trying not to vomit.

*"You are an embarrassment, Teema,"* Zara huffed. *"The 'Fury' does not vomit over something as pathetic as a corpse. Compose yourself while you wield my body."*

*Do you want to take over and dig it out?* I thought at her, not daring to speak aloud. I would *definitely* puke.

*"No,"* she said, too quickly. *"This will be a good exercise for you."*

I chose not to comment.

"Now that we're here…" Lukas started, and I noticed he'd also backed up. Coward. "… shouldn't we address the towering xandi in the room?"

"Hmm?" Was all I could say through tightly pursed lips.

"The queen's letter didn't tell us *what* we had to do with the corpse—only that we had to get it to Ravenna. Alas, she is probably swimming in a chamber pot back in Moonvale."

"Did you have to say it like that, Lukas?" I asked, holding my nose as I stepped away. I'd made a hole big enough for me to reach into, glimpsing horns and what looked like shriveled intestines along the way. That had been about all my stomach could handle.

"Are all people on Earth this sensitive when it comes to bodily functions?"

I heaved, though it was becoming easier to breathe. Maybe I was getting used to the smell.

"I'll take that as a yes."

"We might not know what Ravenna planned to do with Thaddeus, or why we have to keep him away from Calamity… but we know how the rakna get Void Mana," I said, not wanting to say the next bit out loud.

"Oh no," Lukas said, looking in horror from me to the grave. "You don't think… but he wasn't even a slug thing. Or maybe he was? I have no idea. I have no idea about any of this—it's pure dumb luck we're not dead by now!"

"Look, let's just get Thaddeus out of there. Once we're clear of the Keep and anyone else who wants to stab us, we can figure out what to do," I said, not wanting to go *anywhere* near the body again. Lukas must have taken pity on me because he sighed dramatically, the flesh of his right-arm swirling as it grew—a thick layer of fur coating it as it became twice, then three times as large.

"I didn't know you could partially shift," I said, surprised.

"Neither did I," he said with a shrug. "I couldn't back when I could only shift into molger form. But something's changed since…"

He trailed off, peering up into Thaddeus' grave.

"What's wrong? Oh, what is *that?*" I asked, peeking over his shoulder at a small, soft light. Taking a step closer, it brightened. Curious, I backed away, and the light dimmed. "Well, that's not terrifying."

Lukas reached in, grimacing as he rummaged around. I heard a snap, and then something squishy, and he pulled out a lump of gray, shriveled meat—Thaddeus' heart.

My stomach gave up, and I promptly vomited.

*"Pathetic,"* Zara muttered.

"Why is his *heart glowing?*" I coughed, wiping my mouth.

"It's not the heart," he said, peeling the muscle apart, revealing crystal clear glass. "It's the... *flower* that was buried inside it."

## Chapter Forty-Six

Eternity awoke to a slap. She gasped, pain rocking her body. Curling up onto her side, she groaned, coughing up what felt like an entire chimney.

"You're awake!" Malik said, looking relieved. "Come on. Gallow gave us new orders."

Eternity didn't answer—she couldn't. Her insides were on fire, every breath a blunt dagger scraping the flesh from her lungs. Pressing her hands to her chest, she tried to focus on breathing—and saw her fingers. Her arms. Her *legs*. Burns coated every inch of her body, and while the charred flesh was already healing and turning a rosy pink, her nose twitched at the scent of cooked flesh… and burnt hair.

Horrified she brought her hands to her head, almost weeping when she found only an inch of straw-like hair—the rest burned to ashes. She chided herself for being stupid and vain—she'd let Player Two catch her unawares and had almost died for it. Her hair, or lack of, should be the last thing on her mind. Yet she kept running her fingers over her skull, hoping to find her long, luscious locks magically returned.

"Eternity, we have orders," Malik said softly, getting down on his knees. The smug, condescending look he usually wielded like a blade was gone. Instead he looked terrified out of his mind, and she knew he'd realized what she had in the last few weeks—their victory wasn't guaranteed. That his and the sages' proclamations they would easily best Calamity were nothing but daydreams and hot air.

"What… what did Gallow say?" she forced herself to ask. Her doubts and questions didn't matter. They'd failed to stop Gaj, and thousands of people now stood directly in the path of destruction. But the look on Malik's face derailed her thoughts, a frown cresting her brow.

She knew that look—he was debating how much to say.

"Malik, you will tell me *exactly* what Gallow said, or I will split you open on a mountain," she said. She didn't shout. She simply said it as it was—a matter of fact.

"Gaj will consume the people of the Ivory Keep and open a gate to the Void—allowing Calamity to come through," he said, not meeting her eyes. "We are to wait until the ritual is complete and the rift stable. I will then distract Gaj and Player Two while you bind Calamity. Alone." His tone told her exactly how successful he thought they'd be.

"No, absolutely not!" Eternity said, wincing when she moved too quickly. She flopped back down, breathing hard. The wounds on her hands were nearly healed, but she still couldn't get up. She'd never healed so quickly, hadn't even known she could, but then she'd never been hurt so badly before. "We're not sacrificing everyone in the Ivory Keep. Nor am I throwing you to the wolves."

"We were always going to die, Eternity," Malik half-whispered, "I just... I always thought it would be with Calamity on his knees before us, broken and beaten. The entire Ivory Keep would stand at our backs, applauding our sacrifice, our names guaranteed to be remembered for thousands of years to come. We were supposed to die *victorious*. Not... not like this."

"I am ready to die," Eternity said, managing to sit up this time. "But I will not let hundreds of people..."

She didn't finish the thought. Couldn't. She finally saw the twisted body mere feet from her, his back bent nearly in half.

*Lazander.*

She half dragged, half crawled through the dirt.

"Eternity, don't," Malik said, moving to bar her way, but one look from her and he wisely backed up.

"Lazander," Eternity whispered, hands hovering over his body, her own pain forgotten. A layer of dust and dirt covered him, and he lay as still as a corpse. Bending over, she ignored the burn in her ribs as she turned her head, relieved when hot breath tickled her ears. Alive. He was *alive*.

Lightly resting one hand on his forehead, she placed the other on his chest. She didn't know if this would work, had never seen a Champion come back from wounds so grievous, death was but a breath away.

But she had to try.

Taking a deep breath, she poured her own magic into his body—pushing it to heal the overwhelming damage.

**"LEAVE HIM,"** Gallow's orders rang in her ears like a death sentence.

"We need to go, Eternity," Malik said, sounding sad and ancient. She almost wished he went back to his snide, biting ways. "I can carry you, let's—"

"Do not *touch* me," she snarled, her hand locked onto Lazander's forehead.

**"GO TO THE IVORY KEEP,"** Gallow commanded, his voice a storm in her mind. **"I WILL NOT ASK AGAIN."**

Her only reply was to grit her teeth.

"Eternity, you'll drain yourself dry, and he'll still die. If we don't follow orders, Gallow will *punish* us. I… I let fear and doubt cloud my mind, and Gallow hurt me for it. But it won't happen again." He straightened, a spark of his old self coming through. "We need to go."

"… no."

"What was that?"

"I said *no*." Eternity had skirted the edges of Gallow's approval for years, choosing to aid when he'd been silent, saving lives when he'd been vague, praying she never invited his anger. But never in her hundred and twenty years of service had she ever told the God of Judgment *no*.

**"YOU ARE MY CHOSEN."** Gallow's voice rattled her skull, and she clutched her head, a trail of blood falling from her nose. **"YOU WILL FOLLOW ORDERS."**

Eternity shook her head, but hands were grabbing her, throwing her over a rough shoulder. "Stop it, Eternity," Malik barked as she struggled. "He's ordered me to take you to the Keep. This is happening whether you like it or not!"

"I. Said. *No!*" Eternity's cry was echoed by a resounding crack as she blasted her magic into Malik, sending him flying. She hit the ground face-first, coughing as her ribs screamed, the dirt dragging along her still healing burns. Then she was scrambling to Lazander's side, hands on him as she poured every last drop of her magic into him. His eyelids didn't so much as twitch.

"Have you lost your bloody mind?" Malik roared, a wild look in his eyes. "We have to do what he says! It's *Gallow*."

"I have spent my entire life wishing for other people's approval. The disciples. Sages. Gallow. *You*," Eternity said quietly. "I told myself that as long as I did as I was told, I was a good person. I was worthy."

Beneath her hands Lazander's heart came to a slow, resounding stop. Her vision blurred—her mana was almost gone. "I am tired of living my life for other people."

**"DO NOT DARE,"** Gallow's voice boomed, and the pain in her head increased, but she barely felt it.

"It is past time I lived for myself."

She flung the door open to Gallow, but it felt jammed, as if something was blocking it. The God of Judgment was trying to stop her, she realized. But she had wielded his magic for over a century and knew it as well as her own. Furious, Eternity shoved past Gallow, ripping the god's own magic from him as she poured it into Lazander, threading it through his body like a delicate needle. A snapped spine and shredded organs knitted together at her touch.

And then she felt it—a layer of Gallow's magic wrapped around Lazander. She hadn't noticed it before—it was too deep and too subtle. Her anger threatened to overwhelm her when she realized what it was: a spell to dull the senses and soften the mind. To make someone more obedient. More *malleable*.

This was what had changed Lazander. This was what her god had done to his "favored." Why hadn't she seen it? Why hadn't she done something?

No, she realized, that was a lie. She *had* noticed, and she'd looked away—too afraid of the choice she'd have to make. Eternity didn't know what would happen if she removed the spell—Gallow was so deeply embedded in Lazander's brain, it was hard to tell where the God of Judgment began and ended. But the Lazander she knew would rather die than live under the thumb of another.

She pressed her forehead against his. "I am sorry. Sorry I did not see how much you were hurting. Sorry that I let my own fear stop me from doing the right thing. But I *will* fix this." Bracing herself, she ripped Gallow's magic out of Lazander with the skill of a seamstress and the brutality of a predator. Heart in her throat, Eternity leaned back, shaking.

Lazander's eyes fluttered open, and when he looked at her, she saw the dull, cloudy look that had haunted those green eyes was finally gone. He smiled weakly, looking like himself for the first time since becoming a Champion.

"Eternity…" he whispered.

"Welcome back, Lazander," she said, squeezing his hand. "I have missed you."

"My lord…" Malik cried, his voice shaking, and Eternity didn't need to ask who he was talking to. Her eyes remained fixed on Lazander, trying to take in every detail while she still could. "My lord, please… she won't do what I say, I can't—argh."

A thud, and Eternity knew Malik had fallen to his knees, gasping in pain. She waited for Gallow to strike her down for her disobedience, bracing herself.

But nothing happened.

Curious, she watched Malik writhe on the ground. "It is I who disobeyed you, Gallow, not Malik," Eternity said, getting to her feet. "If you desire punishment, then punish me."

Malik screamed.

Why was Gallow hurting him but not her… Eternity's fists clenched when she realized what was happening. "You cannot wound me as you do Malik, can you Gallow?"

Silence followed her proclamation.

"You cannot manipulate me either, as you did Lazander. Otherwise I would be like him—loyal, unquestioning, *obedient*. Why? Is it because I have wielded your power for so long? Or am I too strong for you?"

Gallow's only answer was Malik's cries of pain. The Champion gripped his hair so hard he ripped a chunk out of his scalp.

"You claim to be the harbinger of justice—the protector of this world." Eternity was shaking, tears of rage in her eyes, but she refused to let them fall. "Yet you treat us like playthings and punish us for your mistakes! *You* sent us to Freyley. *You* are the reason we could not stop Gaj coming through. Stop hurting Malik this instant, or I swear you will have to kill Calamity *without* me."

Malik gasped, but flopped onto his back, white-faced—his relief palpable. She might not like the Champion, but she refused to let anyone be hurt in her place. Gallow was silent, and she wondered not for the first time how much of her mind he could see. Did he know her entire world was collapsing around her? Breaking under the weight of his lies?

Taking a deep breath, she forced the panic down and told herself none of it mattered—only one thing did. "Tell me this, Gallow—can you do it? Can you really kill the Tyrant? Lie to me again, and I will leave."

**"I CAN. THERE IS NO OTHER,"** came the immediate response.

It wasn't lost on her that he'd spent years ordering her about like a dog with single word commands, but the moment she refused him he suddenly spoke in full sentences.

Something dark pushed against her mind, but Eternity didn't flinch. She knew it was Gallow lurking on the outskirts, looking for a way in.

He would find none.

"Swear it," she said. "Swear that you will kill Calamity."

**"I SWEAR IT.**

**"I SWEAR IT ON ALL LIFE IN THE UNIVERSE.**

**"I WILL KILL HIM."**

Eternity wanted nothing more than to grab Lazander and leave. She wanted someone else to be brave. But she couldn't do it. She couldn't abandon this world—no matter how much she wanted to.

"I am no longer your Chosen, Gallow," she said, "but… I will not abandon this world. So let us strike a deal. I will go to the Ivory Keep. And in return you will do as you promised—you will kill Calamity and save us all."

She had only a whisper of mana left but she coated her words with it. Heart thundering, she felt Gallow's magic reach out in turn, answering hers. Together they weaved a spell, forming a binding. And just like that, a pact was made.

**"IT IS DONE,"** he intoned. **"NOW GO."**

The God of Judgment vanished from her mind, and she let out a shaky breath. The spell they'd cast together was *Unbreakable Oath*. It was extremely powerful, and one she'd never used before, but she knew the theory—it bound both parties in an eternal promise. Should either break it, the death that followed would be both swift and painful. While Eternity had no idea if it would work on a *god*, it was the best she could do. The only thing she could do, really.

Malik groaned as he got to his feet, glaring at her with open hatred. "You happy now? You did a little song and dance, and for what? To do exactly what we had to anyway?"

Frowning, Eternity reached out to him with Gallow's magic, searching his mind for the same threads the God of Judgment wrapped around Lazander.

And found none.

"You are not…" she stammered, thinking of the years he'd spent manipulating them, first with smiles, then with barbed words.

"I'm not *what?*"

"All those times you made me feel worthless. The cruel things you said to Lazander and me. How *small* you made us feel… Gallow did not force you to say any of it. You were never under his control, were you?"

Malik stared at her for a long moment, and she could see him flicking through possible responses, trying to turn the situation to his advantage, even now. He settled on, "He only did that to the stubborn. Those too proud or too stupid to see that Gallow is the *only* way we will survive. I just did what I could to keep everyone in line. And if you're expecting an apology for giving a damn about saving the world, you'll get none." Malik wasn't even looking at her. He calmly sheathed his axe and adjusted his armor, while for the first time in her life Eternity truly considered killing someone. She finally saw him for what he was—a fanatic who would say anything, *do* anything to get what he wanted.

"If there is any justice in this world," she said, "you will get the end you deserve, Malik."

Eternity didn't wait for him to reply. She knelt by Lazander, brushing curls damp with sweat from his forehead. He was still unconscious, but his heart was steady, his pulse even—while her own heart felt like it was about to burst. She could almost see it—the life they could have had. A small farm by a creek. A yard full of animals. Perhaps even the pitter-patter of small feet in the garden.

To her shock, tears ran down her cheeks—and all at once she understood what her heart had been trying to tell her for weeks.

"I love you, Lazander," she said softly, kissing his forehead. "Your kindness. Your strength. Your *compassion*. Thank you… for everything."

In hours she would be dead—such was the cost of stopping Calamity. But it was a death *she* chose—and she took comfort in that.

**"Bless mine body, so I might better tread your path,"** she said, the words false and hollow. To her surprise she floated from the ground. Though she'd turned away from Gallow, she still had his powers, it seemed. Floating high into the air, she flew toward Gaj, the craters and trail of death and destruction the giant left easy to follow. Below her Malik hesitated for a moment, but then his hand came to his head, and he winced.

He soon sped ahead of her.

She smiled sadly. That was the thing about cowards—you couldn't trust them to do the right thing, but you could trust them to save their own skins.

## Chapter Forty-Seven

"What are we supposed to do with a flower?" Lukas asked, holding it close to the torch, turning it this way and that. "A flower that, need I remind you, was trapped in the body of a man with goat legs and horns and not the adorable doggy I was expecting."

The flower glowed as I reached for it, the colors of the rainbow bursting from its crystal-clear glass. My hand dropped from the unexpected weight—it was *heavy*.

*Fury's Claw Activated.*

My claws lengthened, and a thrill went through me—they'd almost doubled in size since the upgrades.

"You should take a step back," I said, still taking care not to give Lukas a direct order. He was no longer bound by a blood-debt, but old habits die hard. When he didn't answer, I looked up to find him already at the end of the corridor.

"What?" he called. "You might have forgotten about the wallow-tail and setting yourself on fire, but *I* haven't."

I sighed but closed my eyes.

*Lightning Claw Activated.*

Electricity burst from my claws, lighting up the glass flower. When it dimmed, there wasn't a scratch on it, nor did the glow within change.

"Damn," I said, twisting it around. "I thought it was like Calamity's Ability Stones—you have to crack them open to use them."

I brought up the System Menu, jumping to the Operator Tab. I'd never tried to use the Menu to "identify" something. I didn't know if it was even possible, but the moment I locked eyes with the strange flower, a pop-up flashed.

**ETERNITY DETECTED.**
**COST TO OPEN—2 VOID MANA.**

**VOID MANA AVAILABLE.**
**3/9999**

Wait... *Eternity?*

I stared at the glass flower—it couldn't be connected to the Eternity I knew, could it? Unless it was nothing to do with her but rather Gallow—that might explain why Calamity wanted it. But that didn't make sense either. If this belonged to the God of Judgment, it would've been hidden in one of his temples. Maybe if I open it...

*"Do not dare,"* Zara said. *"That Void Mana is to get you home. I refuse to let you use it on a trinket we neither know nor understand."*

I had to agree with her, though not about getting me home. All we knew about this thing was that we had to keep it from Calamity. Opening it might be as good as giftwrapping it for him and leaving it under the tree.

"What's an 'eternity'? What does it do?" I said aloud, my right eyelid twitching. Using the System when I was awake took my complete attention—if my thoughts strayed, or I became distracted in any way, it vanished. Instead of answering my question, however, the System said:

**ORIGIN: ERROR.**
**ADDITIONAL UNLOCKING PATHWAYS AVAILABLE VIA BLOOD OF ORIGINS OR CHOSEN.**

"Chosen," I knew—Eternity was Gallow's Chosen, so maybe it *was* connected to her, but I had no idea what an "origin" was or why I needed their blood. And that still didn't explain why Thaddeus, a shapeshifting dog, had it.

I groaned, closing the System. This wasn't getting me anywhere. Once we got out of here I could... the thought vanished as a memory from my first few days in this world surfaced. The first time I'd been to the Void, I'd asked Calamity why? Why kidnap me and bring me to this planet?

He said three words: "to Summon Eternity."

I stared down at the strange flower. This couldn't be it, could it? Did Calamity hurt and kill so many just to find a piece of *glass*? I knew he needed Player Two and me to break out of the Void, but I didn't know how or why. Was there a connection between us and this "eternity" thing?

"Lukas!" I called.

He sprinted to me before I'd finished saying his name, and I explained everything I could before I lost my mind to the possibilities.

In typical Lukas fashion, he neither panicked nor told me I was crazy—he just scratched his chin thoughtfully. "Teema, I mean this in the nicest way possible, but what does it *bloody matter?* Ravenna and Thaddeus hid this from Calamity for a reason. Now, I don't know about our boy Thad, but Ravenna took a one-way trip to chowtown for us, and that's enough for me to trust her—I say we grab this thing and run off into the sunset."

*"For once I agree with the cub,"* Zara said.

"You're right. Both of you," I said, "let's—"

*Boom.*

The crypt shook, dust raining down on us.

"What was that? An earthquake?" Lukas asked. We stood still, but something twisted in my gut. I'd been in an earthquake before—I didn't know when or where, but the shaking had been drawn out over several seconds. It hadn't felt like a single—

*BOOM.*

I jumped, chunks of debris falling as spider-web cracks formed in the ceiling. "That's no earthquake," I said, shoving the "flower" into my Inventory—it was easier than calling it an "eternity"—only one person had earned that name in my book.

"Come on," I said. "Let's slip out of the Keep while we still can."

\*\*\*

Getting out of the crypt was much easier than getting in—a combination lock and two heavy doors were all that barred the way, and the queen's impossibly neat handwriting detailed every step. The timing between the explosive booms never wavered, but they were getting louder. By the time we threw open the last door some of the older tombs had collapsed on the long dead and whatever rats weren't quick enough.

Lukas took a big, dramatic breath when we emerged to a dusk-filled sky. "May I never smell another dead body *again*."

The heavy iron door clicked shut behind us, blending into the yellow stone of the mountain—I couldn't even see the ridges where it closed. Even if I somehow found myself back to this exact spot, I doubted I'd be able to find the door again.

"Right," I said, trying to figure out where the hell we were. We looked to be about halfway down the mountain—one of the Keep's marble towers was just visible high above me—and a desert of ruined forests and ashen soil lay before us. "Let's get at least a couple of hours away before setting up camp. Then I'll open up the System again and see if I can't figure out what this 'eternity' thing does…"

I trailed off, squinting at a dark shape in the distance that was growing larger with every second. From here, it looked like it stood head and shoulders over the trees. I blinked, thinking it a trick of the light until I realized the tallest scarlet sunders didn't even come up to its *ankles*.

Zara growled.

The sound of bells reached us from high above.

### *Tithe of Beasts Activated.*

I closed my eyes, trying to focus on the noise. Over the clanging I could hear people in the Keep shouting, panic in their voices, but I couldn't make out what they were saying.

"Righto," Lukas said, gesturing in the opposite direction. "Let's get moving, we're losing daylight!"

"Lukas…"

"I have dried spike-hog and egg. I could whip us up an omelet when we make camp?"

"Lukas."

"Wait, we had spike-hog yesterday... I think whippertusks are native to this part of Navaros, but with everything being all barren and what not that might be a—"

"Lukas!"

"Don't say it," he said, a finger raised. "We're here to figure out whatever that glass thingamabob is. We are *not* here to fight the giant monster that may or may not have made me pee a little. Maybe that's Gaj, maybe that's Gaj's pet goober-pig, I don't care. What I do care about is stopping Calamity, and we can't do that if we're *dead*." He gestured up at the Keep with his thumb. "Evergarden has smarts, Freyley has beer, and Navaros has an *army*. They'll be fine."

"Did you *see* an army at the Keep?"

"Well, no."

"Did you see an army on the way here?"

"I mean... maybe," he said. "We can't know for sure."

"We saw their banners in the distance, Lukas—they were heading east. Maybe they're already on their way back, or maybe they're *days* away. Until then, the Keep has, what—a hundred soldiers? And you saw how they did against you and Zara. What are they supposed to do against *that!*"

I pointed at the dark shape, broad shoulders now visible. Somewhere in the Keep I heard a scream.

"But..." he trailed off, clearly angry.

I frowned. "You're not scared—well, you are, but that's not what this is about. What's going on?"

"You heard what the soldiers said about us," he said. "How their *king* wanted us handled."

"Ah," I said, suddenly understanding. "They were ready to kill us... for the crime of not being human."

"I spent most of my teens running away from the molger and hiding in human towns—but in the end, I always went home. Why? Because it didn't matter how well I hid my scent or how good I was at talking and acting like them—humans *hate* us."

BOOM.

The dark shape was close enough now that I could make out some details—long, gangly arms that swung back and forth. And a face as white as snow. The sight made my guts twist.

"Zara?" I asked aloud.

She'd been silent the entire time, buried so deep in the darkness I couldn't tell what she was thinking or feeling. *"Lukas is right. The humans fear us, or rather they fear our potential, for they know they will never measure up to us,"* she said, and my heart sank. *"But... whatever that creature is, it serves Calamity—which means it must die. I say we kill it."*

I relayed what Zara said to Lukas. He threw up his hands and sighed. "Fine. Guess we're killing it. Let's go."

"No," I said, stopping him gently with my hand. "You didn't ask to get tangled up with gods, monsters, and a weirdo from another planet."

He smiled at the last one.

"Yes, we're friends, and yes, I know you came because you wanted to help, but this isn't your fight. You don't have to risk your neck to pay back your blood-debt anymore—you're free. Go home, Lukas. I won't blame you."

*"I will,"* Zara muttered.

I ignored her, focusing on Lukas' face—the creases in the corner of his eyes when he smiled. In years to come they'd settle into deep laughter lines. The dimples in his cheeks and the mess of blond curls that had a life of their own. He'd been dragged from the life he'd known to chase after me, and while he'd loudly complained along the way, he'd risked everything to save me—because he didn't have a choice.

He did now.

I dropped the satchel Mara had given me, knowing I couldn't take it when I transformed. *You ready?* I silently asked Zara, head craned as I sized up the distance between here and the Keep.

*"Always,"* she replied.

I was about to hand her back control when Lukas gripped the rock beside me, his claws digging in.

"Not a word," he muttered as he started to climb. "Not one bloody word."

# Chapter Forty-Eight

Queen Firanta stood on the outer wall, gripping her cane tightly as she looked out at the kingdom she'd slit her own throat for. Only weeks ago the view had been breathtaking—the sharp incline of the Widow Mountain cut the forest of scarlet sunders in half while the Sweetdawn river curled around the base like the lazy finger of a lover.

Now the view was breathtaking for entirely different reasons.

The forest was gone, the Sweetdawn river nothing but dried mud. Hundreds of people lined the roads, some dangerously close to the cliff edge as they trekked for the Ivory Keep, hoping and praying for refuge. It was what made it so easy for the shadow-fiends to tear through them like parchment.

It was too soon. The sages had sworn it would be months before the Tyrant arrived, let alone do something as brazen as attack—the wallow-tail was simply testing Navaros' defenses, they'd said. But her husband had prepared for it anyway. Soldiers manned hastily made lookout towers that ringed the base of the mountain, each armed with a simple iron bell and a wand that blasted harmless red sparks into the air—the signal for an incoming attack.

But no signal came. No shrill ringing or useless red sparks. Only the heavy clang of the Keep's gigantic bells cut through the air, telling her what the screams already had.

They were under attack. And they were going to *lose*.

Fists hammered on the front gates, a cacophony of flesh on metal as the hundreds trapped outside pounded on the doors.

"Help! Help us!"

"Please, take my child!"

"They're coming! Gallow help us, they're coming!"

Every single one was a dagger in the queen's heart.

The mountain shifted, lying still and barren one moment, crawling with pitch-black limbs the next, like a sea of ants swarming a fresh kill. Shadow-fiends ran on all fours, some climbing up the side of the mountain, others charging straight through the hordes of people stuck on the road—a deadly fall on one side, a monster's claws on the other.

It was an impossible choice.

"We need to open the gates," the queen said, proud of how steady her voice was. "Our own people are being *slaughtered.*"

"We can't, my queen," Commander Rhys replied, one hand instinctively on his sword. "We lack the resources to protect the Keep *and* man a frontal assault. All we'd do is feed the Tyrant more soldiers—when given a choice, most choose to serve. I've seen it with my own eyes."

Had anyone been eavesdropping, they'd think Rhys cold and unfeeling. But Firanta had known him since he was a boy—he'd grown up with Leon, the two as close as brothers. She was probably the only person other than the king who could hear the cracks in his voice as he watched the carnage out on the green, tens of lives lost every second they dithered.

"How many soldiers do we have?" Firanta asked.

"Forty palace guards, seventy-five soldiers—all my men—and twenty palace mages. We have no battle mages—the king requested all of them to deal with the wallow-tail's attacks."

Firanta risked a glance at the Gallowed Temple. The followers of the God of Judgment had barricaded themselves inside the moment the bells rang, but she knew Head Disciple Harrow. Had Zara and Lukas been discovered he would be outside, yelling about intruders and demanding every soldier be sent to apprehend them, regardless of what was happening.

Gallow's justice came first, after all.

The cynical part of her wondered if she'd been a fool. For all she knew Lukas and Zara served the Tyrant, and she'd just handed the corpse of her closest friend to the enemy. It was at times like this she missed Thaddeus the most, her fingers clutching the memory gem in her pocket. The light within was barely a glimmer—maybe he could still hear her. Maybe not. But having even this small piece of him gave her strength. Now was not the time to doubt herself. The Tyrant was coming, and she'd be damned if she went down without a fight.

No, she thought, remembering the steel in Lukas' eyes—*Calamity* was coming. If she was about to die, she might as well use the bastard's real name.

"I need those doors open, and my people safe. Tell me how," she said.

"We need to force the shadow-fiends back and thin out their numbers, or we'll be overrun the second we open the doors. Arrows do little against them unless spelled, but I have the palace mages working on that as we speak. That leaves us only one option—pour oil over the sides, and torch it," Rhys said, gesturing at the tangle of limbs, claws, and blood that spilled onto the grass, turning it crimson. "We discovered that fire works almost as well as enchanted weapons, of which we have painfully few."

"Fire doesn't distinguish between friend or foe," the queen said, "our own people will burn."

The archers on either side of her took aim and fired, a volley of arrows striking at least ten shadow-fiends. But the dark beasts barely flinched as they closed in on their victims, slicing and screaming along with them. Though the queen had never been on a battlefield, she thought she'd known what to expect. But no one ever mentioned the *smell*.

"We either beat them back with fire, or we lose everyone trapped on the green outside *and* the road," Rhys said quietly.

A blood-soaked woman ran screaming for the Keep, a shadow-fiend hunting her on all fours. An arrow struck the monster, then a second and third. It stumbled and Firanta's breath caught—but then it leaped forward with a moan, tackling the terrified woman. They fell together into the trenches where sharpened spikes had been hammered into the earth.

Firanta looked away when only the shadow-fiend emerged, shadows already knitting the hole in its stomach closed.

"Do what you must," Firanta said, hating the words but swearing she would stay and watch. She was about to murder her own people—it was the least she could do.

A roar cut through the moans of the shadow-fiends and the cries of their victims. Firanta looked up to see a huge, winged beast, its fur as white as snow, soaring through the air.

"Archers, ready!" Rhys shouted. "Load the catapults! Mages! Where are my damn mages?"

Firanta stared at the monster, transfixed—she'd never seen a beast like it. A silver mane haloed its face while a long, reptilian tail snaked out from behind. Powerful wings curved as it descended, heading straight for them.

They were doomed, she knew. The Keep was designed to handle attacks from the ground, not the sky, and while Leon had run the mages ragged doing drills after the wallow-tail's attack, they didn't have the numbers to take it down. Firanta held her ground as mages swarmed the battlements, refusing Rhys' repeated request for her to evacuate to a siege room.

Her mother had always told her a queen's place was with her people—and that was where she would stay.

Firanta was sure the beast would land in the inner courtyard where it could do the maximum amount of damage, but it gave a ferocious roar and crashed into the middle of the shadow-fiends—*attacking* them head on.

"Rhys!" Firanta called, but he was already leaning over the outer wall to get a better look, palm raised for his archers to hold. The beast spun, its huge tail sending five shadow-fiends over the edge of the cliff before its fangs bit down on the head of another, ripping it off with a savage tear. A figure leaped off the beast's shoulders. All Firanta saw was a flash of blond hair, and then a six-legged molger appeared, saving life after life as it barreled through the monsters with reckless abandon.

"Zara and Lukas," Firanta said in disbelief. She'd given them everything they needed to flee this place and never return—yet they'd come back. She silently offered up an apology to Eternity and Lazander. They'd pleaded Zara's innocence, none more than Eternity, and she'd scoffed in reply, thinking she knew better.

A pathway cleared, the molger forcing the road open while Zara approached a bedraggled group of survivors—many clutching bleeding stomachs and legs. Rhys made to drop his hand, raining arrows down on the beast.

"Hold. She will not hurt them," the queen said.

Rhys didn't look so convinced. "What manner of creature *is* that?"

"I have no idea what it is, but I know *who* it is—Zara the Fury," she replied.

Rhys couldn't hide his incredulous look.

"Look at the eyes," the queen said with a small smile. "Who else has irises that burn like melted gold?"

Zara stopped a few feet from some of the survivors and dipped her head. About two hundred people huddled outside—some hiding among the trees while others had dared to take their chances in the trenches—but the most hurt lay sprawled on the ground. To the queen's surprise, the able wordlessly helped the injured onto Zara's back, her white fur turning pink and red from the blood. When twenty or so people clung to her, Firanta realized what the Fury planned to do.

"She's coming here," Firanta called when Zara took off at a sprint. "Clear the way, Rhys, and if a single person lays a finger on her they will answer to *me*."

Firanta didn't bother waiting for a reply. Cane in one hand, the other flush against the wall for balance, she headed down the steep steps, cursing her mechanical leg no fewer than five times. By the time she made it past the inner walls and to the courtyard, the once crowded space was half-empty as people pressed themselves into corners—even those Zara had saved were limping as far away from her as they could.

"My queen!" a nervous soldier called, his spear held tightly in his hands. "My queen, we've been ordered to stand down, but shouldn't we—"

"Silence," she snapped, pushing past him.

People threw themselves out of her path almost as quickly as they did for Zara.

Up close the beast was gigantic, the delicate scales of her wings iridescent in the setting sun. Claws the length of a sword rested on cobbles, and the queen knew all it would take was a press of her paw for Zara to split the very stone. Yet she sat on her haunches, her wings held loose and relaxed at her sides. Eyes as golden as the sun's dawn looked down at her with a keen intelligence, waiting for the queen to make the first move.

She was happy to oblige. "Greetings, Zara the Fury," the queen called, making sure her voice carried. The cries and whimpers of the hopeless faded as she spoke, a flurry of whispers following.

"Did she say *Zara?*"

"The bandit killer?"

"Magnus' fiancée?"

The last made Zara growl. The courtyard instantly fell silent.

*"You do not cower as the others do. Good,"* said a voice in her head.

The queen was one of the few who didn't gasp. Firanta glanced around to see people looking at one another, the same question in their eyes. "Did you hear it too?"

"A helpful gift," the queen said, as if it was an everyday occurrence for a magical beast to speak in her mind. "Tell me, can you also hear my thoughts?"

*"If you direct a thought at me, then yes—within a certain proximity,"* Zara said. *"But I cannot hear your general thoughts, nor do I know the boundaries of this ability. I am still taming my voidbeast."* Cat-like eyes twinkled at her, and the queen smiled when she realized the Fury was enjoying this.

"Voidbeast? A fitting name for such a beautiful creature." It was pointless flattery, and they both knew it, but Firanta wasn't saying it for Zara's benefit. She was saying it for the people who stared at her, their heads cocking to one side as they realized their queen was right—the voidbeast *was* beautiful.

Zara's lips curled in an imitation of a smirk. Outside, the pounding on the Keep's doors began anew. *"I will ferry the injured inside until the way is clear. Once the shadow-fiends are dead, you will open the doors and allow those who still breathe within,"* Zara said.

The queen nodded, as if that had been the plan all along. "Navaros is grateful for Moonvale's aid," she said, raising her voice to make sure every single person heard. "We will remember it in times to come."

Zara huffed, but she said nothing. The voidbeast crouched low and leaped high into the sky. The queen couldn't help but marvel at Zara's powerful wings as she flew skyward, her silver mane barely rustling as she headed back into battle.

# Chapter Forty-Nine

It took four more trips through the skies and scores of dead shadow-fiends before it was safe enough for the Keep to open its doors. Lukas hobbled over to Zara in his molger form, head low, almost every inch of his huge, barrel-chested body covered in claw marks. She eyed the wounds, searching for any that looked deep enough to cause him serious pain. But when Lukas collapsed dramatically with a loud sigh, Zara relaxed—if he was well enough to complain, he was fine.

*"This is no time for a nap, cub,"* she said, one eye on the doors where the humans shuffled inside. Why was it taking so long? And why were they wasting their time on useless things like *crying?* She kept glancing back at the road, sure the shadow-fiends would reappear at any moment. At some unseen signal Calamity's servants had retreated, scuttling away like the vermin they were. While Lukas was relieved, it made Zara uneasy. The slug was clearly planning something.

*"This is ridiculous. How come you don't have a single mark on you?"* Lukas huffed, his voice reverberating in her mind. They'd been pleased to discover her telepathy worked on him even when he was transformed. *"Too busy running off and being a hero."*

Zara's tail swished in irritation. Lukas chuckled, a deep sound closer to a purr. *"Admit it,"* he said. *"It's fun being the good guy for once."*

BOOM.

The giant's steps were impossibly loud, and Zara narrowed her eyes at the monster—as if the force of her glare could beat it back. It had just reached the dried riverbed that curved around the forest closest to the Keep, though its pace had slowed considerably, its body shaking with every step. Zara could see its bleached bone skull, the ivory daggers that stuck out from its chest and wrists, and was, quite frankly, unimpressed. To her, true evil was a man with silken robes and lustrous blond hair. If this was Calamity's attempt at scaring her, he was doing a poor job of it.

*"That* must *be Gaj,"* Teema said, her voice low though only Zara could hear her. *"How are we supposed to stop her?"*

*The same way we stop everything,* Zara silently replied. *By cutting off her head.*

A shout from the Keep's walls drew her attention, and Zara's irritation only increased when a soldier beckoned her with his gauntlet. "Her majesty wishes to speak with you, Lady Fury!"

*"Ohhh, it's* Lady *Fury now,"* Lukas said, shaking enthusiastically as he stood, most of his wounds already healed. *"Go on* Lady Fury, *royalty calls."*

Zara spun, making sure her tail caught him in the side. He just laughed—in his solid molger form, it was like striking a mountain. With a huff, she sprinted for the cliff edge and jumped as far as she could—allowing herself a few seconds to enjoy the cold air that whipped her mane intro a frenzy before snapping out her wings. She'd given Lukas a heart attack the first time she'd jumped but had found it much quicker than taking off from the ground—which felt like trying to fly through thick soup. The injured she'd carried on her back hadn't appreciated it, but that didn't bother her—let them scream. They were safe, and that was what mattered.

Zara tilted toward the courtyard, amused to see a large space had been cordoned off for her. The queen waited just outside it, a circle of guards at her back. The strange old woman intrigued Zara. Her pale complexion, sightless eye, and lack of limbs would have marked her for death with the vaxion, yet she led these people.

*"Zara, do* not *say that to the queen,"* Teema said.

*It is a compliment to her leadership. Had it been up to myself or Ashira, she would have been slaughtered as a babe.*

Teema sighed.

While people had thankfully stopped screaming every time they saw Zara, they still skittered back when she landed. A growl escaped her—she'd risked not only her life but Lukas' to save them. They should be falling at her feet in *thanks.*

*"They will,"* Teema said, and she could feel the girl smiling. *"Just give them time. Who knows, maybe a statue or two of a certain* Fury *will end up in this very courtyard."*

Zara just grumbled—it was a horrifying thought.

"Lady Fury," the queen called formally, "we owe you our thanks. Your heroics have saved hundreds of lives today. Navaros is in your debt. *I* am in your debt."

Zara stared down at the queen.

*"Say you're welcome, or something,"* Teema said, a little panicked. *"You're being rude."*

*I will not. This is their own doing,* Zara silently replied. *Had they been better prepared we would not have been needed. The deaths today lie on her head, and that of the so-called king. This is the burden leaders bear.*

The silence stretched from uncomfortable to awkward, but the queen smiled as if she hadn't noticed. "With the road clear, we've raided our stables and aviaries and sent every man, woman, and child who can ride. They won't make it to the king before our hawks, but I'm taking no chances. With luck, King Leon will receive word before the moon is high. His armies should be here before dawn."

*"Everyone will be dead by then,"* Zara said calmly.

Teema sighed. The queen looked more amused than offended by her candor.

"You are not a woman who minces words, are you Lady Fury? But I am afraid this is all we can do. Our allies are either too far away or too busy fighting their own battles. We will have to last until dawn, or as you rightfully pointed out, die."

Zara chuckled. There was a bite to this queen she admired—these people might have a chance after all. *"The giant is called Gaj. She is Calamity's lieutenant and the catalyst of his arrival. This is no simple invasion of your lands—this is the site where he will be summoned."*

The queen blanched, eyes darting to the Gallowed Temple. Zara had been inside it once before. The people within were fat with power and arrogance, not even stirring when she roamed their halls. Zara was about to suggest they throw them outside the gates as fodder for the shadow-fiends, but Teema gave her the mental equivalent of an elbow in the ribs.

"Then it is all the more important for us to not only survive but take down this *Gaj*," the queen said finally. "But I did not call you here to give in to melancholy. Rhys?"

A man in heavy armor stepped out from the guards who circled her—moving in his full-plate with ease. Not a guard, Zara realized, a soldier—one who'd seen his fair share of battle. He raised a hand to his brow, snapping out a salute.

"During the next attack, I will lead an assault outside the gates alongside thirty of my men," he said. "We will have a mix of palace guards and mages on the walls while the remainder of my soldiers will protect the courtyards should the gates be breached. Until then, we will repair the trenches and dig more should we be graced with time. This battle will be a marathon, not a sprint, and so we will work in five hour shifts. Food and water will be available for you and the molger—"

"Lukas," the queen said primly.

"—for you and Lukas," Rhys said, stumbling.

Zara tried not to look bored—she didn't understand why the human was telling her these things.

He stopped, looking awkward. "It would be of great aid to us if you would explain your approach for the coming battle."

Ah, that was why.

*"Kill everything,"* Zara said.

Teema laughed. The queen's lips twitched in the ghost of a smile.

"I see," Rhys said, not bothering to hide his clear disapproval for what she'd always considered a foolproof plan.

At Teema's insistence, Zara added, *"You will deal with the shadow-fiends. We will deal with Gaj. And the wallow-tail, should it appear. I doubt Calamity will hold anything back during this battle."*

The man brightened. "I can work with that. Very good, Lady Fury." He offered her a salute but dropped it when Zara just stared at him.

She snapped out her wings—the conversation was over as far as she was concerned. They would either live or die, and nothing said would change that. But as she rose into the air, struggling to gain momentum in the tight space, the queen's thoughts reached her.

*"I was wrong about you, Zara,"* she said, sadness threaded throughout her words. *"And for that I am sorry."*

Pride rolled off Teema in waves. Zara grumbled but couldn't deny that part of her was pleased. Magnus, the queen, the molger, even Lukas—so many people had misjudged her. Then again, only months ago she was a very different person. The old Zara, for instance, would never do something as stupid as risk her life for a bunch of humans. But now she had people she wanted to protect—Teema, Lukas, Ashira, and the other vaxion back in Moonvale. And while she knew she'd probably die for her newfound heroics, that didn't bother her.

Because for the first time in years Zara the Fury had a *choice*. And dying for the life she'd chosen, for the *people* she'd chosen… well, perhaps that wouldn't be such a bad thing.

\*\*\*

When the attack came, the shadow-fiends didn't bother hiding. They raced up and over the Widow Mountain in waves, digging their claws into the ground and throwing themselves forward, moaning with anger and need.

Rhys stood in the middle of the green outside the Keep, soldiers at his back, the red and gold of Navaros emblazoned on his cloak. The ground in front of him was slick and heavy with oil—even the trees Zara had hidden in only hours before were doused in it. Rhys stood; hand raised. The shadow-fiends charged him, heedless of the oil, the wet slap of their claws sending drops flying into the air. When the first monster was almost on him, he brought his hand down, slicing it through the air like an executioner's axe.

At his signal an arrow dipped in flame hit the oil, the green exploding in a blazing fireball as thirty or so shadow-fiends fell prey to the trap. They struggled, flailing as the fire cut through their protective shadows, burning the flesh of the hosts within. But for every one that fell, five more monsters appeared to take their place, running through the still burning corpses.

A handful of Calamity's servants raced up the near vertical summit of Widow Mountain, trying to breach the Keep from on high. The walls lit up with spelled arrows and bursts of flame from the mages.

Zara longed to run into the fray and rip the shadow-fiends apart, despite the sour taste they left in her mouth, but she forced herself to wait. She stood at the very top of the mountain, higher than even the shadow-fiends and their claws could reach, her eyes locked on Gaj.

The giant was minutes from the Keep, Gaj's skeletal form a corpse of horrors. But Zara felt no fear of the fight to come—only anticipation. She looked to the skies, eyes peeled for the wallow-tail, but only the velvet soft navy of the coming night greeted her. No matter—she was about to change that.

Her human skin shifted, shimmering like a river in moonlight as tendrils of flesh swirled around her skull, her lightning crackling with bloodlust as she transformed into a vaxion. The sky darkened, and Zara threw her head back with a *roar*. Her call was a cry, a demand—let them come: Gaj, the wallow-tail, Calamity—it didn't matter. She would kill every last one.

**Wrath's Storm Activated.**

The sky answered her battle cry, forks of lightning striking Gaj over and over, the air alive with power. Several bolts hit the mountain, the screams of the shadow-fiends drowned out by her defiant roar. The dark clouds cleared as quickly as they'd come.

Gaj hadn't even slowed.

"Well, we knew that was a longshot," Lukas said, patting her shoulder. "Let's go and teach skelly belly why she picked the wrong world to mess with, eh?"

Zara's reply was to growl as her flesh coiled around her, her bones breaking anew as she grew and grew until she towered over man, vaxion, and molger. Lukas clambered onto Zara's back, his human hands gripping the silver mane of her voidbeast.

Had *Wrath's Storm* not worked, she'd planned to circle Gaj alone, searching for a means to attack, but Lukas had insisted on coming—an idea she thought moronic. He had no wings, which meant if he fell, a swift death was all that awaited him.

"But think of how funny it would be to make it to the end of the world, only to die because I tripped," was his reply. It wasn't much of an argument, but he'd proven himself in battle. To coddle him would be to disrespect him.

Zara took off at a sprint, her wings catching an updraft, taking her high into the sky. The sun had just dipped behind the horizon, but already an ice-cold wind nipped at her through her fur. She felt Lukas' entire body tense when Gaj turned her eyeless sockets toward them, the creak of her skull like nails on a chalkboard.

*"I'm here for you,"* Teema said, and Zara felt the ghost of a hand gripping one of her huge paws. *"Whatever happens, I'm here."*

*As I am for you,* she replied, the words thick in her mouth.

Gaj slowed to a halt; head bowed. And then the giant swung for Zara—her bony fist a blur of speed at odds with her halting walk.

Zara flattened her wings against her body, fearlessly dropping like a stone. Lukas yelped as an impossibly large fist shot past, grazing her fur—the blast of air sending them spinning. With a snap, her wings shot open, shaking at the sudden drag. Lukas buried his head in her mane, but Zara had no time to comfort him—it took all her focus to zip around Gaj's legs as she dodged a second, blisteringly fast strike.

Flying skyward, Zara focused on the righteous fury she felt when she found Teema in Calamity's prison—naked and half-starved. Her sobs when she wrapped her arms around Zara, hugging her like a life buoy. A warmth began at the back of Zara's throat as a power built inside of her. A power that yearned to be unleashed.

Gaj came to a crunching halt, her huge body turning to face Zara. The Fury unhinged her jaw.

**Skyscream Activated.**

A beam of destruction shot from her mouth, hitting Gaj square in the chest. It cut cleanly through muscle and bone and out the other side—striking the ground. The world held its breath for a split second, and then an explosion of fire and light burst into life behind Gaj.

"Hell yeah!" Lukas yelled, whopping loudly. "Shove that up your—"

Gaj raised her head, the muscles around her neck unfurling like snakes.

"Oh, *shek*."

The flesh-like vines shot forward, their speed and reach astonishing. Zara tried to dodge, but it was too late. They wrapped around her, piercing flesh and bone as they bound her. She screamed at the spear that dug into her side, tasting blood.

One of her wings beat frantically, the other pinned to her side as Gaj pulled Zara toward her, the Fury fighting every second. A lone figure in gold armor stood on Gaj's shoulder, half-hidden by the bones that burst from her like blades. He raised a hand, fire brimming at his fingertips—Player Two.

"I've got you Zara, hang on!" Lukas cried, hacking and slashing with his claws, chunks of Gaj's flesh falling from the sky, but it wasn't enough. If Gaj didn't rip her apart, Player Two would.

And then a weight leaped off Zara's back, and Lukas was running along a narrow tendril of dried muscle, a dark blur in his vaxion form. Player Two banished his flames with a smile, drawing a wicked blade from his back.

*"Idiot cub!"* Zara yelled, ignoring the pain as she thrashed, driving the spear deeper into her side. *"You cannot take him alone!"* She brandished her anger like a shield, biting and clawing at her bindings. In this form, she couldn't use her fire—and if she shapeshifted while impaled...

"Zara! I have a Healing Void, *one second,"* Teema cried.

*Not while I am bound,* Zara barked. *Or I will heal with the flesh-vines inside me!*

She could feel Teema's horror, but Zara focused on ripping into Gaj with everything she had. She couldn't reach the main spear that skewered her like a pig, but she refused to give up.

"Zara..."

*Not now, Teema.*

"Zara, look out!"

The Fury froze. Gaj's neck slithered open to reveal a gaping hole where her throat should be. Useless teeth lined her top jaw, but she didn't need them. Soft globs of graying flesh wriggled like fat fingers, and an acrid scent hit Zara's nose—*acid.*

She was going to be burned alive, and then swallowed whole.

"Gaj, no, we need her!" Player Two roared, driving his blade into Lukas. The cub whined, falling back, his claws scrabbling to find purchase. "You can eat the boy, not—"

And then an arc of darkness cut through Zara's bindings, and she was falling.

# Chapter Fifty

"That white-winged beastie is the one who gave Lazander and me matching scars," Malik said, grinning. "Guess Ravenna decided she wanted a bigger piece of the pie than the Tyrant was willing to give. Let them at it, I say."

To Eternity's dismay, some of Malik's old swagger had returned on their journey here. They stood in the dried mud and scattered corpses of the Sweetdawn river, their heads low. Shadow-fiends rushed past them in the distance, but none gave Eternity and Malik a second glance—they were too intent on the Ivory Keep.

"The Keep is being overrun," Eternity said, her voice tight. "I can feel the shadow-fiends from here, there are... too many to count."

"Makes sense," Malik said, his eyes locked on Eternity. "When it comes to Calamity, a fishing village and a bunch of vaxion aren't going to cut it. The dark god needs hundreds of lives to come through, and where better to find them strung up like livestock than here?"

"So this is the plan? To sit back and watch hundreds of people die?"

Malik hissed in annoyance. "Not this again. Right, let's say we do things your way. We charge in like the Gilded Knights, fighting with everything we have. On the off-chance we don't die, how are you going to kill Gaj or bind Calamity if you're in tatters from killing a couple hundred shadow-fiends? For the sake of your own ego, you want to save a bunch of humans only to doom the *entire world* because you couldn't do the hard thing. How are you not getting this? If you're going to die, make it bloody count!"

Eternity almost smiled. "I was Chosen on my nineteenth birthday, Malik. I have lived every moment since knowing I must die for the world to live. But I will do it on *my* terms."

Malik didn't see the rock hovering behind him, not until she slammed it into the back of his head, knocking him out cold. Eternity's fingers twitched as she used her magic to lower it to the ground, knowing she only had seconds before the Champion was up.

**"YOU JEOPARDIZE YOUR PEOPLE."**

Gallow's voice echoed in her mind.

**"YOUR WORLD."**

"I swore to come to the Ivory Keep—an oath I have kept," Eternity said, eyes locked on Gaj and the strange, winged creature. It was odd, but there was something familiar about the white beast, though she knew for a fact she'd never seen it, not even in books of old. "I will be back when you are ready to fulfil your end of the bargain, Gallow—do not think I have forgotten."

She flew toward Gaj. The giant dug its vines into the white-furred beast and fear lent Eternity speed. She gathered Gallow's power in her hands, ignoring the fire in her skull, her body struggling to contain the god's presence. She'd lost count of how many times she'd used her gifts today, but she wouldn't let pain stop her.

**"You have been judged. And you have been found wanting,"** she cried, firing a whip-like blade of shadow with deadly aim.

\*\*\*

It was her.

It was *Eternity*.

I hadn't seen her since I'd woken up in Magnus' castle—a lifetime ago. She hung in the air, eyes pitch black, once long blonde hair cut so tight it brushed her skull. My heart twisted. She looked like she'd been through a war zone.

And then we were falling.

I pulled up my Inventory, jumping to the *Healing Void*. To my relief, there was a falsling specific option to "auto-apply." If Zara had to drink it mid-air and without thumbs, we were both dead.

*No,* Zara said. *Do not use it on me, save it for... for...*

And then she was gone, her mind going dark as she fell unconscious. Any other time I would have rolled my eyes at her stubbornness, but I just braced myself as I used the *Healing Void*—and took control.

Pain lit up my voidbeast body, delicate trails of smoke hissing from my wounds—the acid from Gaj's tendrils. Knowing I'd kill Zara too was the only thing that kept me conscious. Stretching out my wings, I gasped when the wind tore at the membrane, ripping open wounds almost as quickly as the potion healed them. Zara had insisted I try her vaxion and voidbeast forms on the way here, but it felt like walking around in someone's stolen clothes. I didn't have her control of them, so I made do with keeping my wings level, hoping the *Healing Void* worked quick enough to stop us from crashing.

I grimaced, the ground rushing to meet me as I fell, still too fast.

*This is going to hurt,* was my last thought as I hit the dirt, tripping head over tail. Crack. Front paw. Crack. Back left. I tumbled to a stop, groaning in pain, but miraculously alive.

The tingling sensation of the potion faded. I shakily got to my feet, happy to be alive, and even happier I could still move. I checked my wings, relieved the tears had healed, but when I put weight on my left paw, something slid around inside it—making my stomach flip. Zara healed quickly, even quicker since the upgrades, but it would still take about an hour to reach full strength. I had to get back into the air, back to Lukas—who was fighting Player Two *alone.*

"I am sorry I could not aid you when you fell," a soft, serene voice called. "The vaxion was thrown from Gaj, and I helped lower him to the ground. Know that he is safe and unharmed, for I have no quarrel with you or Ravenna."

Eternity landed lightly in front of me. I was still reeling from the fact that she was actually *here,* but my happiness at seeing her was tainted by how awful she looked. Her clothes hung loose on her too-thin frame, and there was a new sadness in her sapphire eyes. But alongside it I saw a strength and confidence that wasn't there the last time we'd met. I smiled. Guess I wasn't the only one who'd changed since that fateful night.

"I know you serve Ravenna but not where her allegiances lie," Eternity said calmly, hands raised like I was a rabid animal. "If you attacked Gaj to stop her, then you and I have the same goal. But if this was some ploy to earn Calamity's favor, then I cannot—"

She gasped when my skin shifted, and I couldn't help but groan, my broken arm burning from the change. Her eyes went wide when I stood on two legs once more, my left hand clutched to my chest, my dark armor reforming in time with my skin.

"Zara... Zara is that you? How—"

I wrapped my good hand around her, pulling the smaller woman into a tight hug, memories of my first day in this new, terrifying world overwhelming me. My injured arm screamed in protest, but I didn't care. Thin arms wrapped around my waist, returning the hug.

I don't know how long we stood there, my head resting on hers, or who pulled away first, but when I looked down, I saw there were tears in her eyes too.

"Hi," I said, heat flaring my cheeks, suddenly embarrassed. I hadn't even said *"hello"* to the poor woman before practically tackling her. For all I knew she barely remembered me, yet here I was acting like she was my long-lost best friend.

"That was how you first greeted me so long ago. It really *is* you."

"You... you remember that?"

Eternity laughed. "How could I not? You rescued me from Magnus when others stood by. During my darker moments, the memory of your courage... gave me strength, and more. And for that I owe you thanks." A light pink lit up her cheeks. My own burned brighter in return.

"What are you doing here?" I asked, eager to change the subject. "What happened to you? Why are you..." I gestured at her, taking in her dirty, bedraggled appearance.

"It is difficult to explain," she said. "But I am here to help. As are you, I take it?" She smiled, but I could see the fear in her eyes as she wondered whose side I was on.

"Don't worry," I said quickly. "Ravenna is, *was*, against Calamity. So am I. And... so is Zara."

Eternity frowned, and I could see her confusion. Zara stirred in my mind, shaking her head like a dazed cat. *"I see we are not dead. Well done, Teema."* I felt her surprise as she looked through my eyes, grinning wryly when she realized what was happening. *"Ah, it is your precious Eternity. I wondered when next your paths would cross."*

*Not helping, Zara.*

"It's complicated," I said to Eternity. "But the real Zara is also up here." I tapped the side of my head. "I'm just a passenger. A temporary one, but Zara knows about me. We're... we're friends, actually."

I felt oddly bashful at the proclamation. Against all odds, she'd become not only someone I trusted, but also one of my closest friends.

*"We are more than friends, Teema,"* Zara said.

*I know what you're trying to say, but that's not what that phrase means, Zara,* I said, having moved from "bashful" to "mortified." I was happy Eternity couldn't hear the conversation going on in my head, but my relief turned to concern when her eyes widened.

"Player Two mentioned Valerius. Spoke of him as if he was one such 'passenger.' I thought it madness, but is this true? Is he… are you like him?"

"No! I mean, technically I am. But I don't serve Calamity, I swear it," I said quickly.

"But how are you… sane? I have seen what it did to Player Two—his mind is polluted. Lost to a madness that threatens the entire world."

"Because… well, because of Zara. And people like you. People who were kind to me and helped me—even at great cost to themselves," I said, thinking of Lenia and Waylen, who nursed me back to health in the molger village. Ashira and the vaxion. Lukas. "I don't know what happened to Player Two to make him so angry, but I want to save this world. You can speak to Zara if you like. Lukas too, I'm not—"

"I believe you."

"—going to… Wait, what? Just like that?"

"You saved my life—more than once, in fact. But even if you had not, you wear your heart on your sleeve, and the truth shines through it. However, this presents me with a problem." I tensed but she smiled. "I have only ever known you as the Fury. What should I call you, passenger?"

"Zara calls me Teema."

Her eyes widened. "The Fury named you her teema? You grow more extraordinary by the second. Well, if she is all right with it, then I too will call you Teema—you earned it that night in Magnus' castle."

*"I like this one,"* Zara said, making me jump. *"She may call you Teema."*

"Hi, hello, how's it going, *terribly* sorry to interrupt what I'm sure is a beautiful moment," Lukas said, his skin rippling as he came to a skidding halt next to us, his human head forming first, arms and legs following. "But we have a problem."

Gaj's bones groaned like metal in the wind as she turned, resuming her slow walk to the Keep. I was struck again by her pace. She could move blindingly fast, I saw it when she fought Zara—but now she acted like she was trudging through treacle.

"Player Two is still up there, but there's something wrong with him. Other than the usual insanity and serving a god who's trying to kill us all," Lukas said, hands on hips. "He could have cut my head off at least twice, he fights like a demon, but his sword kept jerking to the side at the last second. Oh!" he said, offering a hand to Eternity. "Hi, I'm Lukas, molger-cum-vaxion extraordinaire, it's a long story. Thank you for stopping me from falling to a painful death."

Eternity took his hand, focusing on his eyes and face with an uncomfortable intensity. It took me a second to realize why—Lukas was completely naked. My armor changed with me, but he had to make do with his birthday suit. I'd seen it so many times now it didn't bother me, but this was a first for her.

*"Now is not the time to linger on Lukas' manhood, Teema,"* Zara said.

*I wasn't! I'm not—*

*"Gaj will reach the Keep any minute now. I will go."*

*Just… give me a second.*

"The real Zara is going to take over now," I told Eternity.

The Fury was chomping at the bit to attack Gaj again—she considered it a personal failing that she hadn't anticipated Gaj's horrifying flesh vines and a mouth full of acid. I knew better than to argue with her. "She's… intense."

*"I am focused."*

"But she's a good person," I finished with a smile, and then I was back in the darkness. I wondered what Eternity thought of the switch, knowing it must look strange. One second I was smiling, the next Zara was back in her body, loudly cracking her neck as she rolled her shoulders. She didn't acknowledge Eternity or Lukas. She was too busy focusing on her body with laser-like precision, assessing her injuries. When she came to her injured arm, she wrapped her hand around it and without warning jerked it sharply—breaking it a second time.

"Zara, what are you *doing?*" I called, horrified.

"The bone was not set after the fall, which meant it healed incorrectly," she said aloud, no hint of pain in her voice.

Lukas hid a smile with a well-timed cough while Eternity looked like she was regretting all her life choices.

"Eternity, Zara, Zara, Eternity," Lukas said, gesturing between the two. "And yes, Eternity, she is like this all the time."

"The darkness you wield like a blade," Zara said, golden eyes fixed on blue, "is this an ability you can use freely?"

"Yes. And no," Eternity said. "I have a limit, one I'm steadily approaching."

"So, you have at least one blow left, good. You will strike at the neck while I attack with my skyscream. Together we will cleave its head from its shoulders. Teema, can you see someone's… magic numbers like Ravenna did?"

"Ah," I said, cursing myself for not thinking of it before. I couldn't see them on regular people—they weren't plugged into the System—but I should be able to for Player Two. "Get me close enough, and I'll try."

"Good," Zara said. "Lukas, you will ride on my back, but you will *not* engage. I would leave you here on the ground, but you would probably do something foolish like die."

"Aw, you *do* know me, Zara," he chimed.

"If Player Two attacks I will handle him," Zara said, ignoring Lukas. "Eternity will focus on Gaj. Let us move."

Then she was on all fours, shifting into her voidbeast form, her front paw screaming in protest, but she didn't even flinch, her wings slicing the air like blades.

As we took off, I heard Eternity whisper, "She really *is* intense."

## Chapter Fifty-One

The Ivory Keep was a cacophony of noise—the moaning cries of shadow-fiends, screams of the terrified, and prayers of the dying. And there were so many dying. They lay curled up by the front gates, collapsed in the courtyard, or simply sobbing in a corner. Only one thing cut through the wall of sound—the Keep's gigantic iron doors being torn to shreds.

Metal screamed as claws punched through. Mages hurled flames the size of candlewicks, their mana all but empty while desperate soldiers swung torches—the only weapons they had left that could hurt the monsters. But for every claw that pulled back, three more took its place until a shadow-fiend broke through. Then a second. A third.

A soldier grappled with a shadow-fiend, its body halfway through the door. Sword abandoned, he fearlessly wrapped his arms around it, holding it in place.

A woman leaped forward, flame-tipped arrow in hand, and drove it into the monster's skull. It screamed, slashing wildly—catching both soldiers with its claws, but retreated. Clutching bleeding stomachs, the man and woman fell, trapped by the doors as more shadow-fiends pushed through.

"Out the bloody way!" Liddy roared, charging forward. The healer had no weapons or armor. She simply ran into the fray, ignoring the claws that swiped at her as she grabbed the injured and hauled them to safety with nothing but strength of will and stubbornness.

Soldiers swarmed, fighting to cover her.

The old woman wore a long vest with slots at the front, back, and sides for potion bottles. It was full when she'd first arrived, telling Firanta she'd better things to do than cower in the healing wards. Liddy had moved at speed, treating everyone from soldiers to civilians with the same care and attention. But now her vest was empty, and Firanta watched Liddy's hands shake when she placed them on the injured soldiers, fighting to stop the bleeding. While the queen was no mage, even she could tell the healer was a single spell from mana backlash—but she wouldn't disrespect her friend by telling her to stop. At this stage, every life saved was a victory.

The plan to fight in five-hour shifts was long abandoned. Rhys and his men had been overwhelmed out on the green before the moon was fully risen. Of the thirty or so who'd volunteered to fight outside, only three made it back alive—Rhys included. For every shadow-fiend they'd killed, ten more appeared, some even giving birth on the battlefield as they shoved the heads of wounded soldiers into their chests, new monstrosities bursting from their backs.

Firanta forced herself to watch every single one.

The Ivory Keep, center of Navaros' power for centuries, home to soldiers, zealots, and royals alike was lost. Rhys knew it. And the queen knew it. Firanta's grief and fear loomed like a tidal wave, and she knew that if she allowed herself to feel it for even a second, she would lie down and die where she stood.

"I need a progress report on the evacuation," she said quietly. As quietly as she could with the screaming, that is.

Rhys ran a hand over tired eyes. Claw marks trailed down his neck—it was a miracle his head was still attached—but he only let Liddy work on it long enough to staunch the wound before telling her to focus on the others. "Only two hundred people so far, my queen."

The queen couldn't hide her grimace. Three siege rooms dotted the Keep, each with a hatch that led to the tunnels below. But the way down was long and narrow, designed to make it difficult for the enemy to follow and easier to collapse should the need arise. That very design was what slowed them down now. By her last count almost a thousand people were in the Keep.

"My queen," Rhys said, his voice gentle, "please make your way to the siege rooms—I beg of you. One of my men will escort you while I oversee the fight from—"

"Firanta!" a voice called, sharp and indignant. The queen didn't bother turning around—she knew who it was. At her side, Rhys' hand went to his blade at the use of her first name.

*"Harrow,"* she said, her voice ice.

The Head Disciple didn't notice. "Your so-called *soldiers* have barred Gallow's followers from the evacuation! What is the meaning of this?"

"Civilians are first, with women and children given priority," Rhys said, a muscle in his jaw twitching. "Since you are neither, you will have to wait."

"Firanta, this is ridiculous. I demand we—"

The queen let a hint of steel thread her voice—just enough to shut the man up. "Return to the temple and organize your people. When you hear three knocks on the front door, that is your sign to evacuate. I will have Rhys personally escort you all down."

"My queen!" Rhys said, aghast.

"Thank you, Firanta," came Harrow's smug voice.

She heard the swish of his ridiculous black robes. Rhys waited until Harrow's footsteps had faded to speak. "My queen, Harrow and his sages are the reason we're so unprepared. They swore Calamity wouldn't arrive for months—that there wouldn't even be a battle, so quickly would Eternity and her Champions best him. I... I do not know if I can stomach—"

"Once Harrow is back in the temple, bar the doors," Firanta said calmly. "Brick him and the rest in if you must. They will not set *foot* outside this Keep until everyone else is safe."

Rhys blinked once, twice, and then dipped his head. "Yes, my queen. My deepest apologies for questioning you."

She almost smiled. "They are not the only ones to blame for this, Rhys. Just as much fault lies with the king and I. We are the reason we lack the men to protect the Keep. That is why I shall leave with Gallow's followers and not a moment before."

Rhys paled, opening his mouth to argue but she raised a hand—this was not a subject she would budge on. "How long?" she asked instead.

He didn't need to ask what she was referring to. "We have maybe fifty soldiers left, and we've exhausted what few mana potions we had. They'll break down the doors in the next hour—if we're lucky."

*Before the king can make it,* was what he didn't say. Firanta was not a woman who believed in miracles, but in that moment, she desperately wished for one. Her gaze strayed to Gaj—the lumbering monstrosity of flesh and bone was minutes from them. She knew if the shadow-fiends didn't kill them, Gaj would. She didn't know which she'd prefer.

A streak of white zipped across the sky, catching her eye, and Firanta smiled when she saw Zara diving for Gaj. The queen had watched Zara fall to the monster once already, sure the Fury had died—yet there she was, fearlessly throwing herself at the giant with everything she had. Maybe they didn't need a miracle, the queen thought.

Maybe they already had one.

"Once Harrow is dealt with, head down to the tunnels, Rhys," she said, not looking at him. "Leon should know what happened here."

"With the greatest of respect, my queen—no. My place is here," he said, trying and failing to cross his wrists behind his back. Wincing, he brought a hand to his neck.

"Damn it, boy, stop moving!" Liddy snapped from the stairs. Sweat dotted her brow while purple shadows marked her eyes—she looked on the verge of passing out. "I just got that neck of yours closed, and here you are jostling about like we're at a carnival."

"Will you stand with me, Liddy?" Firanta asked quietly, suddenly overcome with the need to have her oldest friend by her side. She knew better than to ask Liddy to evacuate—queen or not, she'd be told to "shove it."

Liddy huffed, and it was a sign of how exhausted she was that she joined them without comment. The three stood together, watching claw after claw burst through the Keep's doors.

\*\*\*

Valerius saw the Ivory Keep through Player Two's eyes, the coward half-hidden on Gaj's shoulder. Shadow-fiends swarmed his childhood home, his *kingdom*, in a sea of twitching darkness. While he couldn't see her from so high up, he knew his mother would be standing on the battlements. That she could see him riding Gaj's shoulder like a stallion into battle, ready to kill everyone and everything he'd ever loved. He wanted to call out to her, to scream it wasn't him. That he'd slit his own throat to save her!

But he didn't say any of that.

Instead he *concentrated.*

He imagined he was back in his own body—pictured Player Two's golden armor and dark blade as his own. It was his hand that rested on Gaj's shoulder, his feet that balanced in the gaps between the giant's strung-out muscles. So deep was his meditative state, he could almost feel the wind against his skin.

Weeks of practicing, of testing every wall that surrounded Player Two's mind, had led to this moment. He'd never been able to break through and take full control, but he was getting close. In Player Two's fight atop Gaj, Valerius had made his captor flinch right as he was about to cut off a pitch-black vaxion's head—saving the man's life. It was only one person, but Valerius told himself it was proof. Proof he could stop Player Two if he only fought hard enough.

He took a breath.

"Argh, that *hurts!*" Player Two spat, gripping his sword hand as it twitched, trying to turn his own blade against him. "Stop, or I'll bash Mommy's head in. You hear me?"

Valerius' concentration almost broke, but he knew that doing nothing was as good as killing his own mother. And so he pushed down his fear and imagined Player Two taking a step forward, his body tumbling through the air as he fell from Gaj—how it would feel when they hit the ground, every one of their bones shattering. Player Two howled, hand digging into Gaj while his body leaned forward ever so slightly—and then pain exploded in Valerius' skull, breaking the connection. Back in the darkness, the prince fell to one knee, head pounding, drenched in sweat—and utterly furious.

*Get up. Your mother is about to die thinking you killed her. Get. Up.*

"When you hurt him, you hurt yourself, Prince Valerius," Magnus said quietly. "I don't know how much more your mind can take."

"Then *help* me, damn it!" Valerius snapped.

The mage hunched down, shaking his head, terror etched into his face. It wasn't the first time the prince had pleaded with him for help, but every single time the mage shut down—too scared to raise a finger against Player Two and Calamity.

Valerius screwed his eyes shut. He'd been fighting against his captor for *weeks*, and the fruit of his efforts was a flinch—that was it. There must be something he could do, he told himself, he just had to *think*.

\*\*\*

The gristly muscles in Gaj's neck uncurled as we flew closer, but Zara stayed high in the sky, just out of reach. Lukas held on to her mane tightly. He'd barely said a word since we'd taken off—a sign of how dire things were. From here I could see the Keep was swarmed by shadow-fiends, the walls covered in pitch-black bodies—they'd breach the courtyard in minutes. Gaj slowed to a creaking halt the moment she saw us, the Keep only a few steps from her—apparently she couldn't walk *and* fight at the same time. This was it. We had to stop her right now, or everyone in the Keep was *dead*.

I tried to shut out the thought and pulled up Player Two's stats—it turned out one of the perks of being an Operator was I could see any System User's Character Sheet at zero cost. But the numbers only hammered home how impossible this was:

| User: SYSTEM ERROR Aliases: Valerius, Player Two | |
| --- | --- |
| Stamina | 1900/2300 |
| Hit Points | 2190/2200 |
| Mana | 800/1200 |

Ten points of damage was all Lukas had done to Player Two—and he'd nearly died for it. I relayed this to Zara, who simply huffed, unconcerned.

*"Do you see anything we can use against him?"* she asked. *"Any weaknesses?"*

I looked over his base stats, feeling hopeless.

| Base Stats*<br>*Note—these figures are unstable.* |      |
| :---: | :---: |
| Strength    | 350  |
| Essence     | 300  |
| Resistance  | 975  |
| Recovery    | 1110 |
| Speed       | 206  |
| Luck        | 80   |

He was almost twice as strong as Zara's human form, if not more, which didn't make any sense. Yes, he'd been in this world longer, but when we fought back at Moonvale I'd beaten him. What had changed since then? I frowned at the note under his base stats—"these figures are unstable." A pop-up appeared that made my blood run cold.

---

Note: Three souls fight for dominance in a single host. This grants the System User increased base stats and abilities at no additional cost. However, the degeneration of the host's body is rapidly increased. Time to full breakdown estimated at five to seven days.

Note: Option to destabilize Player Two unavailable. Insufficient Void Mana.

---

"Three souls"—Player Two and Valerius were obviously two of them. But who was the third? Someone from this world or Earth? I shuddered. It was crowded enough with Zara and me in the same body—the thought of adding someone else... well, that would explain why he acted so erratically in his fight with Lukas. If Valerius and whoever else was trapped in there were fighting back, that might give us an edge. And while I wasn't sure what "destabilizing" Player Two meant, the pop-up had given me an idea.

"Can I use Void Mana to kill Gaj?" I asked.

**COST TO KILL RAKNA #8700 UNAVAILBLE.**
**INSUFFICENT VOID MANA.**

I felt my jaw drop. *Gaj*... was a rakna? Just like Ravenna and Calamity?

**RAKNA #8700 SYSTEM ACCESS REVOKED.**
**RAKNA #8700 HAS BEEN STRIPPED OF VOID MANA AND ASSIGNED "THRALL" STATUS BY SYSTEM OPERATOR CALAMITY.**

I frowned. Zara had told me the gist of Ravenna's story—about the war where the rakna fought one another, eating each other alive. But she hadn't said anything about rakna being made mindless servants—had Ravenna known? And... if Gaj was a rakna, did that mean the wallow-tail was too?

Eternity drew up alongside Zara in the sky, darkness growing in her hands. Covered in dust, patches of her skin red raw, she looked nothing like the meek, picture-perfect woman I'd met in Magnus' castle. Magic rolled off her, her eyes turning as dark as the night sky. A shiver went down my spine, and I felt both awe and a hint of fear at the sight—I'd known she was Gallow's Chosen, but I hadn't understood what that meant until now.

Zara's jaw unhinged, power gathering in the back of her throat.

Gaj stared up at us with shadow-filled eye sockets, head cocked to one side. We'd expected her to grab trees, rocks, or anything else she could get her hands on and throw them at us—had prepared for it—but she simply looked up at us, curious.

*"Ready?"* Zara asked. Her throat burned as she held the magic there, pushing it to its absolute limit.

"Ready," Eternity said, the darkness growing until it eclipsed her. She held it above her head, muscles straining—eyes alight with determination.

*"Now!"*

**Skyscream Activated.**

Purple light and darkness swirled, molding into one as Eternity and Zara threw everything they had at Gaj in an explosive burst of power.

It was so small. A spark of flames flashed in front of the giant, but those sparks turned to wildfire as the wallow-tail appeared from nowhere. It looked exactly as it had when I'd released it. Flames licked its wings while its eyes burned with a pure white fire, and then it was gone—blasted into a thousand pieces as it took the full force of Zara and Eternity's attacks.

"No!" Eternity cried.

Zara cursed.

Gaj was already turning, taking one colossal step, and then another, and suddenly she was standing over the Keep. Her limbs creaked like a derelict house as she raised her fists above her head—casting the Keep in shadow. One hit was all it would take. Fire flickered in the air around us as the wallow-tail started to reform.

"Zara, hurry!" I shouted, the world slowing, the image of the queen and the hundreds of others trapped in the Keep flashing in my mind.

"Again!" Eternity cried at the same time, blood pouring from her nose as the darkness grew in her hands.

---

**WARNING.**

**SKYSCREAM LIMIT REACHED.**

**FURTHER USE WILL RESULT IN SEVERE BACKLASH.**

---

I expanded the warning and saw *skyscream* had a max usage of twice a day. Before I could say anything, Zara whispered, *"I know."*

She opened her jaw as wide as she could.

Gaj's arms shook, her fists high above her. I'd noticed before that she could move with the speed of lightning in a fight but walked like a glacier. As I watched her fingers dig into bone, I realized why—she was fighting back. Fighting against Calamity's control.

"Now!" Eternity yelled, darkness bursting from her hands as Zara's *skyscream* followed—her head exploding as our vision blurred with flickering shadows. Darkness and light combined to catch Gaj squarely in the neck—and kept going, severing muscle and bone, cleaving the giant's head from her shoulders.

"Yes!" Lukas cried, punching the air.

Trying to see through the blur in Zara's eyes, I watched Gaj with bated breath. Her skull shook, slowly inching back as the weight became too much—and toppled from her shoulders. Dirt and ash exploded when the skull hit the ground with a resounding boom. I finally let myself feel hope. We'd done it—we'd killed Gaj!

But then the giant tilted forward, swaying like a scarlet sunder as she began to fall. I realized what was about to happen, and my heart stopped. "Look out!" My scream of warning was as instinctive as it was pointless. Gaj, Calamity's slave and servant, fell—right on top of the Ivory Keep.

The mountain shook, sending shockwaves outward that we felt even from here.

A deathly silence followed.

"No…" Eternity whispered, that single word driving home the horror of what had just happened. Lukas buried his head in Zara's mane. The Fury didn't say anything, but she didn't need to—I could feel it: anger, guilt, and shame that came in waves, each vying for dominance. She should have seen the wallow-tail, she should have attacked quicker, all the should, should, should making her head spin.

Eternity swayed mid-air, fighting to right herself—blood pouring freely from her nose. And then she was half-flying, half-limping toward the fallen Gaj. Zara followed, her wings beating slower and slower as she struggled to stay in the air, her head splitting.

I wanted to tell Zara it wasn't her fault—it was Calamity's. But that would have made her angrier. I settled for, "Some people might still be alive. We'll dig out who we can, then check the escape tunnels below—they might have had time to evacuate."

She didn't answer—just kept her eyes locked on splotches of red peeking out from beneath Gaj's fallen body.

# Chapter Fifty-Two

Firanta was about to die.

To her pleasant surprise she wasn't afraid. Since a debilitating illness as a child, she'd felt she'd been living on borrowed time—everyone but Liddy had been shocked she survived to see her twenties, let alone fifties. But one eye and limited mobility hadn't stopped her from marrying the love of her life and leading their kingdom as best she could. While there were many things she'd have done differently, she couldn't say she had any regrets.

But as Gaj's huge body fell forward, eclipsing the moon so her entire world fell to darkness, the queen realized that wasn't true—she did have one regret.

A smile crept over her lips as she thought of a summer's day twenty-one years ago. She'd been in labor for hours, flitting in and out of consciousness while Liddy gripped her hand. Firanta had been ill for so many years that every mage this side of Evergarden had said it was madness to go through with the pregnancy. Everyone except Liddy. The healer told them all to jump in the sea and stayed by Firanta's side night and day.

It wasn't magic or skill that saved Firanta and Valerius' lives that day—it was Liddy's hand in hers, and the fierce look in the healer's eyes. Her low, husky voice as she whispered, "If you die, Firanta, I'll rip you out of Gallow's hands my damn self."

Now as Liddy stood by her side, Gaj seconds from crushing her and all of the Keep, the queen saw him—a figure in gold, shining like a cheap brooch on the giant's shoulder. She couldn't see her son's expression from here, but she knew it would be smug and condescending. He'd done it. He'd *won*.

Liddy took the queen's hand, gripping it as tightly as she had the day Valerius was born.

Men and women, soldiers and civilians alike screamed and pushed, trampling one another as they ran for the gates, for the tunnels—some even trying to climb the walls. It wouldn't make any difference, Firanta knew.

"My queen, you—you could still make it!" Rhys yelled, "run to the siege room, I beg of you!"

He looked so scared—scared for *her*—that she couldn't help but drop her cane and offer him a pincer-like hand. Eyes filled with tears, he took it, holding his head high as queen, healer, and commander looked death head on. When Gaj's body struck the Keep, crushing every man, woman, and child within, Firanta's last thought was of her one true regret.

She wished her son had never been born.

\*\*\*

Valerius screamed. He cursed. He sobbed. He slammed his head into the ground, wishing over and over for death, but it was too late. He saw her, saw his mother, and the look on her face right before she died, her eyes burning with hatred.

Hatred for him.

"Her last thought," Player Two said, his voice echoing in the darkness "Was that her little boy killed her."

He laughed as Gaj flattened the Keep, Valerius screaming along with his people.

\*\*\*

It was silent when we landed.

**Tithe of Beasts Activated.**

Zara's senses sharpened as she listened for cries of help, screams of pain, the thrum of a heartbeat—any sign that *someone* was alive. But the Keep was as quiet as the graveyard it had become.

Gaj hadn't taken the entire Keep down. Not all of it, anyway. Part of the eastern wall still stood, the giant's shoulder jutting into but not quite piercing the stone, but that was it. Everything else, from the walls to the towers were gone—crushed to dust. Zara glanced over the cliff edge, then immediately looked away, but not before I caught sight of the bodies at the base. I didn't know if they'd been thrown off the mountain from the force of Gaj's fall or had chosen to jump.

Neither was a comforting thought.

"I failed. I know I failed, but I had to *try*," Eternity said, her voice a whisper. She was only a few feet from Gaj's body, a single human hand visible beneath the giant, so small it was almost comical. "I *had* to."

I didn't need to say anything—Zara knew what I wanted. When next I opened my eyes, I was back in her body and moving toward Eternity. Tears streamed down her cheeks, and her eyes filled with such hopelessness that my heart broke all over again.

"Eternity?" I called, wanting to say so much. That we'd tried. That this wasn't her fault. But I couldn't say a damn thing.

"I said I know!" she said sharply, not looking at me.

I frowned. Who was she talking to? The sound of Lukas cursing reached me, followed by falling rocks. I looked over to see him shoulder deep in the wreckage of the eastern wall, frantically searching for survivors. He knew it was pointless. We all did. But I didn't blame him for trying.

"We can't stay here, Eternity," I said gently, kneeling by her side. "It looks like Gaj took out most of the shadow-fiends, but more could be on the way."

"Not bad, Player Three. Not bad at all," a voice called.

Claws burst through the tips of my fingers, a rage to rival Zara's flooding my body.

*"Player Two,"* I snarled, putting myself between him and Eternity.

He stood on Gaj's back, sword balanced on one shoulder, grinning down at us like a hunter over a triumphant kill. "Now, don't you worry, I'm not going to take all the credit! I couldn't have summoned Gaj without you—though I admit I'm curious how you got that key out of a xandi's thigh. You can tell me all about it over drinks."

I frowned, wondering what he was playing at when a noise made me turn. Eternity backed up, eyes wide with fear, hands covering her mouth.

"No, it's not what you think!" I said, realizing what she'd just heard and the natural conclusion she'd come to. "That was before I knew who Calamity was."

"*You* found the gem that bound Bala. *You* released the wallow-tail. Now that I think about it, none of Calamity's servants would be here but for you, Player Three." He smiled, showing too many teeth. "No one but us, anyway."

"I didn't—" I looked from him to Eternity, but Player Two seemed content to stand there and taunt me. "I didn't know," I said again. "I didn't know who or what he was. The second I did, I fought back, and he... he punished me for it. Locked me in the *Void*."

I saw a flicker of uncertainty in Eternity's eyes, and I kept going. "If not for Zara, I'd be dead or worse—she rescued me. We've broken free of Calamity, Eternity—I swear it."

"She says that, but she's still got the servant boy our master gifted her," Player Two called in a sing-song voice. "Why else do you think Lukas is traveling with her? She bound him in a blood-debt—if she yells jump, that boy is leaping into the sky before he knows it."

"I released him!"

He shrugged. "Only because you bound him in the first place."

Darkness flickered, weak but steady in Eternity's hands.

"I was trying to save his life," I said, the excuse sounding weak even to my ears. "And yes, I did bind him, but that—that was an accident."

"How do you 'accidentally' enslave someone?" she asked, glaring daggers.

I had nothing to say to that.

*"Enough! Stop letting your idiotic mind take control while this* shek *pulls the reins,"* Zara barked. *"Actions speak louder than words, Teema—so act."*

I turned on Player Two with a snarl. She was right.

**Fury's Claw Activated.**

Charging forward, I was on Gaj's back in a heartbeat, claws swinging at Player Two the next. He was stronger, his stats nearly double ours, but I refused—*we* refused to bow down. But Player Two simply stepped back, a blur of speed I couldn't see, and my claws swiped air. Damn it, he was *fast*.

"Oh, it's far too late for that." He smiled, snapping his fingers.

Gaj's body shuddered, making me stumble. I panicked, thinking she was somehow still alive, but the way she jerked and shifted felt like something was moving *inside* her. A sharp crack split the air, and I looked down in time to see spears of grizzled muscle shatter bone as they burst out of Gaj—the same that bound Zara mid-air—and wrap around my legs like snakes.

With a jerk I was yanked back from Player Two and slammed face first into the dirt—my knee nearly popping out of its socket from the force. Eternity screamed, and I could only watch as flesh-vines wrapped around her, more erupting from Gaj's dead body.

*Monstrous Strength Activated.*

With a growl, I flung out my arms, ripping my bindings apart. I ran for Eternity, claws out. But Player Two appeared in front of me, so quick I barely had time to blink before he drove a fist into my stomach so hard, my feet lifted inches off the ground. I retched. It felt like getting hit by a *truck*.

*Steel Skin Activated.*

I fell to my knees, metal sliding over my body, trying not to vomit. Player Two's foot met my face, and my head snapped back with a crack. God, he was strong.

> **WARNING. STEEL SKIN COMPROMISED. WARNING.**

A flurry of blows rained down on me so quickly I could only raise my forearms and duck my head—fighting to take the hits and stay standing.

> **WARNING. STEEL SKIN LIMIT APPROACHING. WARNING.**

"Zara!" Eternity screamed. Player Two's hands were in my hair. He was drove his knee into my face again and again, each blow pushing me to the very brink of consciousness.

I saw a flash of something huge and brown, and suddenly Player Two was knocked back, sliding in the dirt as Lukas charged, his huge molger head bent low. Player Two laughed, his fingers deep in molger fur as he skidded back.

*"Give me control,"* Zara growled.

I said nothing, only handed her the reins as I coughed, blood spattering my hands.

\*\*\*

Zara smiled. Everything hurt—her nose was a bundle of raw, bloody nerves, her vision blurred with what she knew was a concussion. But still she smiled.

She'd been looking forward to seeing Player Two again.

Lukas grunted, locked in a standoff with her opponent. When she saw how close they were to the edge, she knew the cub was trying to throw him off the mountain—only fifty or so feet of green remained, the rest lost to Gaj's corpse—but Calamity's dog was too strong. Lukas came to a grinding halt, growling as he shoved with all his strength, but Player Two simply clasped his fists above his head—and brought them down on Lukas' skull. The cub's legs shot out from under him as he hit the ground, unconscious. Player Two raised his fists to strike again, but Zara was already on him.

**Blazing Whisper Activated.**

Her hands lit up with flames and she wrapped them around his waist, urging the metal of his armor to melt into his flesh. Blows rained down on her back, but she took every hit, digging her clawed feet into the ground, inching them both closer to the edge.

**Partial Transformation Activated.**

Her arms grew in size, pitch-black fur trailing down her shoulders and biceps. Bones rattled in her still broken arm, little rocks of molten pain, but she gritted her teeth and dug her razor-sharp claws into Player Two's back, smiling when he howled—she'd pierced his armor. They were so close to the edge, just another—a burst of pain in her back made her freeze.

> **WARNING. STEEL SKIN BREACHED. ABILITY FAILED.**

Zara's breath caught, her skin cracking as the metal crumbled from her body—useless. She tried to push past the pain, but while her mind was willing, her body was not. Zara's grip slackened, and that was all Player Two needed to break her hold, kicking her so hard she fell on her back—limp and boneless.

Player Two whined like a sickly cub, his hand cupping the fresh blood that poured from his sides. Burns marred his face and neck, yet before Zara's eyes the flesh knitted together, leaving behind skin as smooth as marble. Panting hard, he grinned, holding his dark blade aloft—the first few inches crimson from where he'd driven it into her back.

"I shouldn't," he said, smiling. "But someone's clearly been adding to their stats—even Imani and Vivek didn't make me try that hard. So really… you should consider this a compliment." He took a breath, and though she had no idea what was coming, Zara braced herself. *"Fester."*

Lines of deep green trailed up Zara's arms, her veins bulging as her blood caught fire, burning her alive from the inside. Back arched, her claws dug into her palms as she *screamed*.

"Stop it!" Eternity cried. "You are killing her, *stop it*!"

"Oh, I think she can take a bit more."

Flesh-vines trailed around Zara's jerking body, her neck straining as she fought not to bite off her own tongue. She could feel Teema, could feel the woman yelling something, but she couldn't hear it. Couldn't focus on it. There was only the pain.

And then it was gone, vanishing as quickly as it began. Zara collapsed on her side, spittle dribbling from her mouth, aftershocks of pain making her limbs twitch. Gaudy gold sabatons filled her vision.

"See? I knew you could take it." Player Two smiled.

Flesh-vines gripped her, carrying her over to Eternity, head lolling.

"Enough," Eternity hissed. "Just kill us and be done with it."

"Oh, I'm not going to kill you," Player Two said. "Not after all this. Because it's thanks to you that when she fell…" he jerked a thumb at Gaj, "… she took four-hundred-and-thirteen lives with her. More than enough for my master. All we need now…"

He reached for Zara, and even delirious with pain she snarled when he wrapped his hand around her throat and *squeezed*.

"Player Three, I know you can hear me," he said. "I just have one teensy tiny question for you. Where, oh where, did Ravenna hide the eternity?"

# **Chapter Fifty-Three**

I blinked, shock making me slow. Opening the Inventory tab, I stared at the strange glass flower.

"I'll take it from here, Zara," I said gently, pain radiating from her. She swapped with me without a word, which scared me until I was back in her body—and then I was just amazed she'd heard me.

The wounds she'd suffered in her fight with Gaj were papercuts compared to whatever that dark blade had done to her. Every pump of her heart's blood felt like fire, and my limbs kept twitching of their own volition—I didn't even know if I could move.

"Hey, hey, it's not nice to *ignore people*," Player Two said, slapping my cheek. "Where's the eternity?"

"Calamity is *lying* to you," I said, knowing he was too far gone, but I couldn't stop myself from trying. "If you do this, we can't go home. Earth will be *gone*. Everything here—the shadow-fiends, the sickness, the death—all of that is coming for our families. You said you have brothers, what about—"

Player Two smiled, his dark blade moving like a deadly shadow.

Eternity cried out. A thick line of red now ran from her shoulder to her elbow, inches deep.

"Bastard!" I yelled. "Touch her again, and I'll *rip* your head off!"

"Now, now, this isn't my fault," he said with a sigh, twirling his sword. "It's Ravenna's. Technically speaking, anyway. You see, long ago one of her little servants took something. Something that acts as both lock and key for Master's prison. Yet Master didn't despair. He wove the threads, laid the path, then sat back and waited."

A smile. "You all played your parts beautifully. You—the weeping damsel trapped in the Void. Zara—the adventurer on a quest to save her dearest friend. And Ravenna—who was *supposed* to be the heroic knight who swoops in and tries to save you. She always had a soft spot for humans, you see. Calamity's plan was simple—trap his little sister in the Void and rip from her the location of the last thing standing in the way of his arrival. But then Zara decided she wanted a snack."

He shrugged, arms splayed. "So we watched. We waited. And sure enough Master felt the eternity light up at your touch, hungry as ever for Void Mana." His smile vanished, and he pressed his blade to Eternity's neck. "I won't ask again, Player Three. Where is it?"

Eternity looked at me, shaking her head as much as she could with a sword at her throat. She had no idea what was going on, but she still didn't want me to say anything. Thinking frantically, I tried to stall.

"I don't have it, but I know where it is—it's buried in Thaddeus' heart."

Player Two's eyes widened. He burst out laughing, a harsh raucous sound. "It was under my nose all these years? Hah! Well played, Ravenna, well played!"

I glanced at Lukas and saw he was still out cold, but he was a falsling—he'd be up and moving in minutes. I just needed to keep Player Two talking.

"His body is in the crypts—at least a hundred feet deep under Gaj's corpse. I suggest you get digging."

Eyes locked on me, Player Two flipped his sword and drove it into Eternity's leg. She screamed.

"No! Stop it, stop hurting her, damn it!" I roared.

Eternity bit her lip hard enough to draw blood, fighting to stay quiet. I should say nothing, I knew. But I didn't have it in me to watch her die.

My hands glowed as I summoned the glass flower. "I'm sorry," I said to her. The flesh-vines parted, and Player Two snatched it.

"Exactly as Master described." He smiled, holding it up to the light.

Zara growled, slurring as she came to—*"Have no fear... Teema. I will... I will kill him."*

"You thought you'd escaped Calamity—sorry, 'broken free,'" Player Two said, his tone mocking. "But you never left his service, Player Three. Not really. And now you've given him the very last piece of the puzzle—the 'eternity.'"

"All this for a piece of glass named after me? I did not know the dark god was so easily bound," Eternity said, her face pale, pain threading her voice. She'd seen me stalling and was trying to help, I knew, but I wished she wouldn't—she looked on the brink of passing out.

"Oh, little Eternity, this isn't named after you! In fact, it's the other way around. *You* are named after *this*," he said, giving it a shake.

"My namesake is the First Eternity," she said tightly. "A woman who stood against Calamity with nothing but Gallow's—"

"—Champions at her back, blah blah. I know the stories, but I'm afraid they're just that—tall tales. Porky pies. Complete and utter *lies*," Player Two said, clearly enjoying himself.

"But I—I've seen it. Gallow sent me visions of the First Eternity. She was as real as you or I."

"Oh, there certainly *was* an Eternity, but she wasn't Gallow's Chosen, or even Ravenna's…" He smiled, leaning in. "She was her own—for she was a *god*. Ask him. Ask your precious Gallow about his so-called Chosen. Or better yet, let's ask him *ourselves*."

He pressed his hands over the flower. It began to glow, the air crackling with the thrum of a coming storm. The wind picked up, my hair whipping around me. Above us an inky-black line split the sky in two, ripping through the night like a blade through honey.

"No!" Eternity yelled, struggling. "Val—Player Two, please. Calamity does not care for you, or anyone but himself. He shall kill you once he's done with you!"

Player Two gripped her thigh, ignoring her cries of pain as he pinched the wound in her leg so hard, drops of blood slid from it. He pressed the glass flower against her bleeding leg, catching every drop. The glass flared to life, turning crimson.

I kicked and hissed, fighting my bindings as he stepped behind me. Something cold drove into the wound in my back, and I cried out. In his hands, the glass turned a solid crimson, glowing like the sun.

"Three came together to bind Calamity. Three betrayed him, locking him away for all time. Now, with the blood of those tainted by his betrayers, I open the door to the Void and…" Player Two said, eyes filled with rapture as he cradled the flower, raising it above his head. "I *Summon Eternity*."

\*\*\*

Eternity's mind was spinning. Teema had been a servant of Calamity, a piece of glass was all it took to release the Tyrant, and Player Two claimed her namesake wasn't Gallow's first Chosen—instead she was named after a *god*. Terrified, lost and confused, Eternity instinctively did what she had done countless times over the century—she turned to Gallow. But the god only had two words for her.

**"TRUST ME."**

Above her the purple of night fell away, and the stars winked out one by one like crushed fireflies. A rift split the sky in two, an angry wound three times the size of the one used to summon Bala. And then she saw it—the thing that had haunted her nightmares and those of every Eternity before her.

A hand.

Dark spindly fingers came through the portal first, nails digging into the edges, forcing it open. Flames dotted the sky as the wallow-tail appeared, whole once more, and hurled its fire at the edges of the rift—every spark helping its master break free.

A second hand appeared. Shadows writhed in place of flesh as a wrist followed, then a forearm—the hand so large it eclipsed the night sky. Eternity's heart bullied her chest, terror making her blood run cold.

*No, no, no—this is not real, this* cannot *be real.*

The hand brushed past the mountain, and before her eyes the yellow stone shuddered. Veins of crystal shot out from that single touch, spreading throughout Widow Mountain—turning it the crystal-clear sheen of *glass*. That was it. A touch was all it had taken for Calamity to warp the world, reality fighting against the dark god's presence.

It was over. They'd failed. *She'd* failed.

Eternity closed her eyes, praying that when Calamity killed her, it would be quick.

# Chapter Fifty-Four

Calamity didn't grab Eternity, nor did he crush her to death as she'd expected. Instead he slowed, his palm hovering above them like an executioner's axe, his voice ringing in her ears.

**rELeASE heR**

Eternity's heart dropped, and she fought her bindings, though she knew it was pointless. What now? What was he going to do to her?

But Player Two didn't turn to her, or even acknowledge her. He raised the flower above his head—and crushed it in his fist. Shards of glass fell like rain from his fingers, and he sprinkled them on the ground delicately. Something long and cylindrical started to form where the glass fell, its outline rough at first. It was the size of a cat, its head dull and slimy. As it solidified, Eternity could see a row of teeth, razor-sharp and serrated. It... it was a *slug*. A slug she recognized.

**eTERniTY,** Calamity said, and Eternity's heart almost stopped. The creature in front of her was the image of the thing she'd seen wrapped around Player Two like an ermine scarf. It was small and wretched, and it... was her *namesake?*

"Well, well, well!" a singsong voice called. To Eternity's horror, she realized it came from the slug. "Should've known that spit-hole wouldn't be enough to hold you. Oh, don't look at me like that, *Calamity*—you're as happy to see me as I am you." The creature stretched, arching its back. "Warbling shark-maggots, that thing was *cramped*. How long have I been stuck in there, old chum? A century? Two?"

**aS lONG AS i HAve BeEn bOUNd**

**A tHOUSaND yEARs**

The slug, despite having no lips and only a slash for a mouth, gave a low whistle. "That would explain the mind-numbing boredom. Not that I didn't do my darndest to keep myself entertained, but there's only so much mortal-watching a girl can do. The humans on Earth, though, have this thing called *television*—I can't recommend it enough, Clammy-whammy. I had no idea drag queens and heels could be so much fun."

The slug gave a little shimmy of joy, apparently unconcerned by either god or man as Player Two inched closer to her—blade at the ready. "But if television isn't your jam, you should *see* the weapons they have on Earth. They get *pretty creative* when it comes to murderizing one another. You should check it could sometime. It might give you some inspiration the next time you try to *eat your family!*" It was only with the last words that the slug's cheerful demeanor vanished. She barely reached Player Two's knee, yet she bared her teeth, hissing wildly.

**haD i nOT TRied TO eAt YoU**

**YOu wOulD HAve eaTEN mE, ETErniTY**

"Urgh, stop calling me that, you know I hate it. Call me Nettie, or don't call me at all." The slug cackled. Eternity didn't understand the joke. "And *fine*—I would've eaten you, wanted to in fact! But Ravenna was all 'stop the cycle,' and 'forge a new path.' Speaking of…" Nettie twisted about, her eyeless head swiveling as if searching. "Where is our darling sister? Come out Ravenna, I know you're here! Otherwise little brother wouldn't have escaped the spit-hole we shoved him in."

**sHe iS dEAd,** Calamity said.

Nettie froze. Her head snapped to Teema, who was staring at the slug like she'd seen a ghost. "Dead? *DEAD?* Then why do I smell her on you, little piggie? I smell her stink in your *blood.* What did you do to my *sister?*"

Teema's eyes widened at the sudden change in Nettie, who hissed and spat like a viper. "I—ah, Calamity took me prisoner and Ravenna… gave up her life, her Void mana, to save me."

The slug twitched, teeth bared, ready to lunge for Teema—then she sat back on her haunches, sighing loudly. The mood swing was so abrupt, Eternity found herself blinking twice to make sure she'd really seen it. "That sounds like her. Ravenna always had a thing for mortals. I mean, she spent a couple thousand years eating and ruling you all, but she sang a different tune in the end. Yet that begs the question…"

She turned, stretching up to her full height as she looked skyward. "Sister dearest collected Void Mana like you collect grudges, Clammy-whammy. So why didn't she save the mortal herself, *hm*? Don't bother lying to big sister Nettie—I know you had something to do with it."

The huge god-like hand of Calamity twitched ever so slightly. It would be effortless for him to reach out and squash the creature—yet he stayed still and silent.

"Nothing? You're not even going to *try* to lie? Woof—that means it was *bad*. But you haven't chomped on me like I'm the last bit of popcorn in the bucket, which means you want something…"

Nettie raised her head, and though she had no nostrils, Eternity swore she heard the slug sniff the air. "Stop lurking, Gallow. I know you came through with Clammy-whammy—I can smell the depression from here. Or are you going to leave your 'Chosen' trussed up like a turkey?"

Eternity was so focused on running through everything the slug said, trying to piece together what was happening, that she'd almost forgotten the creature could see her. The slug slithered forward, inching closer. An ancient instinct rose in Eternity, telling her to run and hide, or the monster was going to get her.

And then the air shimmered.

The atmosphere, already crackling with Calamity's power, became thick and heavy—every breath was a struggle. The rough sketch of a figure appeared behind Nettie. At almost eight feet it was tall and rail-thin—too thin for a human. A cloak of velvet, so dark it made the night look pale was draped over its shoulders. Where flesh and blood should be, a tower of bones made up its chest, but there was a power and a presence to it that made Calamity feel small. Insignificant.

Eternity's mind went blank when she realized who she was looking at.

She'd spent weeks doubting him, her sanity pushed to the limits as she toed the line between loyalty and betrayal. But as the skeletal figure stepped forward into reality, Eternity wanted nothing more than to throw herself to the ground and beg forgiveness.

It was *Gallow*—the god she'd served for over a century, who she'd refused to obey only hours ago. No one knew what the God of Judgment looked like, yet he was exactly as she'd pictured, down to the last detail. He held a long curved staff of pure shadow in one hand, the other loose and relaxed at his side. She raised her eyes to his face, his features hidden behind a gigantic, bird-like skull with a razor-sharp beak—the smooth polished bone catching the few stars still left in the sky. Beneath his soft leather boots the grass shimmered, his every step leaving behind a footprint of solid gold.

A god. Her god was really here.

**"YOU CALLED.**

**"I ANSWERED."**

Gallow intoned, and Eternity shook—though not from fear. She'd heard his voice in her head countless times over the years, but she'd never heard it out loud.

**GaLLoW, RavENNA, eTERnITY—My BlOoD MY bEtRAYeRS**

Calamity spoke, echoes of rage in his voice.

**wHAT SaY yOU?**

"I say call me 'Eternity' one more time and see what happens—it's *Nettie*," the slug piped up. "And can the two of you *stop* with the theatrics? A gigantic hand in the sky and a bird who got left in the sun for too long—that's your idea of 'godhood'? Urgh, talk about a *waste* of Void Mana—this is why the two of you are always hungry."

**NETTiE**

"Better. You can drop the whole 'betrayer' schtick too. You weren't the one shoved into a piece of glass the size of a cockroach for a thousand years. Isn't that right, *Gallow*," the slug hissed at the god, who stared down at her impassively. "You've got some nerve showing up looking like the world's shiniest skeleton when *you're* the one who trapped me in that hellscape. We had a deal—lock Calamity away before he serves us up as appetizers. No more wars. No more eating each other—just happy-slappy creation at its finest. But noooo, you had to stab me in the back and then, to add insult to injury, use me as a glorified *lock!*"

The vines around Eternity slackened. Her eyes shifted to Player Two who stared at the gigantic hand above them, a beatific smile on his face. She squirmed, trying to get her hand free. Slugs were "gods," everything she'd been taught about Gallow was a lie, and a thousand years of solitude had clearly driven Nettie insane—that was all the tiny fragment of her mind not drowning had gathered. At any other time, the fact that her entire life was a lie would bring her to her knees, but survival was stronger than panic. Her mind honed in on the one thing she knew to be true—

that any one of these creatures could kill her. And despite having craved it for over a century, the last thing she wanted right now was the attention of a "god".

**THiS iS wHY i STay mY hANd,** Calamity said, his voice reverberating throughout the world.

**yOU tOO wErE BeTRaYED**

**fORCed tO bE LoCK aND KEy TO mY PRiSON**

**STAnd WIth ME aGAINsT thE TRaiTOr**

**sTANd wiTH mE AGaINst GaLlOw**

"Oh, ohhhhh, now we're getting to the juicy bits. This is better than those reality shows Earthlings love." Nettie laughed, shimmying with happiness. "Let's think about this for a second, huh little brother? Ravenna, Gallow, and I wanted to lock you away for good reason—you kept trying to *eat* us. And our sister, despite my very, very strong arguments, refused to go the old-fashioned route and have us gobble you up. I mean, you'd eaten so many of us, we'd probably have died, but still—why change a classic? So what reason could you *possibly* have to want to ally with me, unless..." The slug paused, cocking her head as she turned to Gallow. "Brother dearest, you're the one who's been kicking about the universe. How many of us are left? A thousand or so?"

**"THREE,"** Gallow said.

"Hundred?"

**"THE THREE OF US STAND ALONE."**

Silence. Then the slug threw back her head and laughed, a strange cackling sound. "Oh, this is delicious. You know this is *exactly* what Ravenna said would happen, and while she was the brains, I'm far from stupid. The two of you both want me to help you kill the other, right? Because you need *Void Mana*. Clammy-whammy because he spent a millennium trying to break out of jail, and Gallbladder because he's been waving his god-stick about like it's going out of fashion." She turned to Gallow. While his mask hid his face, Eternity saw the god's fingers dig into his staff. "The sheer *amount* of Void Mana you've spent in this world is impressive—no wonder the mortals adore you. So... what's *your* argument, brother? Why should I help the rakna who left me to rot?"

Eternity held her breath. She should be fighting to free herself but found she was hanging on every word—transfixed. A glance at Teema told her the woman was the same.

**"I LOCKED YOU AWAY.**

**"BECAUSE YOU ARE INSANE.**

**"AND THREATENED MY MORTALS."**

"What, because I like to snack on them? Hah!" The slug barked her strange laugh. "Like you're any better. Do your little piggies know how much you take when they pray to you? How delicious their mana is?"

**"ENOUGH! THIS IS MY WORLD,"** Gallow snapped.

**"I AM ITS SAVIOR.**

**"ITS PROTECTOR.**

**"AND YOU WILL BOTH STAND DOWN."**

"Ha… hahaha…" The slug's entire body shook so hard with laughter it looked painful. "*Your* world? *You* double-cross us, but get all the credit? *You* get worshipped and adored? I don't think so."

Gallow ignored her, drawing himself up to his full height.

**"COME MY CHOSEN,"** he intoned, spinning his staff—and pointing it directly at Eternity.

**"LET US END THIS."**

With a jerk the flesh-vines that bound her loosened, and Eternity fell to her knees before Gallow, Nettie, and Calamity. She felt their gazes upon her—ancient and immense, their presence pressing on her skull like nails.

"Eternity!" Teema cried, fighting her own bindings, the veins in her neck bulging. "Don't you *touch* her, do you hear me?"

"Eternity?" Nettie cocked her head, looking from the kneeling woman to Gallow. "You named your Chosen after *me?*"

Gallow stayed still. The slug slid toward Eternity, and she froze, instinctively gathering magic in her hands.

"Don't be an idiot, mortal. I just want to look at you," Nettie said, sounding bored.

Inches from her, Eternity could see the slug's skin had a rough crisscrossing texture while her stomach was pale and translucent. Something dark shimmered inside the slug, swishing about with her organs.

"Hmm... do you bleed when you use my brother's magic?"

**"ON YOUR FEET, CHOSEN."**

*"Do you bleed, mortal?"* Nettie asked again, her tone commanding—yet Eternity didn't feel the pull of the slug's magic, or any attempt to influence her mind.

"I... I do," she said, her voice a raspy whisper. She stayed where she was on her knees—too scared and too overwhelmed to move, let alone stand.

The slug dipped her head. Eternity felt a rush of power, a butterfly kiss of a presence, and then Nettie was gone—her feelers twitching as she turned to Gallow. But Nettie left something behind. Something Eternity didn't yet understand.

"Right, before I decide whose team I'm batting for, I need to ask you something, brother," Nettie announced, sliding toward the God of Judgment, a trail of flame left in her wake, the grass catching fire at the god's touch. "Why did you name your Chosen after me?" Nettie barely came up to Gallow's bony knee, yet the air shimmered with a power that rivaled the god's.

**"TO REMIND MYSELF.**

**"OF THE COST."**

The slug pressed her head against Gallow's shin bone. "Liar. You hated me. I battered you from the clutzaped nebula to the planet Petraz the last time you tried to kill me. Ravenna is the only reason I didn't finish you then and there—her and her dream of us living together like a big happy family." Nettie froze. "Wait... is that why? Did you name your Chosen after me... because you *hate* me? You couldn't beat me in real life, so tormenting some wretched mortal with my name was the next best thing?"

Gallow's silence was answer enough.

Eternity couldn't move. She could barely breathe. Her fists clenched in the soil while two gods stood over her as if she didn't even exist.

The slug bared her teeth. "Ohoho, that is *messed up*, brother. But hey—I've eaten my share of babies, so who am I to judge? Last question, and if you answer honestly, I will stand aside and let you and Clammy-whammy rip each other apart How did I end up in a zindor's heart?"

**"I GAVE HIM TO YOU.**

**"AND BID HIM TO HIDE."**

"Try again," she said, snuggling closer, her head pressing against him almost affectionately.

A pause.

**"HE FOUND YOU.**

**"AND FLED."**

"There he is," the slug said, pulling back slightly. "The bottom-feeder I have longed to *kill*." With a speed that astonished Eternity, the creature slid inside Gallow with a vengeful hiss.

## Chapter Fifty-Five

I took in maybe half of what the rakna were saying, but it was enough. I knew a little from Ravenna's side—that she'd tried to end the constant war between the rakna, each fighting to eat the other. That she dreamed of living a peaceful life where they used their powers to create, not destroy. And that somewhere along the way, it had all gone wrong.

I tried to imagine what it must have been like for Ravenna. After years of watching Nettie and Gallow try to kill one another, she'd finally convinced them to give her dream a chance. But something stood in the way of that peace—Calamity. Millennia of feasting on his siblings had left him fat with Void Mana, too strong even for the three of them combined. And so Ravenna hatched a plan—come together, bind Calamity, then lay down their arms. No more killing. No more fighting. The cycle of violence would finally come to an end.

But that wasn't enough for Gallow. I didn't know exactly what happened, and I probably never would, but I knew how it ended: Ravenna alone with Gallow—her dream broken, her sister locked away alongside Calamity, one unable to be released without the other. And so Ravenna let go of her dream, spending every last drop of her Void Mana to create the vaxion and molger before curling up and waiting to die.

Leaving Gallow the last god standing.

I knew rakna didn't feel things the way we did, though they could learn—living with the vaxion meant Ravenna had come close. And Nettie spoke and acted completely differently to her brothers—the product of years spent watching Earth, though she clearly thought little of mortals, calling us "little piggies."

But Gallow… I could tell he believed. He really believed he'd saved the world. It didn't matter that he stole mana from his followers. That he'd betrayed his siblings. Or that he'd chosen the name "Eternity" for such a petty, hate-filled reason. He truly saw himself as this world's "protector." In that moment, I didn't know which of them scared me more—Calamity, Nettie, or Gallow.

What I did know was we needed to *run*.

The God of Judgment howled when Nettie slid inside him, writhing and thrashing in his chest cavity. Darkness enveloped his skeletal hands, and he drove them in his own stomach, clawing and scratching at himself. I watched with disgust as he dug into Nettie's flesh, pitch black blood squirting through his fingers, and yanked her out. She screamed, a horrible, high-pitched sound that made my head pound.

Gallow's beak shifted, and he opened it wide—revealing a long row of serrated teeth.

**"YOU CHOSE THIS, SISTER."**

He raised the screeching slug to his beak but got no further. A blur of shadowed-flesh shot through the air, Gallow's bones snapping as Calamity slammed his gigantic hand into the ground, pinning the God of Judgment. A shockwave of air forced my eyes shut.

**"ARGH! NO!"**

**"THIS IS *MY* WORLD."**

Through slitted eyes, I watched darkness erupt from Gallow's hands, much like they did when Eternity's used his magic. The mountain shook, the stone-turned-glass cracking beneath my feet.

---

**WARNING. VOID MANA DETECTED.**
**WARNING. REALITY SHIFT INCOMING.**

---

The pop-up flashed as Gallow's darkness surrounded Gaj's corpse. To my horror the headless giant raised a huge hand and slapped it on the ground, narrowly avoiding Eternity and me. Gaj's bones creaked, snapping like dried wood as she forced herself up.

Gallow had taken control of Gaj.

The flesh-vines that bound me slackened. I was terrified out of my mind, but I wasn't an idiot. I slipped free and ran for Eternity, sliding slightly on the glass. She knelt on the ground, eyes glazed over as she stared at the fighting gods.

"Eternity, we have to run very very fast—right now," I said, eyes darting around the chaos, searching for Lukas. He'd been knocked out cold close to Gaj's body, but in a sea of broken glass and bursts of magic, I couldn't see him. My mind immediately imagined the worst—he'd been knocked off the mountain when Gaj stood, his body smashed to pieces on the rocks below.

*"The cub is not so weak,"* Zara said, the first she'd properly spoken since her fight with Player Two. *"Focus on running—he will follow."*

Gallow was fighting Calamity's hold on him, one hand commanding Gaj, the other still gripping Nettie, who thrashed and screamed. They hadn't even noticed we were free, which was the only reason we were still alive—we weren't important enough.

"Eternity? Can you *hear me?*" I yelled, trying and failing not to panic as I wrapped an arm around her, hauling her to her feet. She hung like a ragdoll in my arms, her eyes locked on Gallow. The headless Gaj stumbled like a drunk, crashing into the mountain. Huge chunks of glass, each big enough to crack a skull open, rained down—barely missing us. I dragged Eternity as far from the fight as I could, but we only had a few feet of space behind us—after that, open air awaited.

Gaj finally stood upright, swaying heavily. I watched Gallow clench a fist, and the giant's mirrored his. Calamity's shadowy arm reached out through the rift, the top of a shoulder just visible. Gaj pulled back, fists high like a boxer and unleashed a flurry of blows on Calamity—hammering every inch of him she could reach. I winced, knowing exactly how hard she hit. But the dark god's grip on Gallow just tightened.

"Lukas!" I shouted, praying the gods were so busy killing each other, they wouldn't pay any attention to me. Despite Zara's reassurance, I couldn't bring myself to leave without him. "Lukas, where are you?"

A lithe shape twisted around a fallen chunk of glass, and a limping vaxion appeared. He was covered in dust and debris, and clearly hurt—but he was alive. I wrapped one hand around his shoulders, squeezing tightly with relief while the other, my injured one, still clung to Eternity, who was starting to scare me. She hadn't said a word.

"We have to get off the mountain!" I shouted.

Lukas nodded vigorously in agreement, his vaxion eyes darting between the battling gods and the rift above.

"Eternity? Eternity, I'm going to change now, and you need to get on my back, okay?" I said, snapping my fingers in front of her vacant eyes. She shuddered, blinking at me.

"Gallow calls for me. He... he wishes for your aid. Otherwise he cannot kill Calamity and... and Nettie," she said, wincing at the name.

"Absolutely not," Lukas said, grunting as he shifted back into his human form. "He lied to everyone about how he 'saved' this world and named you after a *slug*, Eternity—a slug he hates and is currently trying to eat!"

Gaj wrapped both her arms around Calamity's shadowy forearm, her bony fingers digging in as she pulled—fighting to free Gallow. Her body shuddered, bits of dried flesh and bone falling to the ground like hellish rain. In minutes she would fall apart, and then it would be Gallow on his own against Nettie and Calamity.

Eternity was right—he was going to lose.

"What choice do we have?" Eternity asked quietly. "Calamity will rip this world apart, and Nettie thinks of us as little more than livestock. I... I do not want to help him any more than you do, but he is the only one who can stop this. Unless you have a better idea?"

Lukas ran a hand through his curls, and I could tell he was grasping at straws. "Maybe... maybe if we head back to Moonvale and got all the vaxion, we would stand a chance? I know they've only just gotten their powers back, but a pack of vaxion with a vendetta is a force to be—"

"Moonvale is *gone*," a voice said.

I moved on instinct, shoving Eternity in one direction, Lukas in the other. A dark blade whipped past my face, the tip grazing my cheek.

Player Two stood in front of us, but his smug, condescending expression was gone. Eye twitching, he grimaced, a hand cradling his skull. "It was Moonvale's blood and bone that brought Gaj to life. I watched her crush the vaxion's little hidey-hole to *dust*. Oh, don't look like such a shocked maiden, Player Three! Did you think there was no cost for refusing him?" He laughed bitterly, but I could see he was in pain. No visible wounds marked his skin, but *something* was hurting him. "There always is—I just learned that lesson quicker than you."

"You're lying," I whispered.

"Go then. Go and see the ruin you left in your wake. He's won, Player Three. He won *years* ago."

***

Zara heard the slugs prattle. Heard them squabble over who had wronged who, but the more they talked, the less she cared. It only cemented what she'd already known—these so-called "gods" were nothing more than selfish, over-sized children. But when Player Two spoke, she listened. And the cruelty in his eyes when he revealed Moonvale's fate rang true.

"To me, Teema," she hissed, memories flashing. Jaza's smile as she handed Zara plate after plate of food she "happened" to have left over. Fatyr dancing in the moonlight, embarrassed when Zara caught him. Esia's little roar as he shifted for the first time, howling with joy up at the moon.

And Ashira—her aunt's golden eyes locked on hers, love and sadness woven in every word.

Teema didn't say sorry or ask if she was all right—the girl knew better. But what Zara hadn't expected was the strange letters that flashed in the darkness—the shiny gold box of the System suddenly appearing.

---

**GOD FUNCTION EXECUTED.**

**BASE STATS OF SYSTEM USER "ZARA THE FURY" DOUBLED.**

---

"What have you done, Teema?" Zara whispered, but she already knew.

*"Make him pay, Zara."*

"That Void Mana was for you!" she hissed. "To get you home to your family!"

*"Do it for Ashira. For the vaxion,"* Teema said, her voice trembling.

With a blink Zara was back in her body, her fists clenched as strength and power anew flowed through her. The wounds left by Player Two healed instantly, and a fire welled up inside her, begging to be used. She was unstoppable. Unbeatable. She was *Zara the Fury.*

Player Two's eyes widened.

*"Do it for you,"* Teema whispered, pulling back.

"Eternity," Zara barked. The woman straightened, eyes flicking from her to Player Two and the battle that raged only thirty feet from them. "I despise your slug god. But even I can admit that pride and rage will not win this war. Tell your '*god*' that if he can truly kill these slugs, we will aid him. *But*," Zara glanced at the woman, letting her see the full force of her anger. "If it is a lie, I will let this whole world burn just to have the pleasure of watching him die."

Zara nodded to Lukas. "Be our eyes and claws, cub. If you sense even a hint of deception from Gallow, grab Eternity and flee. Now go."

The Fury didn't growl, or hiss, or give any sign of what she was about to do. She just threw herself at Player Two with everything she had—this was it. The dice of fate were cast, and one of them would die today.

***

Sweat poured down Valerius' face and his body shook—Magnus was right. The more he fought Player Two, the greater the toll it took on him. But he refused to stop. Zara attacked Player Two, her wounds healed, a fire in her eyes that gave Valerius strength anew. He pushed back against his captor—determined to help her.

Valerius' skull pounded like someone was trying to crack it open with a hammer, but he knew Player Two was doing far worse. The man panted, bringing his sword up too slowly as Zara struck, her claws finding his neck, wrists, hip, and armpits—every place his armor was weakest. Freshly healed and at his strongest, he might still have beaten her, but not now. Not while Valerius fought back.

He closed his eyes, concentrating on the feel of the blade in Player Two's hands, on making him shift right when he meant left, on making him flinch when he wanted to stand strong.

"It's working..." Magnus said, his voice filled with wonder.

Valerius didn't dare look at him, but he heard the man's chains as he came closer. "You're doing it, you're taking control."

A lightning bolt of pain made Valerius gasp, and he fell to one knee—the connection vanishing.

"Not enough," he hissed, driving his fist into the ground. "I'm not enough, damn it all!"

Magnus was quiet for so long Valerius raised his head, expecting to find the pale, slight man back in his corner again. Instead the mage stared into the darkness, his fists clenched. "It's her," he said quietly. "It's Zara the Fury."

Valerius couldn't hide his surprise—the mage had refused to look through Player Two's eyes this entire time. "It is," the prince said, pride in his voice. "He has beaten her more than once, but still she fights, throwing everything she has into every single blow."

Magnus stared. "Player One hurt her. Tormented her day in day out. *Tortured* her. But she's still... she's still here—fighting to save the world she once hated."

"Were it another time, another life..." Valerius said, running a hand through his hair—his fingers coming away damp with sweat. "... I would ask her to join the Gilded Knights. Hers is the courage of legend. And I will not stand by and do nothing while a fellow warrior fights so fiercely."

Zara was knocked back, claws meeting glass in a flare of sparks, but she barely flinched. Metal coated her skin, and flames burst from her eyes—an avenging angel made flesh. Hand pointing skyward, she snapped her fingers—a tornado of fire exploded to life, engulfing Player Two. He *screamed,* the sound all the encouragement Valerius needed.

He closed his eyes, sinking into a meditative state once more. He waited for the jangle of chains as Magnus backed away, but to his surprise the scent of burnt flesh and ash filled his nose. He could *smell* the air, could feel the heat on his skin. In all his weeks of fighting back, he'd never come so close to being in his own body again.

Player Two was still there, his presence a barrier, but instead of feeling like an impenetrable wall, it was rubbery and pliable. As if with the right push Valerius could do it—he could take control.

A low voice nearly pulled Valerius out of his trance. He risked a glance to his left to see Magnus standing next to him in the darkness, his brow creased in concentration. It was him—the mage was *helping* him. After all these weeks. After all his fear.

Hope sprang in Valerius' chest, and he closed his eyes.

His name was in ruins, his family and friends all but dead and gone—many by his own hand. But this—this he could do. This he *had* to do.

***

Zara had Player Two on the ground, the coward's own blade digging into his throat. The man's skin was charred black, his face unrecognizable but for the eyes that stared up at her in shock and terror. She bled from a wound in her neck, another in her side, but in truth she barely felt the pain. A ferocious joy coursed through her as she watched Player Two realize what she had the moment she struck the first blow—he was going to die.

"For Teema," she hissed. "For Ashira. For the vaxion. And for everyone else you hurt because you were too much of a coward to fight back!"

She drove the blade down just as Player Two screamed, "Master!"

Something dug into Zara, yanking her back. Instinct alone kept Player Two's blade in her hand as she hit the ground, landing flat on her back. Confused and winded, she saw Gallow was gone—the rakna was now high in the sky, his dark cloak whipping about him. Off to the side, amidst a scattering of bones that must have been Gaj was Nettie, her body barely twitching.

But that wasn't what made Zara drop the sword.

Gallow's hand hung in the air above her like a guillotine, blotting out the sky, the moon, and the stars. It grew larger, filling her vision until it was all she could see.

**mUST i Do EVERyTHInG?**

And then the hand came down, slamming into the earth where Zara lay.

# Chapter Fifty-Six

Zara knew she wouldn't get out of the way in time, but she still tried. She wasn't the type of person to back down—not even in the face of an angry god and the death he promised.

*Lightning Step Activated.*

She waited for her body to vanish in a flash of light, a last-ditch attempt to escape Calamity, but a pop-up appeared.

---

**OPPOSING SYSTEM OPERATOR "CALAMITY" DETECTED. CALAMITY HAS BLOCKED *LIGHTNING STEP*. WARNING. INSUFFICENT VOID MANA TO COMBAT.**

---

The Fury closed her eyes, feeling Teema's fear. They were both about to die, yet the girl was only worried for Zara.

*My one regret, Teema,* she said, *is that I did not give you back your home, as you gave me mine.*

Teema's only answer was to squeeze her hand.

Then someone grabbed the back of Zara's armor, and suddenly she was flying through the air. She hit the ground at speed, the edge of Calamity's little finger grazing her back as the furious god struck the earth—crushing Player Two.

**nO!** Calamity howled, his rage echoing through the world. Above her, the night turned crimson as the sun was dragged across the sky at impossible speed. A dark cloud appeared, fat with rain, bursting over Zara, only for it to vanish a second later. Thunder. Sunshine. Snow—the weather changed abruptly like a mighty finger was flicking through a scrapbook, unable to choose. The glass mountain shifted beneath her, turning red and grainy. It was only when Zara started to sink, the ruins of the Keep turning crimson that she realized what was happening—Calamity's rage was turning the mountain to *sand*.

Her skin shifted like liquid, her voidbeast wings snapping out as she dodged sinkholes and crumbling stone. Four paws slipping in sand, she threw herself from the cliff edge, fighting to gain air as the entire mountain collapsed behind her.

Together Teema and Zara watched the Keep, the hundreds of dead, and even the crushed remains of Player Two dissolve into red sand with a languid sigh. Calamity roared, his hands digging into the rift as he fought to open it wider. They didn't speak, both heavy with what had almost happened.

Teema broke the silence first. *"Did you see?"*

*I did,* Zara said, remembering Player Two and the look on his face when he threw her to safety. Of the bright smile he wore. And the tears that filled his eyes right as Calamity crushed him to death. Tears of *relief*.

*I guess the worm found his courage in the end,* Zara said, hating that she had anything nice to say about the man, but unable to deny the truth—she'd be dead if not for him. Both her and Teema.

*"I… I don't think that was Player Two,"* Teema whispered.

***

Valerius was dreaming.

Together with Magnus they pushed Zara out of the way, the shock and confusion in her eyes eclipsed by the joy the prince felt. As the Fury hit the ground, Valerius swore he could see Marito and Gabriel sitting beneath the stars, smiling as they invited him to join them. He saw his mother as she helped him put on his armor for the first time—the pride in her voice and the unshed tears in her eyes. Liddy slapping him on the back of the head when he came home with a broken arm, and her delight when he presented her with a bundle of flowers the next day.

*I'll see you soon,* he thought, unable to stop smiling as he was crushed to death.

***

Player Two was screaming.

He lay in darkness, fingernails digging into his cheeks, leaving deep bloody groves as he fought to take back control. But he couldn't—invisible hands gripped his back and shoulders, holding him in place.

Terror turned his blood to ice. If he didn't kill Player Three, Master would be angry. He'd send him to the Void, he'd... and then he saw his hands. Small pale fingers that belonged to a boy not yet a man. He wore strange trousers that were dark blue and slightly stiff while on his feet bright white shoes gleamed in the dark, an odd checkmark design on either side of them.

"What..." he started, slapping his hands over his mouth. Whose voice was that? It wasn't his! What was this? Another test of Calamity's?

A golden light caught his eye, and he squinted—a bead of sweat dripping down his neck as the temperature spiked. The light grew larger, sharpening into the bright square of a screen. Leaning forward, he felt a solid weight under his forearms, his left hand gripping a joystick, his right hitting the attack, dodge, and jump buttons in rapid succession.

The pixelated form of Lazander, his favorite Gilded Knight, rolled across the screen, dodging Zara the Fury's fireball. With a grin, he yanked the joystick to the right, moving in for the kill. He'd finished *Knights of Eternity* over a hundred times now, but his heart still pounded when he fought the Fury. She was the first boss in the game, but she was tough as nails, especially in a playthrough like his—Lazander as his main, plus two mages and a hunter.

Smoke tickled his nose, but he ignored it—his mom had probably passed out again while cooking, bottle in hand. She'd wake up when the smoke alarm went off. The controls grew hot under his hands, the plastic near-boiling, but he barely noticed. His brothers liked to tease him, saying he lived in a "bubble" when he was gaming. They could be standing next to him, shouting in his face, but so long as he was playing *Knights of Eternity*, he couldn't even hear them.

It was his happy place.

*DUN-DUN-DUUUN!* The game chimed, Zara spinning in a dramatic circle as Lazander drove his sword into her. A flash of red, and the Fury fell down dead.

"Yes!" he cried, punching the air. He'd never beaten her before without *at least* two tanks, so this was a big—the screen flickered, the bright garish colors of *Knights of Eternity* turning black and white. Abruptly the game died—taking his progress with it.

"No, no, no!" he yelled, kicking the machine. "Stupid piece of *crap*." He'd spent *forever* trying to fix it after Dad found it in the scrap heap. Maybe if he unplugged it, it would...

And just like that, the happy bubble of *Knights of Eternity* popped. He blinked to see flames licking the back of the machine. A spark was all it took, but in seconds the discarded couch and piles of dirty laundry lit up, the perfect kindling. Panic made him freeze, and he could only watch as the stairs leading out of the basement, the only exit, cracked and split in the flames—trapping him.

"Mom!" he screamed, immediately regretting it when smoke filled his lungs. He coughed, throwing himself to the floor. "Mom!" he cried again. No one else was home, just her. Even passed out, she'd have to hear the fire-alarm, right? She'd wake up and come save him—she would! All he had to do was find a safe corner, and... and...

\*\*\*

Eternity cut her palm open, cursing when it immediately started to heal. She pressed it into the ground, hurriedly drawing the same symbol over and over.

**"IS IT DONE?"**

"No," Eternity said, trying and failing to keep the sharpness out of her tone.

Gallow clicked his tongue against his beak—or at least that was what she assumed the odd clucking noise was—but said nothing else. The harsh demanding voice that had commanded her to leave Lazander to die was softer now, and if Eternity didn't know better, she'd say Gallow was trying to be *nice* to her.

Trying, at least.

The clucking sound began again when Eternity stopped to watch the mountain and the Keep collapse in a pile of red sand, her heart pounding. It was only when she saw Zara and Teema's white wings in the distance that her shoulders relaxed—they were safe.

Lukas stood close by, the dark eyes of his vaxion form watching Gallow with open distrust. He stalked around them in a tight circle, keeping close to Eternity—he'd clearly taken Zara's orders to protect her to heart. While she had no idea what he could possibly do if the God of Judgment turned on them, having him watch over her made her feel better.

Malik hadn't said a word to her. She'd expected yelling and cursing, but the Champion had fallen to his knees the moment she landed—Gallow at her side. The once proud man sobbed, his words frantic as he begged the God of Judgment for forgiveness, saying he would never again hesitate, never again shy away from an order. The skeletal god ignored him.

Eternity wished she could do the same, but Malik's whispered eighty-first sublimation dragged over her ears like sharpened nails. He'd stood by while Gaj attacked the Keep, killing *hundreds*—sure Gallow had a plan. Sure all this death and suffering had a *purpose*. And not too long ago, Eternity might have done the same.

"**WHY HAVE YOU STOPPED?**" Gallow asked, his tone carefully neutral.

They stood in the ruins of what was once a lush forest near the Sweetdawn river. The soil was ash, the trees charcoal. In the distance the wallow-tail flew back and forth, blue fire bursting from her wings as she scorched the earth—searching for them.

"**I HAVE HIDDEN US FROM SIGHT,**" Gallow intoned. "**CALAMITY'S SERVANTS WILL NOT FIND US.**"

"Why do you look exactly as I imagined?" Eternity asked abruptly—it had bothered her from the moment she saw him. She pointedly held the blade against her palm but didn't cut it.

"**FOR YOU.**

"**TO EASE YOUR HEART WHEN YOU LEARNED THE TRUTH.**"

"What do you really look like?" she asked, blood flowing from her hand when she cut deeper than she intended. "Do you look like… the 'real' Eternity?"

"IT MATTERS NOT.

"I AM A GOD, REGARDLESS OF MY FORM."

*That's a yes,* Eternity thought, her stomach twisting as she thought of the teeth-gnashing, feral creature he'd held in his bony fingers. Of the same creature who'd wound around Player Two. All these years, all the sacrifices she'd made, and it was for a god who looked like a *slug*.

"I COULD LEAVE THIS WORLD TO CALAMITY'S VICES," Gallow said, and she jumped, shocked he'd read her so easily. Silver eyes gleamed inside his bird's skull. "IS THIS WHAT YOU DESIRE?"

Eternity waited to feel fear, to cower as Malik did at her god's wrath. Instead a cloak of calm settled on her shoulders.

"Of course not," she replied, rocking back on her heels to give her knees a break. "I want *answers*, Gallow, to questions I have been too afraid to ask. After a century of service, you owe me that much."

"Forgive her!" Malik sputtered, his face in the dirt. "Since her capture by Magnus, her faith has wavered. But not I. What other god has stood watch over us? What other god—"

"Be quiet, Malik," Eternity snapped in a rare showing of temper. She was so tired of the bowing and kowtowing. "I am *speaking*."

The Champion sputtered, shocked into silence.

"You could have saved Imani. Maybe Vivek, too," she said, remembering Imani's smile as she died. Vivek's head rolling in the dirt. "Why not?"

"YOU HAD TO BE PROTECTED.

"THEY KNEW THIS.

"AND DID THEIR DUTY."

"Only because you sent us in blind! If you had told us… if you had told *me* about Bala and Player Two, we might have stood a chance! Instead you tell me nothing but 'south.' You feed us information piece by piece, favoring one Champion one mission, another the next. You give us vague, one-word orders while we trip over ourselves trying to figure out *what you want*. Why? Why not tell us everything?"

Gallow's elongated skull creaked as he turned to watch Calamity roar. She thought he wasn't going to answer, but after a long moment, he said:

**"MANY HAVE BETRAYED ME.**

**"I SOUGHT TO TEST YOUR FAITH.**

**"YOUR LOYALTY."**

"You mean years of doubt, second-guessing, and fear that we will accidentally upset you was because of your… your *paranoia?*" A fire rose in Eternity's chest, magic flickering in her fingertips, begging to be used. Her blue eyes locked on silver, but she refused to be the first to look away. The god's eyes narrowed.

**"I OWE YOU NO EXPLANATION."**

Eternity almost laughed. What had she expected? Gallow demanded complete loyalty, allowing no doubt or questions from his followers. His decisions were "absolute," his judgment "impeccable."

"This is your fault," she spat. "None of this—Gaj, Calamity, *none* of it would have happened if you had not sent us on a wild whipper-tusk hunt to Freyley. If we had stayed in Moonvale, we could have stopped Gaj. Stopped all of this!" she said, gesturing to the barren landscape, the collapsed mountain of sand, and the hundreds of dead she knew lay buried within.

The skeletal figure didn't strike her, as she'd half-expected. He stiffened; two hands wrapped around his staff—his eyes flitting from hers to the landscape.

**"I SAW CALAMITY'S SERVANT IN FREYLEY.**

**"AND ASSUMED… INCORRECTLY."**

Malik gasped, and even Lukas paused his pacing to stare. Eternity knew it was the closest thing she would get to an apology, but instead of feeling vindicated at the god's confession, it just made her feel worse.

"Tell me—was any of it real? The stories of the gallant First Eternity and her Champions? The woman who gave up everything to save the world she dearly loved? Was… was everything about you a lie?"

**"I CANNOT HIDE US FOREVER,"** Gallow said, ignoring her question. He stared up as the wallow-tail flew overhead, flames streaking across the sky. **"IF WE ARE TO SAVE THIS WORLD, WE MUST DO SO NOW."**

A part of Eternity wanted to walk away. A larger part wanted to blast Gallow apart from the inside out. "Not yet," she said, knowing she was pushing it, but not caring. Gallow might not be the god she thought he was, but he was still all-powerful—he could crush her like an ant. But she had one last thing to say. "You said this ritual will kill us both. That is a price I am willing to pay, but if this is another of your lies…" she said, stepping forward. She was covered in ash and dirt, her hair mere cinders, but in that moment, Eternity felt like herself for the first time in many, many years. "If we do this and Calamity lives, it will not matter if I am dead. We sealed our bargain with the spell *Unbreakable Oath*. If you fail to kill the dark god, I *will* take your life—even from beyond the grave."

The god stared down at her. He raised a skeletal hand, and she couldn't hide her flinch—but he pressed it over his chest where his heart would be if he'd had one.

**"CALAMITY WILL DIE. I SWEAR IT."**

"I will hold you to that, Gallow," she said, returning to the eighth circle. She had been bluffing of course—she didn't know if *Unbreakable Oath* would even work on him, but she had no other recourse. As she finished the final layer of spells, Eternity found herself praying—to the universe, to the dead gods, to anyone who might be listening—that she hadn't made a mistake. That she was doing the right thing.

A glance from Gallow was all it took for Malik to jump to his feet and rush to the god's side, his eyes wide and adoring. Eternity ignored them both, looking skyward as she searched for Zara and Teema—the voidbeast was flying in spiraling arcs, and while they'd passed over her several times, they'd made no attempt to land.

Eternity frowned. Could they not see her? Did the same magic that hid her from the wallow-tail hide her from Zara and Teema?

**"IT IS TIME,"** Gallow said, gesturing to the center of the circles. **"TIME TO END THIS."**

Eternity's guts twisted and she took a breath, trying not to vomit. She'd always known she would die, yet now that the moment was upon her, she was terrified—regrets and wishes washing over her like the tide. Daydreams of exploring Navaros with Teema, which had felt so childish and silly at the time, now felt like precious gems she should have cherished. She desperately wished she'd had more time with her. That she could have gotten to know the woman who'd saved her life and been a beacon of courage for her on her darkest days.

Eternity stepped into the bloodied circle, warmth spreading through her at the memory of Lazander holding her tight, a smile on his face. His ferocity when he defended her. The love in his eyes when he worried for her.

Angry now, she told herself this wasn't about her. This was about saving the *world*. And while she desperately wished there was another way to kill Calamity, she couldn't see it.

The Chosen allowed herself one final look at the sky, casting her mind outward at the last moment.

\*\*\*

Zara's eyes swept the blackened soil. *Anything?*

*"Nope, which worries me. Gallow was chomping at the bit to take Calamity down, so where the hell are they?"* Teema replied.

The ground below was a mess of crumbling soil and red sand. The dark god was struggling to get more than two arms and a shoulder through the rift, especially now that the wallow-tail was as intent on searching as Zara and Teema were. The weather continued to change with the flip of a coin, oscillating between a too-hot sun and bursts of icy cold wind that made even Zara shiver, despite her heavy fur.

Teema stared at the sky with growing worry. Zara knew the girl feared what would happen when Calamity came through, her mind a snowstorm of "ifs," "buts," and "maybes," but the Fury didn't concern herself with such things. She dealt with the problem directly in front of her, and right now that was finding Eternity, Lukas, and the slug Gallow. She had questions for the so-called god, and if she didn't like his answers, well…

Zara meant it when she said she'd let the world burn. It was better than bowing to another god's tyranny.

*"Zara? Zara, can you hear me?"* Eternity's voice rang clear.

*"Eternity!"* Teema called out in relief, though Eternity wouldn't hear her unless Teema took control. They'd swapped once mid-flight, or rather mid-fall, already, and Zara would rather not repeat the experience.

*"I can hear you, Eternity,"* Zara replied. *"Where are you? Tell me what you see, and we will come to you."*

*"Look for the row of blackened trees in a long straight line, right on the bank of the Sweetdawn,"* Eternity whispered. *"We are about to begin the ritual to—"*

Her words cut off abruptly. Zara reached out but found only a blank space where the woman had once been. Her gut twisted with suspicion.

*"There!"* Teema called, though Zara saw it at the same time. Her voidbeast turned sharply toward the distinct row of ruined trees where an ungodly scream made her pull up.

Zara and Teema watched as Calamity gripped the edges of the rift and *howled*. He clung to the portal with shadowed fingers, and Zara was shocked to see the god was trying to get back *into* the Void. His gigantic body changed before their very eyes, long, terrifying limbs shrinking like tin being crushed by powerful hands.

And then something, or *someone*, began to pull the flailing god out of the rift—forcibly dragging him into this world.

Below Zara hot air shimmered, and Eternity suddenly appeared at the heart of rows upon rows of bloodied symbols. Her back was arched, her mouth open in a wordless scream. Behind her Gallow stood, his bony hand outstretched over her bent body, his eyes locked on Calamity.

**"COME BROTHER.**

**"COME FACE YOUR END."**

## Chapter Fifty-Seven

In the distance, Zara could hear a rumbling—the sound of hundreds, no, thousands of feet against the earth. She turned midair to see a long row of pure darkness charging toward them. Eyes narrowed, she growled when she realized what she was seeing.

Shadow-fiends. An army of *shadow-fiends*.

Hundreds had swarmed the Keep, but their numbers paled in comparison to the waves that moved so quickly they shimmered, a roiling sea of claws and bloodlust. Behind them larger shapes moved, ten-foot-tall monstrosities that lagged behind, their claws dragging along the ground, scarring the earth.

"There's... there's so many *of them. How?"* Teema whispered.

*I see now why Calamity almost conquered this world,* Zara said, hiding her fear with disgust. *Most would choose a life of servitude rather than the comfort of death. Cowards—every last one.*

Calamity screamed again, a shriek that made Zara flinch.

The dark god hit the ground with a boom, sand and soil exploding outward. At the center of the crater lay Calamity, but gone was his colossal form. His right arm had shrunk until it was smaller than Gaj's, while his left was no bigger than Zara's. The Fury grimaced when the pitiful god dug his fingers into the sand, finding no purchase. The once stoic "Tyrant" was slowly being dragged, kicking and screaming toward Eternity, Gallow, and the strange circles. The wallow-tail—seeing its prey—dove for Eternity, fire bursting from its wings, but Gallow simply raised a bony hand. Blue-fire washed against an invisible barrier.

*"He was telling the truth,"* Teema said in disbelief. *"He really can kill Calamity."*

*Perhaps,* Zara said cagily. *But not soon enough—look.*

Teema followed her gaze, realizing what Zara had the moment the shadow-fiends came over the horizon. The monsters were moving too fast—they would reach Eternity before Calamity.

Zara growled, wracked with indecision. Yes, Gallow's magic was working, but even from here she could see it was hurting Eternity. She didn't want to leave the woman alone with the god, though she knew Lukas would fight tooth and claw for her.

"*What is it you always say? 'Deal with the problem at hand, not the one in your head'?*" Teema asked, though she was clearly unhappy. "*And right now that's the army of shadow-fiends heading for us.*"

Zara grinned wolfishly. *I will remember that the next time you dawdle, lost in the muck of your own mind.*

Her voidbeast landed with a heavy thump a hundred feet from Eternity, planting herself squarely in the path of the incoming army while Lukas prowled around Gallow and Eternity, lips bared in a snarl. Zara nodded in approval, proud of how at ease he was in his vaxion form. He couldn't kill the slugs—none of them could—but he might be fast enough to spirit Eternity away should the fighting reach her.

Zara widened her stance, took a deep, steadying breath and turned to face the waves of darkness and claws that charged her. There were thousands of them, and even a hero from one of Lukas' stories would say it was insanity to fight them alone. But she wasn't alone, she told herself—she had Teema now. And if this was how they were fated to die, then so be it—she would make it a death the world would remember.

**Skyscream Activated.**

Her throat burned as raw, concentrated energy shot from her gaping maw. It cut through the air, silent as death as it cleaved through the shadow-fiends like a blade. The monsters didn't even have time to scream. They were simply running full tilt one second, the next their shadows and flesh evaporated as skyscream cleaved the earth in two, leaving a scorched path in its wake. Zara's lips curled in a half-smile at the wide, satisfying gap that had formed in the charging darkness.

A smile that dropped when the gap instantly closed as monsters rushed to fill the empty space. Growling, Zara fired again and again, Teema keeping an eye on her new limit—six shots.

By the time she got to the fifth, Teema warned that her mana had dropped to less than ten percent. The monsters were close enough now that she could make out the gaping holes in their chests where their hearts should be. The shadow-fiends had barely slowed despite her slaughter, and she couldn't tell if her efforts had halved their number or barely dented it.

Zara's gaze flickered to the God of Judgment. The skeletal figure hadn't even glanced at her, or the monsters—as if he'd expected Zara to do this. Expected her to sacrifice herself to give him and Eternity the time they needed. And while she would never say it aloud, she knew Teema sensed it—they couldn't win.

Growling, the Fury unsheathed her claws, her fangs bared. If she burst through the center of the shadow-fiends, maybe she could…

The sky darkened, pitch-black clouds forming. In seconds a blistering storm raged overhead, the air sparking with static. The hair of Zara's mane rose, a shiver passing through her as the clouds grew fat and heavy with electricity.

*"That's* Wrath's Storm!*"* Teema said, her confusion matching Zara's. *"I thought you couldn't use that in voidbeast form?"*

*I cannot,* Zara replied, her heart in her throat.

Lightning burst from overhead, bolt after bolt raining down on the shadow-fiends, sending bodies and sand high into the air. The monsters came to a screeching halt, scrabbling as they searched for the enemy, but the lightning kept coming.

A thud of hooves came from the east—a lone rider cresting the horizon, waving a flag of red and gold. Zara frowned, partly in surprise, but mostly at the human's clear stupidity—why was the fool announcing themselves before a horde of shadow-fiends?

The rider brought a horn to their lips, blowing hard—a call that was answered with a roar. Zara froze, not daring to breathe for fear the hope that blossomed in her chest would vanish—it was a roar she knew. A roar she was sure she would never hear again.

A cloud of dust rose from behind the rider. A long line of men and women came charging over the hill on horseback. They were clad from head-to-toe in red and gold armor, the sound of their warhorses a battle cry. A hundred, two hundred, no—three hundred soldiers!

And at the very front of the army, running at full speed like demons, was a man, a vaxion and a molger.

*"Ashira!"* cried Zara, at the same time Teema said, *"Lenia?"*

\*\*\*

I was dreaming. There was no other explanation for it.

The woman who'd found me half-dead on a forest floor. Who'd risked her and her son Waylen's life to take me in and nurse me back to health. Who'd sided with me against her own people to save Lukas' life. What was Lenia *doing* here? And with Ashira! A woman she hated, who should be dead! How…

I didn't finish the thought as I looked behind Lenia, Ashira, and the heavily armored man they ran with. In-between hundreds of soldiers, I caught glimpses of fur in shades of red and brown, black and gray, as fifteen, no—*twenty* molger ran with the army, heads thrown back in a roar. Pitch-black shapes darted among them, their tendrils crackling as they lent their lightning to Ashira's storm.

Tears pricked my eyes. They were *alive*. The vaxion were alive!

The clouds burst again, lightning exploding as tridents of destruction ripped into the shadow-fiends, the monsters shrieking as death and chaos tore their ranks apart. The larger shadow-fiends had finally caught up to their smaller, quicker versions, and they were turning toward the incoming soldiers and vaxion, their claws raised.

Two hundred feet.

One hundred.

Closer now, I could see the man in white armor who rode by Ashira and Lenia. He had dark hair and a rough beard that covered a sharp jawline. Teeth bared, he drew his sword, and I was struck by how familiar he was.

Player Two… no. *Valerius*. He was the image of Valerius—albeit about thirty years older. That must mean he was—

*"For Navaros!"* the king yelled.

Soldiers answered the king's battle cry with their own, drawing swords, hefting spears, and nocking arrows.

Army and horde clashed in an explosion of claws and fangs, blades and shrieks. I was about to tell Zara to hurry, that we needed to get to Ashira and the others, but I stopped when I heard her thoughts.

There was relief and gratitude of course—her pack, her *family* was alive. But what overwhelmed her was knowing that they'd run all this way just to help *her*. Zara had faced gods and death without flinching, but seeing the vaxion alive and well, fighting side by side with humans and molger—something that hadn't happened in over a century—was too much for her.

"I've got this," I said quietly.

She disappeared into the darkness, her words caught in her throat as I took control.

\*\*\*

I couldn't fight as well as Zara, nor did I have her command of her shapeshifted forms, but the sight of Ashira and Lenia fighting alongside the King of Navaros unleashed something in me. I charged into the shadow-fiends like I was possessed, my claws ripping darkness, my fangs tossing bodies left and right as I cut through the army.

The shadow-fiends fought back, claws harmlessly catching my mane. But some got lucky, raking their sharpened tips along my side, blood coating my once white fur. I didn't even slow—with Zara's new stats, my wounds healed in seconds. I kept my eyes locked on the closest vaxion to me, a woman who was fighting a dozen shadow-fiends on her own, her lightning flashing weakly as they overpowered her, forcing her to the ground. Bellowing, I rammed into three monsters as I tore through two more.

"*Jaza?*" I called, whipping my tail around, the barbed edge catching the shadow-fiend that had pinned her, cleaving its head from its shoulders. The vaxion at my feet stared up at me, bleeding heavily, but alive.

"*Teema?*" came her astonished voice. "*What are you—what manner of beast is this? How… how are we speaking?*"

"*A better question—what are you doing here?*" I asked, kicking my back leg at a shadowy form trying to sneak up on us.

Jaza snarled, forcing herself to her feet as she bit down on another. *"We left Moonvale mere hours after you did. Ashira meant her oath to Lukas. It was time to stop hiding from the world. Time to settle the sins of the past. And so we went to see the molger in H'tar."*

*"You did what? Wait, when Gaj arrived you weren't—Player Two didn't... one second."* I paused to drive my fangs into a shadow-fiend's neck, my paw snaking out to pin a second. The acrid taste of rotting flesh coated my tongue, and I tried not to think about it as I ripped off its head. *"Everyone left Moonvale, right? You didn't leave anyone behind?"*

*"No, everyone is—ah, step back, will you?"*

I leaped back just as a burst of lightning erupted from Jaza's tendrils. Three shadow-fiends were caught in the blast, their bodies arching as the vaxion burned them from the inside out. They fell to the ground in a pile of smoke and charred flesh.

*"Ashira, the romantic fool, offered the molger all of Moonvale, as well as her own head on a spike,"* Jaza said, panting slightly, her words harsh but her voice full of pride. *"They were in favor of the spike part, not so much the rest. She tried to tell them of Calamity, and what you had seen, but they refused to listen. It was about to turn violent when Lenia and Jerome intervened."*

*"Wait, Jerome? As in—the-guy-Lenia-had-to-kick-the-crap-out-of-to-stop-him-from-killing-Lukas? That Jerome?"*

*"That is a very short version of the tale Lenia told me over tea, but yes—that one."*

My mind was short-circuiting at the thought of Jaza and Lenia sitting together in Lenia's stone cottage, sipping tea and chatting, when the vaxion hissed. A shadow-fiend drove its claws into Jaza's side, and she swiped at it, cutting it in half. Snarling, I raised my front paws and brought them down on the monster's head with a sharp, wet crack—killing it. Jaza nodded in thanks but had to jump out of the way of another. I growled, inviting the mindless beasts to try their hand at someone their own size, but in truth it was hard not to feel hopeless. It didn't matter how many we killed, they just kept *coming*.

*"Lenia and Jerome agreed Ashira would have to pay for what she had done,"* Jaza continued, *"but that could wait. Punishing her would do little if the world was conquered by*

Calamity. They said a certain 'Fury' was proof the vaxion had changed—that they could be trusted."

If I'd been able to, my voidbeast would have smiled even as my eyes welled with tears. I'd done that—I'd helped someone even when I'd been so scared and anxious of, well, everything. Even when I hadn't believed in myself. Determination ignited in my chest.

"*Wait,*" I said. A spearman up ahead drove his sword into a shadow-fiend while a molger bit down on it, the two working together to kill the monster. "*If that's how you teamed up with the molger, then how did you end up with Navaros' army?*"

A dozen claws dug into my back with no warning, but I was ready for them. I tucked my wings in tightly, threw myself on the ground, and rolled as quickly as I could. It wasn't graceful, and if Zara hadn't so overwhelmed she'd have given me crap about it, but it got the job done. Bones crunched under my back, but no sooner had I gotten to my feet than ten more surrounded me.

"*That was luck or fate, perhaps both,*" Jaza said, and I could tell that while I was tired, she was exhausted. I glanced at my stamina, relieved to see it filling almost as quickly as I spent it. I could keep this up a lot longer than she or the other vaxion could—which made it all the more pressing to get this done, and *fast*.

"*What do you mean?*"

"*We crossed paths with Navaros' army on the road to the Keep. They assumed we were with Calamity, and were all set to kill us, but—*"

A shriek made me look up. The wallow-tail flew straight for us, flames bursting from her wings. They rained down on us from on high, lighting fur and shadow aflame. A molger just ahead of me roared, a trail of fire racing down her back, but she couldn't reach the flames to put them out.

I dropped the shadow-fiend in my jaws and raced for the molger, who was thrashing on the ground. Rising on my hind legs, I was grateful for my massive paws as I slapped at the flames, ignoring the pain as my skin crackled and blistered from the heat. Between the molger's writhing and my awkward attempts at pat-a-cake, we put the flames out, though the molger was left with long, ragged burns down her back and sides, the charred flesh oozing.

With a groan, the russet-colored molger got to her feet, and I nearly screamed with joy.

*"Lenia! It's me. It's, well, it's Zara!"* I said half-shrieking, remembering only at the last second that was the only name she knew me by. *"Are you all right? Is Waylen here?"*

*"What the—Zara? No, I made him stay home with the other kids, though he's sworn to never speak to me again for my treachery,"* Lenia said, small molger eyes staring at me with astonishment. *"Why do you have wings?"*

A shriek came from above, and I dived atop Lenia, stretching my wings out so they covered us both. Flames hit me, explosions of pain that made me hiss as they ripped through the delicate membrane like paper, but the wounds started to close almost as quickly as they burned, leaving only an uncomfortable tingly sensation. I heard the roar of a molger and the yip-like cry of a vaxion and knew others hadn't been so lucky.

The wallow-tail turned, flying away from us, but it would come back around in seconds. I snapped out my wings.

*"I'll deal with the wallow-tail,"* I said. *"Can you keep the shadow-fiends off me while I take off?"*

*"Don't worry,"* Lenia said, nodding to me in thanks. *"He said he'd take care of the bird. We should focus on the ground."*

*"Who?"*

Before she could answer, a flash of gold streaked across the sky as a huge dragon collided with the wallow-tail. Flame and fang fought for dominance as they tumbled through the air, neither giving the other an inch.

## Chapter Fifty-Eight

What felt like wet sandpaper dragged across Lazander's face. He groaned, trying to bat it away, but the sandpaper persisted. He became dimly aware someone was shouting.

"Mabel, no! We can't help him no more, okay? We have to go, *please*."

*Wait, Mabel?*

Lazander opened his eyes. He was lying on the ground, and everything *hurt*. His muscles screamed in pain, and when he tried to move fire burned through his back—throbbing like an old wound that had never quite healed. He grunted, rolling onto his side.

"Mabel, is that—" Lazander began, but wet lips rummaged about in his hair. He heard a familiar neigh of delight as she chewed on her favorite snack.

"Mabel!" he cried, running his hands over her long neck, tears in his eyes when she nuzzled him. It was her—after all these weeks, after Gallow had tried to wipe her from his memory, his horse, his *friend*, had found him. A part of him wondered if he was dead. In that moment, he didn't really care.

"Blessed Void! I'm sorry, Master Lazander, I'm so sorry!" the same young voice called out. The rider dismounted, making sure to keep one hand on Mabel's reins, though judging by how enthusiastically the horse was eating his hair, Lazander didn't think she was going anywhere anytime soon.

A young girl, thirteen-years-old at best, stared at him with red eyes brimming with fresh tears. "I didn't know it was you until Mabel stopped to give you a lick, but then I thought you was dead so I told Mabel to leave you 'cause the rest of the riders are way ahead, and them shadow-beasties are everywhere, they got three riders just on the way out the Keep, but I put my head down and rode as fast as I could—"

"Hold on," Lazander said, his head whirling. The girl spoke so quickly, he could barely understand her. "I need… I need a moment."

His mind raced, trying to piece together what had happened. He remembered Eternity falling, clutching her to his chest, Gaj striking him in the back… but then there was only darkness. A vague memory surfaced of Eternity's voice, and he swore he could still feel the warmth of her hands on him, but he had no idea what she'd said or where she'd gone. He didn't even know how long he'd been out. But he felt… different. Despite the ache in every inch of his body, his mind felt clear and unclouded. He felt like… *himself*.

His eyes darted around, the joy he felt at this new clarity damped by the knowledge of what came next. Gallow would sense he'd broken free and bring the chains down around his neck any second now. He glanced from the young girl, her tears threatening to spill down her cheeks, to Mabel, who'd grown bored and was pawing the dirt. Any second now, the child-like form of Gallow would appear, his icy hand sealing Lazander's fate.

Nothing happened.

"The Keep is under attack, Master Lazander!" the girl cried around big gulping breaths, the dam breaking as tears rolled down her cheeks. "A big giant thing is coming, but Zara the Fury and this molger-vaxion was there. I didn't know you could be a molger-vaxion, I thought it was one or the other, but I saw the man with four legs and then six, so he was definitely a molger-vaxion. Him and Lady Fury killed a whole bunch of shadow-beasties and then the queen ordered us to ride as quick as we could and deliver this here to the king."

The girl held up a letter. Lazander instantly recognized the beautiful cursive—it was Queen Firanta's.

"Right, first of all…" Lazander said, getting down on one knee. "I don't know what's going on, but I do know one thing—you've been extremely brave. There are not many Mabel trusts, so for her to let you ride her is proof you have a good heart. You've done well to find me, all right?"

The girl nodded, her eyes huge and still filled with tears—but they no longer fell.

"Second," he said, smiling as he placed a hand on her shoulder. "You said the Keep was attacked, but you were being helped by Zara the Fury and… Lukas," he stumbled on their names and the memory of the last time they'd met. He'd dared to hope that Lukas had survived, but he was sure he'd killed Zara. Relief warmed his heart, and he had to fight not to squeeze the girl's shoulder too tightly in thanks.

The girl nodded. "I like the Lady Fury. She's a big, beautiful white beastie. It's real pretty."

Lazander's eyes widened at the memory of the beast that had burned a hole in his chest back in Ravenna's maze. "Did you see anyone else? Lady Eternity or one of her Champions?"

The girl shook her head, and Lazander's stomach dropped. He tried to reassure himself that if he was alive, that meant Eternity was too. "May I see the letter?"

She hesitated, looking unsure. "I'm supposed to give this to the king. They gave us all the same letter and sent us out on every horse they had. They said one of us had to make it, that it was life or death."

"May I ask what is your name?"

"Katarina."

"Lady Katarina, I will not force you to give me the letter. I know you have been given a duty, a very important one, but I only wish to help. I do not know if I should rush to the Keep and try to help, or should I join you and meet with King Najar. The contents of that letter will help me figure out where I am needed."

The girl took this in, then gave a sage nod, handing him the letter. Lazander tried not to rip it open. He absently rubbed a hand against Mabel's neck, who had once again decided she was in the mood for Lazander's red curls, and read:

*Leon,*

*I hope the fates are with us, and that by the time you read this the Keep still stands, but alas you did not marry an optimist.*

Lazander's heart clenched as he read about Calamity, the shadow-fiends, Gaj, Zara, and Lukas—everything lined up with what Katarina had said. And then he came to the last paragraph:

*Ride on the Keep. Take every man, woman, child, or beast you can find—it matters not, and kill the demon that threatens our kingdom. I may be dead, but Navaros is more than the stone* walls of the Keep. Do not let my death stop you from being the king I know you to be. Save our people, Leon. Save Navaros.

*It has been an honor to call you husband.*
*Yours even in death,*
*Firanta*

It was only willpower that stopped Lazander from crumpling the letter in his fist. The queen wasn't a woman who gave up, but despair and grief were etched into every word. What had happened at the Keep for her to write this?

"Where are we, exactly?" Lazander asked quietly.

Katarina looked thrown by the question, but pointed east—"about an hour's ride from the border. That's where King Najar was headed."

"I want you to take Mabel and ride somewhere safe. The town of Radiant is about two hours west—it's far enough out of Gaj's path that people might still be there. I'll deliver this letter to the king."

"But Master Lazander, you can't go all by yourself. What if there are shadow-beasties?"

Lazander's throat caught, moved by her bravery. Kneeling he clasped his fingers, helping Katarina up and into her saddle. "Mabel is more than a mighty steed—she's my friend. My family," he said, rubbing her neck in open affection. The Keep might be lost, perhaps even Eternity and Malik were too, but he could make sure these two souls were safe—and that had to be worth something. "I need someone to protect her. Can I trust you to do that?"

Katarina nodded vigorously.

"Good." He smiled, holding up the letter. "I'll get this to the king, you head to Radiant, all right?"

He didn't wait for her to reply. He pressed his head against Mabel's in farewell, preparing to use Gallow's gifts to run as fast as he could, but Mabel headbutted him in the back. Hard. He stumbled, more from surprise. Katarina pulled on her reins, calling—"No, Mabel, this way! Come on, girl!"

But the horse shook out her mane and trotted east in the direction of King Najar and his army. Mabel shot Lazander a look, and while the two could no longer communicate, he didn't need to—her eyes said everything. *"I dare you to leave me behind again."*

Lazander's chest tightened as he wondered what he had done to deserve such loyalty. "I'm going to run ahead and clear the way of any shadow-fiends," he said to Katarina. "Head east—we need to find the king."

***

"I told you, human," the woman said, her single golden eye boring into King Najar with a familiar ferocity. "We are here because we saw the giant marching and know what lies in its path—your precious Ivory Keep."

Lazander hadn't known what to expect from his meeting with the king. What he could not have predicted however, was finding him in a showdown with a powerfully built woman who was almost as tall as the King of Navaros—a man mounted on a warhorse. Her arms and chest were covered in tattoos while dark hair slid over her one shoulder in a heavy plait. She was missing an eye, the scar left behind radiating out to cover her cheek and part of forehead, yet it didn't seem to bother her in the slightest. At her back stood thirty or so falslings, a mix of vaxion and molger, their claws scratching against the dry soil as some growled while others bared their teeth.

Behind King Najar stood an army of three hundred strong. Hooves nervously pawed the dirt as men and women who'd faced down armies twice their size gripped swords and kept bowstrings taut. The air was thick with tension, and Lazander knew all it would take was one wrong word for violence to erupt.

The ground was littered with headless corpses still sticky with blood, the earth scarred with deep gouges. Lazander couldn't tell who'd killed the dozens of shadow-fiends at his feet but judging by the blood on the woman's hands as well as the king's sword, he guessed both sides had taken down their fair share.

"How *altruistic* of the vaxion—a people who have not set foot outside Moonvale in nigh on a decade. And certainly not in the company of the molger," the king called, his voice laden with sarcasm. "I say this once and once only, falslings—

turn back. Whatever the Tyrant promised you is not worth the blood that will be shed today."

The woman snarled, a hint of a fang showing. "*Idiot.* We do not serve the dark god. We march to aid my niece—it is she who fights to kill the Tyrant and rid this world of his evil."

"And just who is your niece? She must be a hero of legend if she is strong enough to kill a god," the king said.

Lazander knew from the man's tone that while his words were phrased as a question, he didn't particularly care for an answer—he'd already made up his mind.

And it wasn't good.

"Zara the Fury," the woman answered with pride.

Whispers erupted from behind the king, and his brow darkened.

"While you are not my enemy, human," the falsling continued, "if you keep me from my Zara a second longer, you *will be.*" Her last words were a growl.

The king raised his sword.

Lazander darted forward with a burst of Gallow's power, appearing in between King Najar and the woman.

The soldiers to his left instantly dropped into defensive positions, their shields held high. But the woman didn't even flinch—she simply raised a curious eyebrow.

"The Keep is under attack—Zara the Fury fights with everything she has to protect the people of Navaros," he announced, holding the letter up high. "And she needs all the help she can get."

\*\*\*

They met Katarina and Mabel on the way back, and Lazander was thrilled to see they weren't alone. An unhappy looking bundle of feathers sat on Katarina's shoulder, but it chirped in delight when Lazander raced to meet them.

"Merrin!" he cried, cupping the hawk in his hands.

She squawked with joy, sounding like a hatchling again, and nuzzled Lazander's cheek. The hawk was in poor shape—half her feathers were gone, burned to a cinder, and a line of blood trailed along her neck.

His heart was in his throat as he gently pushed aside what few feathers remained and examined the wound as carefully as he could. Clutching her to his chest, he thought about the last time he'd seen Merrin—he'd barely waved goodbye to her.

Had Merrin died, that half-hearted farewell would have been her last memory of him.

"What happened?" he asked Katarina, trying to calm the fury in his heart. If he thought about it any longer, he'd charge ahead and try to kill Gallow himself.

The young girl pointed up at the sky. "We was riding along when I spotted her, Master Lazander. She was falling fast, and one of her wings wasn't working so good. The only reason she didn't fall down flat is 'cause—"

A *whomp* reached his ears a second before a dragon the size of a barn landed next to him.

"—is cause of Galora, Master Lazander. She came racing after Merrin and caught her in her talons, all gentle like. Ain't seen nothing like it," Katarina finished.

Galora bent her head, pressing her warm, scaly forehead against Lazander's. Merrin chirped, snuggling against his chest, and Mabel, never one to be left out, joined them, resting her head on his shoulder. They breathed together as one, tears pricking Lazander's eyes.

For months all he'd cared about was killing Player Two. His need for revenge consumed him, and Gallow had used it like a carrot on a stick, promising him the prince's head if he did just one more mission. If he killed just one more person. His desperate desire for vengeance made it all too easy for Gallow to slither into his mind and wipe away everything that wasn't utter devotion to the God of Judgment.

Now with his arms wrapped around his family, Lazander felt the pain and grief of Marito's and Gabriel's deaths fade. He would always love and miss his brothers-in-arms, but it would break their hearts if they saw how far he had fallen.

This was what was important—his friends, his family. Not hate. Not revenge. And *not* Player Two.

"I missed you," he rasped. He had so much more to say, to apologize for, but that was all the lump in his throat could manage. Katarina, to her credit, said nothing. She simply sat on Mabel, her hand gently running through the horse's hair.

Lazander coughed, embarrassed he'd broken down in front of the girl. Galora leaned back enough to press her snout against Merrin, giving the hawk a concerned sniff. The hawk chirped, assuring the dragon she was all right.

"Who did this to you, Merrin?" he asked, wishing for the hundredth time he still had their bond. He looked her over again and noticed the red tag on her foot—the kind used to attach a missive. But whatever had been there was lost to the same flames that had taken her feathers—which told Lazander exactly what had happened.

"Were you on your way to find the king, Merrin?" he asked, gesturing behind him. The army and the falslings, while quick, weren't as quick as he was on foot.

The hawk ducked her head, looking down sadly at her foot and the missing letter. She'd always taken pride in her work, and even without the bond Lazander knew she felt like she'd failed. He patted her head reassuringly. "Did the wallow-tail find you? The bird of fire?"

It was Galora who answered, her growl so low and menacing Katarina jumped.

"Don't worry, Galora," he said, patting her neck. "You'll get your chance."

## Chapter Fifty-Nine

The wallow-tail was fire incarnate, but even flames could be ripped apart by fangs—if the wielder was determined enough. And Galora was nothing if not determined.

Lazander gripped the dragon's neck between his legs, holding on as tightly as he could as she crashed into the wallow-tail with a vengeful roar. While Lazander had been furious the wallow-tail attacked Merrin, it was nothing compared to the rage with which Galora fought. Flames exploded around them, but she drove through them, biting down on the giant bird's neck with all her strength. The wallow-tail's answering scream made Lazander's ears ring.

Tucked against his chest, Merrin squawked, adding her fury to Galora's as they tumbled through the air. The hawk had refused to go with the other injured, shrieking in rage until Lazander tucked her safely inside his tunic. Mabel, upon seeing that Merrin and Galora were going with him, had dug her hooves in and nearly thrown poor Katarina off. Lazander tried not to think of Mabel on the battlefield below, a replacement for a warhorse who'd been hurt. This wasn't her first fight, and he almost pitied any shadow-fiend stupid enough to try its claws against her hooves and teeth.

Galora growled, bringing him back to the present as she tucked her wings in against her sides—making them fall faster. The wallow-tail thrashed and screeched, forcing Lazander to curl around Merrin, but the dragon only growled, biting down harder. Once she set her mind on something, neither man nor god could stop her.

**"His touch is stone, his body eternal,"** Lazander said, hating he still had to invoke the God of Judgment. **"Let my own speak true."**

Lines of gray trailed over him, his skin turning to stone. He kept one protective hand over Merrin as they fell. Below them the earth was a sea of pitch-black with only occasional spots of fur mixed with red and gold armor as humans and falslings fought together, but Lazander felt no fear. He trusted Galora with more than his life—he trusted her with Merrin's.

At the last second the dragon twisted, forcing the wallow-tail under her as they hit the ground in an explosion of flames and bodies as shadow-fiends were sent flying. Calamity's servant screeched, flames bursting from it as the monsters trapped underneath screamed, burning to death in the wallow-tail's panic. Galora roared, ripping and tearing, her eyes squeezed shut—the only part of her the bird could truly harm. But the dragon didn't need her eyes—she'd pinned the creature with her teeth, growling viciously as her claws ripped and tore.

The flames started to fade while Galora's rage only grew.

After what felt like an age, the dragon's claws met soil, and the last of the flames trickled away, twisting into the night. When she pulled back, panting hard, Lazander spotted a chunk of what looked like crystal half-buried in the churned earth.

"There, Galora! Can you let me down, please?" he asked, patting her gently.

Lazander slid from her neck as she dipped her head. They stood in a small crater, the bottom carpeted by the bodies of crushed shadow-fiends while the battle raged around them.

Lazander picked up the crystal, recalling what little he knew of the wallow-tail. This wasn't the creature's first death—it had reformed at least once after Eternity killed it. While Galora casually whipped her tail around, crushing several shadow-fiends that had been trying to sneak up on them, Lazander smiled. At the heart of the crystal, blue-fire sparked—the exact shade of the wallow-tail's wings.

"I think we found the key to the beast's 'immortality,'" Lazander said, presenting the crystal to Galora. With every passing second the fire at its core grew brighter.

"What do you think, Merrin?" he asked, holding it up to the hawk. Merrin's response was to peck it angrily. "I agree. Would you like to do the honors, Galora?"

The dragon took the crystal delicately in her teeth. With a fierce grin, she bit down, and it shattered. As the shards fell from her mouth, Lazander swore he heard an echo of the wallow-tail's scream as it died, once and for all.

\*\*\*

My chest tightened with worry when Galora and the wallow-tail fell, a swirl of gold and blue. The dragon refused to let go, even when they hit the ground in an explosion of fire that made me flinch. I watched until Galora took off again, triumphant, relieved the dragon was all right. But my relief was marred by the shock of red hair and black armor I saw on the dragon's back.

*Lazander.*

He'd almost killed Zara and Lukas, yet here he was fighting Calamity. I knew he now served Gallow like Eternity did, or rather *had,* but where had he been until now? Was he a zealot like Zara thought, or was his delay coming here a sign he'd broken away from Gallow?

My mind was so lost to thoughts of the Champion, I almost missed the dark hair of the corpse at my feet. But when I saw it, the rest of the world fell away. I hadn't known that when vaxion died they returned to their human forms.

I did now.

By some miracle Fatyr's face was mostly intact, but the rest of him was a mess of blood and claw marks. I remembered him drunk out of his mind while he happily danced by himself, the other vaxion cheering him on. Remembered how much he adored Esia, and my heart broke at what the thirteen-year-old would do when he found out his brother was dead.

Rationally, I'd known people would die in this fight. But it was one thing to know something and another to have that fact stare up at you with wide, terrified eyes.

Something bumped me gently, and I whirled with a snarl—to see a pure white vaxion at my side. The ground behind her was scorched carnage, but the eyes that looked at me held no rage—only love and sorrow.

*"Ashira,"* I whispered.

She dipped her head, pressing it to mine. *"The world will know Fatyr's name when we are done. They will know he gave his life to save theirs while they hid in their homes like cowards. But today..."* she said, lifting herself up to her full height. *"Today the gods will learn that it is* us *who should be feared."*

She roared, but not in anger—her battle cry was a call to arms, a call to give everything we had to the fight. I joined in alongside vaxion, molger, and even some humans, our voices drowning out the moans of the shadow-fiends. *Come*, we cried, *come and meet your death.*

Together Ashira and I dived back into the fight, the darkened bodies of the shadow-fiends and the human corpses they left behind blurring into one as we fought with claw and lightning, fang and fury, cutting a path through the battlefield. I kept expecting Zara to say something, or to take over—I could sense her watching through my eyes, but the falsling was quiet. There were still hundreds of shadow-fiends, but their numbers no longer stretched endlessly into the horizon.

I felt a flutter of hope in my chest. Could it be? Were we... were we winning?

*"Eternity,"* Zara whispered after what felt like hours. It was the first she'd spoken since the fighting began. *"We should check on Eternity, and the slugs. We have not seen them in too long."*

*What? Like, right now?* I asked, ripping a shadow-fiend in two.

*"Take to the air, Teema,"* Zara said. *"My gut screams that something is wrong."*

I didn't want to leave Ashira and the others to Calamity's servants, but one look was all the leader of the vaxion needed to read my expression.

*"Go. Do what needs to be done,"* she growled. *"I will hold them back."* She let lose another round of lightning, clearing the path for me.

*"Thank you,"* I said, tensing my legs. I'd never taken off from the ground before—only tried to stop us crashing into it. But Zara made no move to take control. She murmured gentle instructions to me, and I adjusted my footing, stretched out my wings and pushed down hard at her signal.

My take-off was... wobbly at best, my muscles groaning as I beat my wings harder and harder. But the higher we got, the easier it became. Once we leveled out, I looked down at the fight below and saw I was right—we *were* winning, but there were still so many shadow-fiends. Four or five hundred, I guessed, but we'd taken losses, too—dead men and women dotted the field, some naked, some clad in red and gold.

*"Focus, Teema,"* Zara said, and I forced myself to turn toward Gallow and Eternity. At a distance, they looked much the same as before—Eternity hovered above rows of bloodied concentric circles while Gallow stood behind her, still as a

skeletal statue. Lukas crouched like a watchful gargoyle while Malik knelt in the dirt, head bent to his god.

"*Tch. Imagine bowing to a* slug," Zara huffed in disgust.

I would have replied, but I was too busy scanning the ruined mountain of red sand that was once the Ivory Keep and the path that led to Eternity. Because something was missing—something *important*.

*Zara… can you see Calamity?* I asked, trying and failing not to sound panicked. Last we saw him, he was on the ground and being dragged toward Eternity, his body shrinking with every pull. The rift in the sky had doubled in size since Calamity came through, stretching across the sky like an open wound, but I could see no sign of the dark god.

"*There!*" Zara barked.

On the ground mere feet from Gallow a slug lay curled up like a prawn. Its body was cut and torn; a trail of blood leading behind it. It screeched and flailed, each thrash weaker than the last.

"*He is in pain,*" Zara hissed. "*Good.*"

But there was something about the scene below that felt… wrong. On instinct I opened my Operator tab—I hadn't tried to since I spent all my Void Mana, and I was relieved to see that while I couldn't use "god functions" anymore, I was still labeled as an Operator. Narrowing my eyes, I focused on the bloody circles below.

## ETERNAL PRISON DETECTED.
## COST TO CAST—CONTINUOUS.
## COST TO RESIST—CONTINUOUS.
## NO VOID MANA AVAILABLE.

I frowned. An "Eternal Prison" sounded like something to bind Calamity—not kill him, but maybe Gallow had to imprison the god first. But… that didn't make sense either. Calamity spent a thousand years trapped in the Void, and Gallow was happy to leave him there.

"Your instincts are good, little piggie, but you're too naive," a voice said. "Gallow has no intention of 'binding' Calamity or being all noble and killing himself to save you. That would require a *spine*."

I nearly dropped out of the sky in surprise.

*"Where are you, slug?"* Zara hissed.

"Rakna, darling—do get it right. And I've been here the whole time—I hitched a ride on you when Clammy-whammy was throwing a tantrum," Nettie answered.

I looked down in horror to see something curl out from between the toes of my left paw. Something small, dark, and *slimy*. Instinctively I shook my paw, flailing in mid-air.

"Don't make me bite you, little piggie," the rakna said. "Especially when I'm being *helpful*."

*"If you wish to be helpful, then* die,*"* Zara hissed.

"Oh, I'm next on Gallow's list, don't you worry. Annoyingly, he's always been the brains of the family—the rest of us wouldn't have the patience to implant the memories or craft all the lies and propaganda needed to become the *God of Judgment*. I'd have just eaten you all." Though the slug had no eyes, I could swear I felt her roll them. "I just heard the story of how 'Eternity' stood against Calamity alone—my brother's idea of a joke. Let's be thankful he chose to be a god and not a comedian."

*"Wait… how? Who told you?"* I asked, confused. She hadn't even heard of Eternity until a few hours ago.

"Oh, I used some Void Mana to search a couple of mortals' brains. Lotta junk in there, but some gold nuggets too. Don't worry—I didn't hurt them. Probably."

*"Eat her, Teema!"* Zara said. *"Feast on her and take her Void Mana. She sits on our paw and practically begs us to!"*

I thought Nettie would protest or try to convince us to help her defeat her brothers, as Gallow had. But she said nothing. She merely cocked her head.

"You don't fancy a snack, 'Teema'? As Zara knows, we are *very* tasty." There was something about the way she spoke, and the undercurrent of grief I sensed, that made me say the first thing that came to my mind.

*"I'm sorry about Ravenna. I didn't meet her, but I'll always be grateful to her."*

The slug flinched. "Urgggh, you meant that! Why couldn't you be a power-hungry toad-licking troglodyte like most mortals? That would make this *so* much easier."

*"I'm... sorry?"*

"I just wanted to kill Gallow, you know," Nettie said, her head dipping. "I didn't care if Calamity gobbled me up, or all you little piggies. Hell, he could eat the whole universe. I didn't give a damn—none of this is my problem. But... I can still hear her, you know. Hear her whispering in my head, telling me to 'do the right thing.'" The rakna sighed heavily. "Ravenna was the optimistic one. She thought we could change our 'destiny.' That we could finally be happy if we just stopped fighting. She was my little sister—born 0.000798 seconds after me, and I never let her forget it—but I went along with her ideas anyway, thinking I was doing her a favor. Never thought I'd be sitting here, hitching a ride on the mortal who ate her and wondering if maybe, just maybe, she was right."

*"Give me back control,"* Zara said, nearly frothing at the mouth in rage. *"If you lack the stomach for it, then I will eat her."*

"Speaking of, that's what the Eternal Prison is for," Nettie said, nodding at the bloodied circles. "It binds a rakna by stripping them of their magic and Void Mana, forcing them to look like little old me again. It's a hell of a spell, and Gallow has spent about a thousand VM points on it by my count. Calamity has used much the same fighting it, which means my idiot brothers are essentially stuck in the universe's stupidest tennis match. But Gallow has his little Chosen. He's channeling through her, letting her take all the big hits while he stands on the sidelines looking pretty. Calamity started out with more Void Mana, but he'll be the one left holding the hot potato."

I felt Zara's confusion over "tennis" and "hot potato," but she chose not to ask.

"Okay, so Gallow lied..." I said, taking this all in. "... but he's also going to win? Isn't that a good thing?" I knew I was trying to salvage this. Gallow wasn't exactly a benevolent god, but if the choice was between him and Calamity's never-ending destruction, he was the lesser of two evils.

"Depends on what you mean by 'winning,'" Nettie said cheerfully. "The moment he gets his hands on Calamity, Gallow is going to *eat* him, then me. Meaning my brother will finally achieve his dream of being the only special little snowflake left in the universe." The slug shrugged. "Maybe he'll be a kind god. Or maybe he'll be a constipated shoe-horn of a goat-sticker who'll rule over you all with an iron fist. Take a wild guess which one I think is more likely."

*"Why are you telling us this?"* I asked at the same time Zara said, *"You wish us to save you, is it slug?"*

"The funny thing about being trapped in a piece of glass for a thousand years is it gives you a lot of time to *think*," Nettie replied, arching her back as she stretched. I had no idea whose question she was answering, or if she'd even heard us. "Now I'm not the thinking kind of all-powerful being—all I've ever wanted to do is feast and fight. But sitting here now, watching my brothers slobber all over themselves trying to eat each other. *Again*. I find it's all so..." she paused, considering, "... well, so bloody *boring*."

When the rakna showed her teeth this time, I knew it was a smile.

"So let's spice things up, shall we?"

\*\*\*

Eternity saw it. Gallow's mind stretched out like a vast, endless ocean before her, his guard slipping for an instant. Her insides felt like they were being scooped out while her mind hovered on the knife edge of sanity, but she forced herself to look. Forced herself to see the truth. She'd known Gallow had lied, and while she hadn't wanted to help the god, she had no choice, she'd told herself—no one else could stop Calamity.

But as she fell into the fathomless depths of his mind, she wished, just for a brief moment, that she'd let Calamity destroy the world instead.

## Chapter Sixty

When Eternity hit the ground, her first thought was, "I hope I'm dead."

Her second thought was that on the off chance she wasn't dead, she was going to kill Gallow with her bare hands. But the God of Judgment strode past without so much as a glance at her broken body.

*"You swore,"* she hissed, blood bubbling in her throat.

Gallow paused, one hand behind his back.

**"I SWORE TO KILL CALAMITY.**

**"I WILL. WHEN I EAT HIM."**

There was so much she wanted to say, but all she could manage to spit out was a single word— *"Liar."*

Malik shot to his feet with righteous outrage.

"How *dare* you," he barked. "He's done it—he's bested the dark god. Look! Look how the Tyrant squirms before him!"

Malik was right—the "god" was a pitiful sight. He lay on the outer ring of the bloodied circles, a small, shriveled slug that twisted and cried in pain. Gallow reached down, delicately picking the slimy creature up between two bony fingers.

*"Liar,"* Eternity said again, but a wracking cough made her curl into a ball. She slapped a hand over her lips as she vomited, feeling something wet and sticky come up. With horror she looked down to see she'd coughed up part of her lung.

Eyes screwed up tight, Eternity fought back tears. She wanted to scream, but not at Malik, or even Gallow. She wanted to scream at herself—for being so naïve. So *foolish*. "You want… to rule," she rasped. "A world… dedicated to *you*. Mindless… devoted."

She'd seen it in his mind. An endless ocean of worshippers willing to pluck out their own hearts to please him—who gave him everything from blood and bone to flesh and mana in the fervent hope it would please him. People he never had to discipline because they'd take the whip to their own backs and those of their friends and family.

People like Malik.

And the God of Judgment knew just how to do it—Eternity and the Champions had been his testing ground. It was why he'd fed them piecemeal information and changed favorites at the drop of a hat. They were so busy vying for his favor and freezing one another out at the very thought of his displeasure that he'd barely had to lift a finger—he simply had to nudge them along. Eternity had been no different. She'd been so desperate to carry out his will. Desperate for his *approval*.

"Tell him..." Eternity whispered. "Tell Malik... why I bleed."

When Nettie had pressed her head against Eternity's, the slug dropped a kernel of knowledge in her mind. Knowledge she hadn't understood until Gallow tore her apart from the inside out.

The God of Judgment stood with his back to her, one hand clasped behind him, the other holding the squirming Calamity, whose jerks and flails became weaker by the second.

**"THE CHOSEN IS DYING, CHAMPION,"** he intoned, walking away. **"MAKE IT QUICK FOR HER."**

Malik drew his axe.

Eternity wanted to scream. She'd spent her life as a Chosen being mocked and looked down on for how much it hurt her to use Gallow's powers. It happened to all his Chosen, she was told. The fact that it was worse for her was a sign that she was weak. That she needed to be more diligent. More dedicated.

It was a *lie*. Every Eternity bled because their own magic was *fighting* the god. Because their bodies recognized him as the parasite he was—and Eternity bled the most not out of weakness. She bled the most because she fought back harder than any other Chosen—she just hadn't known it.

Malik raised his axe above his head.

Gasping, she tried to tell him what she'd seen, knowing he wouldn't believe her. But a cough left her insides burning. "Malik... please..."

"I tried to help you. Tried to keep you on his path," he said with a smug, self-righteous grin, "but you didn't lis—"

Whatever he was about to say, Eternity never heard it because several things happened at once. A vaxion leaped on Malik's back, biting down hard on the shocked

Champion's neck. Stumbling, Malik drove a vicious elbow into Lukas' side, throwing him off with one hand. Lukas hit the ground with a whine, and the Champion spun, bringing his axe down in a killing blow.

A blow that never made it.

Malik's eyes opened in shock, his weapon falling from his grasp as he raised trembling fingers. He pawed at the blade that burst through his neck, the edges slick with blood.

With a jerk, the sword was yanked free. Malik fell to his knees, staring up at the red-haired man who stood over him. "Zan… Zander… wait…"

"My name… is *Lazander*," he roared, his sword a blur as he swung it—cutting off Malik's head with a single strike.

"INSOLENT!" Gallow roared, his cloak snapping about him as he turned to face them. Darkness burst from the god's skeletal hand, shooting toward Lazander and Eternity.

Lazander stepped smoothly in front of her, bringing his sword down in a wide arc. The darkness split like bone before his blade, but the Champion—no, Eternity thought—the *Gilded Knight* stood strong, his feet planted on the ground as he took the full force of Gallow's rage.

"I SAVED YOU, MORTAL.

"PULLED YOU FROM THE VERY CLUTCHES OF DEATH.

"YOU SHOULD BE ON YOUR KNEES.

"YOU SHOULD *WORSHIP* ME."

The darkness pushed Lazander back an inch, then two, but the knight held fast. "No more, Gallow. You shall be worshipped no more. Feared no more!" Lazander spat. "For on this day I shall see you *dead*—on my honor I swear it!"

Abruptly Gallow ceased his onslaught. Eternity forced her eyes to focus on the god. She had to get up, she *had* to help Lazander, but she couldn't move. Could barely breathe.

Lazander raised his sword—and vanished.

Time slowed as the Gilded Knight appeared behind Gallow in a flash. The god spun almost casually, snapping his skeletal fingers, and from his chest a spear of bone shot out. It drove through Lazander like a blade through parchment, punching out his back in a shower of blood.

"No!" Eternity cried, her words a pathetic whisper.

She could only watch helplessly as Lazander coughed, blood pouring from his mouth, trapped midair by white bone stained crimson. He raised his sword defiantly above his head. Eternity thought he was going to cut himself free or impale the god in turn, but the knight brought his sword down on Gallow's shoulder. With a sharp crack, the blade jammed in the bone. Lazander yanked at it, pushing it forward and back, driving his sword in deeper.

**"BEG, *KNIGHT,***

**"BEG AND I MIGHT SPARE YOU,"** Gallow said, his tone deadpan, his words mocking.

Lazander's eyes looked blurry and unfocused, his skin as pale as a corpse's, but he kept sawing his sword back and forth, splintering bone. With a crunch Gallow's shoulder fell from its socket, taking Calamity with it as both slug and arm hit the ground with a soft *thunk*.

The god glanced down at his cleaved limb, then threw back his head and *laughed*.

**"IT WILL TAKE MORE THAN THAT TO KILL A GOD."**

Lazander's only reply was to grin, his teeth bloody.

"I'm not trying to kill you, slug," he said. "That's *her* job."

Something huge and white barreled into Gallow.

\*\*\*

*"Oh hi, Clammy-Whammy!"* Nettie screamed with delight. *"Did you miss me?"* She sat perched between my ears, and while I worried a gust of wind was going to knock her off—I had no idea how she was holding on—I focused on flying as hard and as fast as I could, Gallow's bony arm clutched tightly in my jaws. Calamity writhed in-between the God of Judgment's skeletal fingers, and I had to hand it to Gallow—he had *excellent* grip.

**yoU hAve choSen... WiSely...** Calamity whispered, his words halting. **tOgetHer we... rULe... tHIs woRLD...**

"Right, you can eat him now," Nettie said with a contented sigh. "I just wanted to see him squirm."

**NO!** Calamity roared, his words sharp with an echo of power. **DO NoT—**

*"This is for Zara,"* I said, my voice a vicious growl. *"For Valerius, and the prince he once was. But most of all..."* I threw my head back, tossing both arm and slug into the air.

**sTOP**

**i COMManD—**

*"This is for me!"* I bit down, soft flesh and bone crunching as I ate the dark god, the scourge known as the Tyrant, *alive.*

It turned out Zara was right—gods did taste like honey.

**VOID MANA DETECTED.**

**250/9999 VOID MANA**

"Oh, that was *beautiful*," Nettie sang. "Very poetic, little piggie. You should write that down. And lookie lookie—what did I tell you?"

Below me the shadow-fiends, which still numbered in the hundreds, froze. Their bodies writhed, the darkness that cloaked them shaking and spiking as if something was trying to burst out of their skin. One by one they collapsed—the shadows that bound them drifting away, leaving behind a sea of corpses. Molger and vaxion, men and women alike stood—some battered, all bloody—their weapons still raised as they stared at one another in confusion.

Zara harumphed. *"A single truth does not make you trustworthy, slug."*

**"YOU DARE!"**

A howl ripped through the air. Far below us Gallow struggled to his feet, his single remaining arm digging into the dirt. Power erupted from him as he threw back his head, his fury all-encompassing.

**"I AM THIS WORLD'S GOD.**

**"ITS RULER.**

**"AND I WILL HAVE WHAT IS OWED."**

He bent over, his velvet rich cloak undulating as something writhed beneath it. At his side, Eternity lay curled up in a ball, blood pooling beneath her. Lukas was shakily getting to his feet, and Lazander… Lazander lay flat on his back, a large bloody hole where his chest should have been. He wasn't moving.

I flapped my wings harder, fighting back tears. If I wanted to help them, I had to follow the plan.

"Wait for it…" Nettie sang.

As if on cue, huge wings burst from Gallow's back alongside a new arm, a nightmare of bone and flesh that whipped about him like blades.

"Called it," the rakna said smugly. "My brother looooves *theatrics*."

A single flap of his mighty wings was all it took for Gallow to shoot into the sky at supernatural speed, the bleached bone of his bird's skull growing closer every second.

"Higher," Nettie said, completely at ease despite the murderous god who was closing in on us. "You need to get higher, or we're cooked."

I flew as fast as I could, fear and adrenaline lending me strength as I burst through the clouds, my fur wet and heavy. Droplets on my whiskers turned to ice, the air becoming so thin it scraped my lungs with every pant, but Nettie only said, "higher."

**"RETURN CALAMITY TO ME.**

**"AND I WILL LET YOU LIVE."**

"Up," the rakna said in a bored voice. I shot up at her command, a blast of darkness grazing my wing—it burned, leaving the tips blackened and numb.

"Down."

"Left."

"Right."

I dipped and dropped, and Gallow's roar of frustration was immensely satisfying despite how sure I was that I was going to die any second.

"Right about *here* should do it," Nettie said.

Despite how indifferent she sounded, I could feel her writhing atop my head in excitement. With a snap of my wings I twisted mid-air, turning to face

Gallow. In a flash, the sun dropped behind the horizon, the sky turning orange, red and then a vicious purple as I opened my mouth—feeling power grow inside of me.

*Skyscream* took raw mana and turned it into "energy." It was designed to cut through organic and inorganic matter like butter—the only exception to this being the rakna. They were born of Void-stars and were essentially energy incarnate. Fortunately Nettie knew just the thing to change that.

The God of Judgment came to an elegant stop only twenty feet from me, his skeletal wings stretching out from his body like the fingers of death. He raised his arms.

"CEASE THIS MADNESS.

"I SEEK TO PROTECT YOUR WORLD.

"TO—"

---

**GOD FUNCTION EXECUTED.**

**BLACKHOLE ACTIVATED.**

---

What burst from my throat was the power of the universe, a force so strong we had to fly this high or risk accidentally ripping the planet in two. It spiraled toward Gallow in a kaleidoscope of color that lit up the sky, forcing me back as I struggled to keep flying.

"Hold onto your butts!" Nettie cheerfully called.

Gallow realized a split second too late what was about to happen. It hit him in the chest, punching into his body so hard he nearly dropped from the sky. There it stayed, the god frantically clawing at the small, dark hole that formed. It grew and grew, inhaling his chest and fingers, rapidly expanding as it gleefully swallowed him whole.

"NO.

"STOP THIS.

"I WILL LEAVE!

"I WILL—"

"Bye-bye, brother," the rakna called cheerfully as Gallow screamed, his skull sucked into the blackhole with a delicate *pop*. "I hope you *rot*."

Just as quickly as it appeared, the blackhole vanished—and with it, the God of Judgment.

\*\*\*

I hit the ground hard enough to sprain at least one of my paws, but I didn't care. Lukas crouched next to Eternity, his head bent. A long trail of blood led me to Lazander, where he'd dragged himself to her, his hand reaching for hers. Galora huddled around him protectively, fat tears rolling down her cheeks. A beautiful tan horse nudged his body with her head, pushing against him again and again until the dragon growled at her. A hawk perched atop Galora, but she didn't look at Lazander. Her back was turned, her small head half-hidden beneath her own wings in grief.

Beyond them people circled, molger, vaxion, and soldier alike—many had removed their helmets, their heads bowed. Maybe it was out of respect for Lazander, a legendary Gilded Knight. But I knew there was no one who hadn't seen Eternity wracked with pain as she gave up her life to save them.

The crowd parted to make way for me. My fur melted, replaced by human hands and feet, and in seconds I was limping toward them. Galora hissed at my approach. I dipped my head, my hand over my heart in the Gilded Knight greeting. After a long moment she shifted to let me pass—my heart in my throat. Lazander's eyes were closed, his lips parted as if he were about to speak. I tried not to look at the gaping hole in his chest. But then I saw how tightly he clutched Eternity's hand, even in death, and the tears I'd been fighting fell from my eyes.

He'd hurt people—hurt my friends. But in the end, he was the reason we'd won. When I saw him kill Malik, saw how hard he fought to save Eternity, I'd reached out to his mind, asking for help.

All he'd said was, "I will clear the way."

Eternity was worse. Blood from her eyes and nose had dried against her skin, forming a sticky pool beneath her cheek. Though I knew it was pointless, I checked both of them for a pulse and bent my head over their mouths, listening for a whisper of hot breath. They were both as silent as the grave.

"No…" I whispered. I took Eternity's hand in mine, the touch of her still-warm skin a blade in my heart. A sob escaped me, and I wept, my head in my hands. "I… I'm only alive because of you. You saved me. You saved us all. I'm so sorry, Eternity."

Lukas gripped my shoulder. I felt the light touch of Zara's hand on my other.

"Bloody hell, you lot are dramatic," Nettie piped up. "She's only been dead a minute or two, same with the boy. You know you can bring them back, right?"

At her words, a pop-up flashed.

---

**GOD FUNCTION AVAILABLE.**
**REVIVE—COST 50 VOID MANA.**
**VOID MANA AVAILABLE 100/99999**

---

I cried out in relief. I could do it. I had just enough, but I could bring them both back. I was about to choose "yes" when I felt Zara tense.

"*Wait,*" she said, and I knew what she was about to say. "*If you do this… you cannot go home, Teema.*"

*And you don't get your body back*, I said, the full implication hitting me.

"*I do not care for such things, Teema,*" Zara said firmly. "*I would gladly share my life with you. But you have a home. You have a family, my friend—even if you no longer remember them. And… if they miss you half as much as I will, then they deserve to have you back.*"

My heart swelled at her words even as something about the word "home"—and what waited for me there—niggled at the back of my mind. I dismissed it.

*I know, Zara, but…*

I looked at Eternity and Lazander. Were their lives more important than Zara's freedom? And who was I to make that call?

"There's also the big old door left swinging wide open in your world." Nettie casually nodded skyward. Frowning, I followed her gaze—my stomach dropping to my knees. The rift Calamity came through now took up the length and breadth of the sky. Through it I could see the blood red sand of the Void and the blackened husks of its twin suns.

"With every hour that's left open, more of the Void will pour into your world—and as ridiculous as it sounds, Calamity's playpen was actually pretty hospitable. There are some *nasties* out there who'd love nothing more than to turn this place into a spaghetti bowl of blood and guts," Nettie said cheerly. "Right now you're looking at aboooout 95 VM to close it, I reckon. What does your System say?"

I pulled it up, my heart sinking when I saw Nettie was wrong. It wasn't 95 Void Mana to close the rift—it was 97. As I watched, the number ticked up to 98.

"So I have to choose between saving Eternity and Lazander, giving Zara back her body, or closing a world-destroying rift?" I asked, my heart breaking. I knew what I had to do. It was the only option, after all.

I gripped Eternity's hand, hating how cold it already felt. "I'm sorry," I whispered. "You too, Zara. You don't deserve this."

*"You owe me no apology, my teema,"* Zara said. *"Close the rift. Save this world."*

*"Or…"* Nettie piped up, dropping from my head to land with a plop on Eternity's chest. "You could just eat me?"

# Chapter Sixty-One

I stared down at the rakna in shock, speechless. For once Zara was equally surprised.

"Oh, you guys are too much." Nettie laughed. "It hadn't even dawned on you? I mean, what else am I gonna do? I'm the only rakna left in the universe! Once I'm gone, all Void Mana is bye-bye. *Kaput*! Sure I could terrorize you and rule like a god for a couple hundred years, but mortals always end up killing each other anyway. Who am I to spoil your fun?"

"But..." I stammered. "You helped us. Gallow would have eaten Calamity if you hadn't warned us. Without you, I wouldn't have had the Void Mana to stop him. Wouldn't even have known how."

"Oh, don't get me wrong, little piggie," Nettie said. "I don't like mortals—never have, never will. But I've lived for hundreds of thousands of years, and if I hoard my Void Mana, I'll probably live a hundred thousand more. And while there was a time when that sounded like a pretty sweet deal, now I'm just... I'm just *tired*."

The slug dipped her head, for once sounding as ancient as she was. "If Ravenna was here, she'd tell me to do it. She wanted to stop the killing and do some good, and while this wasn't exactly what she'd planned, maybe... maybe I fancy being like my little sister. Just this one once, mind you."

The slug's body shimmered, curling in on itself. Her skin shifted from a dark brown to a light, almost translucent green.

It took me a second to realize she'd turned into a *grape*.

"See? I'll make it easy for you and everything—you won't even have to chew! Oh... you mean... ohhhhh."

The grape rolled left then right.

I frowned, unsure if this was just Nettie being, well, Nettie, or if something else was going on.

"Oh, I *like* it, Zara," she said finally, spinning excitedly. "Knew you were the smart one. Right, you get all that, Laaaady Fury? Because I can't exactly repeat myself from your gullet."

I didn't have time to ask what she was talking about because Zara abruptly shoved me back into the darkness and took control. I stumbled—I hadn't even known we could *do* that without the other person's say so.

"Count yourself lucky, slug, for you are the first I have said this to," Zara announced, holding the grape to her lips. "You are a vicious and delightful creature—and it has been an *honor*."

She bit down, and we were immediately flooded with power, sadness, and the sweet taste of honey.

*\*\*\**

I didn't have much time to say goodbye. Zara retreated into my mind after eating Nettie, offering no explanation for what the hell had just happened, despite my repeated questioning.

*"We do not have time, Teema,"* she said. *"The cost to close the rift rises with every second you spend dawdling."*

I hugged Lenia tightly, wishing I had the time to explain who I was, what had happened, or how she'd changed everything by saving me in that forest. I tried to apologize for ruining the dress she'd lent me so long ago, but she simply patted my cheek. "You are *not* going to get hung up on a dress after you helped save the whole damn world. Waylen will be so excited to learn he got to meet a real-life hero—consider that payment enough."

Lukas was harder.

"Nope," he said, a finger raised. "If you hug me I'm going to start weeping like a newborn babe—and no one wants to see that." He held out his hand. I gripped it hard enough to hurt.

"Now I'm not saying I'm *glad* I turned into a ferocious slobbering beast," he said, his voice cracking. "But I'm glad it was you who saved me. Thank you, Teema."

I nodded, fighting my own tears. "I'm going to miss you so much," I managed.

"I'm gonna miss you too. But I also hope we never see each other again because if we do, that means the world is going to blow up or something," he joked.

I smiled, pretending not to see him wiping his eyes when I turned away.

Jaza hugged me tightly, as did the other vaxion. I expected Ashira to press her head to my forehead, the usual vaxion farewell, but she wrapped her massive arms around me.

My lungs screamed as every bit of air left them.

"You returned to us more than our powers, Teema. You gave us back our futures. Moonvale might be gone, but we will build new lives with the molger as *allies*. We will build a future our children will be proud of. But most of all," she bent low, whispering in my ear, "Thank you for saving my little star. I will leave behind a life where she is happy and safe. You have my word."

Ashira kissed my forehead, then turned away, covering her face. Jaza took the woman's hand, winking at me.

In the back Jerome stood. I didn't have time to speak to him—didn't even know what I'd say to him, but there was no need. He nodded respectfully to me, relief and gratitude in his eyes. I smiled in return, happy he'd proved me wrong—people really could change.

King Najar stood before me, helmet tucked under one arm. I was struck again by his appearance—it was like looking at a Valerius from a distant future. Or rather, the man the prince could have been

The king pressed a fist over his chest and bowed low. His soldiers hurried to do the same.

"I won't confess to know what happened here—but I know you fought to save my people. To… to save my wife." His throat caught, but he plowed on. "I am sorry for the role my son played in this and for my failure as both king and father to stop him. What happened here is as much my fault as the dark god's."

To my surprise, Zara whispered, *"Tell him the truth, but do it in two sentences or less. We do not have the time."*

"That wasn't Valerius," I said, and the king straightened. I gave him the shortest explanation I could, pointedly leaving out that I was also one of the "souls"

Calamity had pulled from another world. It took more than two sentences, but Zara didn't interrupt.

"I don't know this for sure," I finished, "but in the end… I think the real Valerius took back control. He saved Za—he saved my life. We'd all be dead if he hadn't sacrificed himself."

The king's face was still, but I saw his fists clench. "As a king, that changes nothing. But as a father…" he let out a breath. "Thank you."

"My lord…" a soldier called, pointing at the horizon.

I squinted. In the distance lay the hill of red sand—all that was left of the Ivory Keep. But something moved beyond it. As the dark shapes came closer, I gasped. Dozens, no—*hundreds* of people were walking toward us. Some were dressed in rags, others in fine silks.

"That's Jeremy—a palace guard!"

"And Loke from the blacksmiths!"

"They're alive? *How?*"

The king chuckled to himself while his soldiers cheered. "Trust my wife to offer me hope, even from beyond the grave."

And just like that his back straightened—his eyes suddenly clear. He called for his horse, mounting the dark warhorse smoothly, already barking out orders. "Mages at the ready for the injured. Let's move!"

As he rode to meet the survivors, Zara gave a pointed sigh.

*I know, I know, we don't have time.* I smiled. Though she acted otherwise, I could feel her relief that at least some people had survived.

Taking a breath, I stared down at Eternity and Lazander. They'd grown pale, their skin taking on a sickly sheen as death sunk its clutches into them. Kneeling, I brought up the System Menu, placing my hand on Eternity's ice-cold forehead.

---

**GOD FUNCTION EXECUTED.**

I expected *something* to happen—a glow of magic, a flash of light, some jazzy sound effects as her wounds healed. But Eternity simply opened her eyes and sat bolt upright—breathing hard.

"Eternity?" I said carefully. "Can you hear me? Does anything hurt?"

"What did you—how am I?" she stammered, a hand coming to her face. "I died. I know I did. I felt it!"

"We did it," I said, putting my hand on her arm. "We *won*."

"We… we did? I cannot believe it. I was sure…" She frowned, looking down at the cold hand that still gripped hers—and saw Lazander. Her eyes went wide with panic and grief.

"He's going to be okay," I said quickly. "Just give me a second."

Eternity's gaze darted from me to Lazander, and I knew she had a million questions. But she simply took my free hand as I pressed the other to Lazander's forehead, gripping it as tightly as he did hers in death.

Lazander's transformation was more dramatic. The hole in his chest shuddered, filling from the inside out in the time it took to blink. Then he was on his side, coughing and spluttering.

"I am here," Eternity said, brushing his hair back so gently I felt like I was intruding. "It is all right, Lazander. Everything is all right now."

"Is he… did we…"

"We did," she smiled. "Thanks to Teema. And Zara," she added.

I felt Zara huff but knew she was pleased not to be forgotten.

"Thank you." He coughed. "When I heard you in my mind, I thought I was dreaming. But you saved us… you saved *her*." He smiled at Eternity with open adoration. "I was sure—"

His words were lost as a dragon, a horse, and a hawk dog-piled him. I lost sight of him beneath a flurry of scales, tongues, and feathers, but his laughter and constant reassurances that he was all right made me smile. I even felt Zara grinning, though she tried to hide it.

"Eternity," I said, trying to put words to the heaviness in my chest. "I have to go now, but I wanted to say thank you. When I first woke up in this world, I was so scared—I could barely move. But *you* made me get up. You made me leave Magnus' dungeon. Without you… I wouldn't here."

I expected Eternity to protest, or to ask what was going on. But she leaned forward, kissing me gently on the cheek.

"Aliana."

"What?"

"My name—it is Aliana. I told you long ago that Eternity was just a title. And I think it is past time I reclaimed my real name."

I smiled. "It's a beautiful name. It suits you."

She flushed. "I wish we had met at a different time, perhaps even in a different life, Teema. It might be a strange thing to say, but…" her cheeks turned a shade darker, "… I would have liked to travel with you. To have seen Navaros and the world beyond together."

I squeezed her hand. "I would have liked that too."

Back in the darkness, Zara rolled her eyes.

"When you go… will the Fury stay?" Aliana asked suddenly.

Her question took me by surprise, but I nodded.

"Good," she said. "Tell her I look forward to our new friendship. And should she protest, I am afraid she has no choice—I am her friend, and she mine—whether she likes it or not."

*"Hm… I will allow it,"* Zara muttered, clearly happy.

Ashira and the vaxion were setting bones, wrapping wounds, and organizing rations. Lenia and the molger worked alongside them. Soldiers ran about, already setting up tents and tending to survivors while Lazander was busy getting his hair chewed on by a very happy horse.

I gave Aliana one last smile, then disappeared into the chaos. My goodbyes were done. There was no use putting it off any longer.

"Let's go, Zara."

\*\*\*

We flew as close to the rift as we dared, red sand pouring from the tear in the sky like a waterfall.

*Zara, are you sure about this?* I asked, fighting the gravitational pull of the rift, its magic threatening to drag me inside.

*"Nettie was clear. The closer we get to the rift the less Void Mana it costs to close it and send you home in one fell swoop. We will use the rift's excess magic to 'ride the wave like a greased-up surfboard.'"*

Zara clearly had no idea what those words meant, but she dutifully repeated them. I was about to ask why Nettie had told her this and not me when the obvious suddenly hit me.

This was the last time I was going to see Zara.

I'd been so busy saying goodbye to everyone else, I'd almost forgotten I was leaving her too. The Fury—a woman I used to be terrified of. Who'd hated me and tried to kill me more than once—yet here we were. Friends wasn't enough to describe what she meant to me, but I had no idea what else to call it. Or what to say to her. How do you tell someone that, despite all the terrible things that happened, you're so glad you met? That you feel the happiest and strongest you've ever been. . . because of her?

Stalling for time, I brought up the Operator tab—but a pop-up appeared.

---

**SYSTEM OPERATOR PRIVILEGES REVOKED.**

**CONTACT SYSTEM OPERATOR FOR MORE INFORMATION.**

---

*What? No!* I yelled in shock and dismay. *Zara, can you see this? What are we going to do? We can't close the rift without—*

The portal shimmered, the edges of the tear pulling together as an invisible needle and thread sewed them closed. The waterfall of red sand was cut off, and my back warmed as the sun rose in the sky behind me, casting the world in the soft orange glow of dawn.

"*All is well, Teema,*" Zara said softly. "*We simply transferred Operator privileges to me when I ate the rakna. I only granted you permission to use Revive.*"

*We? Who is 'we'? What are you talking about?*

"*Nettie and I. She helped me craft that ridiculous lie about riding the rift like a 'surfboard.' It makes no difference where we are, nor did we need to rush to get here—we have Void Mana to spare. It turns out the rakna was fat with it.*"

*But… but why?* I said, not liking where this was going. *If we have so much Void Mana, think of what we could do with it! How many people we could Revive!*

"*That is exactly why,*" Zara said. I felt her smile softly in the darkness. "*Had you known the truth, you would have delayed your return or tried to bring back every corpse on the battlefield. I chose to be selfish for you. Know that I ask for neither permission, nor forgiveness, Teema.*"

My anger flared. I was about to tell her she had absolutely *no* right to do that, but the words died in my mouth. The world spun, and I pressed a hand to my head, feeling dizzy. Wait… hand? But I was a voidbeast, how—

---

**GOD FUNCTION EXECUTED.**

---

*Zara? Zara…* I slurred, my tongue lead in my mouth. *What are you… doing?*

"*Nettie knew you. In all her years of watching your planet, she saw more than just mortals killing mortals—she saw* you. *She saw you die. Watched your blood spill on the floor of an arcade.*"

Her words were sludge, but something stirred in the back of my mind, that niggling doubt I had about returning home hitting me full force. I remembered a gun. A shout. My back hitting an arcade machine. My uncle Jacobi on the floor—his shirt stained red by gun shots. Noah crying my name.

Wait… my name?

*Uncle Jac!* I yelled, a kaleidoscope of memories sending me reeling. *Oh god, and Noah! Am I… Is Uncle Jac—*

"*Shhh,*" Zara said softly. I felt her hand on my face in the darkness. Saw her smile, concern shining in her eyes. *"This next part will hurt, I think."*

# Chapter Sixty-Two

The neon sign outside read "Uncle Jac's!" but only half the letters lit up. Beneath it a catchy slogan once promised a world of fun for all the family, but it was illegible after years of exposure to the elements.

A crowd gathered around the arcade, but then the red and blue lights always brought people. They pushed against the yellow lines of police tape, straining to get a better look. Straining to see who had died this time.

But no one could have guessed what lay inside.

Blood stained the carpet—once gray, now a dirty brown. Jacobi lay abandoned on a stretcher, the two paramedics who'd been tending to him long gone. Adrian stepped in front of Noah and his mother, his bloodied ear forgotten.

A girl lay on the ground, her chest stained with blood, her eyes open and unseeing. But Maggie kept pumping her chest, whispering the same thing over and over. "Come on, my sweet girl, you can do it—breathe for Mom. Please, I'm begging you."

The arcade machine by the girl's head jerked, a dark fist pulling back as it prepared to punch the screen from within. The glass was cracked—one more blow was all it needed to break free. The machines that surrounded it lit up, music blaring, lights flashing. The last of the paramedics fled, running for the only exit. Maggie stayed.

"Come back," she sobbed. "I'll never ask for anything else again, just *come back!*"

The dark fist rose—and vanished. The machines switched off, the music fell silent, and the arcade was plunged into darkness.

Another hand appeared. The fingers were long and elegant, the tips ending in midnight blue claws. Instead of punching through the glass, it gently pressed against the edges of the screen, as if asking for permission. The words *"Knights of Eternity"* flashed briefly, and then the glass vanished. The hand reached out, gripping the edge of the machine. An arm and shoulder followed, and then a shock of dark hair, the tips the same midnight blue as her fingertips.

Zara the Fury stepped out of the arcade machine and onto the stained carpet of Uncle Jac's.

"*Run,*" Adrian whispered to Noah and his mother, ready to distract the strange woman with knives for fingers.

But Noah stepped out from behind him and pointed at her, a confused smile on his face. "Is that… is that *Zara?*"

The Fury nodded to him, a ghost of a smile on her lips, then headed for the large form of Uncle Jacobi. It seemed Nettie was as good of a liar as Calamity and Gallow. She'd claimed to dislike mortals, but the years she'd spent watching Earth had left her with a soft spot for them. Especially the ones who threw themselves in harm's way for family.

Still, Zara had been suspicious. Mortals died all the time, what difference did it make to the slug if Teema did? Nettie simply shrugged and said, "You love that girl just as much as I loved Ravenna. After all this crap, someone should get a bloody happy ending."

Zara knelt by Uncle Jacobi and placed a hand on his back. There was a soft "plink" as a bullet slid out of his flesh and onto the floor. The big man groaned… then let out a loud snore, lost in a blissful dream.

Zara's eye caught on the boy with the strangely shiny hair and bloody ear. When she stepped toward him, he raised his fists.

The Fury barked a laugh. "I'd eat you alive, boy. Now stay still."

To his own shock, Adrian obeyed. The tall woman with beautiful golden eyes brushed a hand against his ear. He felt a warm tingle run through his body. Without a word she walked away. Bringing a shaky hand to his ear, he found it whole once more.

Finally Zara knelt beside the older woman, who still pumped the girl's chest, though she'd been dead for several minutes. Maggie was crying so hard she could barely see, but she couldn't stop. If she stopped, that meant her little girl was gone.

"Enough," Zara said gently, taking Maggie's hands. "Let me."

Something broke in the older woman, and she fell back with a sob, her face buried in her hands.

Zara pressed a hand to the girl's bloodied chest. "Come now, parasite," she said with a smile. "I'm not going to let you die so easily."

Zara pulled her hand away, a bullet following the path of her fingers.

Maggie gasped as her daughter's skin flushed with life, her eyes shooting open.

Girl and Fury looked at one another, a world of meaning passing between them. And then Zara crushed the bullet in her fist—and vanished.

***

They kept me in the hospital for days, running every test imaginable. Newspapers, social media, and conspiracy forums had a field day. I received interview requests almost hourly, ranging from radio hosts who wanted to talk about my "brush with the divine," to online only TV shows that ran specials called, "The chemicals the government puts in your water!"

I declined them all.

Uncle Jacobi was released early after he threatened to throw his doctor out the window if they took one more drop of blood from him. I stayed, mainly because Mom kept asking me if I was all right every five minutes. I figured the best way to convince her a bullet wasn't secretly swimming in my chest was to have the hospital give me the all-clear.

Besides, I couldn't shake the feeling that Zara wasn't done.

The sun dipped behind a row of skyscrapers, and I watched it, remembering the feel of the sun on our skin as we raced through Moonvale. The ice-cold touch of wind when we flew so high the air became thin. When she appeared, I had no warning. I was simply alone one second, the next the bed dipped, and she was sitting next to me. In many ways she looked exactly the same. Her smile was bright and vicious, and the white scar that ran from forehead to cheek only highlighted her fierce golden eyes. Yet one look was all it took for me to see that Zara the Fury was different now.

She was *happy*.

"So…" I said, "how much Void Mana did Nettie have?"

"Over eight thousand."

I gave a low whistle. "You weren't kidding when you said she had plenty to spare."

Zara smiled. "I have spent most of it. It turns out rebuilding the world after a bunch of slugs used it as their playpen is costly work."

My jaw dropped, and she laughed at my expression. "Fatyr is alive and well," she said, somehow sensing my question, "and still enjoys getting drunk and dancing under the moonlight."

"The Gilded…" I said, remembering the plaques beneath the Keep. "What about Marito and Gabriel? And all the other people who died when Gaj fell?"

Zara shook her head sadly. "I could not bring back those who died at the Keep itself—Calamity turned their bodies to sand. But I have not been sitting on my haunches."

While it had only been two days for me since we'd last met, it had been over a year for Zara. After the battle, Ashira had bowed to the molger and said she was ready to fulfil her promise—her head was now theirs, as well as the crumbling remains of Moonvale.

But Chief, Lenia, and the other molger suggested a new deal—Ashira and the other vaxion would help them rebuild Moonvale. Zara offered her Void Mana to help, of course, but the molger and vaxion insisted on doing much of the work themselves—they wanted to make a new home together. And no one had worked harder than Ashira.

Lukas left Moonvale and was busy traveling the world. The last Zara heard he'd somehow earned a spot in a dwarven king's court and was having the time of his life drinking wine and telling stories.

I laughed. "That sounds like him."

Lazander had taken up residence in the newly rebuilt Keep. The king's orders were simple—train a new generation of Gilded Knights with Lazander as their leader.

"Is that… pride I hear in your voice, Lady Fury?" I teased. "Does that mean you've changed your mind about the knight?"

Zara lifted her shoulder in an elegant shrug, looking bashful. "I can forgive him for killing me—but he'll have to work harder to make up for hurting Lukas. Still, Aliana has asked me to be godmother, so I suppose I shall have to."

I stared at her, mouth agape. "Do you mean Aliana…"

She smiled.

"And *Lazander?*"

Zara smiled harder. "The baby is due the same time as this year's batch of molger and vaxion cubs. I shall have my godchild wrestling falslings to the ground by the time she can *walk*."

If it was anyone else, I'd say they were joking—but by the look in Zara's eyes, I knew she was deadly serious.

"Where did you end up?" I asked. "The Keep or Moonvale?"

"I move between them. As my Void Mana has decreased, I've found myself in the Keep more often—the king wants to make me an 'ambassador.'" Zara grimaced. "I told him my idea of diplomacy was slitting someone's throat, but he is most insistent. Lazander, on the other hand, is pushing to make me a Gilded Knight. He was only slightly deterred when I threw him from a balcony—do not make that face, he is fine." She sighed, though it was one of contentment. "Still, I think I will stay in the Keep for now. You should see the new courtyard. It is littered with gigantic marble statues, all built in honor of those who died and those who rose to defend the world at 'Godfall'—their poetic name for our final battle."

I gasped with excitement. "Was I right? Did they make a statue of you?"

She growled. "They asked. I threatened to turn them into jelly if they dared."

I laughed. "So who was the victim?"

"You."

I froze.

Zara smiled softly. "I see now that I got your nose a little wrong. But your eyes—they captured your eyes perfectly."

"Zara…" I said, suddenly wanting to cry.

"My Void Mana is spent," she said, taking my hand. "And perhaps it was selfish, but I wanted to use what I had left to see you. You are my friend. My teema. The woman who saved both my world and hers."

"*We* saved the world," I corrected, squeezing her hand back.

She tilted her head, eyes closed, as if listening. I knew what was about to happen, but I still held her hand so tightly it must have hurt.

"Thank you, Zara," I managed, tears welling.

"And thank you, Teema... no." She leaned forward, her lips brushing my forehead gently. I closed my eyes, her last words a murmur against my skin. "Thank you, Emily."

When I opened my eyes, she was gone.

"Emily! Emily, I got the newest *Gotcha Go!* Do you wanna—" Noah burst into the room, his eyes wide when he saw me wiping my eyes. "What's wrong?" he said, looking far older than any twelve-year old should. "Does it hurt? Should I get a doctor?"

"No, no, I'm fine."

"Am I interrupting?" came a voice. Adrian appeared at the door, yet another bundle of flowers in his hands.

"Not at all." I smiled. "Noah and I were just about to play a game."

# THE END

## **END OF BOOK THREE**

I confess, I had a bit of a cry when I finally finished this book. I've spent so much time with these characters that it's strange to put an end to Lazander, Aliana, Emily, and Zara's stories. But I knew that after everything I'd put them through, they should get a happy ending. I'm biased, but I think no one deserved it more than Zara the Fury. I hope that in some parallel universe she's teaching her two-year old godchild how to do a chokehold while Lazander fusses about like a mother hen and Aliana laughs, telling him it'll be fine.

Also, I told you you'd learn Emily's name! AND you got Aliana's real name too!

I didn't want to make this book too long, so I didn't add this in the end, but while Emily's anxiety continues to lurk in her mind, it never again controls her life like it does in book one. And when those negative thoughts creep in, all she has to do is think of Zara the Fury, *"Deal with the problem at hand, not the one in your head."*

It's advice I do my best to follow too.

If you want a sneak peek at any new projects, you can find me on Facebook, TikTok, and Patreon.

Finally if you enjoyed this book, feeding the Amazon gods a rating helps immensely, (they are almost as hungry as Calamity).

P.S Not only does Lazander return Benjamin the ceramic frog to Emeret the mage once everything is over, he also finds a permanent place for the man in the Ivory Palace, where he and his frogs can retire in peace.

Love,

Rachel Ní Chuirc

# ARISE ALPHA

By Jez Cajiao

**When you steal a hundred grand from some very bad people, the best way to survive is to stay small and quiet...**

Possibly its not to save a pair of drowning girls, not go 'viral' on social media and certainly not to let the local police take your passport, trapping you on a small 'party' island in the middle of the Mediterranean Sea.

But Steve isn't the average guy, he's ex-military, ex-enforcer and ex-human. He's a one-man nanite fueled nightmare for those that cross the line, and he's decided that it's time to clean up his act. He's going to make up for the things he's done, and save 'the little guys'.

It's a nice fantasy, but even he has to admit, it's really just a justification, because he's a very bad man, with horrifying abilities, and he's only just learning what he's capable of. He needs a reason to not go to the dark, and if that's hunting down the creatures of the night and beating them to death with their own femurs?

Well, he's just the man for the job.

**Stolen money. Greek Islands. Werewolves and Enforcers... What could possibly go wrong?**

https://www.amazon.com/Arise-Alpha-Dark-LitRPG-Adventure-ebook

# WANDERING WARRIOR

### By Michael Head

### Punishment for the guilty is coming – carried by the armored fist of Judge James Holden

He's reached the limits of his power, and in the process, he's brought justice to nineteen entire worlds. But now, cast across time and space to his twentieth planet something's wrong.

The darkness runs deeper than ever before, those in power corrupt those beneath them, and the concept of honor is twisted and long lost to those who should know better.

James has had enough, and as the chosen weapon of the gods, he'll bring balance to this world again, or die trying.

If somebody needs to be sent to their gods for that to happen? Well, that's a sacrifice he's willing to make.

### It's time for judgement.

https://mybook.to/WanderingWarrior

# QUEST ACADEMY

By Brian J. Nordon

*A world infested by demons.*
*An Academy designed to train Heroes to save humanity from annihilation.*
*A new student's power could make all the difference.*

Humans have been pushed to the brink of extinction by an ever-evolving demonic threat. Portals are opening faster than ever, Towers bursting into the skies and Dungeons being mined below the last safe havens of society. The demons are winning.

Quest Academy stands defiantly against them, as a place to train the next generation of Heroes. The Guild Association is holding the line but are in dire need of new blood and the powerful abilities they could bring to the battlefront. To be the saviors that humanity needs, they need to surpass the limits of those that came before them.

In a war with everything on the line, every power matters. With an adaptive enemy, comes the need for a constant shift in tactics. A new age of strategy is emerging, with even the unlikeliest of Heroes making an impact.

**Salvatore Argento has never seen a demon.**
**He has never aspired to become a Hero.**
**Yet his power might be the one to tip the odds in humanity's favor.**

https://www.amazon.com/Quest-Academy-Brian-J-Nordon-ebook

## SCARLET CITADEL

By Jack Fields

Gormon Hughes is 19, thin as a broom, and has—not for the first time in his life—been swept into the path of trouble. Poor, recently heartbroken, and indebted to the sort of people who file their teeth into needle points and devour wriggling bloated spiders for fun, Hughes sets his sights on salvation.

That salvation is the Scarlet Citadel, a wealthy organization of pageant fighters, monster hunters, and secret keepers. With the aid of strange oracles, rare good fortune, and a unique power that bubbles like champagne in the core of Hughes' being, he must join the Citadel and advance himself.

But the ladder of progression is harsh and dark. The rungs are slippery.

*And falling means disaster…*

https://mybook.to/ScarletCitadel

# OVERDUE: LIBRARY SYSTEM RESET, BOOK 1

K.T Hanna

**The library once stood proud as a beacon of magic and power. For five hundred years, it has been broken.**

Quinn can barely handle her own life. When the Library of Everywhere discovers her compatible magical signature, suddenly, she is the sole existing potential librarian. Now, it's not only the weight of her world on her shoulders—Quinn must connect with the library system before the universe itself disintegrates.

Once she's settled, it should be quiet, peaceful work—just as soon as she battles a few engorged bookworms, repairs hundreds of years of damage, and figures out why there's been no librarian for the last several centuries.

And once that's done she can start gathering overdue books. All 18,042 of them to start.

There'll be a helluva lot of late fees to process.

BUY

https://www.amazon.com/Overdue-Library-System-Reset-Book/dp/B0D5J4Z9J3

# I RAN AWAY TO EVIL
# BOOK 1

Mystic Neptune

**A reluctant heroine finds unexpected love when she's sent to assassinate a lonely dark lord in the first book of this cozy romantasy series.**

Henrietta Doryn has never enjoyed fighting. She'd rather be in the kitchen baking cookies. But it's her duty as Warrior Princess to face off against the forces of evil. As such, she's unceremoniously shooed from her kingdom to go eliminate the all-powerful Dark Lord next door.

Keith Monfort has never enjoyed ruling with an iron fist. He'd prefer to be in his workroom tinkering with practical magic. But it's his duty to lead the Dark Enchanted Forest and the forces of evil. So when Henrietta shows up at his door, he's only too happy to invite her in for tea to talk it out instead.

Can this unlikely pair prevent war between their two kingdoms? Where do their true loyalties lie? And when will they finally confess their growing feelings for each other?

Blending the best of love stories, fairy tales, and whimsy—with just a dash of mystery provided by the soothsaying Madame Potts's enigmatic announcements—*I Ran Away to Evil* is a deliciously delightful start to a charming romantic-comedy LitRPG series.

**The first volume of the hit LitRPG romantasy series—with more than a million views on Royal Road—now available on Kindle, Kindle Unlimited, and Audible!**

https://www.amazon.de/-/en/Mystic-Neptune-ebook/dp/B0CXSB4QSR

# FACEBOOK AND SOCIAL MEDIA

I have a very fancy author page if you'd like to reach out and chat! I can't promise you witty banter, but I *can* promise you terrible memes:

**OR**

There is a FB group where I often lurk, like Valerius in a library. It's dedicated to two very simple rules:

1: Lets spread the word about new and old brilliant LitRPG books.

2: Don't be a dick!

Come join us!

www.facebook.com/groups/litrpglegion

There are also a few really active Facebook groups I'd recommend you join, as you'll get to hear about great new books, new releases and interact with all your favorite authors!

www.facebook.com/groups/LitRPGsociety/

www.facebook.com/groups/LitRPG.books/

www.facebook.com/groups/LitRPGforum/

www.facebook.com/groups/gamelitsociety/

# LITRPG!

To learn more about LitRPG, talk to other authors including myself, and to just have an awesome time, please join the LitRPG Group

www.facebook.com/groups/LitRPGGroup

# LITRPG LEGION

I am published by The Legion Publishers, a fabulous (and wonderfully chaotic) trio. Jez, Chrissy, and Geneva are taking on new authors, as well as experienced ones, focusing primarily on the LitRPG. They are guided by one simple rule:

**_Don't be a dick._**

That's it. They're also up front and open about their contracts, which you can find here:

www.legionpublishers.com/legioncontract

Got a LitRPG that's been sitting on your desktop, looking for the perfect home? Well, look no further. Submit here!

www.legionpublishers.com/contact-and-submissions

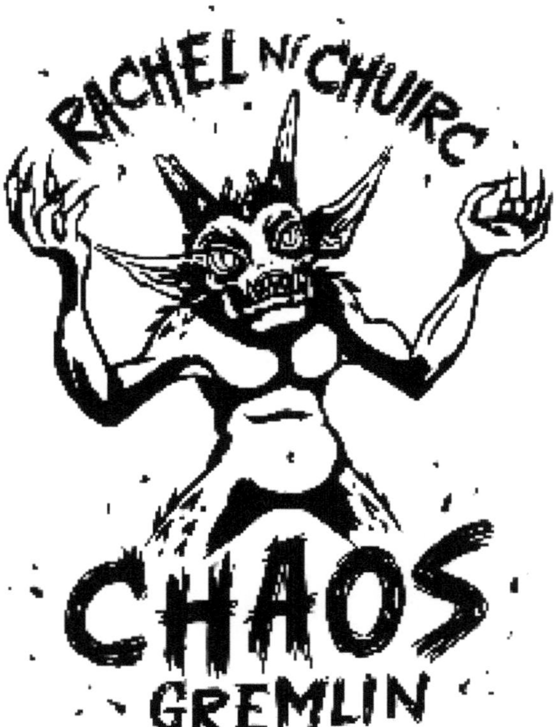
RACHEL NÍ CHUIRC
CHAOS
GREMLIN

Milton Keynes UK
Ingram Content Group UK Ltd.
UKHW020742221124
451186UK00036B/456/J